The Gift of Red Hare

(And Other Epic Tales)

by Billy Ironcrane

The Gift of Red Hare is a work of fiction set in remote history, and based in part on actual happenings. All incidents and dialogue, and all characters with the exception of some well-known historical figures, are products of the author's imagination, engaged fictitiously, and are not to be construed as real. Where real-life historical figures appear, the situations, incidents, and dialogues concerning those persons are entirely fictional and are not intended to depict actual events or to change the entirely fictional nature of this work. In all other respects, any resemblance to actual persons, living or dead, events, or locales is entirely coincidental.

Published by: Mc Cabe and Associates,
Tacoma, WA.
For permissions contact: billyironcrane@gmail.com

Cover drawing and interior map by Renee Knarreborg
Cover image – "Puff Ball" by Doug Goodman

ISBN-13: 978-1-7324154-8-5
Library of Congress Control Number: 2024907460

To those who will not be vassals,
pawns, or lackeys.

Contents

Illustrations
(by Renee Knarreborg)

The Gift
Of
Red Hare

The wizard paused briefly to frame his response.

"The riddle of life reduces to this my friend.

"Our true battle wages where compassion confronts chaos.
It's compassion which proves we are never alone or abandoned.
We puzzle endlessly over how we got here,
and from whence we came.
Or for that matter, to where we will go.

"You'll find no answers but for this:
Between the dawn of each day, and the final setting of its sun,
We'll all have abundant opportunities to show compassion.
And in so doing, bond with those about us
in igniting our treasured essence to full radiance.

"Look no further to conclude we are not alone,
forgotten, or without hope.

"Yet, chaos persists. The most insidious of poisons. Spreading too
quickly, lingering long in the aftermath. Ensuring its victims
cannot readily undo their decline, nor regain what they've lost.

"Heed these words ... It's compassion which matters.
And which overcomes."

Middle Kingdom

Northern
Tribes

Changcheng

Huang He

Western
Wilderness

Wei He

Huang He

Yellow Sea

Shu

**Jing
Province**

Wei

Crystal
Springs

Yangzi Jiang

Ling
Village

Yangzi Jiang

Fortune's
Gateway

Eastern
Sea

Wu

Southlands

Guangdong

Zhuya
Commandry

Southern
Sea

Pearl Cliffs

R.Knarreborg v3 2023

Part 1 - Pieces of a Puzzle

Jing

The once-mighty armies of Wu, now battered and worn, felt the weight of their decline pressing upon them. Desperation drove them to push south and west, their weary soldiers probing for the resources needed to rejuvenate their pitiable state. Desperately, they scoured the land for sustenance, clinging to slivers of hope in a world that had turned against them.

Like other fading empires, Wu inclined to trust in power and intimidation. Quicker than promises and tedious alliances, nothing evoked compliance and acquiescence like what might happen should you refuse.

By their reasoning, expansion made good sense. Endless conflict had finally exhausted once vibrant Wu, leaving it unable to sustain its own population, let alone continue incursions into the north where dreams of empire still lay unfulfilled. They searched for "new elsewheres." When withering within, revitalize from without. Strong must plunder weak.

The West beckoned first, its call more direct and less complicated than the South. A seductive call which inescapably led through Jing.

Embracing the great Yellow River and enriched by eons of soil replenishment, province Jing had been the coveted heartland for aspiring emperors since earliest times. This rice basin could sustain vast armies and replenish stock and steed. But only so long as its inhabitants could be subjugated, placated, then productively engaged.

A story grown old. Tragically finding itself amidst competing empires, this once bountiful province became battleground for warring lords ever since the Han Empire disintegrated.

Taking it by force was one thing; holding it, quite another. Differing prospects tightly intertwined. Many have taken, few have held. Much like when a predator feasts upon a freshly downed carcass. No sooner does the one sink its teeth, than the others come to steal it away.

Surveys of the land recalled images of pigs with rakes[1]. First scraping north, then ripping south, east and west. Crippling natural cycles which underpinned the province's thriving agrarian production. Fields lay bleak and empty; all livestock pillaged. Nothing remained. Residents fell to starvation, disease, want, pollution, conscription, exploitation then abandonment. Loyalties were demanded and extracted. First by incentive, then by fear, retribution; and finally, by terrifying example. Some rebelled with little success. The more practical found ways to ride the chaotic currents. Cautiously, they maneuvered to assure survival

---

[1] A nod to Zhu Baijie, brother "Pig" in the classic novel Journey to the West. Part human, part pig, this one-time celestial commander fell prey to his own base inclinations and was condemned to life among the mortals. There he preyed upon all, using his many talents and skills to deceive and fleece who or whatever he came upon. His weapon of choice was a nine-pronged rake, hence the reference. He is never without it. It is one of the great weapons of eastern lore, and his skill with it can never be doubted. When driven to wrong purpose, it is capable of immense destruction.

until more promising alternatives arose. From within their ranks ascended a new breed of opportunists. Those who misused their own. Finding paths to prominence from harvests of misery, they gleaned wealth and influence. One cannot overstate the load of misfortune which can be set upon the wretched, and how traditional loyalties might be twisted.

Ling Village, once an inconspicuous hamlet in the western reaches of the province, lay untouched as the ebb and flow of contention shifted north and south, focusing on more prominent provincial centers. Luckily, the outlier Ling managed to slip from notice. But its luck ran out when the heart of Jing had no more to give. Eyes then turned westward, toward lands once deemed too distant to conquer. What was once a systematic extraction transformed into blatant pillage.

For Jing, the great change came after the combined forces of Liu Bei and Sun Quan defeated Cao Cao at Red Cliffs. The momentous victory in hand, voices everywhere regarded the alliance as heaven's mandate. Sun Quan's kingdom of Wu possessed distinct advantages that set it apart: unwavering stability, abundant resources, great wealth, and, perhaps most importantly, a fiercely loyal population. Despite the tremendous toll exacted by the siege at Red Cliffs, no one doubted Wu's capacity to renew and flourish. That was after all, what drew Cao Cao in the first place. For him, Kingdom Wu was Jing Province multiplied a hundredfold. His gnawing desire for the remarkable Lady Sun[2] complicated matters even further.

---

[2] Younger sister to Sun Quan. A legendary beauty who from the first, captured the heart of Cao Cao. He does eventually come to regret this.

Cao ... an ambitious ruler whose longings had no bounds. So much need in a single packet of flesh and bones. He wanted everything! Who can fathom his reasons or motivations, without first acknowledging his complexity and his broad talents? Even after Red Cliffs, still licking his indisputably crippling wounds, his agile mind worked tirelessly devising new strategies to catch others off guard. And he did—launching wide ranging attacks all along the common frontiers. If he could not get what he wanted; he would seize what could be had, then build anew from there.

Liu Bei, until that point, held a single, unwavering goal: to safeguard what remained of the Han dynasty. He firmly believed this would quell chaos, assure stability, and return prosperity to the people. From the earliest, he proclaimed his righteous purpose to be resurrection of the Han Empire, leaving no room for doubt about his motives.

In short, he wanted what Cao Cao had already usurped, setting the stage for a bitter rivalry. While Sun Quan and Wu might seem peripheral for the moment, both Liu and Cao knew that eventual success in the north would require dealing with Wu in the south – a unified imperial state brooked no less. Sun Quan understood this.

The intricacies of this tangled political landscape are apparent.

Enduring these cycles of conflict would drive any rational person to yearn for peace, and wish for an end to the swords' dance. Toss them into the sea. Better yet, flatten them into paddles. Use them to mete out needed lessons.

Despite their triumph at Red Cliffs and the professed harmony between Liu Bei and Sun Quan, discord soon surfaced.

It started with Jing Province.

Liu Bei, now acknowledged as a formidable lord and peer, did not have the deep roots of Sun Quan to a territory assuring his future. One might argue he had something better. The unwavering counsel and loyalty of the brilliant strategist Zhuge Liang, along with a devoted band of supremely talented fellows. Zhuge had orchestrated the dramatic turn at Red Cliffs, a story which will unfold further as we progress. Even Sun Quan's once fervent desire to eliminate Zhuge Liang had remitted. During the siege at Red Cliffs, some believed they had forged an unexpected friendship. Might he somehow turn the wizard away from Liu Bei?

Who can say? Much like today, not everything that meets the eye proves to be true or genuine. History bears witness to this. Throughout their years together, Liu Bei never once questioned Zhuge Liang's loyalty or commitment to his vision. While circumstances didn't always align with their initial hopes, Liu Bei's faith in Zhuge Liang remained unwavering. It was a bond that produced the best possible outcomes, regardless of the challenges or twists of fate. This enduring bond was the bedrock of their relationship and an unshakable fraternal understanding.

Zhuge Liang was the one who initially impressed upon Liu Bei the strategic value of Jing Province and its critical importance to their cause. He emphasized this during their discussions in the mountains and reiterated it after the victory at Red Cliffs. "You cannot endure as a nominal warlord," Zhuge Liang insisted. "Without a state to call your own, you and your loyal followers will perish."

Up until then, Liu Bei and his devoted followers were without a true home. Scarcely had they emerged victorious at Red Cliffs when Sun Quan's advisers began to urge Liu Bei's eviction. Why gamble with temptation? The risks of doing nothing were apparent. Powerful allies of convenience and necessity were never far removed from becoming enemies. It is against their nature for armies to forgo mischief. No matter how robust the alliance; once their job is done, send them off! Nearness and divided loyalties among massed troops typically foreshadowed trouble.

For the present, the alliance with Wu ensured mutual survival. But the alliance would grow stale the further Cao Cao retreated into his northern bastions. Zhuge Liang had already emphasized the strategic importance of the western regions and highlands. Still, in the short term, even that couldn't guarantee their survival. Acting on Zhuge's recommendation, Liu Bei seized Jing from Cao Cao's weakening grip, effectively slipping it out from under Sun Quan's coveting eye. Holding Jing secured their sustenance, replenishment of essentials and armaments, and perhaps most importantly, a dignified exit. They would leave Wu of their own volition, with honor intact, and a destination.

Liu Bei Founds Shu

When relating history to Bao Ling, Sying Hao hesitated to reveal all he knew of Jing. Bao Ling had personally witnessed how conflict gutted his native Jing. In his view, those with malicious and self-serving intentions had no qualms about perpetuating ruin. Greedy individuals cared little for the consequences of their encroachments, showing no fear of retribution.

Sying Hao worried how his friend would react on learning he, too, had supported Zhuge Liang's counsel that Liu Bei must take control of Jing. They planned to to use Jing as a stepping stone to annex Ji province and then expand westward into the mountains and highlands. Their ambition was to carve a kingdom from remote lands and engaging those who had been ignored or disadvantaged by history. This, they believed, would provide a platform for the eventual restoration of the Han. It was a difficult choice, but they saw it as a necessity for their survival – succeed in this endeavor, or face certain peril.

Whispers spread among the elite of Wu. "If we keep Liu Bei's forces adrift and in the field for just a year, his army will be starved and easily dealt with. With Cao already weakened, the north would be ripe for our taking. It is we who are destined to unify the empire, not Cao Cao or Liu Bei. We must act now!"

When Zhuge Liang first met Liu Bei in the high mountains, his cautionary words now appeared prophetic.

History would later record this advice as the Longzhong Plan, a grand design for the restoration of the Han dynasty.

Sying Hao couldn't shake the feeling that Liu Bei's actions in Jing, and the subsequent moves on Ji province, foreshadowed the impending misery that would befall Bao Ling's people. He struggled to reconcile his deep respect for Zhuge Liang with the brotherly love he felt for Bao Ling, so he remained silent on the details. He left Bao Ling to figure it out for himself.

The province of Jing, a relentless chant that haunted the thoughts of Liu Bei, Zhuge Liang, and even Guan Yu[3]. Their visceral understanding of its importance was undeniable; everything hinged on it. Yet, they were keenly aware of the exorbitant price demanded. Jing would become the cleaver which severed their ties with Sun Quan and the Kingdom of Wu.

Sun Quan's desire for Jing was unambiguous. He felt a profound sense of shock and betrayal when Liu Bei took it unilaterally. Jing, in his eyes, offered a perfect buffer for the Kingdom of Wu. With Jing under his control, he could safely confine the dogs of war to someone else's domain while ensuring the security, stability, prosperity, and unity of Wu. The principle remains quite alive today, though history has shown repeatedly—the approach will cost dearly. No empire based on this premise has ever withstood the insurmountable burden assumed. Once set loose, the dogs of war are loathe to return to their pens. A fundamental enigma which no one has ever found a solution to.

Sun Quan resolved there would be no repeat of Red Cliffs. "We must secure our realm from future incursions."

---

[3] A full listing of characters and incidentals is provided at the end of the book for the reader's benefit.

His wisdom and discernment in this regard were commendable.

However, his determination set the stage for treachery, sacrifice, and loss. The people of Ling village remained oblivious to these distant matters. Somewhere afar, the presses began rolling their way, propelled by the mounting needs of competing lords, pursuing whatever ventures promised the most gain.

Amid the wake of these turbulent events, only flotsam remained, tossed endlessly about by ill-tempered currents.

In an attempt to counter Liu's advantage, Sun and his counselors devised a cunning strategy: "Tickle gently with a feather while digging the lion's pit." They aimed to find a way to reclaim Jing, despite Liu Bei.

In Wu, discussions revolved around the return to historical borders, which, wouldn't you know, reached beyond Wu and encompassed all of Jing. Such talk rarely occurs without the careful seeding by leaders. Considering the advanced civilization and development within Wu, the inhabitants of Jing seemed primitive, needy, and powerless. Ignorant folk who could only benefit from the gracious assistance provided by their benevolent neighbor. Intermediaries from Wu attempted to persuade Liu Bei to relinquish Jing, but he responded pointedly, "Recognizing my past service to Liu Biao[4], the good people of Jing have

---

[4] Liu Biao 142-208 AD. Fierce warlord, who ruled neutral Jing Province as the once Han dynasty fell into warring factions. Like Liu Bei, he was a distant relation to the once emperor. Honoring their common heritage, he extended sanctuary to Liu Bei when early-on he and his fledgling forces faced annihilation from the pursuing Cao Cao. Liu Bei

accepted my stewardship, acknowledging my prior role in preserving the integrity and security of their land. It should not surprise noble Sun Quan why I am here. None other than Zhuge Liang predicted that without the security and support of Jing, our forces would starve within the year. I suspect our noble friends in Wu would then pick us clean. But I'll consider anything. What do you offer if I relinquish the province?"

They stood in silence, their voices rendered mute by the weight of the argument. All could see how what was, had to be. To take, one must give, or accommodate. Those in Wu appeared to have forgotten the lessons of Red Cliffs and the profound impact of Liu Bei's brilliant ruse (more on that later).

They perceived these new developments as treachery from a once-trusted friend. Their grievances were now declared openly, as they lamented, "Liu Bei stole our Jing."

Much like the mountain dwellers of Shu, the people of Jing possessed a deep sense of identity and purpose. They were a simple, contented folk, in harmony with their surroundings. They held no desires for the possessions of others, nor ambitions for power or empire. Instead, they embraced the natural cycles, accepting of the bounties and the surprises—sometimes unpleasant; but always deserving of their awe.

There was no awe for Wu, nor for Wei, or any other unwelcome guests. Unwanted others whom they tried to accommodate as best they could and persevered, placing their trust in the gales of time to clear the chaff. Their

---

proved to be an able ally and general, making Jing Province under Liu Biao virtually unassailable.

THE GIFT OF RED HARE

patience knew no bounds, and this had served them well in the past, much like the vigilant watch of the noble Liu Biao.

But now, the situation had deteriorated. Without intervention, they risked becoming Wu's helpless prey, trapped and caged. Somehow, they needed to divert the approaching wolves toward new quarry.

Can someone, anyone, ever quiet the great storm once underway?

You will soon see, Liu Bei succeeded in Jing, where others had failed.

From Liu Bei's perspective, Zhuge Liang's recommendations regarding Jing proved wise and fruitful. With Jing as platform, Liu Bei gained adequate foothold in Ji, then cut west to Yi and circled back to Jing, securing a vast western domain from which he eventually declared his state of Shu Han.

In the west and the highlands, the inhabitants were primarily non-Han people. Historically marginalized, they had endured frequent incursions and oppressive taxes. Apart from what could be gotten, they mattered little to others. Their meager existence barely sufficed, yet they found heartfelt contentment in simplicity, much like the residents of Ling Village, Mei Village, and countless other hamlets. Until one day Yama's searing breath blew chaos low upon them.

Recognizing the importance of winning hearts and loyalty, Liu Bei's motivations went beyond self-interest. He aspired to be an exemplary leader, and his actions reflected this laudable goal. To that end, he diligently implemented comprehensive administrative and reform measures, addressing infrastructure, commerce, justice, legal precedent, equity, recognition of rights, resource allocation, unions, contracts, and the abolition of the empire's lingering exploitative taxes and policies. Even his adversary, Cao Cao, acknowledged Liu Bei's previously underappreciated gift for enlightened leadership.

In less than a generation, the region stood secure and prosperous, and Liu Bei had earned the love and respect of the once-suspicious and suppressed natives.

History suggests he should have been satisfied with what he now had. It also says the same of Sun Quan and Cao Cao.

It was not to be, not for any of them.

Fish in the Pan

It's only reasonable we hear from Sying Hao and draw our view of history from his own recitation of what followed.

We learn first that Liu Bei, Sun Quan and Cao Cao have long since joined their ancestors.

Their unresolved campaigns echo interminate. Like barbed tails of lingering follies raking across backs of innocents.

Jing Province, once a flourishing rice basket for millions, lays barren and lifeless, its once fertile fields now desolate with blowing dust.

Remnants of Wei and Wu vie for the eastern empire, an empire only in thought, given the devastation wrought by warring fortunes. Shu Han has disintegrated, save for the determined scions of once-prominent lords striving to carve their own destinies from the gaping carcass.

Despite Shu Han's practical demise, its skeletal remains persist, and the enlightened reforms of Liu Bei continue to influence the isolated western empire. Ever devoted to his people, even in the end days while his armies struggled most valiantly, he carefully strategized to spare the beloved westerners from further suffering and loss. However, Jing Province and Ling Village were not so fortunate.

In the season of Bao Ling's story, warlords, in desperate need of resources and replenishment, turned their gaze to the West and South. Remnants of Wei probed constantly, hoping to harness the Shu Roads to their advantage. Their engineers, explorers and advance guards proved dauntless, thinking all the while, "If the ignorant mountain natives can do it; why can't we?"

From further south, factions from Wu also ventured into the mountains, sometimes as allies, sometimes as competitors with Wei.

As the Lords of Wu gazed beyond their borders, their eyes brimmed with ambition, yet not for the pursuit of new wars. Instead, they turned their hungry gaze to the Southlands, a vast expanse inhabited by an agrarian population, deemed naive, undisciplined, and weak. To the Lords of Wu, it seemed like a land simply waiting to be seized, an age-old refrain echoing in their minds. "We have the smarts and the know-how; you have the resources. If you don't willingly yield, we will take charge for your own good. We hold your best interests in our hearts; our ways will prove superior.

Who can truly fathom the predatory tendencies that lurk in human minds, especially when stoked by the fires of ambition? All too often, giving rise to freshly concocted rationales. These are self-serving wolves, donning the guise of generosity and fellowship beneath their sheepskins. Beware! On their first approach, look closely at their feet.

Through generations of unyielding strife, Wu and Wei achieved little. What were they thinking next? "Look southward!" they proclaimed. "Let us extend a hand in assistance. We'll dispatch our finest emissaries to reveal our vision of the future. Accept our embrace and become one with us!

"Or perhaps, behind the pulled shades and curtains, there's more we can exploit. First, tenderize them. Then pillage and decimate a bit. Get their attention. Reward complicity. Audacity! If we can just get to them first, the tide will turn for victory." A mantra repeated endlessly from one horizon to the next, seeming to spill from lips everywhere.

History reveals the will of heaven is never so simple as one thinks. Its very fickleness reminds. It is far better to align with heaven's grace, than to stalk alongside its sinister twin. As the twin whispers, "Audacity is the key. Take what you need, and you are halfway there." The Tao responds with a deeper truth, "Without restraint, you embrace chaos, and will end with nothing."

If called upon, Abbot Hui could surely lecture these fellows on the great paradox. Causing suffering to innocent others; taking what little they have while growing wealthy and glistening with superfluous fat defines a system which dooms all.
Sages have long known this. Pick any, and you'll see. Read some Laozi; enact his teachings at your peril. You may find yourself with less or nothing, and yet surprised at the contentment within.

In this light, individuals like Bao Ling, Sying Hao, Shi-Hui Ke, and even the enigmatic Zhi Mei and the resolute Colonel Sun, could be considered enlightened spirits in their own right.

Not because they achieved "enlightenment." That's just another illusion, a careless word. One should be careful in seeking or striving for such an ideal. What you actualize may be just another manifestation of greed. History bears testament to the truth that some of the bloodiest warlords were lauded as enlightened figures, or great philosophers, thinkers, artists, poets, and more, all deserving of admiration—or so their followers tell us.

Greed and pursuit persist.

Show me an art or a politic that pulses with life and can nurture the ordinary. Show me an art that can stop the ceaseless race. A fish in the water is far better off than one on the hook or in the pan. Even if someone tries their best to persuade the panned fish otherwise; they are speaking to flesh already simmering to extinction.

Looking South

Until then, they ignored the Southland. Colonel Sun thought the region blessed—home to a great and noble people. A tranquil haven, insulated by remoteness and harsh topography. Its inhabitants favored peace, and averted needless conflict. Culturally, they avoided confrontation, dismissing it as purposeless. An embarrassing waste of time and energy, solving nothing. When in a rare argument, they smiled while making their points. Usually, that sufficed. Music and the arts flourished and a sense of cultural unity prevailed, both with the land and amongst themselves.

Sun frequently recounted to Sying Hao the bountiful wild fruits that seemed to fall from the trees, "They dropped on their own. You almost had to protect yourself from getting thunked!" And how crops grew effortlessly in the fertile, rain-soaked soils, "You could sprinkle your seeds and walk away. Before you knew it, food was popping up everywhere you looked. You'd almost be stumbling over it!"

He felt their culture to be an ancient one, though not quite as old as himself, and jested at the prospect of exploring further. "See who else might be around that I'd like to know!" He marveled at their resourcefulness in taming their environment, meticulously mapping out edible plants, herbs, and medicinal remedies. Even insects played a role, either as a source of sustenance or for flavorings and garnishes. He recalled how the natives referred to him in their playful way as "The ancient one, who always swallowed before he chewed." Though a titan of strength, Sun found no ease in consuming insects, nor biting into what his eyes already rejected. At least not until appreciating with approval the hint of cinnamon in delicacies like the water beetle.

Their land occupied the broad expanse between the emerging Gupta empire to the far south and the failed Han empire to the north, the roof of the world to the west, and the great seas to the east.

The Han Empire, riddled by eunuchs and inbred leadership, had relinquished its former character and momentum. It existed now as little more than a fading whisper, a memory of days long gone. Yet for some, this whisper held a strange allure, tempting those still tethered to ceaseless strife, their hearts yearning for the halcyon past, a time that could never be rekindled.

The emerging Gupta had begun to consolidate the subcontinent south of the great roof of the world.

These fortuitous developments diverted covetous eyes away from the Southlanders. Thus, left to their own devices, stability infused their way of life.

New philosophies and awarenesses bloomed just over the horizons. They eagerly absorbed and drew inspiration from teachings emanating from spiritual centers in the far south. Stars were meticulously mapped, the movements of planets precisely charted, including Earth's. The healing arts evolved to a state of remarkable sophistication. Most importantly, they assimilated the teachings of the great sage Buddha. Lessons on compassion, illusion, distraction and release, had taken firm hold, ushering in new insights and understanding.

Life, body, self, and soul were concepts that had been misunderstood by those in the north, driving them to madness and unimaginable cruelty. For the Southlanders, these were mere distractions, pillars of the illusory world known as Maya, a universe of illusion, itself just another illusion. For them, being meant immersion—doing, and not having been.

The Southlanders even knew of a traveler named Thomas, who hailed from distant lands. He brought news of a deceased friend who, he claimed, had conquered death. He, too, affirmed the importance of compassion, love, respect, tolerance, and charity. These values weren't foreign to the Southlanders; they were already woven into their culture. Perhaps this was because death held a different meaning for them, not a threat but a riddle - not quite alive, yet not truly dead. Just something to be understood and managed, not feared or dreaded.

We said it before, Colonel Sun found them exemplary. "Sying Hao, each one of them is equal in worth to a hundred of our emperors." Sying Hao would echo, "Sun knew his mind and did not bandy opinions recklessly. There had to be something to what he said."

Sying Hao eventually saw and understood for himself. His relationship with Southern Mountain grew from that understanding. Before their paths parted, he swore an oath to Colonel Sun that no harm would come to the Southlanders while he still drew breath.

He loved the mountain, its ever-changing moods, and the secrets it held. There were other reasons, but more will be revealed in due time. He could have stayed there forever, but eventually, the oath beckoned.

What had protected the Southlanders and the people of the subcontinent in the past was the network of impenetrable natural barriers. Great distances separated them from those in the north. The mountainous network deemed to be heaven's gateway stretched between, the frozen ceiling of the world. Though impenetrable to invading armies, rare individuals made it through. Fewer returned. They told of vast riches and wealth to the far south, and of great seas, and trade to distant empires. Most in the distant north considered these accounts to be fabrications. Were they not already the center of the universe?

Their rulers felt otherwise. They simply knew better. To them, new prospects remained a perennial allure.

The western ranges and the imposing Southern Mountain served as formidable natural barriers, flanking the Southland's western and northern borders. While alternate routes existed, they were fraught with considerable disadvantages. To traverse such punishing terrain and torrid expanses would test the endurance of outsiders unaccustomed to the region's harsh exposures. Supply lines would stretch beyond their usual capacities, extending further than even during the tumultuous era of the Three Kingdoms. Additional vulnerabilities lay in the northeast. Any aggressor seeking access to the Southland would first have to gain control of Jing Province, a task that had historically exacted a heavy toll. Jing might seem easily occupied, but no one had ever held it without incurring significant losses.

Only the declining Wu Kingdom, still formidable on their northern border, could entertain the practicality of excursions into the Southland. It was a decision not easily made. Generals from the Wei Kingdom closely monitored Wu's intentions and their probes southward. In aftermath to the sieges at Red Cliffs, Wu had no choice but to maintain forces perpetually deployed to the north, ideally as far from their own territory as possible. Their leaders decided all future battles would be waged outside their own turf—a strategy preserving their essential base and sparing their own from needless suffering. It proved to be an immense strain on resources.

Then there arose the obvious threat. Any major deployment southward would draw reserves from the northern lines, tempting new invasion from Wei. Such were the dilemmas faced by those aspiring to expand their empires. Power rarely delivers on fruits it promises.

For these reasons, the Southlanders had until then been spared. Simply put, they were not a practical target. Now, the situation had changed.

But there's more to the story. Other pitfalls lay in waiting, all too ready to ambush any mettlesome troop tempted to prowl their way.

While it's true that in the south, Wu Kingdom was favored by river crossings which offered access, beyond those waters lay vast expanses of jungle wilderness, considered by some to be no less forbidding than the mountains to the west. Shielded by the dense wilderness, the native Southlanders were fiercely private and notably fierce in responding to any unwanted intrusions.

When incoming probes first challenged their capabilities, they poured forth like nascent streams from the jungles and ancient teak forests. Men, women, and even children spread across the muddy grasslands, all armed for battle. The sight of this unprecedented swarm had more than once unnerved invaders, inducing them to turn completely about.

Those in the north had never encountered the likes of it. Peasants weren't supposed to resist, let alone pose a threat. According to their expectations, peasants should cower and fear.

To Hell With Sun Tzu

Coursing centuries of illustrious rule, the empire grappled with a myriad of spoken dialects. Despite a shared written language, geographical obstacles and vast distances often isolated communities, leading to the evolution of diverse speaking patterns. This linguistic tapestry, woven over ages, defied the best intentions of rulers hoping to unite the land. The issue predated the Han and endured beyond their reign, perpetuating fractious inclinations that eroded support for singular rule, be it from the North, South, or West.

In contrast, the Southlanders possessed an ancient, phonetically based script, giving birth to a dominant tongue and a cohesive identity. Though differences might be found from one region to the next, seamless communication prevailed, bound by shared values and a collective aversion to outsiders whose ways seemed incomprehensible. When the need arose, this unity manifested in a singular purpose: resistance against external intrusion.

If that were not enough, mammoth beasts roamed the Southlands freely, as did ferocious carnivores. In addition, reptiles and insects, whose bites meant certain death, lurked in the shadows. Swamps abounded with treacherous sands and tars capable of devouring the unwary, while unrecognized diseases and ailments seemed to plague outsiders, leaving Southlanders unscathed. Those afflicted held few hopes for a cure or recovery. Worst of all, the unmentionable disease, a curse believed by some to ward off invaders, causing fingers, toes, limbs, ears, eyes, and lips to rot away in putrid stink.

An oppressive heat blanketed the land. A torch of dragon's breath waited in the lowlands. Scorched trails filled with bodies of dead and dehydrated beasts, tended in molten despair by smoldering corpses of men abandoned in the wakes of invading forces.

All this unfolded before the first engagement of arms. Understandably, until now, there had been little incentive to invade; so long as more placable targets lay elsewhere.

The Southlanders had their own expression, a simple "It's nothing." Wild beasts ignored them, venomous snakes and poisonous insects posed no threat, and in the sun, they barely seemed to sweat. Staring into war masks glaring from across the border, they remained perpetual optimists. This was their home; they loved it, and it suited them perfectly. While others might perceive it as one of Yama's hells, for them, it was paradise. Again, the unending mysteries of perception, perspective, and illusion persisted.

In the deeper south, the formidable Gupta wouldn't protect the Southlanders from those in the north. They valued them for their fierce independence, dedication to the sage Buddha, intimacy with nature, and respect for the spirit entities believed to inhabit their environment. The Gupta respected all life and were put off by those who didn't hold this ethos. In practical terms, the Gupta saw the Southlanders as capable of fending for themselves, and this mutual understanding led to a strong trade partnership. Moreover, for the Gupta, the Southlanders served as a buffer, insulating the subcontinent against any immediate aspirations from the far north.

Not quite allies, one might consider them friends of necessity. So long as the Southlanders harbored no designs, the Gupta went about consolidating their emerging empire in the subcontinent. As for the future, well, only time would reveal its secrets.

In the north, generations of conflict without resolution had ground the once great civilization to a standstill—a situation enduring for as long as any living soul could remember.

There are some who profit from conflict. We should all know this; it's a matter of simple reverse logic. Much can be gained and gleaned from what is bad. Skeptical? Until life convinces you of this, just suppose it's true for now. Even in the worst of times, there are vast opportunities. But only for a select few. Tragically, it is the many who must bear the costs and consequences of their choices.

The trick to this has remained constant throughout history and continues to hold sway today. Be invisible. Cultivate friends in high places. Control essential commodities. Eliminate competition. Discourage real change. Build more efficient weapons. Profit from constant turnover. Rely on fear, jingoism, and baited promises in return for dour sacrifice. Be sure to invoke religion and the afterlife—after all, what better friends and allies than gods and immortals on your side? Beckon them, use them, call them down. Interpret for them. Memorials commemorating the gone and deceased are always a welcome touch and certainly worth the effort. No better way to motivate and propel the next waves.

Among the most wealthy and influential, one might find extended family members or close associates serving equivalent roles in opposing camps. Blood and ties beneath shadowy platforms where resources and commodities shifted nefariously through undetected channels, finding endpoints where profits and returns were sure to be maximized and kept close hold.

Curse them all! No plague can match what comes from their machinations.

With the strife, common life everywhere in the north drew to a troubled halt. Infrastructure and resources lay depleted, trades and skills extinguished. With other options gone, warpreneurs on all sides gazed lustily southward … a stark harbinger of Colonel Sun's greatest fears. He cautioned Sying Hao that the day would come when conflict would outstrip the capacity to sustain itself. "The Southland and lands to the west would eventually call to the warring parties. Whoever controlled the west and the south stood to outlast all rivals. The endgame—a matter of simple attrition. Just be patient!"

Great risks deterred anyone looking south or west. Inhospitable territory and the indecipherable network of Shu Roads had long deterred overreaching empires. Saved from their own folly? Perhaps, but now?

None less than Sun Tzu[5] made clear the fundamentals for success in warfare. When you step forward, you must protect your rear. When you step to the right, you must beware of the left. Your force is strongest when it is undiluted and acting with full purpose. Keep supply sources in immediate proximity, and their channels tightly controlled.

Others will mix his precepts with that oft chanted mantra of ambition, "Nothing ventured, nothing gained. Only to

---

[5] Sun Tzu 544 - 490 B.C.E. Renowned military strategist and philosopher, author of *The Art of War*.

those who take the risks, will come the rewards." A mind-numbing concoction of the highest potency.

At this stage, choice mattered little. Options reduced to few. When the only alternative to abject failure is to attempt the impossible, then attempting the impossible made perfect sense. To hell with Sun Tzu and his calculated strategies.

The unbridled fury of the Southlanders and the challenges of moving a properly equipped and armored force through punishing terrain had discouraged ambitions of past lords. So much simpler to look to the Great Northeast, or to the sun-begotten people[6] and the islands off the eastern coast, or even to the seemingly endless plains dominated by mounted tribes in the central north.

Once, other options made the best sense. Now, war engines ran on ambition and hot air, little else. Yama whispered to all who would hear. "Take the west, and the south; victory will be assured."

Colonel Sun knew this and something more. He cautioned Sying Hao, "Never lose sight of the one point on which all else hinged. Only when we starve the beast will it turn its ravenous appetite back onto itself. Only then will the blight be lifted from humankind."

Zhuge Liang affirmed, "Heed Sun's words, Sying Hao. In them you'll find the seeds of change. Look hard at them, don't forget them, or fail in your vigilance. As with the wheel of life, Yang pivots toward Yin. This cycle of unrest will in time tire of its own accord and draw to an inevitable close. From the ashes, an age of quiet will emerge. The

---

[6] Japan. In Chinese, the name for Japan is Rìběn (a piece of the sun). We use this expression, in lieu of the unflattering "land of the dwarfs" which was common during the Period of Warring Kingdoms.

longed-for peace will be at hand. Such changes follow the natural order, as laid bare in the Yi Ching. Even Yama will tire of his own nonsense and turn resignedly toward the realm of stillness. There he will close his eyes and retreat to another kingdom where his endless antics can harmlessly engage the infinite void. Hopefully, when that dawn comes, we will have learned to avoid foolishness."

Is There a Man Who Is Better

By that time, Liu Bei, Guan Yu, and Zhang Fei had long departed, as had Cao Cao and Sun Jian. Zhuge Liang had promised the dying Liu to safeguard the Western Kingdom and mentor his untested son Liu Shan, whose own mettle remained in question. The dying Liu demanded Zhuge Liang swear to depose the son should he not ascend to the responsibilities. Zhuge merely stared at his friend. Both knew he would never undertake such treachery. His integrity remained impeccable until his own end. Above all, with Liu's passing, Zhuge would have preferred retiring to his mountain retreat and to the snow people he loved so dearly. Sadly, by then, those he had known would all be gone, as would likely be their children. Oftentimes, he pondered whether their grandchildren would know anything of the great wizard who brought the ways of fire, awareness, and survival to the snow tribes.

Regrettably, Liu's ambition to restore Han, arguably justified, lingered as a haunting presence alongside Liu's deathbed. The wizard had already planned a new direction for the state, one of rejuvenation and self-sufficiency. But just as Yama readied to lower Liu's eyelids a final time, Liu turned to Zhuge and extracted his solemn oath to continue the northern campaigns until restoration of the empire had been assured.

Zhuge had hoped for a different parting request, but he had prepared himself for the worst and it came to him in this most bitter serving. Having already tested the winds, the stars, the oracle, the shadows, even the flights of strange birds now crowding the skies of his dreams, there could be no doubt.

All foretold failure.

All portended loss and suffering to the many, who should better have been spared.

All spoke to Zhuge of his own end.

Zhuge Liang first emerged as a radiant beacon in a world cast in shadows and darkness. Vested with secrets from the ancients, he delivered them into the practical world hoping to drive the affairs of men. A world muddled in pretense and illusion. Zhuge and Sun both recognized the futility of negating illusions. Just another chain which bound even the wisest to the fabric of mankind's folly. Now trapped within this labyrinth, to succeed they would somehow have to break free.

He had indeed unraveled the secret of immortality, but had grown weary of the game. His soul longed for the tranquility of his high mountain retreat, yet a sworn oath shackled him to the ceaseless ambitions of men. A soured destiny he might once have eluded with ease.

If he could only break his promise.

History reckons Zhuge Liang, Liu Bei, Guan Yu, and Zhang Fei among its most formidable in stature and capability. Collectively, even they were not enough to restore order and tranquility, once heaven presumed to dictate otherwise.

Unlike most, Zhuge Liang did not despair. His far-reaching eye knew another time would come. Three would emerge to take reins left loose behind. Reincarnation? Perhaps. Who knows what opportunities destiny allows to make amends and to right courses wrongly taken. All fevers eventually break. By the time of his end, Zhuge sensed the ascendance of three spirits. Two soon to blossom into human form, pure, unclouded by greed, fearless and free of wanton ambition. It would fall to them, and to a yet unborn poet chronicle to pivot the future and yield the land back to the people, who, following their lead and example, might at last stake their own destinies with courage and conviction.

How could he see these things?

Well, he was Zhuge Liang.

It should be noted, nothing is for certain sure, not even with Zhuge Liang. Wizard and mystic though he might be, when navigating our reality, he too became subject to the unpredictable currents which buffet us all. True, he could detect propensities, leanings, inclinations; and with his multi-dimensional sight, conjure strategies to accomplish what would be impossible for others.

Was he infallible? No!

Could he stumble and fail? Certainly!

And he did. After the passing of Liu Bei, and with the formidable generals Guan Yu and Zhang Fei already gone, Zhuge Liang witnessed fractures spreading like fissures throughout the Shu empire. Wei threatened from the north and the east, and the Southern Shu empire at Nanzhong faced degradation due to uprisings from the Nanman[7]. Led by the barbarian prince Meng Huo, these were the same

---

[7] Nanman - People from the south. A term loosely describing several indigenous ethnic groups habiting the inland south and the southwest. Among those groups were those Colonel Sun came to know as the Southlanders. As to whether Meng Huo was a barbarian, simply a matter of perspective and how those in the north chose to view outsiders.

western Southlanders who had once stood firmly by Shu's side. These developments underscored the obvious.

Three lords vied for ascendancy to the rightful throne of Han leadership, yet generations of chaos had sprouted from their folly. The will of heaven seemed elusive, no longer leaning towards any of these would-be emperors or their progeny.

The Nanman too recognized the will of heaven had clouded. In the fog of suffering and chaos which enveloped the land, they withdrew their allegiance, once firmly with the Shu.

To the southeast, the Wu once again coveted the fertile plains still under Shu control.

But for the cleverness of Zhuge Liang, all would have come to a quick end. Against all odds, he secured a fragile peace with his longtime friend and adversary, Sun Quan of the Wu; then held the Wei at bay in the mountainous north, paralyzed in the never-ending maze of mutating Shu Roads.

He then personally led a string of campaigns to the south, ultimately bringing the Nanman and their warrior king back into allegiance. Heralds spoke of Zhuge Liang's soft spot for Meng Huo, the fierce tribesman whose people had sealed Shu's southern borders for decades, shielding the west from flanking movements by the Wu or the Wei. In the numerous campaigns launched to quell the Nanman rebellion, Zhuge Liang achieved ultimate victory in each instance, but not without some lessons learned. Notably, Meng Huo's wife, Lady Zhurong, supposedly descended from the fire god Zhu Rong and peerless as a warrior queen. She frequently took to the battlefield alongside her beloved Meng Huo. Once, after he had been captured, Lady Zhurong assumed leadership in his stead. Dauntless, she launched an assault directly into the heart of the Shu forces, stunning everyone with her capture of Shu Han generals Zhang Ni and Ma Zhong.

Realizing the loss of two important generals, on hearing the news Zhuge Liang could only voice, "What an annoying woman!" Laughing of course, wishing he had ten just like her.

Once, one of his generals pronounced, "Sir, she stands among the finest woman leaders who have ever lived."

To which the wizard replied matter-of-factly, "Truly? Can you tell me of a man who is better?"

Zhuge Liang is said to have captured Meng Huo, and then released him on seven different occasions to no avail. Not until several times trapping and capturing Lady Zhurong, then treating her with respect and dignity, did he regain the loyalty of Meng Huo. And with that the renewed allegiance of the southern tribes for whom she was a goddess. She more than matched any of Shu's finest warriors in the battlefield. Capturing her necessitated the coordination of thousands, relying on ruse and subterfuge to draw her into exposure. Culminating successfully only when Zhuge Liang devised an intricate trap of nets, concealed by the ordinary, and tripped by Lady Zhurong's unsuspecting steed. Three times he did this. In the first instance, he exchanged her for his captured generals. The final two, he did for the exquisite thrill of challenge.

When done, he had won her respect and allegiance.

Subdued by the brilliance and courtesy of Zhuge Liang, Meng Huo, and the Nanman returned to the fold. They remained loyal until the very end, never wavering.

With the south secured, and a fragile peace with Sun Quan, Zhuge turned his attention to the north, and the looming threat of Wei. His foresight told him time was short, portents weak, and the outcome uncertain. Except perhaps for his own end. This he saw all too clearly.

He took care to make these things clear to Sying Hao. The apprentice on whom so much depended, and who had been so carefully groomed. Within Sying Hao lay the promise of change to come. As to the those who would eventually partner with him, the wizard only knew there would be two, yet unborn, but whose spirits already imbued the land.

These affairs unfolded even as the beast trampled rampant. The "beast" being the engine of Yama's manifest consciousness. Strife!

He frequently reminded Sying Hao of Colonel Sun's admonition, "Only when we starve the beast will it turn his ravenous appetite back onto itself, and thus lift this plague from humankind."

Starving it? Can such be possible?

Let's consider for a moment.

All the philosophers, all the kings, all the generals and their provisioners throughout history have grappled with a seemingly unanswerable question. How does one continuously replenish an ever-expanding war machine? A demon with inexhaustible appetite, consuming all to its front, leaving nothing in its wake. Their only answer, always the same. Growth, new conquests, more bodies. But now, prospects had dimmed. Fresh acquisitions came already dried on the limb, drained from eons of abuse. The demon hungered. But not yet so much as to look to its own end.

Sun saw it right, thought Zhuge. *Yes, it was possible. But timing was everything, and even sages must submit to patience, lest the opportunity be lost forever.*

Liu Bei, Guan Yu, Zhang Fei and all the others were warring for their own purposes. Perhaps righteous—we have our opinions, and prefer to think favorably of them, but only history can judge. Of them all, Zhuge Liang seemed to be occupied on a grander battlefield, targeting Yama and somehow returning the dark lord to his rightful domain and confine.

Once convinced of the same, Meng Huo and Lady Zhurong swore eternal loyalty to Zhuge Liang, carefully distinguishing him from what remained of the Shu Han. Zhuge Liang reciprocated their oath, paving the way for his young apprentice to be the catalyst on which the Southland, and the greater nation, would one day pivot.

Not So Easily Fooled

One supposes it would be all right if, as with other miscreants, war lords and heads of state bore the brunt of their madcap undertakings. Should we think of them as children?

"Yes little piggy, you may have your war, but you must do so responsibly. Make sure you save well in advance. Then you can pay for the havoc you wreak. Never force others to fund your foolishness. Always ask politely, justify your requests, then make sure you leave something standing for the future.

"Whatever you do, don't spend what you don't have; don't destroy what you covet; and don't lose sight of your objective. That's what buffoons do. You're better than that. If it can't be achieved, let it go; you'll have no choice in the end but to sue for eventual peace. Consider that first before pulling any triggers. It's called Dharma, the law of existence—nothing you can do about it, except learn from the pain of consequences.

Lastly, do remember. If your war drags on interminably, there will be hell to pay. You'll have achieved nothing, offended nearly everyone, decimated your present and future, and screwed those you were ordained to serve and protect. Now, finish your rice and wash up. Oh, and be sure you don't let others exploit you!"

Sying Hao spent years preparing Southlanders for the possibility of invasion. In his time, he had witnessed every form of treachery and deceit, and had carefully sensitized their leaders on what to expect.

The Northern kingdoms sent their emissaries.

First they tenderized, employing the time-tested ploys of friendship and generosity. Very impressive gifts flowed to the Southland leaders. No surprises there.

Then, the promises of more wealth and assurances of commerce to follow. "You'll be among the first, get on board early!"

Next, the plays on fear. Guarantees of safety, security and alliance. "Consider this, we'll put sophisticated weapons at your disposal. With these, no one can threaten you. Trust us and what we have gleaned from hard experience. Beware of the Gupta! We'll stage forces nearby to protect you from all threats and eventualities."

None of it worked. Southlanders regarded Northerners as alien and very peculiar. As though risen from another creation, or the moon, or perhaps from hell. Within their entourage, Northern emissaries kept beautiful women, and hoards of riches and valuables. All copiously distributed to whichever Southland leaders inclined to line their own pockets.

Southlanders had no reservations about sex. They embraced the offerings with gusto. After enjoying the beautiful ladies, they returned to their wives, mates, and families, leaving the emissaries bewildered. The Northerners wondered what could motivate these seemingly barbaric people, for whom even the most beautiful women in the world held no irresistible allure. Why, in the north, warlords would sacrifice wives and sisters just to spend the night with any one of them.

For their part, Southlanders never lost sight of what they were dealing with. Sying Hao had coached them well. "You will learn all you need to know just by observing who and what they are."

The emissaries were also in the habit of flaunting costumes, pageant and adornment. Good theater! They knew the power of pomp and circumstance over minds habituated to respond with awe and admiration.

Nothing wrong with costume of course. It's part of life's game, isn't it?

While the Southlanders engaged in what seemed like frivolous exchanges, for the emissaries, much more lay at stake. It was no accident they were where they were and projected such lofty prominence. They possessed a profound understanding of the importance of politicking, rooted in the metaphysical lessons of primordial Wu Chi. They delved into the emergence of consciousness and will, recognizing the divergence of reality into Taiji[8]. This process unfolded in stages – from the actualization of the two, then the four, the eight, and so on, ultimately culminating in perceived reality. To some, this reality might be considered nothing more than an illusion, as espoused by Buddhists and Taoists. Yet, to the emissaries, it was a force to be reckoned with and, more importantly, exploited. Illusion or not, the internal arts were clear on the underlying dynamics. There existed two steps, though not so simple. The first step was to cultivate pliable energies within one's own body through a direct awareness of flow, achieved through purposeful movement. The second step involved projecting oneself into the world about, a process far more intricate than it might at first seem.

You might think of it as mind over matter. Real or not, illusion or not; for them it was as good as gold.

"What does this have to do with politicking?" you ask.

---

[8] Yin and Yang.

First, mind; then intent; then will; then the movement of chi which manifests overtly as li, or energy on the physical plane, and consequentially as jin. Power!

In time, the bastard offspring of these principles became playthings for despots. For magistrates, counselors and emissaries, the outreach of mind over the masses became their governing politic.

For them, to politic meant chi in its full bloom. What they actualized through their focused intent bubbled outward, transformed into power, which when precisely applied, produced desired outcomes and rewards. Great rewards.

Amazing what a skilled hand can garner from metaphysics and mere thought. Even more astonishing, truth or righteousness had nothing to do with any of it. That certainly made things easier. On a broader scale, whoever controlled the politics, controlled the game. They declared their own truth. The web of politics had its limits of course, like everything else. The trick was to push it outward, like an expanding sphere, until it encompassed everything. Then, there could be no counter. Endgame?

Never so easy! Controlling the politics meant thinking for those around you, but as you know, there's always some bug in the ointment. Still, some good news. Most will gladly let you do their thinking. Especially when they're distracted by the harsh realities of life: poverty, survival, illness, starvation, ignorance, greed, fear, and intimidation. Even religion. Most individuals seem to focus on two elemental needs. Survive until tomorrow, and aspire to a better afterlife. Somehow fulfill these two needs, and you can spin the people like tops.

But Sying Hao had now become the very bug in their carefully ointmented enticements. His influence sent ripples through the calculated allure the emissaries had meticulously crafted.

The important people all eventually came. Lords, generals, dukes, and princes, and their endless streams of emissaries. To impress the childlike Southerners, they often dined sitting on skins of tigers and presented carvings of elegant universes carved into tusks from the great xiang[9] beasts. For virility, they milked the poisons from king cobras, then skewered their meaty carcasses over barbecues. Their clothing radiated with threads of pure gold, and they self-adorned with gems and colored jade which Southlanders recognized instantly as having come from their own lands. Tortoise shell buckles, sky flower caps, tips of rabbit horn[10] on their boots. Worst of all, oracle chips from the shells of magnificent turtles, which they bragged to have been over a thousand years old. Almost too much for simple folk to behold.

"Such disgusting people," murmured the Southlanders among themselves.

Their visitors thought, "They will know our greatness merely by casting eyes upon us."

Southlanders, at their core, were animists first, Buddhists second. Wandering sages might have disputed this, concluding the Southlanders were Buddhists in fact, and nothing less. While others searched incessantly, Southlanders saw Buddha everywhere, and in everything, including each other. Right there—in their trees, the plants, the animals, the sky, the earth, the present, the past. It's true, they were unique. A perspective which eluded most

---

[9] Elephants

[10] Horns on rabbits, though hard to believe, result from a viral infection, and can indeed be found in nature.

outsiders, including the emissaries, lords, generals, dukes, and princes. Animists. Buddhists. You pick. Maybe it's the same? Those northern fellows wouldn't understand either way.

Incessantly polite, and never wanting a guest to lose face; the Southlanders, albeit tolerant to a fault, found the strange displays of the emissaries repulsive. Skins of tigers, carved tusks, charred bodies of cobras, horns of rabbit and shells of ancient turtles evoked an immense sense of dis-ease and loss. Shamed by their fellow man and filled with sorrow, the Southlanders struggled to comprehend the outsiders' unbounded ambition and appetites for what wasn't theirs to take or exploit. The would-be usurpers didn't get the disconnect. To them the Southlanders were insufferably ignorant. Seemingly incapable of responding with the anticipated awe and admiration. Indeed, at times their reactions bordered on disrespect. The two sides could simply not find ground or value in common.

As in past dealings with so-called barbarians, when all else failed, it was time to resort to fear and intimidation. The emissaries had pretty much now reached that point.

"We're massing armies along the border to better protect you," they declared, a thinly veiled attempt to instill fear and uncertainty.

When someone hints you should be afraid or fearful, and to put your guard up; a sales pitch is sure to follow. A request for your support, adherence, or a petition to relinquish something of value within yourself or your surroundings.

It's a tragedy when supposed friends deliver needless fear into untainted hearts. When fear becomes their argument, their position holds no merit. The Southlanders, a free and noble people, remained untroubled by the angst which plagued the North. They were not fearful of the unknown or the uncertain.

"We don't need your armies on our border to protect us," came the resolute response.

Sying Hao had been careful to teach them the many ways truth might be bent by lies and deceit. He warned them to be on guard whenever someone seeking their allegiance asked, "Don't you think you would be better off with our help?" or "What would Heaven have you do?" He further cautioned against outsiders who built reputations upon the ashes of others, whom they slandered or slaughtered.

On one occasion, some of the visiting dignitaries spoke of a renegade inhabiting the Southern Mountain, wreaking havoc on all who sought to do legitimate commerce with the south and west. They went so far as to call him a debased earth spirit, a degenerate, a murderer, a monster. We have already heard those things said of Bao Ling, but here of course they meant Sying Hao. Further salting their lies with fabrications, they soiled and slandered the memories of Zhuge Liang and Colonel Sun, whose images remained on prominent display within Southland shrines. How had they somehow missed it?

Blinded by ambition, the Northerners had no notion of how close they came to having their tongues removed.

One group of emissaries came boldly attired in the traditional garb of the Southland elders. Sying Hao had cautioned, "They disguise themselves as their intended victims, speaking their language, engaging in colloquialisms, even singing poems and songs commemorating shared struggles and love of land and nature, praising the old one hundred names as the salt and sweet of the earth. Beware wolves who wear sarongs!"

Thanks to such warnings, Southlanders saw through these shams. They measured one's goodness or baseness and treated one accordingly. When Northerners came disguised as Southlanders, sporting perfect dialects, and intimate familiarity with southern culture, past struggles, and values; the Southlanders deemed it a great comedy. They laughed openly, often directly into the surprised faces of the pretenders. Sometimes even politeness had no place.

This only further mystified the Northerners.

Demonization of Sying Hao, Colonel Sun, Zhuge Liang, the Guptas, the Mountain people, even Bao Ling (whom by then had already been accepted), only complicated matters for the Northerners. Not to mention the poetess nightingale, whose words of truth and sincerity had floated mysteriously on breezes from the north and already danced in hearts throughout the south. The Northerners could find no point of traction.

Southlanders believed in "face." Saving it and respecting it. Demonization of those not present spoke only to the true nature of the party doing the dirt.

Lies and disinformation. First Colonel Sun, and then Sying Hao, had schooled the Southlanders on what to look for. They now knew all they needed to know of these Northerners. "One day they will come. They will come to take, and to enslave. If we let them in, they will never leave. The cycle will continue endlessly, spinning downward as others even more decadent replace those who came first until all is used and gone. What remains will in time be abandoned as worthless."

The Southlanders studied the Northern Emissaries as they skirted questions about the scourge of Jing Province, or the decimation of the Shu Mountain tribes, or the generations of endless conflict and displacement of entire populations, cultures, lives, and ways.

Northerners wondered how remote Southlanders knew so much of what had taken place. They fumbled awkwardly, trying to spin sense from their answers and crippled explanations. This only brought more incisive questions as the Southland leaders pushed to gain understanding of how any people could degenerate so incomprehensibly.

None of the emissaries could prove the fate of the Southlanders would be any different should they be so foolish as to buy into the north's imbecilic (the Southlanders very word) game.

Even the manipulative Northlanders were at a loss on how best to paint this pig to make its smile more attractive to the discerning Southerners.

After unsuccessfully spending considerable time and effort to win over the Southlanders, additional armies of Wu aligned along their borders to the North and East, ostensibly to buffer the Southland from other predators likely to invade.

The Southlanders requested that the armies be withdrawn and returned to their garrisons in Wu. "We have no enemies, just the threat of your armies on our border. Please remove them."

The emissaries of Wu responded that what Wu did in its own territory should not concern the Southlanders.

The Southlanders read that to be a declaration of war and said so.

The Northerners denied and begged the gesture not be misinterpreted.

Overnight, the Southlanders seemed to evaporate into their jungles, simply gone.

Northern spies were stunned, looking everywhere, finding nothing; reporting to their masters the entire Southland seemed like a trap, ready to spring.

The borders sat precariously silent.

Part 2 - Murals Come to Life

Festivities

After witnessing the spectacular conclusion to the archery contest[11], Crystal Springs community erupted into merriment. Joy, laughter, and melodies of celebration echoed throughout the mountain until morning. Bao Ling required no coaxing to join in. As quickly as the arrows had flown in the contest, he surrendered to the revelry and newfound fellowship of the mountain community. Distant feelings from his youth flooded his thoughts. Sparks once dimmed, rekindled in the moment. It had been so long; he sometimes wondered whether what he remembered had been mere dreams or wishes. This day, they poured forth, vivid in their reality. It felt good.

What could be more precious than a sense of place and usefulness, belonging and fullness? Though at peace in the moment, Bao Ling still had gnawing concerns, targeting whoever would strip people like these of their standing ways, carelessly supplanting them with fabricated designs. Selfish constructs catering only to unnatural whims and ambitions. No different than the horns of rabbits or the shells of turtles that adorned their costumes, underscoring their greed with fancies of wealth and power. These types had no qualms and came primed to sacrifice all to their own ends.

---

[11] This vignette follows upon the archery challenge climaxing our prior work, *The Wizard's Testament*.

He knew they would come. He also knew he would be frontmost to meet them.

But again, on this particular day, his thoughts found safe harbor. The fleeting outrage swiftly relented with Zhi Mei's poetic rendition of the day's events, an epic song riding the framework of a tune well known to the mountain tribes. The people were ecstatic, as were Kong Kong and Kuan-Yin Ting, whom Zhi Mei made sure to feature prominently in the narrative.

Masons from the tribe had already planned stone memorials marking from where the final shot first flew and its endpoint, preserving the memory of the event for posterity. Mountain folk were not prone to forgetting. It had long been their custom to mark history and heritage using great boulders with etched stone faces. Even in our times, their scrawlings remain throughout the hills. Detailed accounts rendered in chiseled script, sometimes in pictographs, sometimes in shamanic shorthand known only to tribal elites.

In the hierarchy of legends Bao Ling neared in peerage to Abbot Shi-Hui Ke, though not quite on the same footing as Sying Hao, or Colonel Sun; and barely nudging the distinguished shadows of Zhuge Liang, Guan Yu and Zhang Fei. Such noble hierarchies took their root in broad histories of proven accomplishment. Though simple in their records, mountain folk took care in scoring and keeping measure. They knew who did what and when and seldom forgot. Bao Ling marked his standing in their pantheon and was satisfied.

None of this stood well with the outsiders. They considered the Shu traditions nonsense and took great sport in desecrating monuments wherever discovered. However, their power held no sway against the many songs and poems of the Shu, edifices of vapor and recall that rode the winds everywhere in the hills.

The renewed notoriety meant little to Bao Ling, standing transfixed by the incandescent Zhi Mei, whose golden glow channeled the fires warming the celebration. After several recitations, she and the ladies gathered to perform folk dances, with her mimicking the moves of the mountain people and they attempting to match her lowland style.

Afterward, the men, including Kong Kong, Kuan-Yin Ting, even the elders and martial master Li Fung, all came to the center to play their oft-recalled roles commemorating the exploits of Liu Bei, Guan Yu, and Zhang Fei. Ultimately, they dragged Bao Ling, albeit reluctantly, to the center stage of the bonfire-lit circle. The dance called for the spirit of a dragon to energize the resistance, lest the great battle be forfeit. All stared in anticipation at Bao Ling when the dragon song called out.

Bao Ling had been dreamily studying the profile of Zhi Mei, then looking to the stars above, wondering how one might tame the winds of fate to suit one's heart and quell one's solitude.

As often happens in such quandaries, there were no answers. Just the bliss of the moment, which, as you may have already sensed, should be carefully savored while at hand. Such moments are fleeting, and too prone to become lost memories.

Losing all inhibitions, he ran to their midst, and the dragon Bao Ling danced about from fire to fire, clearing the center ground of evil and intruders. He became more audacious and adroit as his initial reticence lifted away into the darkness. Bao Ling, the man, stole a glance at Zhi Mei, whose own eyes locked onto his in not so well-concealed fancy.

Kong Kong and Kuan-Yin elbowed each other, laughing over the two in their midst, whom all about could readily see were hopelessly smitten.

Later, as the moon finally set, Abbot Hui joined Bao Ling. Together they went off on their own, both quietly taking in the brilliant display of constellations. At times curious bats fluttered through their view, nearly glancing them while foraging for nighttime insects. Occasionally a meteor raced across the darkness, causing one or the other to point and exclaim, "There!" both silently admiring the silvery trail behind.

By the slowly dimming fires, Zhi Mei held the hill people mesmerized with her boundless stream of poems, songs and tales. Many conjured in the moment, bringing their common heritage to life, and revitalizing memories of great heroes and righteous conduct against insurmountable challenges.

Later, as activities finally played their courses to tired conclusion, Bao Ling returned with the Abbot and monks to the temple, where they retired for what remained of the evening. Zhi Mei remained in the village, as honored guest in the household of village chieftain Deshi Ku.

The early morning chill signaled the lateness of the season, foreshadowing change to brutal winter soon to follow the awakening autumn.

Before retiring, Bao Ling raised concerns to Abbot Hui. His time remaining would be short. Sying Hao expected him back at Southern Mountain before winter, and the window for return would fast be closing.

He had hoped to address the status of Zhi Mei but was cut short when Hui acknowledged, "We will talk more of this in the morning."

A Morning Visit

A cool dawn breeze brushed over the mat where he lay, stirring Bao Ling from his sleep.

Sensing a presence nearby, his eyes snapped open to find Hui centered in the doorway. *How long had he been standing there watching me?* Simply there, patient in stillness, watching for the first stir.

"We must talk."

He had news, none of it good. Events had heated dramatically in the South and the East. Armies from Wu have amassed along the northmost borders of the Southland and looked as though posturing for invasion.

Stricken by the news, Bao Ling asked, "That's thousands of lis[12] from here. How do you know it's true?"

Hui acknowledged but continued without answer, "Elsewhere, Wei's armies, newly encouraged by the distracted Wu, have gathered along the eastern plains. They are facing westward—towards us. Presumably timing the change of seasons. It only makes sense. Come spring they will push again through the ranges, looking once more to harness the Shu Roads. For them, a temptation forever irresistible, though prior efforts failed miserably. Even now, anticipated rewards far outweigh the practical constraints. In

---

[12] During the era of our stories, historians estimate the li to have been 405 meters. This works out to roughly 443 yards, virtually matching our own quarter mile.

their shrewd minds, reckoned benefits exceed costs. Completely rational, in their irrational reckonings. They measure costs only in terms of peasant soldiers. Fodder sent forward in overwhelming numbers. Most assuredly expendable. Easily replenished. Driven to doom in the unforgiving unknown. Disappeared into ambushes or dropped from rigged spans over endless chasms. A simple equating of what must be sacrificed to cover the gains."

The Wei would term their strategy, "ceaseless penetration." A simple game of numbers. They reckoned for each Shu eliminated; they could sacrifice a hundred of their own. They would flood Shu with indentured and conscripted humanity, even prisoners. Commodities deemed expendable and easily replaced. For the Wei, a perfectly sensible approach, as there appeared to be an endless supply of bodies. As losses mounted, they saw it as having fewer mouths to feed, fewer bodies to outfit and equip. They reasoned how even in the bad, one might still find good.

But what of the commoners? Why would anyone willingly submit to this life? The answer lay in powerlessness, the absence of other viable options, and a life dictated by circumstances beyond their control. It became a reticent willingness, a submission to service in exchange for the basic necessities of life: rice, warm clothing, and a dry place to sleep.

Riches and authority, on the other hand, were treated with more careful regard. They came only to those who seized them first, held them close, and were unwilling to sacrifice them needlessly. They were never to be taken lightly or sacrificed futilely. Lose them and you had nothing.

'Twas a fact, whoever gained the west, controlled incoming commerce and trade. Precious goods flowed from distant empires beyond the great expanse. The Han had perfected this. It sustained them. They carved and nurtured a network of routes leading to the remote west, as well as to the subcontinent. It enriched them far beyond all imaginings. Silk, an ordinary commodity here, equaled its weight in gold there. Europeans felt silk to be a vegetable product and had no inkling of how it came into existence. Who ever would have thought? Worms! The Chinese carefully obscured the secrets of its production, fully aware of profits enhanced and magnified by exclusivity and concealment. The same for ivory, horn, tea, and intricate carvings beyond the scope of any seen elsewhere—even paper, yet another marvel. In return, the Han received jewels, gold, and wondrous foodstuffs such as string beans, onions, cucumbers, carrots and more. They learned of a mystical beverage; a wine made not from rice, but rather from a berry which until then, had not been known to them. Simply divine!

For the Han, prosperity to this degree rendered war senseless and even counterproductive, leading to a prolonged era of peace.

Now their successors looked wantonly to the same horizons, seeking the surest route to subsidize and underwrite renewed ambitions for empire and exclusivity. Their trust lay in conquest and domination, a departure from the peaceful trade that once defined the prior era.

Hui went on, "Our own people have grown vigilant and protective of the mountains. Forward posts and lookouts cover all sectors. We may be small and few, but we are scrupulous, careful and vigilant. We have eyes in the east monitoring all changes. During his sojourn with us, Zhuge Liang devised his network of Seven Stars—a system of fortress temples much like our own, strategically placed to resist and frustrate any attempts to overrun the mountain networks. You might say the light from these seven stars still shines brightly in all quadrants, ensuring nothing slips beyond our scrutiny.

"While he regrouped our communities, he also engineered and fine-tuned the network of defenses. He further implored Liu Bei to dispatch the forces of Guan Yu and Zhang Fei along the eastern frontier. Against them, all intruders failed miserably, thus securing needed time for our reintegration. In this way, he also sealed their own rear tightly, allowing the armies of Liu Bei to regroup and fortify in the far west and ensuring the survival of the Shu Han. Zhuge's network remains in place to this day, and it has become my responsibility, which I share with the elders."

"How many Wei are there?"

The Abbot answered, 'We believe there are twenty wan[13]. Another ten wan[14] are in the north, held at bay for now by grassland horse tribes who tear at their exposed northern flanks. What remains of Liu's once formidable Shu Han legions exists only in the form of regional states dominated by warlords, usually competing amongst themselves. But still able to unite when dictated by practical need. Like fingers in a common fist against invaders, should necessity dictate. Particularly when the attack comes from Wei and pushes from the north. Old animosities die slowly when they have festered for generations."

"Do you think Wei can over run your mountain sanctuaries?"

"Perhaps. But the cost for them will be very high, as it will doubtless be for us. Nevertheless, we understand our destiny, as well as the gift of independence bestowed to us

---

[13] One wan equals 10,000. Twenty would total 200,000.
[14] *ibid*; 100,000

by Zhuge Liang. Thanks to him, we have returned from systematic extinction. We shan't forget that. To a person, we are prepared to do whatever we must to honor and repay his gift."

Bao Ling considered his many new friends, and the uncertainty confronting them. Nodding to the window opening, he asked "Out there, do they know?"

"As of this morning they will."

"Is there anything else I should be aware of? Anything I can do?"

Shi-Hui Ke nodded, then handed a folded parchment to Bao Ling, who opened and studied it closely. The script was immediately recognizable as Sying Hao's, though there was no signature or mark of identification. He read closely.

In it, he found the answer to his earlier question. It detailed the massive Wu forces aligned against the Southland, voicing expectations of imminent invasion. Bao Ling's eyes raised to meet Abbot Hui's.

"Can this never end?," he wondered aloud.

He could feel the rage simmering within and the unrelenting awareness that for so many, normal existence had been smothered by decades of turmoil. Was no one spared? In the end, would there be even a single seed left from which to rebirth life as he once knew it? Prayer seemed an exercise lost in vanity.

Reading further, he saw Sying Hao's estimate of twenty wan—another two hundred thousand.

"Hui, such numbers are beyond conception. Is there any hope?"

"The answer is simple, yet intricately woven. Indeed, there are vast armies, but their situation is complex and strained. Resources have dwindled, and even with forceful extortion, food is becoming scarce. The very commodities needed for survival are depleting. Everywhere, once exploited populations lay decimated, their land turned barren. Wei's troops are running on near-empty. As we speak, they grapple not just with the will to conquer, but with the pressing need to survive. This mirrors the situation Liu Bei faced when he first ventured west. As you know, Liu won the hearts of those he led, and prospered through insightful leadership. That is, until the germ of ambition touched down once more, infecting even him, who seemed without peer and above them all.

"As for your concerns, the sheer numbers may indeed seem overwhelming, but I caution you not to forget: these are forces desperate for hope—long used and worn from lost causes. They lack the heart for new conquests. Victories are short-lived, marred by greater sacrifice and complications in their wake. Promises made to them were never honored. Many fought for homelands and families they have now learned no longer exist. Now, each conscript must weigh the consequences of current actions against what has been gleaned from harsh experience. Truth and lies, promises and deceit—with time, even an imbecile can discern the difference. At some point, reason must regain its influence over the chaos of insanity. We can't predict when, but we do have patience and determination."

Bao Ling examined the parchment, his curiosity piqued. "How did you get this? And what connection does the Southland have with the Mountain tribes and the Shu Roads?"

Abbot Hui pointed with his eyes to one of the citadel towers where a flurry of birds circled. The significance struck Bao Ling immediately. Abbot Hui and Sying Hao maintained direct contact through a system of winged messengers. Aware of Sying Hao's capabilities in consciousness transposition, Bao Ling toyed with the possibility Sying Hao himself had made the journey, arriving in a form known to Shi-Hui Ke. He struggled with whether to say anything of this, lest he be thought mad.

Sensing the stillness in Bao Ling, Hui added, "Usually he sends his messengers. As it stands, affairs in the south demand his constant vigilance. Still, we have shared remarkable experiences in the past, and one way or the other manage to stay connected when developments unfold."

"I'm not sure what to make of it all," Bao Ling admitted.

Shi-Hui Ke nodded in agreement. "Me too." Then he handed yet another message from Sying Hao.

This time, Sying Hao's message spoke to the timing of events, revealing that bounty bands were scouring the countryside and highland passes for a renegade and his female accomplice. The duo had drawn scrutiny coinciding with the disappearance of a reconnaissance vanguard. Authorities have declared them outlaw reactionaries, a threat to civil order and stability, and promised rewards for their capture. In a touch of playful humor, Sying Hao expressed a desire to meet them, whoever they were, and tender his "Well done!" in person.

In so many words, he implored Shi-Hui Ke take the two under his protection until the seasons changed. They could then safely navigate the frozen southern wastelands, cutting west, looping southward, and discreetly return to Southern Mountain while avoiding population centers, military outposts, and the increasingly frequent patrols. The current situation made any immediate attempt impossible.

Bao Ling's gut sank.

He belonged by the side of Sying Hao.

He yearned for his past.

He needed Zhi Mei.

But where could he find a way which made sense and reconciled with all he deemed important.

A final message from Sying Hao was for Bao Ling's eyes only. Shi-Hui Ke passed it, still sealed.

"Little brother, times grow hard in the South, but our spirits are high. I have been working with our southern brothers and sisters, and trust they will not fail. It will be challenging, and I know you'll understand. I cannot abandon them. Stay with Shi-Hui Ke until the seasons change. He has much to show you. I implore you to learn all you can. For now, he will be your guide. When winter comes, troops will lose their resolve in finding you and your companion. Then it will be prudent to move. Be very cautious, avoid contacts, follow the cold and cut through the frozen basins. Then head west to the shadowlands, turn south to the mountain only when you are certain it is safe. Be wary, don't let them anticipate your movements. I will be on the lookout for you. Use this delay as an opportunity. You have much to learn, and you carry within you many unanswered questions. As do I. There are great mysteries swirling about us, and you center among them. Learn all you can from everything you encounter at the temple. Abbot Shi-Hui Ke will reveal much while you are with him. Use the moment well. Remember he is our eternal brother, both in common purpose and in destiny. When the time comes to move, you will know. Don't linger. I will be expecting you."

Bao Ling passed it to Abbot Hui, assuring there would be no walls between the perceptions of the three.

"What next?" Bao Ling asked.

"Come, it is your time to visit the Grand Hall of the temple. There are things you must see."

The Grand Hall

The Grand Hall unveiled itself, revealing an immense statue of Sakyamuni[15]. In its immediate surroundings, reverent visages of monks, disciples, acolytes, and guardians filled the space. A subtle radiance imbued the chamber, affording a sanctuary of peace and serenity severing any links to the chaos threatening from afar.

Abbot Hui paid his proper respects, then gestured for Bao Ling to follow. Together, they ascended stairs to another level. To Bao Ling's surprise and amazement, the entire history of the three warring kingdoms unfolded around him, explicit murals set in a maze spanning the surround.

Having benefited from the mentoring and accounts of Sying Hao, Bao Ling quickly oriented himself to the nearest image, signifying the very beginning. The moment when the three heroes[16] first met and bound their destinies, creating legends that would endure for all time. Even as their dreams unraveled, the sworn bond held fast. The three locked forever as brothers in purpose, fierce and with uncompromising loyalty. Each to the other, to the nation they hoped to save, and to the people they aimed to serve. Though not born together or on the same day, they swore eternal allegiance to each other and to their noble cause. Praying only when all was said and done, they would

---

[15] Shì Jiā Móu Ní - The Buddha
[16] Liu Bei, Guan Yu, Zhang Fei

depart together to the afterlife. Three as one, until their final sun had set.

From there, Bao Ling traced the threading maze of images to the rebellion of the Yellow Turbans. Then the disintegration of Han by treachery from within. Emperor Ling passed away soon after the rebellion, leaving the weak child Emperor Shao[17] to navigate the tumultuous court, unable to control the influential eunuchs or the power brokers vying for control.

The warlord Dong Zhuo detains, then later topples the child Emperor, installing the eight-year-old Emperor Xian, Shao's younger brother, as a mere figurehead beneath his oppressive thumb. Dong Zhuo's tyranny reaches unchecked heights until those who could bear it no longer arise in protest, but to no avail. Having no alternative, they join their forces in opposition. Among them was the adept Cao Cao, perhaps sensing new opportunities for himself.

Bao Ling traces through the exquisitely detailed chronicle. It feels as though history plays again before his studied gaze. The images possess a life all their own, seemingly enchanted. Cao Cao and other warlords, banding under Yuan Shao, eventually put Dong Zhuo on the run, though not fully defeated. Would what followed surprise anyone? The coalition, already strained by competing ambitions within, soon disintegrates. Dong Zhuo ultimately meets his just end when murdered by his foster son. A tale of competing fancies targeting the same courtly damsel. Though profoundly impacting the turn of events, her identity is unknown to history. A testament that fates of villains are best met by our collective ridicule, never by our grudging admiration.

---

[17] Emperor Shao literally means "Young Emperor."

The next mural shows the disintegration of the once empire into multitudinous factions. Yuan Shao wages war in the north, while Sun Jian and Liu Biao compete in the south.

These events set the stage for the ascendance of Cao Cao and Liu Bei. Both emerge as singularly skilled leaders, capable of forming effective armies and staking their own claims to territory.

Perhaps the single defining event in the unfolding roll of chaos was Cao Cao's "rescue" and detainment of Emperor Xian from what remained of Dong Zhuo's weakened grip. Cao proves to be a brilliant and charismatic leader, albeit very short on restraint and overly inclined to ambition. With Emperor Xian in custody, he establishes the new capital at Xu, defeats warlord rivals Lü Bu, Yuan Shu, and Zhang Xiu and establishes "imperial" control over the heartlands. In essence, uniting the center and north and defining what would in time become the state of Cao Wei, the northern kingdom. By then, Cao Cao has amassed enough power to confront the formidable Yuan Shao, brilliantly defeating him in the Battle of Guandu.

Cao Cao's ascendancy was no quirk of fate. His talents had genuine bite, and teeth which drove deep. All recognized how he made his own luck through diligence and brilliance.

One loses sense of time when immersed in intricately detailed images. To his surprise, Bao Ling's morning had nearly lapsed. Mesmerized, he continues his study, accompanied by the silent Hui. Suddenly he stops. So taken in had he become, he failed to frame its relevance within the context of the present. He turns to Hui, "Why are these here? In a sacred temple? Who produced the images? They come from the hand of a singular artist. But who?"

Hui answered, "Commissioned and placed by Zhuge Liang. He had his reasons, which might perhaps become clearer for you as we move along."

Next, we witness that in the South, Sun Jian somehow gains possession of the imperial Han seal but unexpectedly meets his end at Xiangyang. His son Sun Ce trades the seal for reinforcements from yet another would be emperor, Yuan Shu. With these needed additions, he secures the rich riverlands of the southeast, which ultimately coalesce into the state of Wu. Bao Ling sees where Sun Ce dies prematurely after a ghostly visitation from the imprudently executed magician Yu Ji. His younger brother, Sun Quan replaces him, becoming the missing third piece in the now actualized trinity, alongside the still lightly regarded Liu Bei and the formidable Cao Cao.

The ascendancy of Cao Cao and Sun Quan, as well as the misappropriated Imperial Seal, inclined everyone toward rivalry to Liu Bei. Alongside his brothers by oath, he had sworn loyalty only to the Han. The others praised the Han endlessly but only as greasepaint for their aspirations. Not Liu Bei. He and his companions distinguished themselves in the defeat of the Yellow Turbans and in the campaign against Dong Zhuo. Though considered peripheral players, their talents left no doubts. So long as they might be kept on a short leash, their remarkable skills could underscore anyone's rising ambitions.

Bao Ling processed his thoughts. *How remarkable, Liu Bei truly seems to have risen from nothing before ascending to prominence.*

With Cao Cao's blessing, Liu Bei becomes governor of Xu, where in a play of mixed loyalties, treachery, and fluctuating sides, he loses his province to Lü Bu; but then combines forces with Cao Cao to defeat Lü Bu at Xiapi.

Emperor Xian formally recognizes Liu as "Imperial Uncle" on his return to the capital. This seals his ascendancy into the triumvirate. Doubtless a ploy by the captive monarch to create a strategic counterweight to Cao Cao, knowing Liu Bei had now arrived as a player.

Bao Ling peers at the images intently, noting the aspirations and demeanors discernible in the facial details. He weighs the portrayals against what he already knows to be a history of untold suffering set upon the general population, particularly among his own.

As he edges further along in his contemplation, Abbot Hui silently accompanies him. As though anticipating questions soon to arise, some of which he has answers for.

The next mural depicts Emperor Xian's decree—a message scribed in his own blood for the eyes of the loyal Han general Dong Cheng, and notably, also for the eyes of "Imperial Uncle" Liu Bei.

Better had he never written it.

This was the proverbial straw that tilted and then spun the empire into never-ending chaos, flinging open the gates of hell to spew its dogs of warfare and death to all reaches of the once-grand Han state.

Now only a figurehead, Emperor Xian had become captive puppet to Cao Cao. He knew it and wanted out!

One can argue about the qualities and the inclinations of Cao Cao. Perhaps even the justifications or rationales. But the manifestations were clear. He was carefully maneuvering toward becoming de facto supreme ruler. Possession is nine-tenths of empire. So, the ancients held. Emperor Xian's broadside, written in his own blood, was Han's final call to arms.

The next depiction shows Dong Cheng, Liu Bei, and other lords planning to act and save what remained of the

Han. We puzzle over their true intent. Reviewing such scenarios, we must incline to question everything, even the hearts of the seemingly righteous. Failing in this may have profound consequences.

They plotted to assassinate Cao Cao.

Be careful boys!

Did he deserve such? Perhaps, but who could possibly know with certainty? What or who would stand in his place if he were gone?

The lower right quadrant of the mural illustrates Cao Cao's justice. On discovering the plot, like the great though ruthless general he was, he reacts decisively. He executes the conspirators, their families, their associates, and the families of their associates. History shows Cao Cao to have been generous and loyal to a fault to those who served him well but merciless to those who did not. You might say he plotted with discipline and purpose, sometimes even kindness, but wielded a very, very heavy stick. Among the few who survive is Liu Bei. Thus are their destinies set.

The account of the aftermath depicts the determined pursuit of Liu Bei by Cao Cao's army. Cao had finally taken full measure of Liu Bei, once seen as little more than a minor warlord. A "flea" who, on occasion, might serve a useful purpose or perhaps even the role of a transient ally. Lord Cao knew enough now to realize Liu had become a veritable impediment to the course of his own ambitions.

Emperor Xian had skillfully manipulated the two into eternal opposition by declaring Liu the imperial uncle, and by proxy branding Cao to be the usurper.

Cao pursued Liu relentlessly, defeating him in Xu Province, driving him to the protection of Yuan Shao, then to Runan where he defeats him again. The embattled Liu survives only by retreating with his greatly reduced force (and his two sworn brothers) to Jing Province, where he finds protection under Liu Biao, a distant relation.

All these events play before Bao Ling's eyes as he slowly progresses. The depiction of Jing Province overwhelms his stoic composure. Home! Tears well in his eyes at scenes of once bountiful fields, beautiful streams, abundant lakes, and villages dotting the landscape. Right there before his eyes! All that he recognized and knew to now be gone. His heart grew heavy, witnessing again what his people had lost. Common folk who had nothing to do with, or anything to gain from these dealings. Heat of anger began again to erupt from whatever sealed chamber lay deep within. A molten core of muted memories. Though the images were only murals, it seemed the ethos of those portrayed lived on within them, as did the spirit of the land. Zhuge Liang plainly did not want these matters forgotten.

The gentle hand of Shi-Hui Ke touched Bao Ling's shoulder, just enough to remind him he was not alone.

Elsewhere, the poet maiden sat surrounded by her village hosts, singing her improvised poem of the hero emerging.

Windows to History

We've talked about Jing Province elsewhere. However, its significance runs deeper. Once the fertile pulsing heart of the Han civilization, it served as a wellspring of essential resources, materials, and commodities. Its natural infrastructure, with numerous riverways and ancient passages, facilitated the free movement of people and goods. Imperial strategists long extolled its value as "A breadbasket and storehouse for the necessities of empire."

Controlling Jing ensured a stable and uninterrupted flow of essentials, providing backbone for the empire while keeping military appetites in check. After the fall of Han, competing warlords and aspiring kings coveted Jing. Its strategic location made it a constant target, sitting at the crossroads of their shifting battle lines. From there it beckoned continuously. A needed harbor and refuge for any force requiring respite, either coming from or headed off to another misadventure. It seemed an endless cycle, spinning to nowhere.

However, the province presented its own strategic challenges for any force seeking control. Thinly stretched supply channels argued one might capture Jing, but holding it indefinitely was another matter. It came at the cost of exposing vulnerabilities elsewhere. When you hold one place, your grip loosens on another. Basic military science. In bygone days of Empire, Han had successfully consolidated the nine provinces, including Jing. Under exemplary rule, a singular sense of identity bound the nation together, fostering devotion to the Empire and its rulers. Even remote settlements, like Ling Village, felt part of a greater whole. However, this era of peace and prosperity faded long before the birth of Bao Ling.

Now, as he progressed alongside Abbot Hui, Bao Ling witnessed the unfolding chronicle frame by frame, a comprehensive narrative that left no gaps in his understanding of the past.

Versed in the history of his people and enriched by the teachings of Sying Hao, he felt disoriented by what he saw. *How do I make sense of these things? Where do I fit into these streams of images?* Turning with a troubled look to Shi-Hui Ke, he asked, "When did Zhuge Liang place the murals here."

"The end of his time was fast approaching. The others were already gone, and Zhuge Liang had embarked on yet another major campaign to the north. This effort represented the final link in his chain of promises to Liu Bei: "Never let our story be forgotten!" Without the others and the Shu Han empire disintegrating around him, Zhuge had undertaken more than even he, in his prime, might have assumed alone. He too had become just another marionette of destiny, or so others began to say. Though disappointed, he played true and fully to the course of his fate, anticipating his end without fear, hesitation, or complaint.

Those around him protested his perpetuation of what many regarded as pointless and futile. If he defeated Wei in the north, who, in the end, would assume rule? No one person had the rightful claim to the seat of power, nor the wherewithal to hold it once gained. Certainly, no one in Liu's lineage. The offspring were, in all politeness, deemed wanting. On one single point, none could disagree. Zhuge

Liang would have made an excellent emperor. But that will always be left for scholarly conjecture. He knew taking the reins would not end the bedlam. There seemed to be no answers to causes not yet made evident.

"In the midst of what would have brought lesser men to despair, we learn Zhuge Liang gained new awarenesses. He often spoke of ending the chaos, but his words frightened others. During meetings, he would blurt out 'The real enemies are not the Wei and the Wu, but the minions of Yama who scourge us all.'

What the hell was he talking about?

"He openly bemoaned how even he had fallen at times to the spells of illusion and deception, neglecting the clawed hands shifting strategic pieces from within the shadows. Walking about, speaking these things to himself; others politely stared away in dismay. Had he gone mad? To his generals and loyal followers, he begged forgiveness. 'I have led you to a place where final victory escapes us in our concluding moments together. But there will be victory!' His assurance was bond enough. Though nearly despairing at times, they remained resolute, loyal, and always by his side. They struggled to grasp his meaning when he proclaimed, 'We now undertake a much more vital role. It falls to us not to achieve military victory, or to re-kindle a turned-to-dust empire. It is we who will free Dharma[18] and the underlying Tao from the blight of chaos.'

"This of course left them all mystified. *What does he mean?* But not one argued against the declaration. Such faith had they in him. Enviable. I wish it could be so for all of us.

---

[18] "Dharma" - The way of righteousness, holiness and unity. It is the only thing you can take with you after death. If you protect Dharma, it will protect you.

Zhuge Liang had been tested countless times and had invariably proven himself correct. It mattered not whether mere mortals, or their kings and emperors could or would not get it. Faith and trust! That's what they had come to rely on in the end. As in the very beginning, in the end, it was all they had.

"It was during this period Zhuge Liang hinted to the existence of his Grand Design. His self-heralded 'greatest of plans,' which he promised would, if executed properly, eventually steer the dogs of war back to their underworld confines. He predicted it would restore the land to its natural inclinations, absent overlays of greed, deceit, ambition, and cupidity which had run loosely for too long. He foresaw an eventual end of conflict. The three warring kingdoms would reduce in time to two, then to one, with even that supplanted by a new order. It would take lifetimes; and each generation would contribute its part. He emphasized he stood with the earnest heart of Liu Bei. He would never forget the land, nor the people. Sadly, the onus would be on the oppressed and least favored. Only they could foster the will to turn destiny to where affairs of warlords and tyrants and their profiteering cronies no longer mattered. 'I regret to say, it will not come without great sacrifice on all parts. It is the most noble of tasks. Our land must survive this scourge of chaos.'

"Though he could not predict specifics with conviction, he stressed the importance of the Shu Roads and the role of the mountain people - my people. He conceived and bequeathed the Seven Stars, one of which became the Crystal Springs compound. He tasked Colonel Sun with the Southland, saying 'Prepare the Southlanders in every respect for their eventual roles, particularly as it promises their ultimate survival.' He also foresaw the importance of Jing Province as a fulcrum for what would come.

"When asked to spell out the details of his Grand Design, he refused to answer interrogators directly. 'Forgive me comrades, I don't want "them" to know.' *Didn't want who to know?* In lieu of substantive plans, he commissioned these murals. 'My time has now grown too short. I can only point the way. Trust in this. Though you may despair at times, I will leave signs enough to follow. They are for others to decipher. The others will know who they are and what to do when they see them.'

"He then predicted the day would soon come when he would no longer be there to serve. He instructed his followers to go home when he was gone. He ordered they remove themselves from all conflicts, which he assured would still be raging elsewhere. 'Preserve yourselves, and your kin. Bide patiently. Our time will come.' By then, all would be in place. For now, they should simply forget he ever existed. 'You have all given enough, more than anyone had a right to expect. You have my gratitude. Without your efforts and sacrifice, all would have been lost.'

"As to the murals, he scrupulously instructed the artists on their content and presentation, sometimes inserting finishing touches with his own hand. They were the most skilled artists in the land, yet they marveled in awe of his mastery of their craft. You have before you his message to us, placed on these walls over one hundred and fifty years ago. Speaking through his thoughts as though he were here in the room."

"They all look so alive. I almost wonder if they can see us here, staring at them."

"Yes, there is a bit of wizardry and magic before us. We tend to them very carefully, and study them closely. There is so much to behold within them."

Looking at Hui, Bao Ling asked, "Forgive my impertinence. My head spins from what I see. If there's a message for me, I have only blurs. But tell me, what do they say to you?"

"My words are not the message. I will not have them distract you so early in your study. First little brother, look further into them. Take them in as deeply as you can, like breathing pristine air. Have no preconceptions. Then I will ask you share with me what you glean from them."

Bao Ling expected more from Abbot Hui but got only silence. Together, they turned to study the next mural. This one depicted Liu Bei's darkest years, his first sojourn in Jing to assist its able ruler, Liu Biao. His forces had been relentlessly harassed and pursued, reduced nearly to naught. On entering Jing, all that remained were his loyal cadre and a small tag-a-long population which had grown to trust and support his brand of enlightened leadership. He genuinely cared for these people, and they for him. Though his decisions had cost them dearly, they could forgive him and see his true heart through all the blunders and setbacks. Their loyalty remained firm. Honoring and reciprocating, more than once, Liu Bei diverted his top generals to defending the exposed followers, even when placement elsewhere might have produced a needed military advantage. He would never be so callous as to sacrifice the most vulnerable.

It was during this early period Liu Bei lost his valued counselor and strategist, Xu Shu, to Cao's deceit. We have told that story elsewhere[19]. The depth of Liu's despair ultimately precipitated the three arduous pilgrimages to the mountainous west and the eventual return to Jing with Zhuge Liang.

---

[19] Token Tales and Fragments (2020)

Top Dog

As top dog, Cao Cao began seeing threats everywhere. His strategic mind fixated on Wu, the realm of Sun Quan, a tempting conquest for a palate accustomed to refined victories. Why settle for only Jing when the southern jewel of Wu beckoned. A kingdom teeming with wealth and untapped potential. Added to that, the lingering memory of Wu's Lady Sun, whom he had once encountered and never quite gotten over. Why ignore the will of heaven? The tides of fortune already favored him. He had consolidated the north and Liu Bei lay in disarray. A young and untested Sun Quan stood as open door.

Why Wu? An affluent southern kingdom, rich in resources, far removed from the north. Blessed with a loyal population, brilliant generals and a significant, but untested standing army. In this, Cao wisely foresaw a future threat from the south, but for now, it presented an enticing prospect. The time was ripe for new conquests, and the consequences of ignoring this opportunity were too great to bear.

It would serve well to note there are some, who, though gifted in many respects, can see only threats or opportunities. The great ordinary which fills the broad space between, somehow eludes them. As though standing within a boundless forest; only two trees among the many catch their attention. One to be felled, one to be nurtured. Conquer, cultivate; eradicate, restore. So the throngs of advisers endlessly urge. But what is better, and which is which? Amid ceaseless arguments and endless justifications, decisions often boil down to mere guesswork. *What do I want to do?* Perhaps a remnant fault from a birth's wanting endowment. Many leaders cannot readily differentiate the merits of one course from the other. So they go with their gut—their instincts and their suspicions. Thinking only of where gain is best had.

Among life's more puzzling displays, we witness the frequent drift of reason. Marvel as it grapples to reconcile perceived threats and opportunities. Importuning a functional understanding upon which to solidify a gainful course. Invariably, the calculation reduces to conflict and aggression … seize it, then exploit it. What else is there? Table righteousness for later. First, grab what's within reach.

It appears we have glimpsed into the mind of Cao Cao.

A governed population should keep these types on sturdy leashes. Never have them ascend to leadership or positions of influence or authority, if you have the wherewithal to prevent it. Most tend to fall short in this regard. Whether cream or crap, leaders ascend by tint of nature to the top. But it's the crap which has the weight of numbers and wider distribution. More likely than not, it will rise topside first. Just as likely, you will find it surrounded by more of the same. Between you and I, it would be best for these types to be kept in monasteries or cloisters; better yet, prisons. In those settings, perhaps their propensities would soften. They might find their energies better devoted to the conquest of poetry, calligraphy, or art; or perhaps poverty, disease and suffering.

Everything is possible you know.

That said, we have no practical choice but to recognize the wheel of chaos[20] rolls unimpeded by our protests and flailings. Bumping harshly into just about everything, it moves ever along, dismantling all hierarchy and order.

For Cao Cao, taking Wu promised Empire surpassing even the Han. "Take Wu, and all provinces between will fall, starting with Jing." That's what his advisers said.

In Cao's mind, that settled it!

While the two kingdoms postured like game cocks nearing a reckoning, Liu Bei, guided by Zhuge Liang, broadens his influence in Jing. Rooting there, he trains and replenishes his forces and grows his influence, anticipating the inescapable face off with Cao Cao. During this period, Zhuge Liang refines his Longzhong Plan, envisioning Liu Bei as pivot point amongst those vying for power. In short, the long harassed and pursued Liu Bei, and the now targeted Sun Quan, would do best to align their interests to counter and offset Cao Cao; now commonly viewed as the usurper. A later time would allow for them to reconcile their own issues.

In yet another mural, Zhuge can be seen standing in counsel with Liu Bei and his generals, among them Guan Yu, Zhang Fei, Shao Yun, Ma Chao and Huang Zhong. Others are featured prominently nearby, notably a broad shouldered, helmet-wearing figure, almost tree-like in appearance; accompanied by a young man, whose already wizened eyes immediately draw Bao Ling's scrutiny.

Hui interjected, "He cuts quite a presence, doesn't he?"

"Who?" asked Bao Ling, looking closely at the youth.

"That would be Colonel Sun."

---

[20] On the issue of chaos, one might consider the many implications of the Second Law of Thermodynamics.

"Yes, but I was looking at the young man beside him. Doesn't it seem unusual for him to be there, in a session with the leaders of state?"

"Ah yes, Colonel Sun's squire. As I understand, the two were inseparable. Sun had rescued the young man in the aftermath of a horrific battle. Seeing his family and home now gone, the orphaned boy retreated to a massive rock where he anguished alone for days, wailing at his loss over the smoldering ruins. Finally, bitten by hunger, he reduced to solitude and silent whimpering, appearing only to await death.

"Sun, himself seemingly always alone, saw the boy from afar and at first thought him to be a spy. He ascended to investigate, then immediately empathized when he found the child overcome by sorrow and loss. Sun knew the taste of bitter. Saying nothing, as few can do so well as him, he sat alongside the boy. After several more days with both still fixed immobile and staring into emptiness, the boy turned to Sun and said, 'I think I'll go with you, Sir.' To which Sun replied, 'Suits me.'

"From that day, they were rarely seen apart, except perhaps when the maturing youth became apprentice to Zhuge Liang."

"How can it be?" mused Bao Ling in a barely audible whisper, staring intensely into the boy-man's eyes, recognizing much of his own pain and loss mirrored within.

"You'll see more of him as we move along. He grows to manhood alongside Colonel Sun, and they are like father and son. In time, at Sun's urging, Zhuge Liang takes notice of the young man's remarkable abilities and indoctrinates him into the realms of his own heightened reality."

Bao Ling turned to Abbot Hui, "It's the first true image I've ever seen of Colonel Sun. I had always imagined him looking a certain way—fierce, uncompromising, big, wild eyed, hairy, agile, perhaps barefoot, not handsome, but charismatic. Here, he looks almost like a giant ape, bred for battle. Completely out of his element amongst humans."

Then Bao Ling had a stunning realization. The resemblance between the image on the mural and the remarkable stranger he had once met in his youth was uncanny. It all flashed back. Grandfather He Ling called the stranger "Colonel Sun." They had served together defending the province. The stranger even referred to grandfather as a brother. Then there were his words deemed so significant by Uncle Wei[21]. "They also said the boy was with you."

Uncle Wei recognized what I had missed completely. I was that boy. What did it mean?

The thought flashed like a bolt of lightning. He said nothing of it in that moment, deeming it more coincidence than anything else.

"And my original question still begs answer. You know what I mean. How can it be?"

Hui took some time, attempting to give context to what would follow.

"As you know from my own story[22], there were two who restored my own life. One was Sying Hao, the other, Li Fung. You now know them both. In the distant past, I too have encountered Sun. It is fair to say Sun's appearance bordered on simian. Still, nobility, beauty, and purity radiated from within him, blessing all he considered his friends.

---

[21] An encounter detailed in prior novel in this series, *Token Tales and Fragments.*

[22] Recalled in *The Wizard's Testament.*

"We loved him dearly. An impeccable warrior, the equal of Guan Yu and Zhang Fei, or any of the Five Tigers for that matter. Still, he preferred solitude and life in the shadows, always worried about frightening children or overhearing someone's unkind comments regarding his 'uncouth' appearance. Here, we remember him more for his enlightened mind and kindness than for his ferocity. Truthfully, he fit in well among our people. We tend to celebrate differences and to look upon them with our own sense of childish wonder. Sun seemed more like a god than an aberration. Appearing almost to have been hewn from stone, he wielded immense power.

"He inclined to recite stories, often adding warmth to the campfires during our cold evenings, never running dry, never repeating, just relating his experiences over a lifetime of travel and adventure. He took care to highlight the many lessons he learned, so they would not escape us. We would often reflect how it seemed he had lived the lives of a hundred men. As a young child, I thought of him as a teacher.

"Like Zhuge Liang, he knew many incantations, and could presumably shift shapes at will. This, of course, makes one wonder why he chose to look as he did. He stressed he only wanted to be as he truly was and aspired to nothing else. He told us, 'Disguises had their purposes; but nothing outweighed being who you truly were.' For example, he marveled at the lengths Marshall Guan would go to, meticulously setting each thread, amulet, ornament, or implement before presenting himself to others. He did so even before going into combat, perhaps forgetting or ignoring he'd be covered in blood by day's end. Sun joked about how watching Guan prepare for battle was like witnessing a groom preparing for his wedding, wanting only to look perfect for his bride. He told my people many times over, be proud of who you are. No one, anywhere, can be as good as you are at who you truly are; always make that your first light held out to the world."

Bao Ling, puzzled over the account, "I don't get it. It seems you're sidestepping my question. Again I ask, 'How can it be?'"

Hui continued, "Sun demanded we be awake and aware, just as he was. He stressed the importance of pushing through, getting the true you to the surface, and letting the illusory you drop off like the outer shell of a cocoon. This of course was after his epic journey to the West and his reputed enlightenment."

Bao Ling answered, "Yet he manifests as a killing machine? How does one reconcile that with his being awake and aware?"

Hui looked at Bao Ling, saying nothing; his eyes spoke for him.

Bao Ling could hear the thoughts, just as if they had been spoken, *"As are you, Bao Ling!"*

He would have to be more cautious with his tongue.

Hui continued, "I understand he first came to the Shu Han at the request of Zhuge Liang. Like Zhuge, Colonel Sun had once retreated into the frozen wastelands at the roof of the world. Some say he had his own kingdom, ruling over others just like himself. That may be true, but if there are others like him, we have not yet encountered them.

"It is said Liu Bei, Guan Yu, and Zhang Fei took a quick liking to Colonel Sun. One might consider it mutual admiration. They deemed Sun's loyalty, once gained, an asset equivalent to ten thousand men on the battlefield. I believe that might understate his true worth. Regardless, Liu's history of constant retreat stabilized virtually immediately as Sun's presence secured Liu's exposed northern flanks. Thus, setting the stage for Red Cliffs, and what followed."

"You test my patience brother Hui. I'm sure you know I'm talking about the young man alongside Colonel Sun. Those are unmistakably the eyes of Sying Hao. How can it be his young image stands before us on this mural put here over a hundred and fifty years ago? Perhaps longer. Even Colonel Sun, how do I reconcile him on this image, and as the noble officer who once appeared to me, seeming to know of my existence? Even you admit, the same Sying Hao returned you to life. How long ago was that? How old are you?"

"They are not ghosts, if that is what you're asking. Both will bleed the same as you and me, if cut. I can't speak entirely for Colonel Sun. He is unique. But Sying Hao, if lanced, he will race to his ancestors no less quickly than us or anyone else."

Incredulous, Bao Ling replied, "OK, what is it I fail to grasp? Or that you're not telling me?"

"What you are missing, but starting to get, is that Sying Hao looms large in Zhuge Liang's Grand Design. As do I … and even you!"

He would say no more to Bao Ling's pleading stare.

Out of respect and each genuinely caring for the other, they both elected to avoid discord and turned as one to the remaining murals.

In the following pane, Bao Ling traces Cao's elevation to Chancellor, and his continued efforts to eliminate Liu Bei, seeking at first to gain Jing, thereby setting up a springboard to Sun Quan in the southeast. Thus, by his reckoning, coalescing the empire into a single cohesive entity under his exclusive control. Here, he succeeds only in part. Still, as

Chancellor, Cao Cao now gains full control of the northern kingdom and stands ready to risk all. The time to harvest is when the opportunity ripens.

Zhuge's Strategy of the Crane

Multiple murals depicted the terrible siege at Red Cliffs. No doubt, Cao felt his time had arrived. He risked everything in what he calculated would be the decisive battle. Victory here would mark the birth of his dynasty. Forget the Han. His would be a new and greater empire.

Lord Cao differed from so many others who risked nothing. Lessers who clung tightly to whatever hold on influence they had. He knew power's true worth lay in its unbridled release. Why have it if you're too timid to use it? When he moved toward an end, you always got his best, never less. You might not like what he dealt. Particularly if you happened to be on the receiving end. Against him, holding back in caution, deeming it wiser to keep reserves, hoping to preserve position or assets, meant you were doomed. His legions would wash right over you. Even his poetry radiated his remarkable propensity for seizing the moment, gainfully occupying what lay before him. Sometimes to the point of recklessness, but always with a meticulous aura of calculated abandon. Simply breathtaking in his radiance and unbridled audacity!

The murals immortalized his campaign against Wu. With an eagle's eye, one could see the spread of field below. The staggering deployment of nearly a million troops, half as navy, half as ground legions. In the autumn after becoming Chancellor of the North, Cao encamped alongside the southern Yangzi River. His massive navy dominated the crucial waterway, while his troops consolidated control of southern Jing province. Final steps in preparation for the onslaught. He would personally lead them into the heart of Sun Quan's kingdom, expecting a quick end to all resistance.

Sying Hao's account of events affirmed how Cao considered dominance of the Yangzi as his strategic dagger. To achieve advantage, he would first have to control the Han River to where it met the Yangzi at Wuhan. Until then, Wuhan remained under the control of Lu Biao to the west, and Sun Quan to the east. The two had been warring incessantly, keeping each other in constant stalemate. By neutralizing Lu Biao and later overwhelming his weak son and successor, Liu Cong, Cao cleared any remaining impediments to a grand assault on Wu through Red Cliffs.

The others deemed Liu Bei impotent and not a factor. He had suffered near annihilation at the hands of Cao and had only now achieved some degree of respite in Jing under the sanctuary of Liu Qi, Liu Biao's first son. Liu Qi was a competent general and had been the intended heir to the rule usurped by his younger brother.

But Sun Quan was a different story. Though quite young, he had always been formidable. Blessed with resources, surrounded by talent, and revered by his people.

Liu, at the urging of Counselor Zhuge Liang, regrouped and hastened south into Sun Quan's camp. He then tasked Zhuge Liang with lending his formidable skills. "You are to assist the great Wu general Zhou Yu in mapping an effective strategy against what appears to be an incomprehensible disparity."

A scene with the murals shows Zhou Yu alongside Zhuge Liang, his eyes at first flashing clear suspicion and mistrust of the wizard. However, the suspicion is gone by the next panel when both are facing down impossible odds, as Cao's navy has cut off all resupply from the water. His ever-active army then raids and degrades the border defenses of Wu, threatening for the first time to bring conflict into its heartland.

Before this onslaught, Wu had waged its campaigns from afar—always fighting elsewhere; establishing influence, controlling waterways, annexing territory. Wu's populace had, until then, averted the horrors of war fully unleashed. Their able leaders had deflected the weighty sacrifice thrust upon the not always willing participants in all-out warfare. It's one thing to be a beneficiary of conflict waged afar; another to fall victim as it rips apart one's own household. Cao Cao already knew from long experience. Before all is ended, you can't have one without the other. When you dance with war, you must pay the band. There can be no gambit without a wager from one's own purse. Wu never tasted the bitter agony of occupation. Cao intended to deliver his finest service in that regard. But first, he would tenderize. A little touch of chaos, disease and deprivation would prep them nicely for the anticipated annexation.

But Cao did not calculate the obvious. He, like most everyone else, would not have his quick and easy victory. Great strategists in the past have cautioned: never take lightly those who defend their homes and loved ones. The calculations and likelihoods change dramatically. Forces once deemed adequate for the task now need be increased by a factor of seven. A strategic and logistical nightmare nearly impossible to meet. The mark of any victory predicated on chaos is chaos itself. When you act as its agent, you reap the same as you sow. Put simply, do unto others as you would have delivered onto yourself.

Just as we sometimes prove to be pawns to the likes of Cao Cao, Sun Quan, and even the noble Liu Bei, they too are puppets to Yama, wriggling helplessly on strings to his drumbeat of disorder. Until it is too late, these guys just don't seem to get it. Destiny spits in the face and conceits of would-be emperors. Or anyone else choosing to drive their engines of unbridled domination over the backs of innocents. Ever wonder what thoughts flash through their minds as they meet their ends? I would wager they wonder if it was all worth it.

Would that those thoughts came sooner!

In total, ten murals are dedicated to the battle at Red Cliffs. Depicted are Cao Cao's starvation of the people. His subsequent peace-offering and gift of contaminated silks spreading disease and pestilence among his foes and their families. Then climaxed by his disastrous lust for Lady Sun, showing in the end, even he could be vulnerable.

He had stretched his forces too far southward, subjecting them to unprecedented logistical disadvantages. This he coupled imprudently with conscripts from the elsewhere-conquered who owed him no true allegiance. Despite it all, his strategy seemed faultless. While Sun Quan's kingdom tottered toward disintegration, Cao Cao postured ready and waiting, like a wolf at bay. Even Liu Bei removed his forces from the now uncertain alliance with Wu, fearing decimation within his own units from the rapidly spreading plague. With Liu's consent and blessing, Zhuge Liang remained behind, waiting, watching, and studying patiently—always everywhere, seeming never to sleep. Colonel Sun and his young squire stayed with him, per Liu's orders. "You are to assure his safety and well-being; as well as his escape should all come to naught."

Bao Ling knew the background story well. Sying Hao drummed it into him, stressing everything one needed to know about warfare and strategy lay within what followed.

Perhaps that explained the details preserved in the subsequent murals. Could it be Zhuge Liang felt the same as Sying Hao, making clear what he wanted most for us to know?

Just when all appeared lost, Zhuge Liang sensed a sliver of opportunity emerging. He called it the Strategy of the Crane. In nature, the crane is vulnerable—not nearly as formidable or robust as the bear or the tiger. Frail, and light, it stands susceptible to quick defeat by well-placed strikes and overwhelming force. Arguably, it has balance, and with that the ability to skillfully dodge and evade reckless thrusts. It possesses the instinct to counter sharply to the vitals. But, this crane had been worn and degraded by Cao and the merciless campaign of disease, terror, and starvation. What might Zhuge Liang be thinking?

An opponent would be foolish to conclude the crane, though seemingly down, was permanently out. If you can't confirm its demise, you should remain wary. The martial crane understands one thing above all others: victory is best snatched from the gaping jaws of defeat. Many predators will target the crane and fall prey to the illusion of an easy meal. Just when they feel the crane has become incapacitated and unable to defend, they forgo caution and close quickly upon it. Though defeat seems certain to all appearances, in an instant, the crane's sharp beak pierces one eye, then the next, finishing with an arterial vessel. Before the once confident attacker thinks to curse the reversal of fortunes, the ground melts from beneath, leaving it to stare at bent destiny through reflections in the glassy stare of a wild-eyed crazy bird.

Driven by dire necessity, Sun Quan's counselors and generals insisted he convene a grand strategic summit. For their part, they had seen the writing on the wall, even before matters had reduced to this precipitous level. A decision could no longer be averted. On first becoming Chancellor, Cao Cao had demanded fealty from Sun Quan under threat of invasion by a force of 800,000. Sun Quan's advisers and generals, with the notable exception of the brilliant Zhou Yu, advocated accommodation against contending with certain and overwhelming odds.

Here, Liu Bei was quite clever, and his timing perfect. He had sent Zhuge Liang into Wu to advocate alliance between Sun Quan and Liu as the only alternative to certain subjugation. Helping clarify the deliberations, Zhuge asked Sun Quan, in the very presence of all his counselors and generals, "Who do you trust to better serve and care for your people. Sun Quan, or Cao Cao."

Then he turned to the assembly and asked the same.

Like Liu Bei, ambitions aside, Sun Quan indubitably administered to the benefit and well-being of his people. He trusted no one more than himself to be their benefactor and protector.

Hearing Zhuge Liang's words, he turned to his generals and counselors, drew his sword then declared, "We will unite as brothers and fight a common enemy. That course, and no other, will ensure the security of our people into the future. I thank you all for your honest counsel, but from today, anyone who advocates surrender or fealty will share the fate of my desk." A puzzled meaning, until Sun Quan raised high his sword, then drove the blade down, across and through the gilded receptacle, sectioning its top from the supporting legs below.

Nothing beats clear communication! Most folks prefer their heads right where they're mounted.

Things got much worse in Wu, but all persisted, firm alongside their lord and commander. Committed until the end, which they were now certain, promised to come quickly.

Nearing the last mural of this section, Bao Ling sees the besieged Sun Quan and the patient but calculating Cao Cao. The faces surrounding Sun Quan are despondent, all but for Zhuge Liang, Colonel Sun, and the apprentice. The young warrior had by then tasted hard battle alongside Colonel Sun, and grown into full manhood, looking much more like the Sying Hao of Bao Ling's acquaintance. Bao Ling could see how even Sun Quan began to question his own resolve, doubtless cursing Liu Bei for leaving at the tipping point of crisis. Zhuge Liang consoled, saying one must learn to trust decisions made in righteousness, even when darkness seemed to consume their purpose. Sun Quan listened intently, but his sense of betrayal showed. The others ridiculed the wizard, some going so far as to imply history will show him to have been an agent of Cao Cao, whispered of course only to his back.

To a person, they wondered, "What might be his Strategy of the Crane?"

Xu Shu's Revenge

Cao's waiting game posed its own problems. Sun Quan's domain encompassed the southeast, including portions of the torrid Southlands. Northerners, unaccustomed to the ferocious heat, found themselves burdened by the weight of armor and protective shielding. When seasons warmed, troops, exhausted by overheating, discarded them. Then came the illnesses, some insect borne, some from feculent water, some from who knows what? Though common, and part of life's norm for Wu's population, the contagions proved debilitating, even fatal to the Northerners. It seems they had no acquired resistance to these new afflictions.

Then, an unanticipated problem … the vast navy and the tens of thousands of marines forced to camp afloat grew weary of the constant ebb and flow. Motion sickness ran rampant, seeming to come in waves. Just when one group adapted, another became incapacitated.

In quick succession, epidemics and illnesses linked as charms of ill portent on an ever mounting chain. The persistence of it all baffled Cao's physicians. The standard remedy of opium, but at high cost to fighting efficiency. One of his strategists, the sage Xu Shu[23] (you might remember

---

[23] Xu Shu preceded Zhuge Liang as Liu Bei's first counselor. Through Cao's trickery, Xu left Liu Bei in response to his mother's forged summons. On learning how easily her son had been tricked, the mother committed suicide. Thus

him as the onetime counselor to Liu Bei) ultimately found the perfect solution. "Chain the ships together. This will create the illusion of solidity and ease the never-ending sense of ceaseless movement." Cao approved and thought the plan to be elegantly simple, and thus, brilliant.

Truly, a small subterfuge in the hierarchy of weighty undertakings, but one leaden with direful consequences. In the end, this would prove to be a great vulnerability to Cao Cao. Had he overlooked what transpired with counselor Xu's mother and the sage's possible need for revenge? Until that point, Xu Shu's counsel had been impeccable, putting all suspicions to rest. Bygones should be bygones, don't you think?

A trap being set?

Perhaps. Who can truly know the heart of a sage? Their lofty purposes and principles answer to higher courts than the judgments of you or me. We might question if what followed aligned with the ghostly purview of Xu Shu's mother. By proven action, she clearly valued righteousness over treachery. Would she question where righteousness lay within disproportionate revenge?

It was General Huang Gai, perhaps at the urging of Zhuge Liang, who baited the ultimate trap. Together, they honed the sharpened beak of the Crane for the heart of Cao Cao. Zhuge and his apprentice, Sying Hao, closely monitored the movement of the river and the course of the winds through the gorge as the seasons shifted. Typically, wind direction and magnitude through the gorge favored

---

freeing her son from further concerns distracting him from righteous action. Xu Shu pledged to his mother's ghost; he would not fail her a second time. He promised to meet her in the afterlife, only when honor had been restored.

the seasonal proclivities—mostly constant, seldom shifting. By keeping tables of observations from several strategic points, they claimed to have gained insights into subtle changes, particularly regarding the wind. Predictions! Unbeknownst to Sun Quan, they had been doing this from the very beginning.

Recently, after deep meditation on the seemingly random and gyrating patterns, and perhaps mapping their servitude to the planets and stars above, Zhuge forecast a change in the flow of wind's direction to commence during mid night in concert with the coming new moon.

Sun Quan thought he was going mad, seeing nothing but more ruin rising in the wake of these purposeless speculations. Zhuge Liang persisted. Their charts detailed extensive observations recorded during their extended stay and seemed to hint at definitive patterns, particularly when seasons changed coincident with lunar events.

General Zhou Yu took great interest, as did his fearless right hand, General Huang Gai. Huang Gai knew the value of well-played trickery as you will soon appreciate. Was it not he and Colonel Sun who earlier conjured and feigned, orchestrating the "gift of arrows" attack. Using a fleet of straw boats to draw fire from the wait-weary Cao Navy, they amassed a collection of embedded arrows numbering in the hundreds of thousands, replenishing the nearly depleted armory of Sun Quan's archers. Huang Gai immediately sensed the emerging potential, and Zhou Yu nearly as quickly agreed. They could devise a strategy, but only if the cursed prediction could be relied upon. Both wanted to hear more. To believe more.

All eyes turned to Zhuge Liang. Sun Quan stared only into space and the unknowable, then spoke. "Zhuge Liang. In this time of turmoil, you have become a brother, though I know your loyalty remains with Liu Bei, who has abandoned our cause. From what I see now, even giving due weight to what has transpired and the protests which argue you have failed us, your counsel has proven wise and true. Yet we have paid a great price for your service. Today, all hangs precariously at risk. My people, whom I love and hoped to spare are decimated and ravaged. Cao Cao grows fat, writing poetry just over the horizon. The wind has been blowing westward for weeks, but now you tell me it will turn to the southeast when the coming moon transits to darkness. Our scholars are adamant. No one can predict this! How certain are you? How can this help us in our moment of need? Do you know the weight of consequences should we trust your prediction and it fails? Most troubling is this. How is it possible for you, or for any man, to even discern these things?"

Only silence. Standing in patient expectation, Sun Quan unexpectedly heard a voice floating from afar, seemingly riding the tail of the westward breeze. A young woman singing poetry about heroes to come, and battles yet to be decided. "What could she possibly mean?" he turned and asked those present. Baffled, the others heard nothing. Then Zhuge Liang walked slowly to the Imperial Pipa, picked up the stringed instrument, and began to accompany the maiden's sweet lament.

Recognizing Zhuge Liang's ethereal accompaniment to the spirit maiden's voice which no one else seemed to hear, Sun Quan then knew. His people's destiny lay with Zhuge Liang's recommendation, whatever the counselor's true loyalties might be. For the moment, the wizard would be their guy—their hammer. Their eyes met with understanding.

Sun Quan turned and surveyed his surrounding staff, declaring, "We will never capitulate. Today, we scrape rocky ground on bended knees, bearing the weight of war, disease, starvation, and loss. Across the water, we face impossible odds. Our trusted ally has abandoned us, and a great warrior king orchestrates our funeral at this very moment. Stripped to our essential natures, we have only the choice to succumb or to die as warriors of Wu, proving for history that we fought until the last blade and arrow for our way of life and the land we cherish."

With a slight smile of resignation, he continued, "I expect by month's end we will all be walking around headless, except perhaps for my good counselor and friend Zhuge Liang. Others will doubtless lift him away from Yama's wrath on the wings of dragons," glancing towards Colonel Sun and Sying Hao, his meaning clear.

The wizard in turn assured, "Should doom threaten to fall, I will be there alongside my brother-in-arms Sun Quan, as the celestial dragons marvel at what we do to those who might not fully appreciate our sense of duty and propriety."

Colonel Sun grunted approvingly, sharply nudging his powerful elbow into the side of his now grown squire, emphasizing they would do likewise. This was not lost on anyone present.

Sun Quan walked slowly to the two and put one hand on the shoulder of each. "You two have never failed us. You have stood with us unflinchingly through the heat and horror of every engagement." He turned around and raised his voice so no one would fail to hear his proclamation. "Colonel Sun and Sying Hao have carried our weight of battle when our own determination withered in the moment. Their courage in the flames more than once renewed our hearts. By example they reminded us of who we are, and what we strive to protect, or risk losing forever should we fail. I proclaim them Lords of Wu and declare for all who will hear that we stand with them in full trust and confidence until we have secured our homeland against transgressors or failed while standing unflinchingly to the last person."

Radiant as the Sun

Zhuge Liang turned to Zhou Yu and Huang Gai, his gaze intense. "Generals, do we have a strategy?"

Zhou Yu nodded and deferred to Huang Gai, who began, "We will offer Marshall Cao a prize he cannot refuse."

Colonel Sun interjected, "What might we possess that could genuinely pique Cao Cao's interest?"

Huang Gai responded, "Myself, and my legion of river troops."

Sun took a moment, attempting to see things from Cao Cao's perspective. Colonel Sun understood the importance of viewing matters from multiple dimensions. In less time than most would take for their morning duties, Sun methodically evaluated every nuance of Huang Gai's proposal. He remained silent until Zhuge Liang stared hard at him and asked, "Sun, your thoughts, please?"

"Cao Cao faces numerous challenges. While he presently holds the upper hand, the southern campaigns are now in their second year, lasting far longer than he initially anticipated. Some of his troops are ailing, others are bored or homesick. Some are ready for action, while others desert to aid their families, who remain hostage in occupation. He knows as each month passes without a decisive triumph, his dominance wanes. The overwhelming victory he once envisioned becomes increasingly unlikely. He must seriously consider any offer that promises to undermine our resistance. For him, it will be evident. The addition of Huang

Gai's skills, his knowledge of our defenses, coupled with the legion of hardened marines, will be decisive in the final campaign, sealing our fall."

Zhou Yu interjected, "Then you find merit in the strategy?"

Sun continued, "What makes bait attractive to prey is the premise. In this instance, the premise is indisputable. And the bait, genuine. Should Huang Gai turn, delivering his seasoned troops to Cao's purpose, our demise would be inevitable. Two critical questions arise. Why would Huang Gai turn? Even more troubling, what if he truly turned?"

Sun Quan and Zhuge Liang froze, unwinding the many implications Sun presented. Their minds raced, contemplating the potential fallout, the risks entwined with this perilous play. Swiftly, they arrived at the same dreaded truth. This play risked everything. If Huang Gai did, in fact, turn coat, Wu would certainly fall. The rewards for such disloyalty would be immeasurable. All knew Cao Cao's long history of playing fairly with turncoats, some of whom had ascended to respected leadership in his own cadre.

Nothing is ever simple.

Zhuge turned to Huang Gai, a man with an impeccable history, fearless and brilliant, always the right hand to Marshall Zhou Yu. The wizard wondered, *What might tempt such a person to truly turn*? He already knew the answer; Cao Cao could read greed and ambition like Zhuge Liang read the stars. Cao would have much to offer the likes of Huang Gai, certainly much more than would ever accrue if he remained loyal to Wu, having the younger Zhou Yu forever blocking his ascent.

But as Zhuge Liang studied Huang Gai's silvery steel eyes and weighed the unspoken language of his body, he saw only purpose, not betrayal.

"General, please go on. What happens after Cao Cao accepts your offer to cross sides?"

"To fulfill my oath of loyalty to Cao Cao, I will deliver the entirety of my marines to his service on an agreed date."

Colonel Sun clarified, "Midnight, on the night of the new moon, I suppose."

"Yes," Huang Gai answered. "Under the guise of patrols and harassment, my waterborne marines will depart our shores in darkness, moving cautiously toward Cao's chained lines of vessels. At a pre-arranged signal, we will ignite our torches, confirming the delivery of troops and vessels."

Sun Quan questioned, "What if Cao Cao has set his own trap and launches upon you?"

"Sir, it will not matter at that point," Huang Gai responded, "We will have achieved position."

Colonel Sun and Sun Quan mulled over the thought.

Zhuge Liang grasped it almost immediately, "Fire boats! A brilliant ploy! They embrace your vessels, the wind turns to the southeast, and you set them aflame. Cao's chained boats will sit like ducks stuck in an oven, unable to separate and unable to extinguish the flames. The raging inferno will sear them into cinders. We reinforce with platforms of archers in the surrounding darkness, poised to launch their own bolts of fire. After the inferno is delivered, your marines can swim to our waiting rescue."

Colonel Sun, not forgetting the underlying risk, started to say, "But ..."

To which Huang Gai interrupted, "I appreciate Colonel Sun's reluctance, and his taking care not to offend my honor by raising it." He turned to Sun Quan and added, "I will place my wife, children and household in your charge as surety for my oath to execute truly. I will personally drive this mission to its completion, and then return home to Wu.

Home with my people, where hopefully I will, in time, retire to an old age of boastful stories. Recalling for the children of Sun Quan and Zhou Yu the night we together stared Yama in the eye, and, while holding his gaze distracted, spit in his face."

Sun Quan nodded to Huang Gai, then responded, "General, there comes a time when a leader simply must honor someone who has served and sacrificed for our cause, as have you. Your family and household will be safe and delivered to your care, whatever path you take. To this promise, he secured the word of Colonel Sun. "You are to guarantee the ultimate deliverance of family and household back to Huang Gai at such time as he asks, after each individual's course has played fully to its end."

Sun Quan—a man who understood loyalty, and reciprocation; a leader now ascendant and fully manifest in his prime.

Radiant as the sun.

There may have been moments when doubt cast its shadow. Few let their thoughts be known, understanding the stakes. The fire ships would be loaded with incendiaries and troops made visible on deck, appearing to crowd outward from within. Cao's spies had watched the planning, the loading, and preparations for final launching, and were satisfied Huang Gai's anticipated treachery had gone undetected by Sun Quan. They further confirmed elements of Wu's defending forces remained quarantined in their garrisons, still reeling from disease and starvation.

Zhuge Liang knew this to be an all-or-nothing roll of fate's die. To that end, he urged Sun Quan to ensure all battle-tested troops, even those grievously ill or wounded, be advanced in secret deployment to forward positions. Tens of thousands were strategically placed at the front, parsed into indiscernible fragments under cover of darkness; hidden in store wagons or empty water barrels, under carriages, disguised as farmers, or women. Only their skeletal remnants remained in the garrisons, tasked to maintain campfires and faux activity to convince Cao's spies of their continued presence in the rear.

Huang Gai Sleights Zhou Yu

But for two, one game remained. To allay all doubt among Cao's spies as to his true intentions, Huang Gai hatched a plan with Zhou Yu. Together they agreed, but only amongst themselves, to stage a brazen falling out. It would flare for all to witness when next gathered in open session. A meeting of accountability, allowing proper forum for the generals and counselors to give updates and status to the nobility and gentry.

Before them all, Huang Gai openly declared, "Ere any new and errant ventures commence, I must seize this opportune moment to open my heart and speak candidly as to how we ended up in this terrible predicament. I will point to the very cause. You will judge. I ask all to forgive my impertinence, but things are as they are and beg for scrutiny. If not today, there may be no other opportunity. Our mistakes must be owned by those responsible so as never to be repeated."

He had captured their undivided attention. One could feel the weight of their silence.

Suddenly, he exploded into a vicious tirade, targeting Zhou Yu's handling of the defense up until that point. Searing descriptives such as timid, careless, and ineffective poured from his lips. Followed by allegations of ineptitude, particularly relating to the foolish and self-serving acceptance of Cao's diseased silks by Zhou Yu's frontline troops. He berated, "A stunt which would never have caught my marines. Nor anyone else for that matter." Finally, he demanded the council look hard again at making peace with Cao as only that guaranteed their state's survival. He left no doubts among those witnessing. He would never again allocate his considerable talents to failure, demanding Zhou Yu step down and petitioning Sun Quan for new directions.

Silence and shock gripped the assembly. Eyes shifted first to Sun Quan, and then to Zhuge Liang, who could say nothing. A visibly pained Sun Quan drew his sword and moved toward Huang Gai but was stopped by Zhuge Liang, who stepped quickly between them; pleading, "Lord Sun, it is Marshall Zhou Yu who has been slighted. It is he who must answer these malicious charges and allegations."

To which Sun Quan cautiously eased back, while Zhuge cleared a path for Zhou Yu.

As he stormed forward, Marshall Zhou discreetly signaled his personal guard into the chamber, and in an instant, some very confused and apologetic underlings surrounded Huang Gai.

Zhou Yu never broke stride until stopping before Huang Gai and ordering his detainment. He charged Huang Gai with insubordination, pointing to how his outburst offended his superiors (meaning himself and Sun Quan), denied history, and undermined the carefully considered and agreed upon strategies leading to where they were now. He added how Huang Gai's venomous attack had cast a cloud of doubt and uncertainty over the heroic sacrifices they had undertaken to save their homeland. He carefully reminded how all had concurred in the courses taken and how many of the tactics said to have failed were Huang Gai's very own. While all opinions had their place, the time for second guessing and acquiescence to Cao had long passed and there was no going back. Zhou Yu, though visibly shaken, professed his continued love and respect for Huang Gai, giving full weight and measure to his colleague's long and distinguished service. However, it fell to him, as commander of the resistance, to make one thing unmistakably clear. Huang Gai's conduct that evening amounted to nothing less than insubordination, possibly worse. In fairness, Zhou Yu removed himself and declared a tribunal of counselors would rule on the issue; and if deserved, declare the punishment. He would faithfully execute their decision, whatever it might be.

Acting in the very moment, Sun Quan named the members of the tribunal, then designated Zhuge Liang as inquisitor, instructing they hold immediate session before the group.

Despite the elaborate security precautions, Cao had learned of this assembly and somehow implanted spies even in their midst, some among the nobles, some among the servants. Only a few, but enough to ensure everything which followed came to Cao's immediate notice, corroborated independently from several perspectives.

He knew his Sun Tzu.

The tribunal convened with Zhuge Liang at its helm. The outburst had also taken him in. He listened carefully to Huang Gai's disgruntlement. He then recalled Huang Gai's participation in and contribution to all actions and strategies undertaken to this point, attempting to unravel a puzzle whose pieces refused to fit.

"Why, when you have been so valued and influential in all preceding stages of this difficult campaign, have you suddenly elected to protest and devalue all which has been so painstakingly undertaken?" Zhuge Liang inquired, his dragon-eyed gaze fixated on Huang Gai.

Until that moment, Zhuge Liang had been in the dark regarding the complicity of the two generals, who knew the ruse would work only if it played true and cut fully to the hilt. Huang Gai, usually a steadfast rock, remained silent and motionless, avoiding Zhuge's penetrating stare. The wizard, accustomed to deciphering truths, saw the hesitation in Huang Gai's eyes.

A liar can lie with a straight face, Zhuge Liang mused, *but a staunchly honest man who lies will betray it in his gaze*. Huang Gai's eyes, unable to meet the intensity of Zhuge's scrutiny, drifted downward, a silent confession. Withering under the glare of a wizard determined to see into his heart, shifting ever slightly side to side, as if watching leaves drifting slowly to ground.

And with that, the wizard knew all.

The other two on the tribunal remained confounded. Huang Gai had always been a rock. Yes, he remained as number two to Zhou Yu, but who wouldn't? Huang Gai had already had his day. He was an older man, and Zhou Yu remained at the peak of his ascendance. Sun Quan knew Zhou Yu guaranteed continuity and loyalty in leadership, and virtually all concurred. It was none other than Huang Gai who urged the younger's rise to prominence. Until this evening, no one doubted Huang Gai. Nearly everyone felt him to be properly placed as Zhou Yu's right hand and bludgeon, a role which, to his credit, Huang Gai had executed masterfully.

The other two judges, confounded, sought answers, occasionally probing Zhuge Liang for his thoughts. He professed bewilderment, concealing the depth of his understanding as he too fully immersed into the intricate game.

The Wu judges reached an impasse. One called for Huang Gai's execution, while the other advocated for considering the comments raised by Huang Gai on their merits and weighing or dismissing them accordingly.

All eyes turned to Zhuge Liang, as it became clear his voice would drive the final judgment and Huang Gai's fate.

Zhuge Liang now became a silent co-conspirator to the two generals. He declared "Your outburst offends us all. An inexplicable breach of loyalty and camaraderie between you and Marshall Zhou Yu. A breach until now, unnoticed and undetected." He pushed on, sharpening his voice to its razor's edge, cutting to the heart of the issue. "I attribute the rupture to jealousy and misplaced ambition. You have argued otherwise, but I say the strategic setbacks to date have their roots in failures of leadership and absence of genuine unity, when dire circumstances demanded both."

The words burned Huang Gai to the core. He shuffled uncomfortably, attempting to conceal the welling tears, hoping to shield his vulnerability from the prying eyes of those around him.

Oh yes, Zhuge Liang knew full well how an honest man who lies will all but wet himself in shame.

Even Zhou Yu had stiffened, his hand instinctively reaching for his sword. Had any other mortal spoken like this to his trusted adjutant, he would be headless. The wizard glanced, feigning momentary distraction, catching Marshall Zhou's hand touching upon the hilt.

Zhuge Liang continued, "My decision is this. We cannot change what has already passed before us. Still, we must hold it to full account. Huang Gai is judged to have been insubordinate, yet his motivations are unclear, appearing self-centered. Because of the most unfortunate and ill-considered timing of the outburst, an example must be set.

Huang Gai is to be flogged. Regrettably, it falls to Marshall Zhou as his only peer to execute. That responsibility cannot be delegated. Huang Gai will also forfeit one quarter of his estate, to be held in trust by the state as surety for Huang Gai's anticipated restoration to stature. We remain guardedly hopeful of his eventual return to our love and trust. Our session today was called to discuss coming plans. That will have to wait for a more favorable time."

The other judges quickly agreed, and Zhuge asked for Sun Quan's concurrence and authority to proceed.

The leader yet remained in the dark as to the game playing before him. He hesitated, for once uncertain. Zhuge walked to his front and spoke words only Lord Quan could hear. "You must trust me on this; everything hinges on this moment."

Sun Quan turned to the group, "I have issued my seal of authority, and it will be so recorded; the judgment stands as stated. Given the dire circumstances of the moment, there will be no delay in its execution."

To which Zhou Yu came to his side and declared, "The flogging will take place in the morning. I will personally execute. We will move forward from there."

Red Cliffs Turns About

When the news reached Cao Cao, his spirits soared. After this humiliation, there could be no turning back for Huang Gai.

Cao conjectured, "Better had they killed him! They can never undo this humiliation to one of their finest." But then he rejoiced on hearing they had not. The shame and humiliation would serve as Cao's bond to Huang Gai's anticipated reliability, underscoring the promised turn of loyalties. "He will find his true home, and a better future, with us."

The next day, his spies witnessed the public flogging, describing it as brutal; and confirmed the hatred now flashing evident between the formerly hand-in-glove generals.

Preparations unfolded methodically on all sides, until the anticipated day finally arrived.

The turncoat marines, led from the front by the peerless Huang Gai, were all but embraced by Cao's chained fleet. Though a seemingly confident Zhuge Liang surveyed all from his strategic high post alongside Sun Quan, Huang Gai had at least a momentary sense of reticence as his boat neared the enemy flagship. The wind remained disturbingly calm. Much too calm!

He turned to his men and ordered, "Set the fires, men. Wind or no wind, we go now to our journey's end."

Foreseeing his own annihilation, Huang Gai mounted the
bow of his craft, leading from the very front as it veered
hard to ram the flagship. Those on the flagship sounded
alarm at this unexpected development. Funny how thoughts
take flight as death lingers near at hand. Huang Gai thought
only of Zhuge Liang and the punishment ordered, then
painfully rendered. Even now, his very marrow ached. Then
he thought of Zhuge Liang and the counsel rendered in their
time together, wondering if Zhuge would have been as
harsh on his own failures, given the vision of hindsight.

As he contemplated Zhuge's failures, he registered the
stillness in the air. All trusted the wizard's calculations, and
here before them lay the barren fruit. Zhuge Liang, a puzzle
with no solution. One had to take him as one found him; you
would never get more. In the moment before his now
imminent death, Huang Gai determined he had no account
to settle with the wizard. Despite his words before the
assembly, Huang Gai knew the defense had fared better
than any had a right to expect, even allowing for the failures
and the careless breech which brought plague. Zhuge Liang
did not bring the plague; it came from their own
vulnerability and foolishness. And the failures? Who knows?
In concept the wizard's stratagems were faultless; the
execution however, another matter.

It was then he ran the vision of their final meeting,
recalling the assembly and the role of Zhuge Liang as
inquisitor and judge of ultimate recourse. He thought on
how the ruse played by himself and his sworn brother Zhou
Yu had fooled them all, and but for the stillness of the wind,
Lord Cao would this very moment be facing ruin. Again, he
excused the harshness of Zhuge Liang's punishment. After
all, had they not hoped for something like that when he first

proposed the charade to Marshall Zhou. Thankfully, Counselor Zhuge Liang had not recommended execution. He whispered some words into the stillness of the night, "I forgive you wizard; be assured we part as friends. I will have a banquet table waiting for you in the next life."

As he focused to his front, a rain of arrows now poured all about. He braced for the ramming of the boats. Again, his thoughts raced to the assembly, he laughed thinking of the confusion he read on the counselor's face. He had never seen that look on the wizard before, quite unbecoming for him. Then he remembered the inquisitor's probing questions, and the glare of the stare. It came back to him now; just how he felt in that moment; like a kettle boiling within his abdomen; its boiling contents scalding all within; holding him to task. It meant nothing at first, perhaps just the stress of all being risked in the charade. Then he remembered the counselor finally turning to a very conflicted Sun Quan, whispering softly to Lord Quan just before the Prince turned to the assembly and gave full authority to the decision.

Huang Gai paused to reflect, impact into the flagship now imminent and irreversible.

He muttered under his breath, almost laughing as he did so, "The son of a bitch found us out!" No sooner said than he felt the hint of evening breeze gently awakening from his rear.

Cao's mariners continued raining squalls of arrows upon the exposed Wu craft. Moments before, all had seemed poised for sacrifice. Then a lightly dancing breath exhaled from their rear, jumping flames from the now lit fire boats to Cao's chained vessels. They spread and wound through their midst; feeling almost to be an invisible dragon, evident to all only by its scorching breath, and the fiery exhalations now racing explosively forward and along the front, spreading wildfire the likes never witnessed before or since.

Before dawn, well over a hundred thousand were cooked dead, and an equal number burnt, moaning, and floating helplessly about.

As the chaos unfolded, Liu Bei returned unannounced in a completely unanticipated lightning strike. In a grand pincers movement, Guan Yu, Zhang Fei, and their tiger general brethren, slammed Liu's forces hard into Cao's northern flank, decimating his rear guard.

Zhuge Liang set his arm about Sun Quan, gaze riveted on the cauldron to his front, and turned him to the left, where flames and screams in the far distance told of another unfolding major battle. "Liu Bei returns as the loyal ally he had always sworn to be."

Sun Quan now recognized the hand of Zhuge Liang in everything, and though wanting to behead him for deception and subterfuge, could only hold him, locking him to his front and staring in admiration.

Zhuge only said, "Now is our time."

Sun Quan ordered steeds for himself and Zhuge Liang. They were headed to the front, and by morning would be driving the decimated forces of Cao Cao to their northern rear.

Colonel Sun and his squire, Sying Hao fulfilled their oaths to protect Huang Gai's people. Cao Cao, unforgiving of treachery, that very night sent an army of held-in-reserve assassins to collect their due from that which Huang Gai held most dear.

When a battle-depleted and flog-worn Huang Gai returned two days later, he found an exhausted Sun, alongside Sying Hao, both badly wounded but singing folk songs of the south with children of the household, as the ladies tended meticulously to their lacerations and injuries. Outside the compound lay the corpses of over two hundred of Cao's elite assassins.

All safely delivered, as promised.

Overwhelmed by the miracle, Huang Gai fell to the ground and prostrated himself before the two.

They would have none of it of course, rather insisting Huang Gai join in their drunken musical reverie.

The combined effort had cut Cao's forces in half. Liu Bei and his ferocious generals decimated Cao's northern flank and rear, and with that, his most battle hardened and loyal cadre. Of the hundreds of ships on the water, only the rearmost twenty were able to unchain, and escape the conflagration. Once freed, they never stopped moving, and to a person, their crews abandoned their ships and their battle roles for the foolishness they now saw them to be. Those caught in the wildfire suffered mightily for the havoc they brought to Wu. Even Sun Quan's pursuing troops felt pity on seeing their sorry fate. But pity did not temper the sentiment for any of them.

"Better them, than us" was their only common thought.

In uncontrollable rage, Cao called for Xu Shu. There could be no doubt what he intended to happen. Now, too late. By his own hand, the sage had already joined his beloved mother. Though his body was with Cao, his heart forever remained with Liu Bei and the Han.

While Huang Gai and his two friends sang songs and celebrated, Sun Quan, Zhuge Liang, and Zhou Yu pursued Cao Cao's retreating armies doggedly. Liu Bei secured the northern front, keeping Cao's retreat to the river's edge, and predictable.

Sun Quan later came to realize this too was part of Zhuge Liang's Grand Design. Having his forces pursue Cao Cao upriver left the province of Jing to Liu Bei's army, and after crippling Cao's flank, Liu took Jing for himself setting up his eventual sweep to the west.

Despite his defeat, Cao managed a brilliant retreat to the north, saving enough of his residual forces to ensure his continued reign, albeit in a diminished empire.

In the aftermath, kingdom Wu survived, and before long, returned once again to prosperity under Sun Quan. Though Sun was grateful to both Liu and Zhuge for their roles in saving Wu from conquest, the loss of Jing Province ultimately proved bitter salt on a wounded aspiration. A wound which never healed. Regrettably, it poisoned their futures.

Loose ends? Zhuge Liang did what he was supposed to do. Liu Bei did what he had to do. Sun Quan got his decisive victory. Liu Bei got Jing. Cao Cao kept his head.

As to the others.

Millions died from battle, untreated wounds, infection, disease, starvation, collateral loss, victimization, exploitation, treachery, misuse, and abuse.

More than likely, history will ignore the innocents, and the accounts of permanent record will glorify the decisive leadership, legendary deeds, and displays of courage. By characters whom historians will prop up and enshrine for all who follow to admire and emulate.

But the poor, and the ordinary. Their story lies where blood pools in the dirt. Learn to read this special script, and you will appreciate the truth.

The battle, chase, and consolidation afterward raked the entire continent east of the mountains. It spared no one. After his retreat, Cao Cao had to replenish his forces, and for nearly another generation, adolescent males were torn or seduced from their homes and turned into killing machines.

From the ashes, three kingdoms emerged, and the stone wheel of chaos shifted into lower gear, grinding the land and people, milling the grist for generations to come.

The final mural depicting the aftermath shows a parting of the principals. All were there—Sun Quan, Zhou Yu, Huang Gai, Liu Bei, Zhuge Liang, and the tiger generals. Bao Ling touched where he saw Colonel Sun directly aside Zhuge Liang. Between them as always, Sying Hao, their shared protege.

By then, the no longer young and inexperienced squire had mastered the art of war under Colonel Sun's fatherly tutelage and the way of knowledge and awareness under the close guidance of Zhuge Liang. Colonel Sun formally pronounced the squireship to be ended and proclaimed Sying Hao to be his peer. Liu Bei affirmed, and immediately declared the rank of Colonel, which Sying Hao, remaining always with his two mentors, never openly assumed.

Staring hard at the image of the boy, now a man, Bao Ling saw much of himself in the portrayal and recognized the shared look of resigned acceptance to horror. Something which had come to be an ordinary part of his own life. Locked into the gaze, Bao Ling also saw the spark of hope, knowing that somehow, in some way, good would ultimately come from what they had accomplished.

"You see yourself in him, don't you?" asked Hui.

"Don't we all? More than that, I know him. He has the eyes, face and demeanor of my sworn brother Sying Hao. A relative perhaps? Great grandfather?"

Abbot Hui answered, "No, Bao Ling. For certain, it is him."

Bao Ling couldn't quite yet grasp what he now sensed to be true, "You told me the murals have been here more than one hundred and fifty years. The Sying Hao I know is a mature man, neither aged nor young. The man in the mural has certainly been dead for most, if not all that time."

Then Bao Ling thought, *Unless he was in fact, a spirit, or an immortal.*

"No, Bao Ling, not a ghost, not an immortal. He served Zhuge Liang, a man through whom almost all things were possible. But for his clear mindedness, and his devotion to Colonel Sun and Zhuge Liang, those not knowing him better might conclude Sying Hao to have been a victim of destiny and cursed to walk the earth beyond his natural time as a result. I would argue that Sying Hao stands as the headstone to Zhuge Liang's Grand Design, tasked by his master to wait."

"For what?"

"The right moment."

Though the murals continued and told more of the warring kingdoms, both agreed the day's visit to the Grand Hall ended there, with Abbot Hui promising to share what he knew in due time, but only after first attending to the affairs and needs of the Temple, and the people.

They left in silence.

Part 3 – Interactions

Apprentices

Bao Ling understood the importance of usefulness. Back
in Jing, life meant utility. Survival required inter-
dependence and mutual respect, necessitating relationships
based on trust, movement with purpose, and a unified
commitment to needed ends. There were no layabouts; time
pushed forward, prodding everyone along.

Continual challenge filled their lives, giving meaning to
every aspect. Creative, purposeful, useful—at home with
one another and their surroundings. It doesn't surprise; they
held little fear for death. Just another challenge to be met. To
be answered as they had in life. A threshold marking their
bold and final step into the unknowable void whose essence
gave shape and meaning to all they appreciated while here.
The thought of death something different for them than with
us. Life included death, and simply went on. Like a great
stream—rippling, reflecting, shimmering. Always there.
Being of this mind, Bao Ling took critical measure of others
by the degree they feared death, or the unknown.

When thinking on these things, he would muse on the
words of Sying Hao, perhaps recognizing the irony inherent.
"Bao Ling. There is no mystery to the stupidity of warfare.
Ignore everything they tell you; never let them incite your
fear or your hatred or bridle you with greed or ambition.
Never let them take hold over your sense of propriety or
compel you to their airs of slanted righteousness. Always
stand ready and apart, and watch. Watch the leaders and

what they do. Look carefully at the language of their bodies, then study their actions. Try to see what drives them, using only what you already know; never what they tell you. And always test what you find. You'll be surprised at what you call forth. Even in this, nature has given us the tools necessary to recognize and to avoid folly. True, it involves work and effort on our parts. Awareness isn't easy, nor does it favor the lazy. Therein lies the difficulty. Once they hook you in their spell, work and effort on your part serve only their ends. Nature fails only when we surrender who we truly are to the tricks and guiles of others or imprison its guiding influences in the remote recesses within, surmounted by greed, ambition, and arrogance from without."

Sying Hao spoke invariably of troops who, when not engaged in the act of killing others, were idling endlessly, looking for ways to kill time. "A recipe for trouble," he would say. Like Bao Ling, Sying Hao had been forged to finality in the heat of battle, but he detested it, recognizing it for what it was: the abandonment of humanity. This is not to say he would not defend himself, his principles, or those in need if called upon. He simply felt killing fundamentally altered our very natures, and, within his purview as one man, he had not yet seen where the changes wrought could ever be undone or unwound.

"Bao Ling," he would say, "when not active in combat, or preparing for combat, or training for combat, or waiting for combat, or gaming for combat; troops idle aimlessly about. They squander vast resources until staring the true enemies hard in the face: uselessness, dependency, insignificance, and boredom. Then they reflect on what they did to get there, and the anticipated outcomes unrealized. Thoughts which turn their minds toward the shadows. There's no telling what mischief will result. One glance at troops milling about helpless villages and towns tells the story. Everyone and everything become their prey. Subjects of their interest, scrutiny, and suspicion. The heat of battle is one thing. There, the fiery moment of crisis and the barking orders of superiors decide and seal their fates. That's the easy part. But before and after, they stand idle. Life's reflections casting light on their surrender of what they once were. Once thinking entities imbued with creativity and compassion. Gone! Now like insects trapped in an urn of rice wine. Enclosed and suspended, no way out. Pickled in place!

So, Bao Ling understood the importance of being useful and never idle. In the days following the contest[24], he took opportunity to spend time with Kuan-Yin Ting and Kong Kong. Carefully, he refined their skills and drilled them on tactics he had honed to perfection during his years on the run. While Kong Kong had exceptional skills with the bow, the simple humanity underlying Kuan-Yin's actions most drew his admiration. Even Kong Kong couldn't dispute that, growing to equally respect the generous and self-deprecating heart of his younger friend.

Given the constraints of time, Bao Ling carefully selected from what he knew to ensure they had the essential tools to survive. He knew that his words and the subtlety of his art would be wasted on novices. As mountain tribesmen, Kuan-Yin Ting and Kong Kong already knew how to fight and survive in the wild. With luck, that would be enough for them to benefit from what Bao Ling intended to share.

Drawing from his own travels, observations, and lessons from Sying Hao, Bao Ling concluded that man evolves over time, as does everything else for that matter. The mountains

---

[24] Detailed in our prior work, *The Wizard's Testament.*

held evidence everywhere, with prior life forms preserved in rock telling stories of times past when things had been quite different. Sying Hao had once spoken of tusks from giant hairy beasts uncovered when the deepest snows melted, or of strange footprints in the baked western desert left by creatures larger than anything now walking. Nature's flow inclines we adapt to our surroundings, to threats and to the uncomfortable reality of unanticipated change. The ancients knew of this and carefully encoded these influences into the Yi Ching and other modes of portent.

Bao Ling believed every life and form had its own path toward survival and continuation if played well. The fatal impediments were foolishness, or inability to adapt. As for foolishness, animals had deep-rooted instincts that served and protected them. As humans, we instinctively avoided foolishness for the most part. However, lapses invited unimaginable consequences, and no one had yet learned how to manage that. As to adapting to change, we could learn to flow like water and trust in our ability to act in the moment. But even with that, no guarantees.

Bao Ling would tell his young apprentices, "That's why we identify with water. Water has no mind for foolishness. When it comes to change, water is quick and without peer, in the end, always finding equilibrium with the surround."

Frequently, he reminded the lads, "Remember! Flow like water!" They would nod their heads, seeming to understand his words. He would admonish, "I don't need your nodding affirmations. I need to see you flowing like water. Remember, water never flows like a head nodding!"

Easier said than done. Monks spend lifetimes trying to understand lessons like this.

Young warriors meet quick death when they don't.

The young apprentices did, however, understand change. It manifested everywhere in the high country, and had marked their history and the lives of their people. Bao Ling's beliefs on the evolution of energy found receptive ears. He shared all he gleaned from his own teachers and his elders.

We all possess energy bodies. Like our intellectual and spiritual bodies, they evolved in ways over time to ensure at least the chance of survival against whatever odds or challenges we might encounter. Just as our outer shells altered over span of time, in step with the ever-changing creation, our spirit minds grew from their most primitive states to where they are now. Within us exist vast stores of information, symbols, myths, instincts, reactions, insights, and answers to whatever tests and struggles once crossed the paths of our ancestors and which might still threaten. Among us, many have chosen to become blinded to these gifts. A very few have learned to channel them. Bao Ling explained that teachers of the internal arts were clear on one thing. Everything you needed to know was pretty much already there for you to tap into. He told the story of Ah Ju Na, and Erge Lafah[25] and assured that even their knowledge, or the knowledge of the likes of Guan Yu, or Colonel Sun

---

[25] Chinese for Ekalavya. In the The Mahabharata, rejected by master Drona, Ekalavya returns home, where he enters the wilderness and fabricates a mud and straw image of Drona before which he undertakes a disciplined program of self-study. Resolute to mastering archery, he achieves exceptional prowess ... rivaling, perhaps surpassing Drona's best pupil, Arjuna. Learning this, Drona demands payment in full for his lessons, asking for, and receiving the thumb of Erge Lafah's release hand.

had already been lifted and secured by nature's preserving hand through the mysteries of change and adaptation and gifted to those who followed. He pointed both saying, "Even you two have benefited." But it went beyond that. He opened their eyes to the lessons of the animals, how each had all it needed to survive so long as it were true to its nature. This could be a locust, a rabbit, a tiger, a bird, or a bear. He shared how teachers of the internal secrets knew and stressed that at any point in time, the human energy-body resided in the moment, fully evolved. This meant only one thing. Life had already assimilated all of creation, and the totality of human experience within that creation. It lay there within our collective storehouse of innate knowledge, awareness, and instinct, subject to our need and beckon. Preserved and wanting for renewal, with a life of its own, answering first and foremost to our will and intent.

"From that very essence, emerge our energy bodies. Your energy bodies."

This left them befuddled of course.

Like them, he had at first been skeptical. Over time, he pared away non-essentials, or risked discovery and death. Under hardship's tutelage, he identified everything standing in the way or impeding his ability to go on. Eventually, he figured out what had been there all along. He learned from hard trial what worked; and what did not. Within himself, what worked replaced all which did not. That brought him peace with the lessons passed to him by his elders. Though he had once resisted and been skeptical, they had proven true.

"We have the awarenesses of all creatures within us, their gifts, their weaknesses, and what they have learned either by surviving, or by their failures." He assured even their own village teacher Li Fung knew this to be true, citing his cat stance, crane position, dragon fist, chicken hand. "All inspired by the actual movements of animals. But unless you understand the movements as a universal language within, you will not find the linking thread. That thread represents the basis for all living movement."

Bao Ling promised to guide them on the first steps of the path, but only if he could trust they would act upon the lessons.

They eagerly assented of course. Who wouldn't?

The Animals Within

He started with Tiger.

"The tiger is distinguishable by its adeptness using its paws, or arms to attack and control an opponent. It blends well with the flow of other animals, particularly the dragon. It possesses the trademark ability to execute with power, grace, and balance. When the tiger moves, it is always with characteristic feline agility. When it attacks, it moves inside or around the opponent's rooted stance, precluding the target's chance for recovery. The tiger instinctively attacks only the vitals. On this, it never errs. Its movement ends only when the opponent has become still.

"Like all principles of movement, the characteristics of animals apply equally to large field engagements as to individual combat. One must discern this over time, processing direct experiences to understand its broader scope, delivering an advantage to those who grasp it."

Next, he spoke of the Bear, master of energy and determination.

"The bear embodies power, fearless determination, and the ability to resist pain. The fight of the bear is to take pain to give pain. The bear knows only one direction, forward. It fights to the death, selflessly. However, like other clever animals, the bear can deceive and surprise. For example, despite its power, size and great strength, the bear can transform its appearance to look harmless and docile. In that way, it can play the moment to its advantage."

Bao Ling and the acolytes shared personal recollections of bears walking around on all fours, scrounging for food. Appearing no more threatening than raccoons or feral dogs. The same animal, standing on its hind quarters and moving forward in attack, would panic even the most formidable hunter, causing him to lose composure while trying to set the shot which might save his life. Bao Ling shared personal recollections of bears in the wild, emphasizing their ability to throw sounds to trick the mind. He recalled when one projected growling sounds to his rear, then raced off when he turned about to find nothing. He urged the boys to think about this, and to study from within themselves how the animal did it, taking what they learned to the wild and witnessing it firsthand, and then making it their own.

On surviving when vulnerable, he praised the Cobra.

The boys had heard of cobras and of people in the south who could persuade them to rise and dance about using nothing but musical wizardry. They felt these were only stories, exaggerations. Bao Ling assured them they were true, but as with everything, what met the eye was not always the same as what bore out in fact. "If one came across a cobra in its habitat, the controlling roles might well be reversed. It would be the cobra reaching out to your mind, numbing your attention, and holding you spellbound and unresponsive while it readied its strike." Though vulnerable, perhaps more so than any other animal, the cobra compensated for vulnerability with guile and patience. "Its reflexes move like bolts of lightning. At first not there, then filling the heavens. But cobra knows to choose opportunity carefully. Motionless before you, it measures the beat of your heart, connecting its own metre to that of your limbs, striking only when you are leaden footed, stiff, ill-timed, and unable to spring away. How does it accomplish this?"

Bao Ling explained how the answer lays within. A gift of birth, just as with all of us. While undoubtedly there, a skill only understood if one puts in the work necessary to hone it like the precious gem it is. He repeated often, "These insights wait patiently for your efforts to free them into the light. They will not rise without effort on your part, just as they will not rise from my words alone. Hearing the possibilities from another counts only as the first step."

Recalling what the young men said of people in the south who could persuade cobras to dance with their musical wizardry, Bao Ling stressed one should always think closely over who was persuading whom to dance in every moment and in every situation.

Of all the animals, the favorite for the lads was, of course, the monkey. Mountain people, much like their lowlander counterparts, had countless stories of Monkey, the simian king whose impeccable martial skills vanquished all enemies and invariably saved the day. To the lads, Monkey epitomized the freedom of movement and spirit to which they aspired. Within Monkey's seemingly purposeless antics lay innate natural abilities, impeccable timing, watery flow, and supreme belief in self. True, he might be immature at times. Or perhaps just creating a ruse to hide his vast arsenal behind a veil of seeming foolishness.

"Masters often regard attributes like timing, flow, strength, and confidence as inborn talents or natural inclinations, existing independently of acquired skill. With proper tutelage, these attributes might be perfected through careful training and nurture, tightly bonded with acquired skills such as strategy, discipline, restraint, poise, and purpose. Inborn talent can carry one far, but unharnessed and undisciplined, it can lead to great turmoil and unhappiness. The metaphor for this dichotomy lies in

Monkey and his never-ending stream of challenges on the path to enlightenment.

"To the initiates or other admirers, Monkey symbolizes skill and mastery over the surface environment. You know what I mean. The surface environment—the tumultuous deck on which we all stand, exposed to the gales of life and destiny. Struggling unstintingly for firm footing from which to act our purpose. For monkey, proficiency over the surface environment is a birthright; for us, a gift of internal evolution, released only by our diligence and relentless pursuit of the impeccable.

"To understand flowing like water, think like a monkey. On seeing someone executing a move, and finding it appropriate to his own talent, monkey instantly makes it his own, integrating perfectly with the unfamiliar. Imagine how when first introduced to trees, the young chimp's clumsiness dissipates within minutes as it integrates perfectly into the unfamiliar environment. You can do these things too! Learn to channel monkey!"

At some point, Bao Ling deemed it wise to clarify, "These concepts of animals are not styles per say, but ways— imprinted by time, experience, and constant challenge, deposited by our ancestors within each of us for safekeeping and sure transmission. Teachers of the Nei Gung (internal energies) carefully explained how man represents the pinnacle of evolution, capping all currents of change. In the realm of the internal, they declared we were the highest evolved, and served as ultimate repository for all accumulated experience. From the perspective of energy, and the knowledge of movement and flow, the spirit natures of all creatures and their very essences lie dormant within us. Each animal descriptive portrays an accessible essence, a portrait of unique physical movement, mentation, attitude and resourcefulness, which combined with skill, refines to its silken essence, subject to our command. In time, one masters each of these attitudes, learning to flow from one animal to the next, stringing them into new forms as the situation requires. For those in the know, they compose the language of our very essence, our essential person, assuring our survival.

Bao Ling took care to add how even the humble and sometimes ignored creatures had much to impart, stressing that many, though less conspicuous in our esteem, had their own unique gifts to share.

One example, the grasshopper.

"What can this lowly insect teach us about strategy we don't already know? Have you ever tried to capture one? Do you remember how, just as you were about to put your cupped hands over its unsuspecting body, the grasshopper sprang suddenly into space, landing off to your side. When you came at it again, just as unpredictably, it lifted off to another location, maybe to your side, probably elsewhere. Though considered ignorant, the creature knows full well not to repeat or leave careless trails of predictable behavior.

"The grasshopper represents constant vigilance, and spontaneous reaction. It is a master of surprise, and like the cobra, has a seamless command of timing. Poised under stress, it possesses the innate ability to move suddenly to where you least expect it. As the attack unfolds, it disappears, ultimately surfacing off to the angle or behind, leaving you momentarily bewildered. That is the grasshopper."

And then, the not so lowly ant.

"This creature embodies diligence, determination, impeccable spirit, and readiness to face the unknown. Imagine being pinned down by an avalanche, your strength, speed, and cleverness rendered futile. By the time your panic ran its course, you'd probably see your entire life flash before your eyes, right up to where you are knocking on the door of the jade kingdom. The ant would survive. It would know what it could do in the now. First, believe in himself. Then, avoid distraction, have the courage to execute, and the discipline to persevere.

"See for yourself. Bury it in a mountain of dirt. No sooner imprisoned, the ant begins moving grains left, then right, forging paths where none existed moments before, treating every shift as life-determining. Nothing is wasted. It doesn't know precisely when but is certain that if it remains true to his nature, it will resurrect from this grave of the unfortunate moment. Returning again to life's uninhibited flow, where undoubtedly, it will party jubilant on arriving at the surface."

The lads smiled at the thought but recognized the import of the message for those like them, on whom others depended for their very survival. The realization settled in, a silent agreement passing between them—a shared understanding of the profound responsibility that rested on their shoulders and the wisdom the ant's example held for their journey ahead.

Then there's a seemingly simple creature like the donkey.

"Though often a faithful companion, you probably already know of its tendency toward stubbornness. It can be the embodiment of resistance. When the donkey refuses to move, nothing will make it move willingly. That is the mind of the donkey. When you are hurt, injured, starved, ill, captured, tormented or depressed, you still hold constant to what you know comes first. When choked, or clinched tightly in a lock, you will have the discipline to move, and step out of it, even with the pain. When enemies tear your

136

hair, cut your limbs, crack your nose, you will stand firm, even though others might collapse in surrender and defeat.

"Though easily spoken, these skills demand great conviction to execute. Master them, and you will already be far along the road to survival. Simple though they may be to your intellect; finding them leaves little doubt what at first seems simple and easily attained proves to come only with great investment of time and effort. When foes goad you, humiliate you, insult you, spit on you or otherwise push you into inopportune antagonism, you must have the will to resist, and to control the final timing. Just like the donkey."

One day, Kuan-Yin asked, "Master Ling, how many animals are within each of us?"

Bao Ling replied, "All of them, and their implicit natures. That represents life's greatest promise and bounty. They're there the day we're born. They exist as a separate reality within, and provide road maps of options, but only if one channels their potential."

Bao Ling explained how internal masters dedicated lifetimes developing these awarenesses and grew intimate with all the skills. "Understanding these lessons requires you create unimpeded conduits to places within; rather than using language, descriptives, or complex explanations, which might spin on forever and only detour you from the direct experience."

He emphasized how knowledge must be tactile, tangible, at one's fingertips, ready on the tip of one's tongue. Always there!

Bao Ling noted how the imagery of animals and their skills paralleled the wheel of life and the energies of the five elements, as well as their relationships, each with the other; and their conflicts, synchronicities, partnerships, and oppositions.

The major wheel consisted of Tiger, Bear, Crane, Snake and Monkey. They portrayed the five governing flows just as the five elements represented the metaphoric building blocks of our perceived realty. The other animals also had their parts within us, as supporting branches. One only had to beckon earnestly for their energies to emerge.

Then with a perceptible reverence, Bao Ling spoke of the dragon.

He put it simply. Beneath the major wheel, as the positive energy governing all karma, lay the dragon.

Though allowing it could be different for different people, Bao Ling described his own vision of dragon to be a huge fire breathing reptile, possessed of massive body, mounted upon strong formidable legs, and grounded perfectly by a powerful elongated tail. Almost always, its arms were disproportionately small, nearly non-existent. If the dragon were an opponent, one would likely count the diminutive upper limbs as detriments. That would be a false read.

The power of the dragon is not in its upper extremities, but rather in the body, legs, and tail; and the mystical geometry within, wherein lies the dragon's true domain. With arms virtually useless for anything but blocking and clenching, the fight of the dragon becomes one of position, and subtle interplay of angles with balance.

Using its massive legs and low center of gravity, the dragon instinctively positions itself to maximize its strengths and deflect its vulnerabilities. The dragon means position, stance, and closing yourself to attack, while opening your opponent to counter. Its small arms demand it be deep inside when executing, think eye-to-eye and chest-to-chest. It is the highest skill and requires the heart of a dragon to master. No fear! No trepidation! When executed properly, you have all the openings; your opponent has none. For those reasons, the dragon rules the decisive moment just before death!

Word Spreads

As fall transitioned to winter, the lessons continued. Like ripples in a pond, word of the remarkable teachings and rumors of newfound insights permeated the village, reaching even the ears of those in the monastery. The lads, Kong Kong and Kuan-Yin, swelled with pride in their growth, showcasing their newfound skills at every opportunity. The curious were drawn in, eager to see for themselves, and the once-private gatherings burgeoned organically.

Seizing the opportunity, Shi-Hui Ke and Master Li Fung recognized the potential impact. Encouraged by their support, monks and villagers alike started arriving serendipitously, now a curious audience along the periphery, hoping to glean wisdom from the unfolding lessons. Eventually, Bao Ling, acknowledging the growing interest, conceded to the inevitable and graciously invited all to partake.

Amidst the unfolding events, Bao Ling couldn't shake the suspicion of even this being part of some purposeful scheme conjured by his friend Sying Hao. He chuckled at the thought, realizing the game was still in its infancy, and the true extent of its scope remained unknown.

The hillside soon teemed with aspiring warriors, each immersed in the foundational teachings of movement—meticulously studying and meditating on the behaviors of animals, understanding their instincts, attributes, gifts, weaknesses, and heightened awarenesses.

The gatherings continued unabated through snow and storm. As had his own teachers, Bao Ling intensified their training in adverse weather. He viewed exposure to the elements as a direct glimpse into the soul of the dragon. He said as much. The rain, the cold, the wind, even the driving ice and snow; all imparted unique energy imprints onto the spirits of those readied and receptive. "You learn of them by experiencing them. Just as they shape the earth into what it's become, they work the same magic on you. Open yourself to the gift," he urged. It wasn't long before they sensed tactile manifestations of these energies within their own centers. At first, they thought their minds tricked them. But just as Bao Ling had promised; their techniques powered to unprecedented levels.

In just a few short weeks, Bao Ling wove a rich net of understanding, promising to elevate each participant's awareness to match the full innate potential of their movement.

This was not lost to the monks, who practiced rigorously in the temple, and had previously mastered the foundations of martial movement. Even with their underlying and formidable skills, they still struggled helplessly when looking to find openings moving on Bao Ling.

"While your movement is crisp and quick, and your techniques powerful, you are expecting me to be the same as you, and that is how you base your attack. You are trying to beat me, and you believe I am trying to beat you. You use and rely on all you have have and expect the same from me. So, you look for us to meet like mountain goats, banging heads until one drops or succumbs. You must understand this. For the goats, it's a ritual, and establishes rank. In life, it's real. Second place means subjugation or death. That's how 'they' intend to fight you (pointing to the ominous east). If you respond in like kind, their overwhelming force will annihilate you. We call that wu-wu-shi, or 50-50. The place where force, size, and numbers dominate.

"Someone who understands the animals never postures 50-50 to an opponent. Think about it. When the tiger pursues its quarry, does it map strategy based on an even chance of success versus failure? That would mean every time it encountered prey, it might lose readily as win. At best, failure could simply mean not eating. At worst, it could mean death; or disabling injury. In nature, even a mighty predator like the tiger diminishes his ability to survive any time it sustains injury, no matter how small or insignificant. Likewise, should it miss a needed meal. You are no different. Without your land, your domain, your culture, your history, and your people, you are finished. Just like the tiger without his nourishment. You become somebody else's plaything. Why go on?

"No! Of these things, animals know something especially important, which humans seem inclined to overlook or forget. 50-50 is never smart," he declared. "One must understand his or her underlying nature and rely on one's natural gifts to leverage advantage. The keys to identifying your underlying nature and which gifts best serve your needs lay within the constellations of animals and the grand coalescence of human experience already residing within you. Just beneath the reach of your biased-ridden consciousness.

"Remember, when a cat fights a dog, it must fight like a cat, not try to fight like a dog. When confronted by a menacing dog, the cat relying on its natural inclinations will have an eternity of insight at its command when it acts to survive. Mimicking the dog renders it helpless.

"Problems and opportunities define the situations you encounter. Depending on your focus, you may lock yourself into problems and impediments. Or with a more skillful eye, you may find opportunities, sometimes in the same places where others see only problems and obstructions. Engage your informed judgment to distinguish between the two. Then rely on your strengths with total commitment, striking with full intent and purpose when opportunity presents."

Bao Ling paused, allowing the wisdom to settle. "That too is the Dragon, embodying the essence of recognizing your nature and seizing opportunities."

"For sure, the time will come when you are tested. There is your certainty! Your fate! Remember, having to defend yourself will be like floating in a great sea, marooned in a small boat. That becomes your reality. They have overwhelming numbers. When the wind howls, and the sea becomes turbulent, you may find yourself stiff in panic. Double weighted. Unable to move or to think. When choice has disappeared from your will; all your energy will center on only one thought. Survive! Your future may be only to sustain your existence to the next wave. Go with it, never abandon hope. Then, like the ant, you will know exactly what to do.

"Yet even as you agonize over survival, and what terror might follow next, remember, there are some who routinely manage this seemingly impossible challenge and survive as a matter of course. It becomes routine! Over and over! The difference? They are never 50-50. Using their knowledge and their faith in innate skills, they maneuver their destiny on a field of 100-zero. It's all the same field. The difference is in the seeing. Mind over matter, they control themselves and the options of others, acting with awareness and confidence, and executing cleanly. Though the sea hasn't been tamed, their careful choices have turned the tide in their favor, assuring their survival; and the promise of their next move, and the next after that; executed clean and without impediment. While you battle a raging sea, they move in concert with energy, using its force to propel them to their journey's end. They go where they want, how they want, and when they want, trusting their innate awareness. Wide awake to what is going on!"

Master Li Fung, sitting as an honored guest, carefully added, "Just like a spider, suspended in emptiness, trusting its existence to a barely perceptible silken thread emitting from within."

It was Kong Kong who asked, "But teacher Ling, what if those who come also have this same knowledge; where does that leave us?"

Bao Ling responded, "I have not shared these teaching with them, nor have my teachers. In my past encounters, I have only found their natural awarenesses trapped within shells of greed, domination, ambition, and selfishness. These are great weights to lug through life; and constitute great distractions; especially when carried into battle or encounters."

Kuan-Yin added, "Really, can this truly be so?"

Bao Ling answered, "For me, nothing's certain, except I will act if the moment dictates." Thinking then of the story of Ah Ju Na, Bao Ling wanted to say that it was truly so. After many encounters, he had come to firmly belief that the one principle supreme above all others was that greed, domination, ambition, and selfishness came with openings, faults and fissures; and indeed, left those who harbored such traits stuck and vulnerable. He had long ago concluded it to be the unseen hand of Ke Li Xi Na. The subtly placed one ounce on the delicately balanced scale of life which assured sooner or later the true and fearless heart would always prevail against the off balanced weight of uncertainty. Could he prove it? No! One only had to look at the world to remain skeptical. Again, nothing was certain. Recalling the account of Shi-Hui Ke's torment, he thought to himself, *particularly if one starts with a very bad day*. He could say none of this to those listening. They would likely brand his supreme principle the arrogance of a loon.

He wondered what Zhuge Liang would have thought.

It was Master Li Fung who then gracefully added, "Friends, certainly there are evil titans on the other side. I have met them. But never forget, our people had the honor of guidance and tutelage from the likes of Zhuge Liang, Guan Yu, Zhang Fei, Colonel Sun, and Sying Hao. No one else, anywhere, can say or match that. Each of them taught the same. Bring a righteous and compassionate heart, well-honed weapons, and a good steed when you head for battle. Though they may defeat you in greed, ambition, and cruelty, the enemy will never match you in righteous purpose or skill."

Bao Ling could only smile and nod his approval at yet another example of the old master's penetrating insights.

By month's end, changes in the group were evident to all. Though they couldn't say for sure what had happened, they knew to a person they were different from when they started.

For one thing, their movements had become fluid: no starts, no stops, no pauses. Simply a unified flow, as though there existed only one movement, the flow itself. They learned the secret dragon stance of Bao Ling's grandfather, a position which forever settled the question of first move.

Shifting to dragon dissolved the incoming attack and instantly provided openings for a counter. When asked in the very beginning to demonstrate their power and speed, they instinctively assumed their long-rehearsed combat positions and executed. Always, they ended stunned to silence when each time Bao Ling, standing casually across from them, easily neutralized and defeated their attacks. This stumped them all. He didn't seem faster or more powerful, but they couldn't beat his hand to their target. When they worked to add power to their efforts by breaking tiles; Bao Ling seemed almost nonchalant in crushing them to powder. There too, always besting their hit.

Bao Ling held nothing back. For him there existed only solutions, and as he liked to say, "There should be no secrets between true friends."

He explained how their movement had become bound to mechanical action, an aspect of reality subject exclusively to Yang. "Easily discerned," is what he said. Whenever they moved, they first had to set, then initiate, and only then did their energy coalesce within the climax of their effort. The acceleration pushed outward from the geometry of their stances, moving to intended targets along trajectories now all too predictable.

True movement, he emphasized, rides on a bed of relaxation, springing from a sea of emptiness or Yin, seemingly unengaged and uncertain. That place of emptiness existed just as certainly as did the Yang world of mechanical action, only it wasn't there to be seen. You had to discover it for yourself by mastering the art of emptiness and relaxation. Bao Ling pointed out their considerable progress toward that end, but stressed much more work needed to be done, now on a rigorous conscious level. He shared exercises and flows and sequences of movement, such as Grasp the

Bird's Tail, certain to open new windows of awareness. He had them standing like posts, balancing on thin boards set over streams, and listening for sounds in the far distance — sounds which at first none could hear until he removed each of the nearer distractions, one by one, leaving only the elusive target. This amazed them all. The tactical implications weren't lost on any of them.

One day, he drew a long line on the ground, bisected by a small cross line at its center. Pointing to the cross line, he said, "Here is your body, and to the right is the world of Yang." Placing a rock on the farthest right, he continued, "… and here is your intended target. He paused and asked them to consider the left side of the line, emphasizing its substantiality. "What is it? Where is it?" he questioned. "Until now, all of you perceived only the right half of the line, representing the visible, tangible world. But look! Isn't the left just as substantial?"

He explained further, "When you executed against the target, you started from the cross line and pushed outward, directing your energy in a straight line to the target. At the onset, there was no energy. You were like a bag of rice. As you pushed outward, the energy accumulated until reaching its maximum level just before impacting the target.

"There is a problem inherent in this. Relying on force and effort reveals your intent to the defender … long before your attack is in full bloom. For a skilled defender who understands how to read these signs, negating the attack requires little more than a shift of angle at the last instant, then countering through the first available opening."

These were concepts they had heard before from their own teachers but paid little heed. Youngsters! For them, it was only what they saw, and what they did when they saw it, which defined their board of play. Not visible meant not

THE GIFT OF RED HARE

there. Now, they puzzled over Bao Ling, who had shown
time and again that he could stand right in front of any of
them and still be unassailable. He was there but he wasn't.
Whatever he understood about movement hinted to an art
as high in degree as his archery—for now, a riddle beyond
their reason's reach.

Bao Ling assured them he would elaborate and directed
their attention back to the line. Placing his finger on the
center cross line, he traced it to the left. "This is the domain
of Yin. Imagine lifting this entire line from the ground and
folding it into a circle connecting both ends. Then you will
have the Taiji[26], and you can think of it that way if you wish.
The left side represents Yin, where the mind, spirit, heart,
and intent of the warrior lay when in relaxation. It is only
the physical body and the manifestation of one's intent in the
form of energy that sits to the right of center."

Kong Kong voiced a question, "Allowing what you say is
true. What is the practical effect? Why would it be important
for us? Have you not said, 'What works works, what doesn't,
doesn't.' Shouldn't we prioritize what works over what
doesn't?"

Bao Ling smiled at the question and responded, "Because
in the world defined by emptiness, your mind, spirit, heart,
and intent lay unencumbered. Rooted in stillness. When they
glide within that harbor, there is no resistance, like a vessel
on still water. Place them on the right side of the centerline,
and every action becomes labored and subject to resistance."

Pointing to the left side of the line, Bao Ling explained,
"When you learn to relax completely, keep your weight
underside, center your mind, heart, spirit, and intent, and

---

[26] "Taiji" - What we in the West think of as the Yin-Yang
emblem.

extend your Chi; this is where you will abide. The spark of life within you, with which you emerge into the visible world, is here, and not there" (pointing to the right side). "When you move against me, this is what happens. I am here." (he points to the far left) "My physical body and you are here." (he points to the far right). "When I move against you, my intent forms on the far left and moves toward the center line. Chi, akin to a dog chasing intent as its prey, charges after the thought, moving without encumbrance to the center line. As they merge, energy blooms fully. To the observer on the right side of the line, the movement is explosive, seemingly starting from nowhere, arriving at its intended target before any reaction or avoidance can be staged. No one can defend against what they don't see. That is what happens when I move on you. That is why you can't time me. It's like an average horse winning every race if running full speed from the starting line. That is what you are missing. That is what you must learn to do."

In the village, word spread that not since the days of Colonel Sun and Sying Hao had anyone so profoundly impacted the development of their young warriors.

Though talent takes great time to develop, a week with someone like Colonel Sun or Sying Hao would be like a year with any other teacher. Now folks may be saying the same of Bao Ling, though perhaps in his case it might be an exaggeration. Then again, maybe not.

Masters understand the profound rule of ten thousand repetitions. Only after an act has been repeated and refined ten thousand times can it be deemed fully learned and trustworthy. Very few things in life receive this level of commitment from anyone. Even when some degree of physical proficiency has been achieved, the mind must also be developed in like fashion—taught to focus multi dimensionally, capable of seeing every threat in every aspect and knowing how to flow unimpeded within the perilous surround.

Abbot Hui and Master Li freely recognized the great gift bequeathed by the young archer. When it comes to survival, 50-50 leaves you dependent on physical prowess, speed, power, and whatever else (treachery perhaps?) you require to overcome the threat confronting you. While such skills have importance, they guarantee nothing, and allow survival to fall mostly to chance, tending to favor the dominator. The 100-zero mind perceives openings and knows how to penetrate them, closing all incoming doors. Whatever the attacker attempts leads conversely to exposure and defeat.

Entering the second month, Bao Ling praised their growing skills and commitment, but urged they push to broaden their perspectives and awarenesses. Yes, they were competent fighters, and could now handle the roll of 50-50 quite admirably. Survival, however, can be a brutal challenge, demanding nothing less than focus on the underlying dynamics and transposing that understanding into instinctive awareness. Despite their enthusiasm, finding 100-zero may not be readily achieved, at least not initially. "It takes work. And direct experience. You will need to develop the ability to read an attacker's intent, sometimes by feeling it, or sensing it through 'listening,' just like we've learned to hear sounds in the distance. Once malicious intent is determined, you will need to close your openings, and attack with full abandon, holding nothing back, as the opportunity or opening presents. Remember, if there is no attack, remain still; if an attack occurs; only then, strike first."

To a person, their eyes rolled skyward as he said this.

Bao Ling assured them they were making progress but emphasized the path required total commitment and great personal sacrifice over the course of a lifetime. That, of course, presumes one be so lucky as to survive to that end.

They understood personal sacrifice intimately. Not a person before him had been spared from loss, sorrow, and hopelessness. All understood. Their time of community in this mountain hideaway bordering on Shangri-La, constituted no more than a reprieve against a threat certain to come. For each of them, Bao Ling represented brethren from afar. As had his forbears, he brought deep understanding into what it took to root and hone their skills just as the moment of crisis dawned upon them. Among themselves, they spoke of fate's guiding hand. Most importantly, the very existence of someone like Bao Ling and the stories of his exploits elsewhere assured them of perhaps the most important thing of all if they were to maintain their will to continue.

They were not alone!

As training flowed toward the third month, each passing day brought fresh new faces to the group. Master Li Fung summoned his own students, already dispersed to field duties, instructing they participate in this path to deeper awareness.

Abbot Hui tasked his most senior warrior monks to take full advantage of "Dragon" Ling while he remained among them, stressing a time would soon come when fate called him elsewhere.

No one welcomed the prospect of his leaving. Though no one spoke of it, they all hoped he would remain and fight by their sides. They had been taken by the ways of this outsider, his clarity, and his diligence in sharing all he knew to be of value. Most of all, though he wouldn't acknowledge it, they admired his compassion. He often commented how he had become jaded and skeptical about the affairs of men and whether order would ever return. He apologized, allowing how his past had changed him, and by his admission not for the better. He regularly cautioned them on that very point, reminding that unlike him they should never forget to look first for the good in others, and to try working with that before concluding there was only evil.

It did not go unnoticed. He and Zhi Mei made daily rounds among the elderly and infirm, attending to their needs, seeing they were properly fed and not wanting for wood and heat as the cold descended upon the range.

Energy in Songs

Zhi Mei, too, saw fit to bring her aspiring poets and
songsters to the sessions. Ostensibly they sought to root their
voices in what they found. Notably, admiration for those
who will likely be called upon to make the great sacrifices.
More romantic poets might have reduced this to simply
another instance of young ladies admiring young men from
a respectable distance. Even with winter's approach,
youthful attractions warmed and pushed to the fore.

For her part, Zhi Mei became a participant. In doing so
she hoped to better understand the heart and spirit of her
soft-spoken paladin Bao Ling.

When training sessions concluded, Bao Ling
reciprocated, making sure to accompany Zhi Mei as she
made her rounds in the village. There, she and the others
would gather amidst the warmth of crackling fires. Sitting in
a circle, they took turns reciting events of the day, either as
poems, reflections, or sometimes as songs. Their progress
under Zhi Mei's tutelage amazed Bao Ling. He wished he
had sat in more frequently with them, if only to learn her
approaches for collecting one's thoughts into lyrical feasts.

He listened intently when Zhi Mei explained how she
knew so many folk tunes. She seemed to conjure them at
will. Engaging old melodies as vessels for myriad
combinations of freshly minted words and thoughts. How
skillfully she transported listeners to better worlds and new
heights of perception. Attentive and silent, he sat with chin

on hand, elbow on knee; trying to absorb all. She spoke of how poetry, songs, music, and dance were integral to the refinement of our finer natures. As a counterweight, they more than offset the poisons of strife and chaos. She related her father and brother's words, "These skills must be carefully nurtured and safeguarded. Projected outward, they shower their distinctive blessings on all who would receive them."

Much like Bao Ling, Zhi Mei encouraged each person's participation, carefully uncovering something in each person's efforts that could be refined, polished, or improved. In awe of her gift, all could attest how in the end beauty and truth emerged. Despite their admiration, she blushed when they praised, attributing her gift to a voice much larger than her own. A voice which flickered everywhere in the very spread of life. According to her, we had all become too distracted to hear it, entangled in our daily affairs, complicated by the storms of change and threats of turmoil. The songs which permeated our environment had fallen from our awareness and lay dormant in the realm of absent but not quite forgotten memories. She spoke of their power and how the voices of frogs and crickets as well as the songs of the wind and the birds were nothing less than nature's calls for the world to turn toward regeneration, and to unleash blessings for all.

On one occasion, Bao Ling seemed perplexed. Only when urged did he venture to ask if there were songs hidden in the clash of battles and whether they too held value or deserved our attention. The group froze at the thought, not certain of Bao Ling's intent on asking. Did he mean to stump her? A challenge? Even Zhi Mei hesitated, carefully collecting her thoughts so as to leave no threads untied. She answered, "Yes" then told of how the sounds and words were always there, to be plucked like ripe fruit from trees, if only one knew where to look, and how to pick; carefully steering away from those certain to do harm.

Bao Ling pressed, "What if those are the only songs one hears. Can any good come of it?"

Zhi Mei wondered over the question, then saw it was for himself. She could sense he was in earnest, just as she could see he was looking to her for an answer he could not find within. The thought pained her.

"This has no easy answer. Father and brother taught the songs we hear emerge from the void, forming the bridge over which emptiness blooms into our reality. In their positive form, we have nature; in their negative, we encounter conflict, pain, and chaos—sometimes heard as the clash and cacophony of battle, more often as the words and urgings of those consumed by greed and ambition. On this, Father stressed our individual development inclines toward the sounds we hear the most. He taught there were sounds which acted like spells. Incantations rooting evil and chaos to unknowing and vulnerable ears, distracted from the nurturing voices and melodies which were our birthright. Despite this, Father always stressed there remained hope. In his words, 'A true heart, rooted in righteousness, will always, in time, prevail.' For me, he meant that even for one who heard only the songs of battle and suffering, the return to the Way was a promise still certain."

Their eyes met as she spoke.

While others inquired further, she delved into how so many have spent their lives disregarding the whispers from the gates of perception. As though on the other side of awareness, where shadows now dominate, immortals lie in wait for our call and beckon. As she spoke, Bao Ling, like some others, contemplated his 'line' and the hidden left side.

He too had spoken of where stillness, intent, spirit, and heart lay in repose, awaiting our call to manifest. He had emphasized how the gift can never be unilateral. "It is not for you to take, steal or to demand. Rather you earn what is given as it is given, and each step taken to that end, produces two more in return, reflected in a corresponding awareness and a finely tuned skill." Some among them wondered, "Were their teachings not the same? They must have worked it all out together!"

She stressed how the act of creation aligns one with the Tao and encourages the well spring of truth to open wide. It was how she said it, which drew Bao Ling's attention. "The more one strives toward awareness, the more one will become aware. Truth passes right by the lazy and the passive; just as it passes by the greedy and the selfish."

She taught that when she created, sang, danced, or improvised, she exerted herself to lift truth from the shadows beneath reality. "My art is to bring it into the light of common awareness." If Zhi Mei were to be believed, truth, once released, would never return to its unborn confines. It becomes part of us.

"It only needs one birthing. From there, it has a life of its own, beyond anyone's reach and control."

She talked of structure, and showed how songs and verses, though having what seemed to be endless variations, fell into families, or groups. One could learn to recognize them over time, especially with practice and mindfulness.

She explained how the major archetypes reduced to a handful of distinct families. In fact, she preferred to think of eight distinct groups, paralleling the structure of the Bagua and the incantations of the I Ching. In those arts, each of their eight fundamental symbols rooted with an element of nature, which defined its very essence. There were Heaven;

Earth; Fire; Water; Mountain; Air; Thunder and Lake. Each also spoke to certain rhythms and patterns of sound. As vehicles for words, phrasing had to respect the inherent nature of each song's family. When orchestrated properly, truth pushed through and flew unimpeded from its cosmic center to all who would receive the finely polished gift.

Bao Ling reckoned that for someone like Zhi Mei, possessing the requisite know-how, a song or verse could be just as powerful as the Dragon Bow, or even the thought arrow of Shi-Hui Ke.

When asked, as often happened, if these arts could turn the world from its troubles, Zhi Mei, usually after considerable silence and reflection, would answer, "Yes, I can say they have the power to change the world. I cannot say for certain whether the changed world will be a better one or when and how the changes will occur. We can only control our within. Apart from choosing to emanate truth and its close ally, compassion, we cannot control out there."

This of course left everyone in a quandary. We all require certainty. Not to have it leaves us where we we started; except perhaps now, a bit wiser. Some had heard her words repeated enough to adopt them as mantras. Even today, you might yet hear hill folk, as they go about their singing and poetry or their daily labors, pausing to recite these very phrases; then stopping dead in their tracks to think upon their meaning.

Part 4 - Pieces of Gold

(Lessons From Ancient Tales)

Ah Ju Na's Dilemma

Bao Ling came to associate Zhi Mei with thoughts of Guanyin[27], particularly as her words somehow delivered him into a realm of peace. From there, he would revisit lessons gleaned from Sying Hao's ancient scrolls and find deeper meanings. Particularly those relating to Ah Ju Na[28]. Like Bao Ling, Ah Ju Na was esteemed as a great archer, with Sying Hao describing him as the equal of Colonel Sun, an accolade not to be taken lightly. Bao Ling vividly recalled the story of Ah Ju Na, a narrative that intertwined humankind's fate with events on a sprawling ancient battlefield, with everything hinging on whether Ah Ju Na could come to terms with the challenging choices ahead.

Ke Li Xi Na[29] guided Ah Ju Na's chariot to the center of the field, where he surveyed the vast expanse of armies about to engage. Faces he recognized dotted the landscape. He saw friends, acquaintances, subjects, even former enemies. Among the leaders on both sides, he saw members of his own family, as well as revered teachers. He also saw

---

[27] Bodhisattva of compassion.

[28] Arjuna. Third of the five Pandava brothers and protagonist in the Hindu epic Mahabharata.

[29] Lord Krishna; eighth incarnation of the Hindu deity Vishnu and in his own right, the Supreme deity. Embodiment of compassion, tenderness, and love. Lifetime companion and charioteer to Arjuna.

the faces of those who were innocent. Possessing no reason or heart for involvement, except for having been sucked in by events. Grasping the enormity of the imminent tragedy, Ah Ju Na became despondent. He questioned the very justification for his even being there and the possibility his presence meant death to them all. He knew precisely how dangerous he could be.

As a mortal, Ah Ju Na knew Ke Li Xi Na to be a celestial being, though until that moment, he had only seen him as his beloved companion, adviser, weapons bearer, and gifted charioteer. We know Ke Li Xi Na was no ordinary charioteer. The Creator had assumed human form for a purpose, and all events converged toward this critical moment. Ke Li Xi Na and Ah Ju Na had shared childhoods and all life's experiences. They were closer than brothers.

Turning to his companion, Ah Ju Na sought solace for his uncertainty and anguish; and to voice the clarity with which he now understood the pointlessness of it all. He simply could not sanction or participate in the death of those before them.

All the others registered the chariot mounted archer's pause to be only a fleeting moment on the battlefield. For Ah Ju Na, standing in the chariot, time had ceased to flow.

With boundless compassion, Ke Li Xi Na turned towards his friend and began to unravel the complexities of his awareness.

"Ah Ju Na, you are here because it is your personal dharma. Every soul assembled here today is bound by their own dharma—choices made, paths taken. Though their journeys may have seemed to diverge, leading them in different directions, or to different ends, they all converge here. Now, all stand before destiny on this field before us. You are the embodiment of the supreme warrior, and I am your vehicle; we are one. Your heart trembles because you wished to avoid this moment, but avoidance was not your path. Each of them standing before us might have altered their own destiny by one change of heart, one shift in goal, one relinquishment of jealousy, a touch less greed, or an attempt at compassion. A small step to the right or the left at some point in the distant past could have spared them. They failed to act! Instead, they chose chaos, inching carelessly into its grasp with each flicker of life's flame. For this reason, they stand here, many on the brink of their own journey's end.

"Yes, Ah Ju Na, many were my friends as well. With you I shared childhood among them. Like you I studied and trained with them. Together we witnessed the slow change and tried our best to guide them. We endured their rebuke, trickery, treachery, and even banishment. Because you and your brothers carried my blessing and unwaveringly upheld compassion, justice, and love, you survived and even thrived in the direst circumstances. They couldn't tolerate that. They sought your ruin once; and they would seek it again. Today, they will feel the brunt of their folly.

"You see, chaos would make a selfish deity. Give it ten percent, it demands twenty; offer half, it craves all. This stage before us was not shaped by your hands, Ah Ju Na; it's the creation of chaos, in alliance with those now standing against you. Reflect on this clearly. What will prevail if they succeed? What will become of Dharma when all that you represent lies wasted and ruined?

"Understand that you were born for this task and your only choice is whether you can act as who you truly are. By that, I mean standing against all obstacles, including chaos, even though it has taken the form of those you may call friends and relatives. This represents the greatest deception, but I trust your discerning eye to see through it. Not an easy task, but you've been honed for this purpose over many lifetimes. And to firm your resolve, I stand with you as a brother. Be the supreme warrior you have the potential to be. Overcome all self-doubt. Destroy that which threatens to destroy you and the wheel of life. Pour your essence into and through the darkness. Banish chaos!

Ah Ju Na gazed helplessly at his friend. The prince of warriors could see only the field before him, and his concerns, fears, trepidations, and horror over the absence of alternatives. Ke Li Xi Na looked to him, comprehending his pain and the dilemma he faced.

"Ah Ju Na. You needn't carry the weight of this impossible concern on your shoulders alone. All before you, even your doubts or your distaste for the coming slaughter; they are my doing, and my responsibility. Even as you carefully place an arrow, directing it toward the heart of your foe, ultimately, it is my hand that lifts the shaft, sets the breeze, trims the feather, and carefully delivers it to its end. Everyone stands where they are because of choices they've made for reasons they've self-justified.

"You and I, together, serve as guarantors of Dharma. While you agonize over the fates of your once friends and relations who have elected to stand with chaos, I, Ke Li Xi Na, have one single responsibility. I protect Dharma. All other considerations, all other concerns, all other trepidations stand second to this."

While Ah Ju Na understood his friend's words, they gave him no peace. Even his stout legs began shaking beneath him. The enemy before him reveled in what they perceived to be Ah Ju Na's sudden affliction with cowardice.

Ah Ju Na would never surrender to uncertainty so easily. He looked to his trusted companion, who had been almost as his shadow from the very first memory, then turned fully toward Ke Li Xi Na and asked, "Beloved friend, may I see you as you truly are?"

He didn't know why he asked this, or what it might do to change his frozen fever. He did know he had reached the end of his earthly means and could step no further on his own.

Ke Li Xi Na turned to his friend, knowing Ah Ju Na believed any human looking on his true nature would meet instant death. It was true of course.

"Are you sure of this?"

Even Ke Li Xi Na, who knew all, had a sense of the moment, and couldn't resist playing lovingly with his companion.

"Yes, my friend, I have nowhere else to turn."

Ke Li Xi Na nodded and smiled benignly.

As Ah Ju Na faced toward the warm smile, he saw the lips spread left and right opening to a limitless horizon, as his own reality receded to darkness. Even the battlefield had vanished, little more than a fleeting thought, once there, now departed.

Weightlessly, he floated into the crack rending his creation. Passing through, he witnessed an infinity of worlds swimming amidst constellations near and far, some recognizable, some gone, some yet to come, parts of different awarenesses. He saw his birth and death repeated ten thousand times through ten thousand lives lived. Worlds and constellations, driven by greed, selfishness, desire, and wanton ambition, reached unrestrained in all directions, eating away through the very fabric of creation. He witnessed scions of underworld kings flaunting their necklaces of skulls, attired with endless lost souls slung about their girdles like skins from shells already emptied.

He also saw rainbows of color pushing through the darkness and rolling waves of light and truth over endless blankets of space, gravity, and time.

As he looked, he knew he beheld with an awareness outside his own. A spectacle of such power as to assure instant death to any witness. He also knew he was seeing through the granted eye of Ke Li Xi Na, which opened for him and through him into everything.

At that very thought, the infinity before him became but a speck, subsumed into the ten thousand manifestations of Ke Li Xi Na, whose hundred thousand faces radiated love, truth, understanding and compassion through creations more numerous than the grains of sand on the banks of the sacred river. He realized then that there had been an infinity of Ah Ju Na's, all his equal or better, just as there had been an infinity of battlefields and an infinity of Ke Li Xi Na's in the form of charioteers.

His mind reached out to embrace the combined awarenesses of all his manifestations, and what can we say? As a gift perhaps, Ke Li Xi Na touched forefinger to Ah Ju Na's forehead, thereby exploding his awareness with eternity's string of endless experiences, lessons, and consequences.

Ah Ju Na heard Ke Li Xi Na speak in his true voice, and as he did, all of creation danced, moved, birthed, lived, grew, and ended in submission to his will as it raced and vibrated within eternity's oscillating stream. A vehicle upon which life itself staked its root.

Viscerally, Ah Ju Na understood the touch to his forehead. Everything before him came to be only because Ke Li Xi Na thought it to be.

But along with that divine thought came a great and powerful gift. Freedom!

Freedom of will that is dominant over endless possibilities.

"Why is that significant? Because it is true. Freedom of will means freedom even from Ke Li Xi Na's will, a true gift of compassion, love, and trust. We stand as equals with no strings attached. Just as with Ke Li Xi Na, creation coalesces around our thoughts, propelled by our intent, reaching ends which are very real to our consciousness of the moment.

All that registered to Ah Ju Na's grasp of the scene unfolding—reduced in the end to the thought bed of Ke Li Xi Na. Ke Li Xi Na might blink his eye, and all could disappear.

But he doesn't.

Instead, he watches.

We move with freedom and make our choices. Just as with Ke Li Xi Na, once our intent forms and manifests, our thoughts oscillate in cycles of yin and yang, curving with all others round the endless wheel of life, creating first the two, then the four, then the eight, the sixteen, and the sixty-four. It never stops.

Because we are truly free it is our right to choose evil, and many will. Or otherwise cater to the basest of selfish interests.

Ke Li Xi Na watches.

Because we are truly free, we may kowtow to chaos, and as two become four become eight become sixty-four, bear witness to the great wheel cycling into death and suffering.

Ke Li Xi Na watches.

As humans, some of us might look at this troubled reality and write it off, deciding it is better ended than permitted to continue.

You-know-who doesn't give a whit about our opinions.

Still, Ke Li Xi Na watches.

We might, as does Ah Ju Na in this moment of supreme trial, curse our destiny, bemoaning the trap wherein we find ourselves bound, double weighted, unable to find within our natures the capacity to act or even move.

Ke Li Xi Na watches.

Chaos threatens to envelop all.

Ke Li Xi Na acts.

Not as Ke Li Xi Na, but as us, first with Ah Ju Na, then with each one of us; acting to banish chaos, and to restore Dharma to his freely gifted creation.

"Why doesn't he do it for us?" you might wonder.

Well, it is our reality and our freedom. If we reject the gift, then where are we? Will it or we even be? Where would the fun go?

Because ultimately, this is a gift of love, Ke Li Xi Na never surrenders to his fear on our behalf. He watches, he gives, he acts, and guides us to victory, leaving us at the end once again with our freedom. He knows that in time, the cycle repeating endlessly will assure his eventual return in the role of protector and supreme guardian, acting again as he deems fit in the moment. He is always there, contained within the moment, right beside you!

Transfixed, Ah Ju Na sees the faces of humankind racing through his awareness, just as had the constellations only an instant before. He recognized the roles, the costumes, the acts and the interplays. There were musicians and poets, beggars and princes, fisherman and farmers, mystics and monks, tradesmen and scholars, priests and untouchables, heroes and victims—countless identities spinning into circles of diversity: some awake, some not; some aware, some not. All with the potential to soar and experience Ke Li Xi Na's gift of freedom; but most of whom have foolishly chosen otherwise.

It had seemed like an eternity had passed, but it was only a moment before when Ke Li Xi Na had chided Ah Ju Na for faltering in his resolve. He reminded we are who we are because we willed it to be so. As we stand in the moment of who we are, our only choice is to become impeccable and actualize, or to fall into chaos. As he stared across the field at the tens of thousands, armed, ready, and intent on his demise, Ah Ju Na radiated compassion, knowing that among them were musicians, poets, beggars, princes, fishermen, farmers, mystics, monks, tradesmen, scholars, priests and untouchables, who had departed from Dharma and had abandoned their true natures, and their freedom.

Finally, he nodded in comprehension to Ke Li Xi Na. It didn't matter where he shot his arrow. Those before him had made a lifetime of decisions putting them right where they ended at this moment, soon to savor their return to righteousness, albeit with the added weight of their karma, and the descending arrow. Had they chosen otherwise, they would not have found themselves bound to chaos, this place, and the truth of consequence.

In the end, the scene before him spoke to a solitary reality. Awareness meant banishment of obstacles seeded by others, and perhaps even ourselves, intent on burying our freedom and enslaving our wills.

Ah Ju Na knew now he would stand with his charioteer against all foes. Thus had he done for all of history, thus will he do for all of time.

Bao Ling recalled the sessions with Sying Hao, the two sitting passively by the fireplace, bathed in its comforting glow, shadows rippling about. It seemed just a moment ago, still tangible in his thoughts. Sying Hao would reach for some scroll or text and simply start into a story or lesson. He had no system for this. Frequently he would reach and let some invisible guiding hand determine what they were meant to share in the moment.

But the story of Ah Ju Na always seemed close to his reach. Sying Hao, sorcerer's apprentice; the once feared companion to a warrior man-myth; and for a time, high counselor to a now fallen empire, made one thing foremost to younger friend's benefit.

"You must pay full mind to the dilemma of Ah Ju Na, and his reconciliation to Ke Li Xi Na. Learn to see through Ah Ju Na's very eyes and look deeply into his quandary. Understand how that speaks to us and where we stand on the path. For you, Bao Ling, the story is particularly important."

"How so?"

"I pray it will keep you sane."

And to that end, Sying Hao repeated it at every opportunity, but the narrative didn't end there.

Bao Ling of course asked, "What happened next?"

Sying Hao related that before Ah Ju Na returned to the battle at hand, he pointedly begged his friend's instruction into the proper life, and the path to supreme consciousness assuring they would be forever as one.

While the world perched on the brink of cataclysm, Ke Li Xi Na patiently expounded the many paths[30] assuring humankind's return to union with the Creator. They all boiled down to three essential roots. Action in detachment, which Ah Ju Na had now come to appreciate; committed worship and reliance on divine grace, radiating it outward and unselfishly to all; and finally, direct immersion into

---

[30] Their exchange can be found in all its detail in the Bhagavad Gita. Many translations of this sacred Hindu scripture are readily available.

knowledge manifest as wisdom. The last of course, perhaps most difficult if only because the mind tends to get in the way, setting up many false substitutes for the divine.

"Is that it?" asked Ah Ju Na.

"No" replied his friend. "The gift already given assures all of their eventual return to the one."

Now Ah Ju Na's brow furled in puzzlement.

The hammer of Ke Li Xi Na's reality was that ultimately, all courses led to oneness. For those who sought the Creator in earnest there could only be the one.

Sying Hao emphasized this to be the key. He often said that for people like himself, and Colonel Sun, the temple monks, and even Bao Ling, Dharma acted as a compass, demanding they bring their impeccable attitudes to fruition in restoring order. It fell to them, and others like them, to rescue awareness from the ashes of interminable chaos. All depended on this.

Bao Ling would only smile, "Little chance of that, Big Brother. Vipers under rocks is what we've become. Insignificant, dangerous only to those who turn our cover and step our way. Perhaps in the future, others like us will find our remains and wonder who we might have been."

To this, Sying Hao responded sternly, a rare downturn of his brow, "Never underestimate the power of one person's focus to stir change in a world locked helplessly in darkness. Never forget Bao Ling, when something is stuck and unable to move, sometimes an act as insignificant as a finger's glancing touch will restore it to life. It is making the finger move and finding the moment of touch that is hard."

Bao Ling recalled what he had heard many times in his youth, "One ounce can move a thousand pounds, but only for one who has found the way."

Could it be the same with men under the weight of their foolishness, which is infinitely heavier?

The Dream of Han Fades

Speculation on the nature of extraordinary beings like Zhuge Liang is boundless. Are they gods, immortals, or simply flesh and blood, different in some unknowable way, or fundamentally the same as you and me?

What of their talents? Manifestly boundless. Aware of all. Able to read stars, faces, lines on palms, tea leaves, silence, the Yi Ching, flows of rivers, shadows, shifts of wind, flights of birds, notes of music, fates, destinies, inclinations, propensities, characters, medians, strategies, colors, dreams; the list goes on of course, but you get the picture. They are transcendent!

Whether god, saint, demon, spirit or mortal; Zhuge Liang stood as that one special personage above them all. Peerless. Without equal. There will not ever be another like him.

However, he died. This fact is undisputed. History attests to it, confirmed by many eyewitnesses.

It came about during the fifth Northern campaign against Wei. By then Zhuge had devoted his life to serving Shu. Some claim he had visibly aged beyond his fifty-four years, while others suggest he had fallen ill, whispers of the lung disease circulating. Who knows? He bore an immense weight of responsibility. More than any other man. Is it any wonder the load took its toll? Slowly grinding him down to an untimely demise? As Marshall and Protector of Shu, he had resisted the temptation to heed Liu Bei's deathbed suggestion he replace Liu Shan should the son prove less than competent to rule. Despite public perception of Liu Shan as a nincompoop (the whispers had spread for good reason), Zhuge Liang would never stoop to the indignity of deposing his friend's son.

Besides, Zhuge Liang was never one to give up on others. He always anticipated one's best to eventually push outward to the surface, where it might be actualized and nurtured. This belief extended even to those labeled as nincompoops. That might explain his unwavering patience with the young prince, now king. Others in his position might have had the kid's head, or at least arranged for an accident. There would have been complications of course … the matter of the eunuchs surrounding him; followed thereafter by his personal army of power craving sycophant administrators, law proclaimers, back door strategists, opinion shapers, flirtatious would-be princesses, and their too accommodating witch mothers. The potential spectacle arising from any misfortune befalling the king would be unimaginable.

But Zhuge Liang was a patient sage, endowed with perseverance. He knew Liu Bei to be equally singular among men, as too were Guan Yu and Zhang Fei, and even the Tiger Generals. Zhuge Liang had borne witness, they all had their sour moments and shortcomings, as well as their own indelible stamps on achievement; establishing standards of courage, honor, discipline, loyalty, love, and pursuit of righteousness that would shine as eternal beacons for all to emulate. Loving them as he did, and respecting their memories, he never lingered on their failures, their quirks, or their faults, which now, even he would have to admit, ultimately cost them all dearly.

Isn't it true? Everyone carries their own foibles and personal baggage. Attempting to discard them only results in their return, much like lost puppies. Zhuge Liang understood this to be the nature of things and accepted the inevitable consequences with grace and dignity.

And so, it unfolded. In the end, only he remained. Left to deal with the ashes of the once vibrant western empire, and with the troublesome proclivities of the vulnerable Liu Shan.

Zhuge understood well the lessons of Ke Li Xi Na. Though aligned in righteousness and love to Liu Bei, he nonetheless rooted in the moment, trusting action. Striving to execute perfectly and always with an impeccable attitude. Above all, always looking to end chaos, and facilitating eventual return to harmony.

Somewhere in the reversals of fortunes, it became clear to Zhuge Liang. Shu would never emerge supreme over the competing kingdoms. The restoration of Han ended as an unattainable dream.

One of the inherent pitfalls of early success lies in the abandonment of restraint. When you believe the world is your oyster, you are as comfortable opening it with a sword as with a slice of well-placed persuasion. Why it's yours, why not do with it what you will! That's how you'll feel. Close on the tail of first success will follow honor and reward; often self-orchestrated. Then grows the influence over others, all too natural. Eventually, we learn to love our heroes, just as we admire the wealthy, the successful, and the powerful. Often, they reckon on our doing so. Some view this adoration as the ultimate commodity. Acquiring it, one can do almost anything. When honor, reward, and influence get strong in the mix, ambition begins reaching outward from the concoction. Drawing on the three, it pushes hard and forward. Some will argue ambition to be a positive trait. I believe it may be, though not so often as some suppose. See first who can disassociate it from the tendency to line one's pockets. Or to enrich one's family and cronies over the sacrifices and remains of others.

To Zhuge Liang, the once glorious narrative felt almost like a dream—a soiled story that might not have happened at all. With luck, he might one day snap to consciousness and find himself safe in his mountain sanctuary, awakened from a deep meditation which ended as a troubling dream, but thankfully not real.

Liu Bei had successfully consolidated Shu, transforming the once-neglected, remote west into a thriving inland empire, albeit not the restored Han. He might have held the others in check indefinitely, particularly in the aftermath of Red Cliffs. He had weakened Wei and earned the goodwill of Wu and their helmsman Sun Quan. Recognizing the decimation of Wei's forces, and the effects of war on the Wu, Zhuge Liang saw Shu emerging as a power of reckoning. One conceivably able to survive independently from the others. He counseled restraint, suggesting to Liu a return to the once state of Han would not be possible in the now fractured and partitioned empire. He argued it best to simply wait, and harness the full potential of the moment, riding it to wherever it might lead. He argued "To do so would better serve the cause of righteousness than to rekindle Han."

Liu Bei gave full weight and due respect to Zhuge's counsel, knowing its honest intent and intrinsic worth.

Other counselors in his court intended to make their own mark. "Shu stands supreme! A superpower among lessers, and capable of altering the course of history with timely committed action." They argued it would be irresponsible not to accept the role and to act accordingly. History would judge harshly if he failed in this. They said, "Restraint is for those who will be forgotten."

Doubtless, such voices echo even today.

Behind them were the war merchants, the arms makers, the land grabbers, the breeders, the satisfiers, the intoxicators, and the gold pickers. Takers all! Eager beneficiaries of chaos, catastrophe, cultivation of fear and the threat of damnation or doom. Their assurance of wealth and new horizons of fresh opportunity doubtless to follow.

Swords should be bent into plowshares. Zhuge Liang knew this well. The damned things had a mind of their own and it always meant disaster. Once drawn, they might never be re-sheathed.

The zealots counseled Liu Bei assimilate and hold Jing, that he move north against Wei, that he move Southeast against Wu, that he push west to the foreign territories, or head far north and seize the grasslands from the horse nomads, or even cut south and west to the great subcontinent where rumored richer targets awaited. All sitting simply for the taking, particularly for such as the now proven warriors of Shu.

An empty land, once remote and isolated, had become a perfect springboard for outreach in virtually any direction. The possibilities seemed endless.

The term "superpower" echoed through the court, a seductive notion for those inclined to games.

However, Zhuge Liang, wise to the manipulations of Yama's whispers, despised the term.

He recognized it as another ploy, the old "Us versus Them—a call to assert superiority, offer help, skills, insights, and guidance, and seize opportunities under the guise of moral duty. If not us, then who will fill the current void and seal the moment?"

Yama's poisoned whispers!

Liu Bei, in the twilight of his years, found solace in these suggestions, and liked hearing them.

Now, don't go belittling his folly; I wager you would like it too. It made him feel good. Affirming he was not somebody to be taken lightly. "Ruler of a superpower," he would murmur loftily when alone in his chambers, "the once sandal maker has gone far in the world." Zhuge Liang, witnessing this transformation, would shudder as he sometimes read the ruler's lips, hearing the very words in their movement, recognizing the dangerous mantra over which he had no influence.

On this matter, Zhuge Liang and Liu Bei would not find common ground.

Zhuge Liang spelled it out, "Before Red Cliffs, Wei was the superpower; then it was Wu; now they say it is Shu. In the blink of an eye, it will be another. Predicating governance on the supposition one stands supreme above all only invites disaster. It runs against the flow of Yin and Yang, which even the lowliest knew to be the single principle on which everything hinged. Once, shockingly out of character, he lost patience and screamed at his friend, "The Yi Ching is called the Book of Changes for a reason!"

Liu Bei listened patiently to his trusted companion's concerns, even smiling while absorbing his wrath. "I am sworn to restore Han. One might persuasively argue the reason there are three kingdoms today, and countless warlords acting to their own ends, is because I have dallied. But for us and our having partnered with honor, Wu and the provinces would now be enslaved. Cao would be emperor, neighbors to the south, and north would be engulfed. As you well know, others chastise me regularly for not finishing the job I once started.

The wizard listened and marveled at how wrong thinking might be persuasively woven to accommodate any misguided purpose.

"They tell me I should be looking north, west, and south. Between you and me, I look only north and east to the traditional capital. My intent is to fulfill my oath to someday return there and restore Han's civilized order, it's even-handed system of justice, and its prosperity."

Though he knew its aim to be wrong, and that it would lead to disaster, Zhuge Liang also recognized Liu's righteous character remained intact. The wizard marveled at the paradox, "How is it possible for righteousness to lead someone so far astray?"

A question which has resonated through time and has never found its answer.

Though Guan Yu and Zhang Fei remained ever ready for battle, this unremitting commitment to the dream of resurrecting Han had exacted a terrible toll on the people of Shu. Both knew it, and it disturbed them greatly.

Guan Yu, a compassionate man, understood the situation too well. On occasion, after a few draughts of wine, he would confide in Colonel Sun and Sying Hao. "I sometimes think the good people of Shu might have fared far better had we never come."

Had others heard these words, they would have declared, "Treasonous blasphemy!"

But the knowing ears of Colonel Sun and Sying Hao were vast caverns, where such careless words might hide forever.

Sadly, perhaps connected to the same, Guan came to rely more on his wine over time; if only to sleep through the troublesome conclusions he had fashioned from his lifetime of dedicated loyalty and righteousness.

Guan's End

The good people of Liu Bei's kingdom, previously spared the ravages and harsh realities of war, were now being tutored firsthand in loss and hardship. Villages vanished from the periphery. Once thriving populations transformed into desperate refugees seeking safety in the barren wastelands. Advancing enemies relentlessly gnawed away at their exposed and retreating rear, seemingly closing in from all directions, even breaching what were once considered impregnable mountain sanctuaries.

Compelled to satisfy the insatiable demands of his diminishing war machine, Liu Bei issued conscription orders targeting all able-bodied men of fighting age. As attrition mounted, he reluctantly enlisted the old, the elderly, the young, and, eventually, even children. Self-disgust etched his face as he grappled with the consequences. Often found brooding on his throne, Liu weighed countless scenarios, only to see each hopeful outcome thwarted by the rising destiny of some formidable adversary. Days, weeks, months passed, and nothing changed, while the great kingdom and its war engine staggered under the weight of overreach.

"This is the inevitable end of every so-called superpower," he reflected in solitude.

Liu Bei remained unwavering in his mental exertions. Continuously testing possibilities, he hoped to stumble upon the fleeting solution that had eluded him thus far. Had he not managed this in the past? Liu sought inspiration, recalling a legend from the distant west about a king confronting an impossible knot. On close study, the king looked for points of end or beginning where he could untangle the knot conventionally. He found none. After trying all combinations and considering all possibilities, he could bear it no longer. Emboldened by desperation, he slashed it with his sword, creating loosened threads and tatters with which he quickly unraveled the whole. Liu Bei envisioned a similar breakthrough. But where to strike? And how, with such dramatic effect? Even the brilliance of Zhuge Liang seemed incapable of providing an answer. "Sire, you have surpassed my capacity to be of use," Zhuge Liang confessed.

Farms lay untended, starving livestock roamed wild, their misery ending only when slaughtered to feed famished soldiers rushing to yet another front.

The cloud of starvation, once a relentless specter over Wu and Wei, now descended on Shu.

This demon certainly gets about.

Bodies of young ladies and girl infants dotted the waterways, resembling strange water flowers detached from their pods. Their sad fate sometimes envied by others who paused to witness, knowing the alternatives promised no better.

Left perpetually questioning his purpose and haunted by the toll it had taken, Guan Yu arguably lost his edge.

Lord Guan eventually met his end, falling victim to the flattery of a conspiring young enemy officer who had crossed lines under the guise of message bearer.

Guan Yu liked the boy. Spending time with him provided a brief respite from the incessant suffering, offering moments of solace in the company of someone for whom the future seemed boundless. More importantly, Lord

Guan would never allow it to be said that he failed to treat an enemy's delegate with proper respect and graciousness.

The young officer had banked on this.

Come evening, they drank as friends. The officer, whom I will not dignify by naming, addressed Guan Yu as "uncle," citing him as a beacon for his aspirations of serving with honor and distinction. In return, Guan Yu affectionately called him "nephew" and insisted he spend the night in safety, guaranteeing his return through the lines in the morning. They exchanged stories, with the young man attentively listening as Guan Yu reminisced highlights of a lifetime befitting an immortal.

Early next morning, the young officer departed Guan's compound, bearing what appeared to be a gift from his noble encounter, elegantly wrapped beneath Guan's unmistakable seal. The attendants, familiar with Guan's generosity, found nothing unusual in this gesture.

True, Guan Yu's generosity matched his boundless valor. He had bestowed upon the young officer his treatise on combat and strategy, one of only five copies in existence at the time, the others since lost beneath the winding sands of time.

Placed within a gilded rosewood box, the scrolls bore his mark along with words of encouragement, urging his "nephew" never to forsake duty and honor for personal gain or, worse, ambition.

It was a singular treasure.

Given in exchange for a hollow promise made.

Instructed by Guan Yu, his guards safely escorted the young officer to the enemy lines, where he crossed unmolested to his own encampment.

When Guan Yu failed to rise with the morning sun, his aides entered the compound to wake him. To their horror, they discovered his headless torso, left where he had earlier set to drunken rest. On the ground alongside lay the treatise on combat and strategy, scrolls unrolled and cast chaotically about, soiled by the master's spewing blood which had earlier bridged the distance, arcing to where they had sat in their rosewood box, baptizing all in rich saddened redness.

In the pre-dawn hours, acting in the moment; cleverly we must admit; the fiend saw the value of the rosewood box as the perfect vessel to conceal his intended treasure from prying eyes. The scrolls meant nothing, but for their practical use in wiping the bloody residue from the box's exterior. Rice paper torn from the scrolls served this purpose just fine.

Liu Bei and Zhang Fei were devastated at the news, doubly so on seeing the deathbed and the beheaded corpse. They were inconsolable.

It was Sun Quan who had ordered the execution, and understood the strategic importance. So long as Guan lived, Sun's western flank remained vulnerable. While he did not expect the young officer to return with the trophy, he was relieved the officer had taken it upon himself to do so. Without the head, no one would have believed Guan was gone, and soldiers would still be seeing likenesses everywhere, fearing his rage and fabled presence on every battlefield. Sun Quan mounted it on a stake and left it where all could regard it to their own satisfaction. Guan Gung was no more.

After finally convincing his generals, it is said Sun Quan delivered the head as a token of reconciliation to Cao Cao, with whom yet another major confrontation threatened.

The Gift of Red Hare

Sun Quan thought it to be a peace offering, accompanied by a message proposing, "We share a common foe; why deplete our resources and reserves warring against each other?"

Stunned by the nature of the "gift," Marshall Cao looked on with a mix of dismay and disgust at his friend and once nemesis's already rotting head. With sorrowful dignity, he recalled their time together. Long ago, his overwhelming legions had somehow managed to capture the invincible Guan Yu, dispatched by Liu Bei to defend a remote outpost with only fresh recruits. An impossible task for any commander, even the then scarcely known but talented Guan Yu, whose legend as a war god had not yet ascended.

It looked to be an easy sweep, but Cao Cao's finest soldiers struggled for nearly a month to subdue the garrison. They reported daily on the fierceness of the resistance. Cao couldn't believe the reports, then visited the front lines to see for himself. What could this enigma be? This force of nature, which even his best found beyond their capabilities to subdue? Soon enough, he saw it in its full manifestation. His generals had understated the phenomena. Cao Cao watched and studied from afar as the days trickled by, so entranced by what he witnessed he lost interest in the escaping Liu Bei. At month's end, with Liu Bei's escape assured, Guan walked forward through the lines, presented to Lord Cao and said he would resist no further, "No point in valiant men dying needlessly."

Guan's personal surrender stunned Lord Cao and his legion. While they processed in confusion, the remainder of Guan's novice charges made their own escape. Guan, of course, had planned it so.

Lord Cao was no fool. He knew he had been had. But so intrigued had he become with this new enigma, he forgave the con readily.

Cao was captivated by Guan Yu, especially considering the tales he had heard beforehand, and now what he had witnessed firsthand. Even at this early stage in his remarkable career, the stories about Guan were spreading. Impressed by what he had seen, Cao treated Guan with generosity, dignity, and honor, asking for nothing in return but good company and fellowship.

This surprises?

Certainly, as with everyone, there is more to Cao Cao than we think we already know of him.

In time Cao invited his "guest" to accompany him on some campaigns, securing only Guan's promise he would not flee if granted opportunity to move freely about.

The opportunity was granted; he didn't. The promises of real men are like the ground we stand upon. Cao's admiration grew proportionate to his own measure of Guan's sense of propriety and honor. In those times the rarest of traits. Perhaps still so.

The clincher was the Battle of White Horse[31].

---

[31] Baima - "White Horse." First in a sequence of battles leading ultimately to Cao's decisive victory at Guandu, consolidating his hold in the northeast.

During this campaign, Liu Bei played no significant role, as his forces were recovering from recent defeats elsewhere. At this early stage, his small but loyal band gave him claim to nothing, except perhaps status as a warlord. Cao Cao's strategic concern centered on his once ally, the formidable Yuan Shao, whose forces controlled the area north of the Yellow River, while Cao's forces controlled the south. Cao identified Baima as strategically valuable, particularly for the decisive battle he foresaw at Guandu. Yuan Shao also recognized its strategic significance, knowing his ability to move forces discretely necessitated excising Cao Cao's probing eyes from in and around Baima. He entrusted this important task to General Yan Liang, whose impeccable record qualified him above all others as the man for the job.

And indeed, Yan Liang proved to be formidable. Within thirty days, his forces decimated Cao Cao's garrison, prompting the start of a retreat and evacuation. Cao Cao himself, commanding an army of over fifty thousand, led the charge to stall Yan Liang's advance, securing a rear corridor for reinforcements, food, and crucial supplies. Despite Cao Cao's brilliance as a strategist, he had his hands full countering the lightning-like moves of the impetuous Yan Liang, resulting in a stalemate. For Cao Cao, this spelled disaster. Getting entangled with Yan Liang at Baima exposed his grossly weakened flank to Yuan Shao's larger army, already amassing at Guandu.

Cao's advisers implored he enlist the aid of Guan Yu. By then, Cao Cao had grown to value the companionship and sagely advice of the not yet immortalized Guan. Never losing sight of this crucial factor, Cao knew that Guan's ultimate loyalty lay with his sworn brother, Liu Bei.

He knew Guan to be a righteous man. One who would not leave without first fully repaying the full measure of

Cao's generosity and friendship; only then would he make a clean break. In the end, this question of friendship triggered Cao's hesitancy. If Guan Yu returned the measure of his generosity with an equal measure of valor against the army of Yan Liang, nothing would bind him further to Cao and Wei. He would leave forever. Lord Cao had grown accustomed to Guan Yu, almost feeling as though he needed him nearby. He had hoped in time to win his loyalty, and to turn him from Liu Bei. Losing him now would be a bitter price to pay; even for turning around this all-but-failed campaign.

But no other options emerged. Reluctantly, Cao summoned Guan to the battlefront, along with his trusted general Zhang Liao. Zhang had become Guan Yu's constant companion and eventually a trusted friend during the period of "captivity." Cao designated Zhang Liao to lead the all-or-nothing counter-offensive, while Cao secured the flanks and the rear. He implored Guan Yu to accompany, and to offer guidance freely. Even then, he kept Guan out of the direct action, trusting first to his own impeccable skills as a strategist, supplementing the vast field talents of Zhang Liao; whom even Guan Yu clearly held in the highest regard.

As the battle unfolded, waves of men and animals rolled in from the surrounding hills clashing mercilessly in the fields below. Rivers of blood oozed beneath the fallen warriors and their steeds, creating an eerie tableau, as though redcaps were rippling in the wind.

In the far distance, atop a hill overlooking the chaos, a banner fluttered in the breeze.

Guan Yu, standing beside Cao Cao turned and asked, "That's him I suppose, the seemingly invincible Yan Liang?"

"Yes" answered Cao, gritting his teeth over the mounting losses unfolding below. Even his hardened stomach churned at the escalating slaughter.

Guan Yu surveyed the field and focused on its midst, spotting his companion Zhang Liao fearlessly pushing forward ahead of his troops, working to split Yan's forces.

Guan turned to Cao, "You have chosen well, I know of no better man for the job than Zhang Liao, except perhaps my brother Zhang Fei. He will prove valiant, resourceful, and tactically brilliant. But he will not have this day. The geometry favors Yan Liang, by sunset the final wave will over run Zhang Liao."

Cao, visible shaken by the remark, responded, "Then why does Zhang Liao push forward with such a degree of reckless abandon?"

"Because he already knows what we know, and as an honorable man he has no other choice than to serve his lord to the best of his ability, regardless of the odds or the likely outcome."

Cao replied, now comprehending the clarity in Guan's assessment. He spoke as though to the wind at the front. Thinking perhaps the breeze might lift his words to those who needed to know, "I will care for his family always. They will want for nothing; his children will be as my own."

Guan stared at Cao intently, then spoke, "How can it be we are so much alike, but so far apart when it comes to what is right for the nation."

Cao Cao had no answer, except to add, "Zhang Liao often spoke of you as his older brother. I would be honored if you would accompany me when I return his decorated body to his family and home."

Guan Yu stared intently at the far battlefield, "Look, there in the distance, Yan Liang gloats over his victory not yet even won."

Cao Cao acknowledged, seeing the adversary toasting and smiling as he milled about with his staff. Cao spat, then turned away, enraged and unable to stare further.

Guan Yu ordered his attendant bring Red Hare forward.

Many regard Red Hare to be the greatest warrior's horse ever to have graced the battlefield. You might say he was among horses, what Guan Yu was among men. Chroniclers record he could cover five hundred li in a day, and that he never even broke stride ascending mountains, or crossing deserts. In battle, he moved forever forward, fearless, and completely attuned to his master. His coat glistened red, not a single hair of any other shade. When he moved in battle, the sweaty sheen on his coat took on a light of its own, casting a red glow on the faces of all those who closed to do harm. A colored beam shaded blood red. He first served Lü Bu, and though he served him with distinction, it represented a horse's duty, and not his love or devotion.

They can be like that, dutiful, and respectful; but not devoted. Particularly if one be deemed less than matching in skill, talent, or character. On Lü Bu's death, the remarkable steed found its way through capture to Cao Cao. Just another of the many treasures harvested among the spoils of war. Cao could do nothing with the beast, except recognize its great spirit and limitless potential. It seemed for a time no other man would ever rule the animal. Cao Cao might have kept it forever, perhaps even written poetry about it. But along came Guan Yu, the imperial prisoner become house guest. One day, on a lark, he took Guan to the field which held Red Hare. There it stood. Alienated in the new surround. Alone and without purpose; motionless, as if in waiting.

Guan Yu stared at Red Hare, for once unable to speak. His eyes reflected the red hue of the steed, still in the distance. Glee radiating as though from the eyes of a child. Seeing what he now recognized to be the one thing in all creation which had always been missing from his life.

Cao Cao appreciated Guan's pained expression of hopeless desire. After all, he felt exactly the same about building his empire. Lord Cao calculated that as his prisoner and bound by promise not to escape, Guan had no hope of getting the animal, at least not without crossing his principles. *Too bad Lord Guan. My thoughts are with you!*

Guan walked to the fence and locked gazes with Red Hare; soul mates, knowing only now what they had always hoped for, had finally come.

The poet within Cao drank in the full import of the moment. He cursed himself, thinking within, *Don't do this!* Then, as though wrestling with his own will, he walked ever so slowly to Guan Yu's side. There he whispered, almost half-heartedly as the mentations within finally ceased.

"I give him to you."

The words shocked even Lord Cao. Had he thought more carefully about it before speaking, he would not have said them. But the poet in him rejoiced! Given the moment, the words, and their timing, all were perfect!

"Please Sir, no jokes," was all Guan Yu could say, looking almost despondent, "Even if you were serious, I could not in good conscience take such a gift without dishonoring my loyalty to Liu Bei."

Riding the moment to its full potential, the poet king responded, "The beast is yours Guan Yu. It is worthless to me. You owe me nothing. I will be the first to remind you of your duty to Liu Bei when the time comes." Guan Yu turned to Cao Cao, unable to say anything further, his hot desire for the beast consuming him.

Silently, he vowed that someday, in some way, he would even the ledger for this great and freely given gift.

He bounded over the fence in a single leap, walked briskly to the animal's side, then jump-mounted the beast. Cao Cao saw no resistance from Red Hare, noting the red aura of Guan Yu's warrior spirit melded instantly into the glow cast from Red Hare's ashen tinted crimson coat. Guan giggled like a child bursting from within a cocoon and the horse reciprocated, neighing in symphony to the laughter. Guan finally issued a bone chilling scream and, in an instant, the two berserkers jumped the enclosure and darted toward the horizon, not to return until three days later.

None of Cao Cao's generals believed anyone could ride the devil horse, but when the two returned, it became clear to all the two were born to become one.

Guan Clears All Accounts

Guan Yu and Cao Cao continued to survey the battlefield looking for any pathways in the ever-shifting currents. Anything which might work to the favor of Zhang Liao. They saw nothing. The lid on Zhang Liao's coffin seemed to be quickly descending. Guan signaled his squire to bring the Green Dragon Crescent Blade[32], his signature battle weapon. Cao puzzled momentarily as Guan's attendant delivered the weapon to his now mounted master.

After one final scan of the unfolding disaster below, Guan turned to Cao Cao, "The time has come for me to thank you for this beast that in friendship, you declared to be worthless to you."

"Guan Yu, you're not wearing armor. You can't save them. Stay here. There will be another day and we will have our justice then."

---

[32] The legendary Green Dragon Blade - a stylized pole weapon, topped with a crescent-like blade, counterbalanced by a weighted tip or spike at the bottom. Today, known as the Guandao (literally "Guan Blade"), no doubt an acknowledgment of its most prominent technician. Built to Lord Guan's personal specifications, incorporating a unique alloy which gave it extraordinary weight, and made it virtually indestructible.

Guan's impatient spirit exploded to the surface, animating both he and the horse, as they initiated their dance of death, spinning like a cyclone before Lord Cao. Over his shoulder Guan screamed to Cao, "There is only NOW! Look at that bastard Yan Liang gloating while tens of thousands die beneath him. War is one thing, but gloating over the suffering of others offends me. And it is me he will account to before this day closes. If I do nothing today, tomorrow that bastard will be out of our reach, and our Zhang Liao will be stewing in the stomachs of worms. I choose for myself to act NOW!"

Stunned by the roar, Lord Cao remained motionless in silent wonder.

And with that, the king of warriors turned his steed toward battle and charged with reckless abandon into the boiling fray.

From his command perch, Cao witnessed the now demon Guan atop his blood red steed, whirling the Green Dragon blade in all arcs and directions simultaneously. Like a mad drummer working frantically to sound all the world's drums at once. Heads and arms dropped from torsos. Blood erupted from once whole appendages and rained down upon the mad dervish, reinforcing the already reddish tint of his warrior mask.

Cao marveled as Guan single handedly cut, sliced, knocked, and trampled a path clear to the hopelessly besieged Zhang Liao.

Staring in disbelief at Guan Yu's arrival, Zhang Liao's first words were, "Guan Yu, you've brought reinforcements; my prayers have been answered, we might still turn the battle!"

Guan Yu turned to his friend, smiled, and answered, "Better than that my friend. Only you and I and our

uncommon destiny can turn this battle. Let history speak of
our deeds."

Zhang Liao nodded in grim understanding. Then smiled
broadly. This would be their moment. For a fleeting instant,
he appreciated the rarity of the opportunity. Here, the two
war brothers would seal their lives' scrolls. So many had met
their ends unceremoniously, and seemingly without
purpose. Both recognized the uncommon gift of a slice of
time wherein, unlike the many who simply disappeared,
they would prove by deeds in this otherwise hopeless
forum, just where they ranked in the pantheon of legends.

They turned about and faced away on their steeds. Guan
Yu called over his shoulder, "Taiji."

Zhang Liao understood immediately. One would assume
"Yang" the other would assume "Yin" and together they
would actualize movement in common flow, expanding
outward from the center of this battle cauldron which held
them trapped and surrounded. A spinning saw, radiating
menacingly from the field's core.

The attackers knew to be wary of Guan Yu, having just
witnessed how he decimated their comrades slicing his path
to Zhang Liao. They wanted nothing to do with him; and
looking for easier prey, sought to amass upon Zhang Liao.
Take the lesser, then target the other. That's how they thought.

When they did so, Guan immediately circled about,
cutting to their rear dropping them legless to the soil, then
spinning about and finishing them. As Guan moved, Zhang
Liao adjusted his position, circling toward the rear of Guan.
From the opposing heights, both Cao Cao, and his nemesis
Yan Liang witnessed what appeared to be a red circle,
eventually swirling, then assuming the shape of an
expanding Yin-Yang, its spinning serrations emerging from

the center of the death field and pushing its radius ever outward as Yan Liang's forces proved no match for the two.

As they witnessed, this very same thought passed between Yan Liang and Cao Cao, *How exquisitely beautiful the moment had become.*

Yan Liang fought to return to his senses. What the hell was he thinking? The two bastards were decimating his personal vanguard.

Cao Cao also struggled with the moment, finally putting his admiration and concern for the two warriors over all thoughts of kaleidoscopic beauty emanating from within blood-tinged geometries. He dispatched reinforcements forward.

As to those in the battle's midst, you must remember: It's one thing to fight for your life and honor like your life and honor depended on it. Another thing entirely to fight for your life and honor like you're hoping to survive until sundown. They were the former. The others were the latter.

As the Sun traced across the heavens, Zhang Liao and Guan Yu never faltered. In fact, the valor of each lifted and inspired the other to even more audacious displays. My heavens ... are they still laughing?

By late afternoon, the enemy could no longer come forward without stumbling awkwardly over the bodies and limbs of their fallen comrades. Riderless steeds wandered master-less and without purpose, stretching for several li outward from the center of the death wheel.

Zhang Liao signaled for his remaining cavalry to cut an opening through the now combat torn and demoralized enemy, effectively splitting the opposing forces and opening opportunity to wedge them from where their critical mass had earlier assured prospects for victory.

On the western slope, Yan Liang studied, reacted, assigned, adjusted, compensated and countered. In constant motion, his adjutants darted to all reaches of the field with streams of new orders and instructions.

Cao Cao acknowledged Yan Liang's brilliance as manifested in the changes. Already new fronts and penetrations opened for Yan Liang as his instructions turned the battlefield from the wedge strategy of Zhang Liao to the moths on carpet tactic of Yan Liang whose war-proven finest opened multiple penetrations in Cao's advancing line, any of which might allow a new corridor for committed counter-offense. Doubtless, Yan Liang's famed cavalry, held yet in reserve, postured eager and ready to add their talents to the forum of slaughter.

Cao Cao stared at Guan Yu in the distance, knowing his fate and that of Zhang Liao now hung precariously under the tactical brilliance and maneuvering of Yan Liang, and his famed "hammer," the northern cavalry.

Ever practical, Cao Cao vowed never to underestimate the pivotal role of cavalry in turning the final momentum of a battlefield. It is true that in time, his name would become synonymous with the integration of cavalry into tactical warfare.

For his part, Guan Yu felt the burn of Cao Cao's stare.

Sometimes in the heat of battle, projected thoughts prove to be the only reliable vehicle of contact. Sensing concern, Guan turned and looked first to Cao in the distance, then followed his focused gaze to the western slope where Yan Liang's cavalry massed and readied for the deciding offensive. Though others might have missed it, Guan Yu knew Lord Cao's concern when their gazes met from afar. Two hawks, their fates entwined in the turbulence of uncertainty, locked eyes across the battlefield. Guan Yu grunted in understanding.

Turning to Zhang Liao he ordered, "It is now for you to turn the battlefield. I have promised to pay a visit to Yan Liang."

Zhang Liao stared in disbelief as Red Hare spun about and tore westward, racing with its master up the western slope to impending destiny, or disaster.

The combatants ahead gaped in disbelief, their only instinct to yield to the charging demon. For a brief moment, the arena fell into a stunned silence as none could resist witnessing Lord Guan's fabled fury.

From west of center, a wide path opened across the hillside. No one possessed the will to confront Guan Yu or stand before his frenzied steed. It appeared, for that moment, that Lord Guan might race unopposed to Yan Liang's command post.

Except for the cavalry now positioned strategically in waiting.

These elite warriors, hungry for confrontation, had awaited their leader's order throughout the day, ready to lay waste and destroy all in their path. They harbored no fear of legends, except perhaps the fear of diminishing their own. Skills always looked most formidable when tested against the weak and exhausted. Fully aware that battlefield appearances could deceive, they acknowledged Guan Yu's achievements thus far, crediting him with stalling what had earlier promised certain victory. Yet, each had their own history of valor and heroic deeds, and the opportunity to overcome Guan Yu held the promise of boundless riches, honor, and influence. Death seemed a small risk when weighed against the anticipated rewards.

A miscalculation of course.

Red Hare bore Guan Yu into the heart of their assembled mass. He came upon them before they reckoned possible. Guan's blade carved through their front, while those on the side and rear attempted to close around this sinister firebrand who had unleashed the rare glimpse of true power. It brought to mind Ah Ju Na's return to the fabled battlefield after his exchange with Ke Li Xi Na. On this day, some among the victims even smiled as death greeted them, seemingly appreciating the exquisiteness and singularity of the encounter.

Guan Yu could not be contained. In disbelief, Yan Liang screamed for his attendants to move forward to assist, then ordered his archers to take down everything in proximity to Guan Yu and his cursed blood horse.

By then, Red Hare's advance had quickened, and the arrows, spears, and missiles fell futilely to the rear of their charge, further decimating what remained of the once proud cavalry. The remarkable creature ran blazingly fast, darting like a rabbit, hence its name. Witnesses described it as "sneaky" fast, meaning the animal moved quicker than one could perceive. What you thought you saw was already a step behind when you saw it. An archer's nightmare. The bowman who could hit this steed had not yet been born.

Like Yan Liang's troops, Cao Cao also disbelieved what his eyes told him, but not so much that he hesitated to seize the moment. Charging forward on his own steed, Cao Cao rode the turbulent wind away from the security of his command post, down the hill, and to the side of the valiant Zhang Liao. There, Lord Cao planted his own life and stakes at the still pulsing heart of the battlefield, where all could witness his true valor.

In moments too short to measure, Yan Liang's archers and attendants fell to Guan Yu's Green Dragon Crescent

Blade. Finally, just as the sun lowered, the scene quieted. Red Hare came to a stop, facing the now mounted and armed Yan Liang, who had his men stand down.

"Colonel Guan, all know of your sworn brotherhood to Liu Bei. How can it be you serve the cause of Cao Cao, his dire enemy; our common foe?"

Guan answered, "I am in Cao Cao's debt. He once gifted to me something which I valued, but which he deemed utterly worthless, and I swore to reciprocate the meaningless act, if only to teach him a lesson about conduct, honor, and humility."

Yan Liang sat on his steed, momentarily confused, acknowledging only when it became unmistakably clear. "The horse, of course! A most magnificent beast!" Then, resigned to the possible turn of battle, and his intent before all to personally deal with Guan Yu, a sinister smirk crawled from his center, momentarily darkening his expression, then grew into a malicious and intimidating stare-down directed toward his nemesis.

Guan Yu continued, "But truthfully, it was witnessing your imbecilic gloat today as tens of thousands died and suffered at your feet. That clinched it for me."

Yan Liang thought to attack Guan Yu. In his mind's eye, the attack had already played—Guan sat headless upon Red Hare, and Yan pushed the warrior corpse from the steed's back claiming the valiant steed for himself. The scene played at light speed and began to shape outward from his intent where it would soon enough become reality. He had already full throttled his horse forward to surprise Guan who remained foolishly still and statuesque, completely vulnerable to bushwhack, his Green Dragon Crescent Blade lowered and still dripping blood from the day's work.

Yan Liang puzzled momentarily, wondering why he was getting no movement from his beast when suddenly the beast ambled across his view, removing his focus from Guan Yu. It was only then Yan Liang realized what had, in fact, happened. Mounted on his own steed, high above the line of his gaze, sat his headless corpse, now tilting forward.

And with that realization, his gloat, and then his smirk lifted forever from his decapitated head, supplanted by an eternal mask of perplexed but unmistakable awareness. A faux Buddha!

Those left of his attendants and his cavalry could only register horror and shock, parting as Guan Yu dismounted and strode slowly forward, Red Hare dutifully covering his rear glaring at any who dared think to approach. Guan secured the headless torso to Yan's mount, then pointed the horse to the battle below, slapping its rump; sending it down with its clear message to all who saw. The day now belonged to Zhang Liao and to Cao Cao.

He wrapped the head in the fabric of Yan's command banner, tied it to his saddle, re-mounted, then turned to what remained of his enemies.

"Remember always, a true warrior acts first from a compassionate center, and never from disdain directed against those he opposes. In no case, presume victory; but if won, treat it with the gravity it deserves; just as if it were your own funeral."

We might suppose he finished them all off, but the meat of Guan's message lay in his simply riding away, leaving them to reconcile their thoughts against what they had just witnessed.

We have said, Guan was a compassionate man!

By that point in the day Cao Cao and Zhang Liao had turned the battlefield, doubtless aided by Yan Liang's spiritless corpse drifting aimlessly and without head over the blood, bone and flesh carpeted expanse, undermining what little fight remained in the spirits of his men. Cao Cao's skill in the martial arts equaled his gifts as a poet, and for a few harried moments, he stood back-to-back with Zhang Liao. Together, they repelled repeated onslaughts of Yan Liang's elites, who sought only to save face for a day lost by returning with the heads of the opposing chieftains.

Cao Cao and Zhang Liao were more than their match, but it was Guan Yu who assured their survival simply by riding casually across the death strewn field. His mere presence seeded terror into the core of whatever enemy resistance remained, spreading like a plague through them all. Some thought they heard him singing folk tunes into the upturned ears of Red Hare.

Red Hare liked when Guan sang. It usually meant the day had gone well and promised tasty rewards to follow.

What remained of Yan's troops disengaged, then rolled back and away, frantically removing themselves from the demon war god's sinister gaze. Best not to tempt the monster. That's how they thought. By then, the only residual of Yan Liang's strategy was each individual's pathetic drive to somehow hide and perhaps survive until darkness offered concealment. Few slept that night and those who chanced to survive never slept peacefully again. Their deepest memories and dreams forever tainted with the horror, and the boundless suffering. Unable to reconcile what had become their new reality against the unforgiving serendipity of their now unwanted and nightmare ridden survivals.

As to Guan Yu, they held no ill will. To a person, they recalled Guan's battlefield deportment, and spoke with great admiration of how the man-demon never moved on anyone, who had not already moved first on him.

The Substance of Worthlessness

Though it seemed an eternity, night eventually cloaked the field. An exhausted Marshal Cao returned to his command post. As a special tribute commemorating Zhang Liao's valor, he ordered a feast prepared for three; nominally in Zhang's honor, but being sure to leave a prominent seat for the anticipated return of Guan Yu. Even then, the noble warrior policed the near perimeter of the field, scouring like a vigilant banshee, until all who were able, returned safely.

Guan withdrew from the field only when the cries reduced to silence. The ground chilled, and the night darkened as he returned to camp late in the evening. At Cao's behest, perhaps more of a suggestion than an order, he was directed to the now subdued victory celebration. There he found Cao Cao and Zhang Liao, surrounded by troops, already incapacitated from repeated wine consumption and toasts to each other's heroism. They poured streams of praise, poems, and songs celebrating the deeds of Guan Yu. They swore as eyewitnesses to record the events for all time, ensuring at the very least his deserved immortality in the minds and hearts of men everywhere. Officers, attendants, and others simply too weary to move lay about the compound, listening intently to the stream of homage to the day's hero, all concurring in every detail. At one point, Cao Cao called for silence. In humble gratitude, he proclaimed that never in recorded history have the acts of a single man been so decisive in turning the tide of battle. All bowed their heads in reverence, tears falling to the still blood-tainted soil, each knowing that but for Guan Yu, their death warrants had already been sealed.

As the weary Guan approached, the surrounding warriors cleared a wide berth, many dropping to one knee in respect, then issued forth a prolonged outcry of unmitigated sound, a drum roll of human thunder culminating in silence, a warrior's salute befitting the man become god.

Touched, Guan turned, his gaze surveying the ranks, his eyes carefully connecting with each before him. After a deferential pause, he spoke. "Boys, you did well today. It has been a singular honor for me to share this victory with you, a day I will never forget. I will wear the memory of your faces and your spirits wherever destiny carries me, and will forever consider each of you as part of my family and kin."

Even the ground seemed to rise with the explosion of emotion and love for their warrior saint. By then Cao Cao and Zhang Liao came alongside, Cao gently taking the arm of the clearly affected warrior, invincible but momentarily overwhelmed by justified adulation.

The three retreated into Cao's private compound. Zhang Liao saw Yan Liang's command banner loosely rolled and coiled beneath Guan's arm, assuming it to be Guan's memento of the day. Cao remained silent.

Guan Yu turned to his host, "In my meanderings this day, I came across something which I deemed to be worthless but still of possible interest to you. Certainly, it is of no use to me. You may recall once having given me something you deemed worthless. For me, it remained a matter of honor to ensure your worthless gift received its true recognition with an equally worthless gift reciprocated. What better way for two such as us to know where we truly stood."

Cao slowly nodded in anticipation, already sadly sensing his beloved friend would soon be leaving, all debts of honor finally met.

Guan Yu motioned to Zhang Liao, who, sensing the moment, brought a small table and a lantern to the room's center. Guan Yu set the worthless token down, signaling for Zhang Liao to stand close by with the light.

Guan cut the parcel open. There on the table, Yan Liang stared into eternity, resting peacefully on his once earthly banner of command.

Cao Cao, the poet, grasped the moment. He walked slowly to the mask once topping Yan Liang's fearsome battle figure, then said, "You know brother Guan, sometimes I feel little more can be gained in life beyond understanding the full value of what might be deemed worthless."

Guan grunted. Cao Cao continued staring intently at the head, "Look Guan, no gloat, no sneer, no smirk."

Guan Yu walked to the front beside Cao, then took the lantern from Zhang Liao, setting it directly before the blank, Buddha-like death mask.

"You know, I could almost like a man with a face like this."

Guan Speaks of His Method

Cao Cao agreed, thinking only of the limitless and expressionless void now illuminated before them, all traces of life purged from the once ego weighted nemesis Yan Liang. He faced Guan, asking, "How? How were you able to do this?"

Guan Yu looked to Zhang Liao, then answered, "Well it was clear to me brother Zhang could manage the battlefield without my further interference. I thought of re-positioning to the west when I caught your concern as you stared to Yan's command post. I then understood immediately. He might still be able to launch effective counters, and perhaps turn the tide of battle to his favor.

"So, I figured best to pay him a personal visit.

"It is with deep regret, I must tell you I had to pass through the heart of his cavalry. His finest, which he still held in reserve. Waiting presumably for the decisive moment when he might rain them down upon our lads and cut them to shreds. Many fine warriors, excellent steeds, they never wavered for a moment. I can only say their defense impressed me as nothing less than exemplary. Likewise for Yan's attendants and personal guard."

"How in the world did you get around them?" Cao asked.

"Get around them? I would never dishonor such valiant warriors doing any such thing. Certainly, Red Hare could have dashed to their rear. But then in the time wasted, Yan

Liang might already have departed, or disappeared. Both Red Hare and I decided it best to plow through the vaunted cavalry, and the personal guard. Even Yan Liang would not expect us to succeed in such foolishness. What better tactic than surprise?"

"Of course, and brilliantly executed. But what specific strategy did you engage to penetrate their defense? You did what no one else could do; I'm asking what specifically made you different. Tell me now, no secrets between us, wherein lay the germ of your success."

Guan Yu nodded then mused momentarily, as though reconstructing the steeple of logic which resulted in his succeeding at the impossible, "Why the obvious one of course."

"The obvious one?"

"Certainly. As time raced forward, every moment I lost might prove decisive on the field below. I took them on. All of them. Red Hare rode her fastest and I rose high in her saddle, wielding the Green Dragon in all directions, trusting my steed to push forward while I cut mercilessly from above."

"Mercilessly?" asked Cao Cao.

"Well, you understand they might have wounded me or even hurt Red Hare had I held back even the slightest."

"Of course."

By now Zhang Liao fought to stifle the urge to burst out laughing at his friend's humble and candid replay of what would be remembered as one of the greatest battlefield accomplishments of the age, in fact, of any age.

Guan Yu spoke little of the specifics, except to say that in due course, he and Red Hare had cleared a path leading to the very feet of a most surprised Yan Liang. He confessed how the cavalry and the attendants had taken him to his very limit but could not turn him or match him in the final stretch. A pity he murmured, almost absentmindedly.

"Did any survive?" questioned Zhang Liao.

"Assuredly so! I'm not entirely without mercy. After taking out Yan Liang, I gave distance to the others, passing them without malice, provided they reciprocated the courtesy and chose not to close on me."

Cao Cao looked puzzled, then stared earnestly directly into his eyes, almost as if trying to gain needed insight into a troubling conundrum. "Tell me Guan, where does your compassion begin? Where does it end?"

A musing only poets might undertake, hoping the answer might reveal yet another facet of truth's diamond-faceted face.

"I battle for righteousness, to the extent I can recognize it. I despise arrogance, disdain, and disrespect. For me, they offend propriety and righteousness. I battle for those to whom I've sworn allegiance, and I battle for those whom I love. I never forget my past. I once walked the earth as a lowly criminal, scorned by all, and slept in the streets with the dogs. There I learned and mastered compassion. Each day, some person, or beast, man, woman, child, monk, tradesperson, or warrior demonstrated compassion directly to me. Clear and unmistakable, a kind act or random kindness, or just some token of generosity. I battle for them also. My past remains with me. Every moment. Everything else threatens to distract me from that sworn purpose. But I remain staunch, without compromise. On today's field, I had hoped and prayed they would let me leave unmolested, and they did. They tasted the fruit of compassion. Hopefully, they will remember its benevolent glow."

"And Yan Liang, what of him?"

"He asked me how I justified taking to battle on behalf of my lord's enemy, meaning you of course. I told him my loyalty remained with Liu Bei, but that I had a lesson to teach to someone who had once seen fit to measure my sense of honor against what he proclaimed to be a worthless gift. Again, meaning you of course. It took the old fox a few seconds to catch my meaning. Then came his gloat, and the smirk. Most unbecoming a man of his stature I might add. I sensed his eyes on Red Hare, and his plan to take her for himself should he succeed in doing away with me. He sure knew how to prick my sensitivities."

Cao Cao's eyes closed, as though he were listening into the broad spaces between Guan's words of recount, then replied, "Many regard Yan Liang to also be a peerless warrior, I can't imagine he would give you his head and banner without some degree of protest."

"Indeed so Lord Cao. I suppose it was the foreshadowing of his smirk which spoke of his intent to close on me while I remained distracted and responding to his questions.

"Needless to say, I expected ruse and deception. Long before arriving before him, I had been careful to see all possibilities and to map out the details of how I would bring him back to your acquaintance."

"You mean to say, while in midst of battle, and then while ascending the western slope against insurmountable odds, you developed the plan which you enacted upon Yan Liang."

"Yes, I believe that characterizes what I said."

"But no one can do that!"

"Surely they can. So long as they remain completely immersed in the now, free from the chains of time, and undisturbed by thoughts of greed, outcome, enrichment, victory, or defeat. I came to Yan Liang floating on the moment, like an empty mirror. He saw only what he chose to see, mostly projecting his own thoughts. That proved to be a serious flaw in his style. A weakness. He chose illusion. I knew fully the moment, staying firm within it—he wandered elsewhere."

Cao Cao nodded in full appreciation. Looking to Guan, he responded, "Fucking brilliant! Unprecedented!"

Cao could scarcely breath, so overwhelmed was he by his incontrovertible comprehension of what had occurred. "Guan Yunchang! Now as I stare intently at the empty mirror before me, I can say only one thing with certainty. Your brilliance is surpassed only by your valor!"

Cao turned about quickly, called for his scribes, and beckoned all to exit and stand with him before the remnant battered army still keeping their respectful vigil outside. The king asked that all bear witness to what he was about to say.

With Zhang Liao and Guan Yu at his sides he turned to Guan, dropped to the ground and kowtow'd, lying prostrate before the giant. The mass of battle drained warriors anticipated their leader and fell likewise to the still bleeding soil, knowing and acknowledging what had in fact turned the day, and their destinies. Zhang Liao, who had nearly matched Guan in the day's scale of valor, considered whether he should feel slighted. For a brief moment he turned to his friend and mentor, nodded, smiled then also dropped.

Guan Yu had never seen the likes of this. His own legions expected him to do the impossible, as did Liu Bei. It was merely his duty. But here, for once, he saw his own earthly visage in the empty mirror of his once and future enemies, lying prostrate before him.

Whether from friend or from foe, never take freely given respect lightly. The noble Guan Yunchang surveyed the scene. Silence embraced the community of heroes as tears welled in Guan's eyes. No, he mustn't allow others to see this vulnerability. He rolled his sleeve casually across his brow, hopefully removing all traces; then reached down to Cao Cao with both hands, taking the king's hands into his own and guiding him to standing. He then looked out to the sea of men and signaled they also rise. As did Zhang Liao alongside.

Cao walked forward and proclaimed to his troops, "You must forgive the shortness of my humble message. Like you, I am worn from the day's toil."

Having seen their leader standing fearlessly with them in the heat of battle, a loud cheer erupted from the mass acknowledging the rarity of a warrior king willing to go with his troops to the brink of uncertainty. Most others would have long departed the scene, justifying they save themselves for another day.

"Still, tired and worn as I may be, it would be dishonorable and remiss should I let another moment pass without acknowledging today's victory stands squarely on the shoulders of one man. Noble Guan! On his own, and despite his being our prisoner of war, General Guan saw fit to engage our enemy; assisted ably and with equal valor by our own peerless Zhang Liao. Together they cut the enemy's heart from the battlefield. As Zhang Liao continued to consolidate gains below, General Guan single-handedly attacked and engaged the famed cavalry of Yan Liang, pushing through their midst. He then likewise engaged the wall of personal guards and attendants, in the end removing the enemy's command from the battlefield. You may have encountered the mounted General Yan Liang wandering about in the aftermath." That drew some reticent laughter. All recognized but for fate, it might have been any one of them, headless and alone. Even Cao held the same thought, glancing momentarily at his friend. Only Guan seemed free of the concern. A pity, considering what would come.

"We will never forget the final vision of Guan Yu mounted on the incomparable Red Hare. Remaining in our midst assuring our victory, then covering our rear as we cleared the field to safety. Recognizing his noble gift to us this day, I now reciprocate. Standing before you all, imploring you be my sworn witnesses, I proclaim Guan Yunchang to be Guan Gong, Lord Guan, General of Wei, and, with the Emperor's express blessing (yes, Cao Cao spoke for the emperor, whom he still kept on tight leash), Marquis of Han Shou." He motioned to his attendants who in turn retrieved a chest from the interior. "Not to be outdone by our guest's gift of this day (turning to Guan, he mumbled 'A worthless display on your part, as you and I both certainly know.')I reciprocate in balance and kind to what he has done for us (again turning to Guan, adding, 'No false humility please, it was either give this to you, or throw it into the latrine.')" He opened the chest for Guan Yu's inspection, showing it brimming with gold. Their eyes met and fixed for some time as reverent cheers and cries erupted from the warrior mass.

Cao Cao's Repugnance

In this new moment, many years later, Lord Cao wondered if perhaps he had simply dreamed it all.

Reminiscing on cherished memories from that day, Cao Cao mused, "And today, Sun Quan deems it fit to dispatch Lord Guan's head as a tribute, calculating to gain merit and reduce tension between our states.

"What could the bastard be thinking? This is what you do to fiends, and demons; or to those who have allied themselves with evil and atrocity. But to heroes such as Lord Guan, never! If he's an enemy, kill him, or try with your best effort. But desecrate him, never. Among men, Guan embodied righteousness. A paragon, bettering us all by his example. When you defile him, you defile the Way and stand for nothing. Sun Quan, you have cursed yourself with this ignoble deed, just as your brother cursed himself when he murdered Yu Ji[33]."

Cao Cao knew well enough that when one views the shimmering reflection of a dead enemy's life-gone spirit, one

---

[33] In Luo Guanzhong's Romance of the Three Kingdoms, elder brother Sun Ce sees fit to kill the Taoist priest and sorcerer Yu Ji. While recovering form assassin's wounds Sun Ce thought himself haunted by Yu Ji's ghost now intent on vengeance. Seeing the ghostly image in a mirror, Sun Ce struck out and burst open his wounds, resulting in his premature and unanticipated demise.

sees only the self. Sun Quan, brilliant though he might be, clearly had not grasped this. What he did will turn on him. For a brief moment, Cao wondered over what this might portend for Sun Quan. He hoped only for karma's fair hand in the play, which he knew was what Guan would have wanted.

Summoning his artisans and craftsmen, Cao Cao declared a day of mourning throughout Wei, proclaiming the loss of a great general. When Zhang Liao first heard the news, he became disconsolate, finding comfort only in the company of Cao Cao whose own grief would have been beyond bearing but for Zhang Liao's companionship. Together, the two spent days in the funeral chamber, keeping vigil over the man now become truly immortal.

They drank, and shared stories, and drank, and spoke of impossible deeds, and drank, cursing their once friend for losses eventually inflicted on their own forces, and drank, then in the same breath praised their still beloved adversary for his unerring righteousness, forgiving even when his wrath had waylaid their aspirations.

Oh, that we should all come to appreciate our foes in such manner. Who knows? We might become friends before war bells chime to final silence. Together we could laugh at other fools flushing their lives into cesspools of nonsense and chaos, while blessings blossomed from our newly uncorrupted spirits.

Cao Cao cursed the reality about him, and cursed Sun Quan. Now much older and weary from his unrelenting campaigns, he saw lingering trails of foolishness in his wake, no small part of it his own. He envied the certitude of Guan Yu's peerless life course. It made the loss no less poignant, knowing that Guan's memory would shine for all time, while his own accomplishments would be little more than history's tread stones, becoming invisible among the many.

Enough self-pity. He commissioned fabrication of a new body so that his friend might cross immortality's threshold fully intact, clad in suitable regalia. Their time raced against further deterioration, but all knew Cao's determination to suitably honor his friend, and all acted accordingly.

Within days, artisans fashioned a noble body from the finest woods, adorned with jewels, and gilded with gold. The exquisite combination of aged and tightly grained bamboo, sandalwood, ebony, teak, boxwood and aloeswood, resulted in an elegant, aristocratic, and thankfully fragrant comportment for Guan's final departure. Legions of soldiers, some who fought with him, most against him, lined the byways for a final glimpse. They stared in disbelief at the lifeless hulk, set upon by its crown of human flesh, which by then had soured. A lingering remnant balanced only by the fine scent of sandalwood and aloeswood. Incense clouded the atmosphere. Though stark, and sometimes frightening in its unconcocted asymmetry, a certain beauty emanated from the combined effect of colors and adornment. The care taken to match hues to actual tones of flesh, the red of the face, the exquisite beard, the smoothness, and lifelike sheen of the wood-replicated skin.

Cao buried Guan with full honors. The display made clear for all what he thought of Sun Quan's foolish gesture. He positioned Sun's emissaries frontmost at the ceremony so there would be no mistake in their report back to their leader. It has been said one should be very careful about whom one chooses to annihilate. Sometimes it makes spirits terribly angry, and only vengeance can sate their rabid anger. That has oft been said of Sun Quan's desecration of Guan.

The likes of Guan's prowess were seldom seen again.

It is said his influence clearly rubbed off on his enemy brother and friend Zhang Liao, with whom he shared the transcendent moment at Baima. No one knows why or how it happens, but in truth, something of Guan Gung did remain with Zhang Liao, and radiated within him from the time they first parted to his own end.

Though no one ever replicated Guan Gung's feat against Yan Liang, there remains a wrinkle within history's blanket which might interest you.

After Red Cliffs, with Cao Cao in disastrous retreat, Sun Quan eventually pushed north in punishing pursuit. With the re-vitalized Liu Bei eroding Cao's influence in the west, opportunity opened for Sun Quan to eventually do unto Wei what Cao had once tried to do unto Wu. Sun Quan's battle-hardened warriors now dominated the southeast. His ministers looked hungrily to the north, counseling that Wu had become a superpower and that the time for action was now! Sun Quan liked the idea of being the superpower, especially after surviving near extinction just a short while prior. Sometimes his concubines recalled among themselves how he whispered in his early morning dream state, "Wu, supreme over all."

Singularity and the Measure of Duty

When Sun Quan elected to push into the north, he led combined forces in excess of 100,000 battle proven warriors with another 100,000 blood-hungry recruits ready in reserve, eager to reinforce, replenish, and glean glory. Equal numbers secured the homeland borders, and amidst it all, he felt rather good about things.

During the extended northward retreat, among those entrusted to protect his rear, Cao designated Zhang Liao. Cao's forces were in disarray, weakened, and outnumbered, and it fell to Zhang Liao to stave off disaster. His opportunity arose during the defense of Hefei.

Admittedly, all appeared lost in the south. Cao Cao left cryptic instructions, causing some to wonder, "Has the great man lost his mind?" These instructions were beyond the ability of his generals to decipher, except for Zhang Liao.

He read and immediately understood. The situation was hopeless. Only he had truly been there before, and that was why Lord Cao hand-picked him to be there now. Others had become accustomed to decisive victories or organized retreats. There would be neither at Hefei. He read the instructions and saw the poet's spirit in the words: "When no options remain except to do the impossible, then one must do the impossible."

Whispering words of prayer and gratitude to his enemy, friend, and mentor, Guan Yu, Zhang Liao would have agonized indecisively but for Guan's influence now stirring within him. He turned to the co-serving generals and said, "The instructions stand clear. We attack. I will go now, before opportunity passes and the enemy fully entrenches. Who goes with me?"

Horrified, the others felt their elder had lost his mind. None of them lacked competence. It's just that one becomes easily accustomed to the stability and comfort of power and position. From there, one looks down upon and directs the fates and destinies of others. It's those lowly others, who but for want of opportunity and alternate paths, look forward only to the theater of death; and if lucky, tomorrow's meal.

Except for only one, General Li Dian, all hesitated to commit.

They tendered the usual balking rationales.

"Our duty now is to save ourselves. The future depends on our being there to serve Lord Cao."

"We cannot save Hefei. Sun Quan has amassed over 100,000 men; our intelligence warns of an equal number of reinforcements fast on their heels. We stand no chance. Don't be a fool."

Perhaps most insidious, "General Zhang, General Li, you both forget your sacred duty to Cao, and to the Emperor Xian. Don't selfishly put yourselves above your responsibilities to the empire."

Zhang Liao turned to them all, "Cowards! Ungrateful leeches! I don't require tongues of hyenas to rationalize how we might better serve the empire by neglecting duty, honor, and orders."

They quieted under the weight of the insult, some thinking to mass their influence and act to remove the insubordinate bastard.

If not for his distinguished standing and history with Lord Cao.

General Li Dian, always the quiet one, ever polite and reserved, walked alongside Zhang Liao. With a slight nod of his head in agreement, he cast his fate and fortune to the winds of chance, trusting to the certitude of concerted effort against the weight of the moment. He proclaimed, "No time to linger any longer, I choose now to do my sworn duty."

The others shied away, wanting no part of where this contaminated thinking led.

The two warriors walked out to the troops and asked who would be willing to follow them into certain death. Even then, vast numbers of Sun Quan's forces shadowed the southern horizon, spanning its broad line in the distance—a plague about to begin its spinning descent from the endless storm.

By nightfall, they had eight hundred volunteers. Zhang Liao spent the evening in their midst, sharing rice and laying the groundwork for the morning's work. He spoke of the great battle of Baima and the rise of his spirit in the face of adversity. He explained how all things became possible in situations such as these. "You must never abandon your hope or cower from your duty." He shared from his personal experience how one never knew the full measure of one's own spirit until it has faced its certain end, yet somehow returns, forever tempered, forever changed. He told of how once in the past, all seemed hopelessly lost until suddenly, the peerless Guan Yu partnered with him. "As together we faced the sea of enemy, my guiding mantra simply became this, 'Follow his example, and all will end well.'

"Lads, in the morning, we head to our likely doom. As did my brother Guan, I will not fail you. Wherever you are, no matter the odds or how precarious your moment, look to your side, and you will see me. Think only, 'Follow his example, and all will be well.'"

When daylight came, Sun Quan's advancing army began to occupy and consolidate the approaches to Hefei.

His generals surveyed the city and the terrain, discussing strategies and the anticipated push north once Hefei and its surrounds had been subdued. They were already thinking past this otherwise minor obstacle in their grand strategic planning.

Their discourse came to a quick end when attendants drew their attention to what appeared to be a battalion of mounted cavalry exiting the citadel, now picking up speed and seemingly positioning to attack.

"What the hell?" they muttered almost in unison.

At the rear command, Sun Quan took notice of the suicide charge. Laughing, he commented to those nearby. "A tragic waste. Whoever is responsible should be barbecued and fed to the dogs."

The field command called infantry to the front, supported by lines of archers, with cavalry in reserve. By then, Zhang Liao, at the very lead, had already breached their perimeter.

His boldness stunned the Southerners. How quickly the Wei cavalry had closed the gap between. Before their well-choreographed defenses could be engaged, Zhang Liao came upon them, decimating their ranks with his lance, leading the mounted phalanx deep into the heart of the not yet staged, and now precariously exposed southern legion.

He repeatedly screamed his name, declaring, "I am Zhang Liao, protector of Wei, and stalwart disciple of the peerless Guan Gung. Your leaders have murdered and desecrated my comrades[34] and offended my honor. Come, see for yourself what retribution lies in the eyes of those who fear you not."

"He's no Guan Gung," the enemy murmured, if only to subdue their terror. Even so, they knew to a man the celebrated exploits of Zhang Liao, the other hero of Baima.

No matter what they did, they could not stop this eviscerating contagion, spreading like a fiery blade through their middle.

By midday, the front lines of the Southerners had become depleted and exhausted. Those witnessing in the rear became demoralized. It seemed those in front could do nothing to solve the riddle of Zhang Liao. Now, Li Dian and his newly emboldened troops seemed equally unstoppable.

Zhang Liao never hesitated, never wavered. It seemed as though he expected Guan to emerge at any moment and for the two to again share the impossible experience. These were idle imaginings of course; Guan had returned to Liu Bei. Zhang never spoke of it to anyone, but Guan always seemed to be with him, a voice resonating in memory. Sometimes suggesting, sometimes chiding, sometimes prodding and cajoling, but always there. Even then as he pushed forward, setting sights on the command post of Sun Quan, and Sun Quan himself, prompted and encouraged by the voice within, he recalled the corridor of emptiness so aptly described by Guan Yu, which long ago proved to be the doom of Yan Liang.

---

[34] Alluding to the fiery onslaught at Red Cliffs.

By midafternoon, Sun Quan's discomposed troops stirred chaotically about in disarray, inexplicably looking for enemies where there were none. Stunned, they saw no other forces emerging from Hefei. Those safely quartered within its walls had agreed to let Zhang Liao and Li Dian stew in their mutual foolishness.

Not suspecting any of this, the Wu leadership deduced (with self-reckoned high confidence) the probe by Zhang Liao would prove to be nothing more than an amateurish ruse, meant to divert their defenses from the frontal assault yet to come in its wake. In counsel, they strategized for the anticipated assault expected to emerge at any moment from the enemy's rear, where the defending legions would soon enough assume the full load of battle. The Wu trusted their own rear guard to see to Zhang Liao and his soon to be extinguished battalion, then ordered their main body to disengage and position forward for the decisive battle.

There is something we all know that appears to have slipped their purview. Never trust others to manage a job only you can properly do. They would regret their faith placed in the rear guard, relying on untested champions.

By late afternoon, Zhang Liao had penetrated to the feet of the imperial guard. To the shock and dismay of all, particularly Sun Quan, the war-mad Zhang Liao charged forward on his savage horse (an offspring of the famed Red Hare, gifted by Guan to his friend, but that is another story). He closed the gap to less than a lance's toss from Sun Quan. There he pulled his steed to full stop. Tall in the mount, for all to witness, he proclaimed his name and purpose and threw a personal challenge to the Southern King to test his hand in mortal combat with someone who feared him not. Winner take all! Whatever the hell that meant.

Sun Quan studied him, visibly shaken, weighing the just witnessed impact of a single battalion against his legions, which already outnumbered the attackers a hundred to one. He could not make sense of it and, for once, felt helpless and vulnerable, perhaps even afraid.

They say, "It's not the size of the dog in the fight, but the size of the fight in the dog which truly counts."

Guan Yu knew this well, and he drummed it into Zhang Liao. As they argued strategy and tactics, Lord Guan always emphasized how he became more effective when the numerical odds against him escalated. Not in jest, he stressed to Zhang "Let others have the easy pickings; you and I are made for the impossible. Anything else will only dull our shine." Zhang laughed when he said it, at first considering it idle boasting, though honored to be included in the boast. Guan chided, "Seriously my friend, you must understand this if you are to understand anything."

Guan explained, "Take for example where two attackers come upon you. Alone, you have a single mind and are free to act instantly upon your thoughts and impulses. Their two minds become an obstacle; their thought processes less efficient. Their attempts to coordinate effort and timing stall and hesitate, quickly degrading to less than optimal. Why, before you know it, one of them is preparing to sacrifice the other if only to save his own skin. You, on the other hand, have singularity, a most prized commodity on the field of combat."

At first unsure, Zhang couldn't let go of the thought. What exactly was Guan getting at? He decided not to raise any objections, then asked Guan to excuse his ignorance and walk him through the concept. He needed to grasp a deeper understanding of its true significance.

Guan let out one of his robust laughs, slapped him on the back, and said, "Of course little brother, that was my intention."

They reached the practice field, and Guan turned to Zhang Liao with a commanding order, "Attack me!" No slouch in the least, Zhang had already anticipated and timed the request. No sooner said, the attack was underway. Guan howled in delight, "Perfect, you almost had me. Savor the feeling, prize the moment, it will be our little secret. Now, pick your most fierce warrior, he will be your partner, and together, come at me again, but this time even harder."

Zhang demurred, "Lord Guan. Please, I almost had you; with another beside me, you'll be even more vulnerable."

Guan burst out laughing, slapping his knees and ascending with a raucous horse snort. "Brother, that's precisely why I'm teaching this to you. You don't know it yet!"

Zhang nodded and smiled, now more eager to see where this led. Holding nothing back, he picked his most savage and battle tested knight, whose outward appearance nearly matched Guan Yu and who clearly had no concern or reservation over confronting the legend.

Guan looked at the two, "Excellent. Take a few moments to plan; give yourselves a fighting chance."

They did, launching themselves with reckless abandon, expecting to get Guan off his feet and to the ground, where they could better control him. However, Guan seemed to disappear between them, somehow always finding a position where the two ended one behind the other and never alongside. Their thoughts crossed purposes, each trying to monitor the other while targeting Guan and executing the agreed upon strategy.

Perhaps too quickly for the comfort of their now bruised egos, both were on the ground, with Guan delivering his faux death cuts.

Not yet finished, Guan had them add others to their side, increasing the number of attackers to three, then five, ten, even a whole company of seasoned war veterans.

Finally, Zhang Liao raised his hand to signal, "Enough. You have made your point Brother Guan, I believe what you said is true, but I don't understand it."

Guan bellowed, "Brother Zhang, the understanding lies in the doing."

Then Guan signaled for more volunteers. He had them attack Zhang Liao one at a time, then two at a time, then three at a time, and so on as the day ended and passed into the next, and again the next.

At first, Zhang hesitated when facing multiple skilled attackers. Then Guan took him aside, "Too much thinking." In the dirt, he drew geometric patterns outlining the positions of attackers, their likely trajectories, and avenues of response or neutralization available to the defender. Given his own history, and already well-honed skills, Zhang began to see how subtle movements and changes of angle completely negated the advantage of numbers and arguably turned the weight of quantity into a disadvantage. What he found most important became clearer to him over time. The efficient mind gravitates toward simplicity. The more attackers, the more minds; the more minds, the more thoughts; the more thoughts the more uncertainty. Efficiency required certainty, and confidence in execution. Without that, only failure and death remained. Once the attackers numbered more than five, they spent half their focus figuring how not to hurt one another and the balance on getting out of each other's way.

Over the course of days following, Guan drilled Zhang Liao relentlessly in the process, trusting only to the doors of perception and their promise to open their treasures to one whose concerted efforts and diligence never wavered. Guan never mentioned to his friend, but of all whom he taught until that time, Zhang Liao had no betters. Oh, certainly there were some bigger, meaner, stronger, faster; but as to total package, only Zhang Liao approached Lord Guan.

Finally, the day arrived when Zhang Liao came to his friend and proclaimed, "I think I've got it."

"Tell me, what is it?"

"Against someone with a focused mind, and committed purpose, the attackers don't stand a chance. The more they throw into the mix, the more muddled they all become. In the field of the blind, even the one-eyed warrior emerges supreme."

"It is deeper than even that my friend; but for now, you have a solid foothold. May it serve you well. We have finished the lesson. Someday you'll find an opportunity to bring it to perfection."

Now, as if possessed by the spirit of his beloved friend, he again proclaimed his name and purpose, and threw a challenge of honor to the Southern King demanding they test their resolve in mortal combat, the winner owning the day and the field.

Zhang Liao Channels Guan

Thus had Zhang Liao come to this moment.

Rejecting the challenge, Sun Quan hurriedly mounted his steed and retreated to higher ground, with Zhang Liao in relentless pursuit. It was then Sun Quan turned suddenly about to spring the trap he had personally choreographed for just such eventualities. He signaled his cavalry and rear guard to collapse inward and around the madly approaching dervish.

Only when confident his mass of troops closed in and upon Zhang Liao could he relax, trusting what was out of sight would soon be out of mind.

The expected outcome took an unexpected turn. After a momentary pause, what first seemed certain went terribly awry—bodies fell from mounts, heads dropped from shoulders. The encircling mass, instead of tightening, jerked, thinned, and then unexpectedly bulged until an opening ballooned at one side, and out charged Zhang Liao, resembling more than ever the incarnation of Lord Guan.

He called again to Sun Quan, so loudly no one could fail to hear. "I am a man of honor. My challenge stands today, tomorrow, or whenever we two shall meet. I tell you now. The road to Hefei passes through Zhang Liao. I give you my oath, I will be here to greet you properly. Until Sun Quan comes to terms with this, he will never cross its threshold."

For Sun Quan, a precipitous loss of face; for his legions, an unprecedented failure of leadership.

Turning away from the battlefield, Zhang Liao resolved to return to the garrison at Hefei where he planned to seize full control. No more games or politics. Come daybreak, he would initiate a counteroffensive, catching the Wu leaders off guard with his audacity. They had planned for a routine siege upon a grossly weaker foe—encircle, isolate, and render impotent. None had anticipated an open field engagement with madmen. Sun Quan, as had his brother Sun Ce, began to see images of vengeful ghosts rearing their heads for a final reckoning.

Just as he prepared to bolt away, Zhang heard cries from his valiant battalion still afield. "General, don't abandon us!"

And from depths within, the voice of Guan Gung, "Remember little brother, you are their guiding spirit, their inspiration, and the wellspring of their valor. Think of them as your children. Guard them well, as I have shown you."

Zhang Liao turned around purposefully and headed back to the field's midst, where his men continued their gallant resistance within a narrowing circular amphitheater.

Realizing the situation, he called out, "Follow me, boys. We return to the garrison. Save some of them for tomorrow." Then, turning to the legions of Wu, he screamed in rage, "Leave now while you can. Hefei belongs to Wei. If you're here at dawn, it will be your death. Take our mercy and run while you have the opportunity. You'll not have our mercy twice."

The soldiers of Wu had never seen their leaders so outmaneuvered and vulnerable. Even Sun Quan, whom they idolized, seemed more concerned with saving his own neck than with the capture of Hefei. The field then parted like a weary sea. The leaders of Wu stared in disbelief as Zhang Liao led his men out without opposition or protest from their own.

Zhang Liao proved true to his words and his duty. He returned to garrison along with Li Dian, both begrudgingly acknowledged as heroes of epic stature. The cowards who remained behind really had no choice but to engage the tactic of using adulation and praise to save one's own head.

The once recalcitrant generals now saw the will of heaven tilting again toward Wei and scurried to secure ride upon the tails of Zhang Liao's valor and achievement.

Zhang Liao, exhausted beyond human limit, called the generals to council and declared that he and Li Dian had decided to launch the counteroffensive at first light.

Though coming around, the others were not quite prepared for something so brazen. They advocated a more conservative course, defending from the garrison and targeting strategic weaknesses in the enemy's front. In effect, more of the same nothing which had become their mark.

They had much to lose if they weren't careful with their words.

Zhang Liao thanked them for their counsel. For the moment, he chose to ignore the imagined voice of Guan from within, which demanded he behead the cowardly, self-serving insubordinates on the spot.

He went directly to the garrison and took his case to the troops. He told how he planned to take the fight to Wu, and though the other leaders strongly disagreed, it was clear to him they could glean victory only through audacity and quick action. Any hesitation at this point, even for good reason, spelled failure. He asked who would follow him in his folly. To a man, they swore with Zhang Liao, "Victory, or death."

On the war plain, the Wu camps heard the seemingly endless chant. Terrified over the repercussions from this terrible day, none among them slept.

History recalls it as the Battle of Xiaoyao Ford.

As if the battlefield humiliation, the purposeless loss of his finest men, and the calling out by Zhang Liao weren't enough, the following day Sun Quan learned the demoralized front line of Wu showed signs of plague. He cursed, "What more could go wrong?" Just when he hoped to quell their panic and rally their spirits. Hadn't he done so countless times? He wondered over the troublesome tidings. How could it worsen? He told himself, "Stand firm! Things will only get better from this point."

Losing no time, Sun Quan quarantined those most ill. He froze the frontal units in place, while ordering his substantial reinforcements to occupy their rear guard and flanking positions. "Allow no one to pass through, absolutely no one!" Doing this ensured the contagion remained isolated.

Then, he assigned a battalion of battle proven cavalry as a defensive barrier to protect himself and the high command from further embarrassment by Zhang Liao.

From a distance, Zhang Liao's trained eye recognized weakness in their battlefield geometry, wondering at first if it were a trap set to entice his attack. The geometry recalled Guan's very lessons, and in the mix of angles and curves, Zhang saw many minds and many thoughts moving about without clear purpose or focus. A ruse?

Hearing the voice of Guan calling for patience, he stood on the ramparts looking out while his troops remained at the ready. The hours passed.

The troops, their spirits high after swearing commitment, began to speculate as to the delay.

Some wondered, "Had General Zhang lost his nerve?" Others retorted, "Impossible!"

Waiting quietly, Li Dian remained statuesque alongside, unmoving and patient. Without show, a storm of thoughts and concerns weighed his consciousness as he looked to the field. He knew only that they must not fail. A loss here would open the heart of Wei to Wu's fatal thrust.

They remained in garrison that entire day. The planned counter at daybreak never occurred. As sun set, Zhang sent teams of spies, scouts, and reconnoiters to intelligence the riddle of Sun Quan's all too apparent sleights of battlefield hand. Something was amiss in their camp.

The probes returned before next day's dawn. Puzzled more than informed, they related how significant reinforcements were stationary and encamped to the rear. This, even though front lines remained weakened and under orders to hold their positions. Along the front, bodies were being buried, quicklimed or burned. Reports from informants, yet unverified, indicated some troops in the far rear were returning to their boats, while others crossed south in the darkness, over the bridge at Xiaoyao Ford. Regretfully, they could not decipher the meaning. Might it signal a flanking maneuver? Desertions?

Zhang Liao listened for the voice of his mentor. Guan would surely know how to cut through this riddle ... only silence.

Linked by common destiny, the two courageous generals remained motionless at the rampart, studying intently until second cock's crow when the voice whispered to Zhang Liao, "The time to attack is when the opportunity presents. Beyond seeing and recognizing, one mustn't ponder the opportunity to the demise of the moment."

He turned to Li Dian, "After some thought, my conclusion is we must act decisively and attack now, using all forces and means at our disposal. If it proves to be folly, the failure is mine alone. I will issue the order under my name, and you needn't be concerned about consequences. In fact, I will dutifully record any objections you raise."

Li Dian turned to Zhang Liao, momentarily silent, recalling how the two had in the past incessantly feuded over responsibilities, authority, and stature within Cao's hierarchy of command. Now expecting his imminent demise, he couldn't even remember what they had endlessly quarreled about. Thoughts seemingly vanished from his memory, supplanted by images of the valiant and heroic Zhang Liao, the lion of the battlefield. Zhang Liao looked too to Li Dian, also with newfound respect, recalling his noble words when all others lacked the gall to face off against the enemy.

Earlier, when Zhang Liao asked the remaining garrison commanders who would join him, all remained mute, united in their shell of self-serving non-action. Only Li Dian spoke, declaring, "For myself, the time has come to put Wei and my sworn duty to Lord Cao before my personal concerns and ambitions. A true general could do nothing more, or less."

In his thoughts Zhang Liao reckoned, *He's a far better man than I had regarded him to be.*

Li Dian finally responded to Zhang Liao's extension of courtesy, "Nonsense, it's our decision. Tomorrow, you and I will act decisively and rain hell upon Sun Quan and his troops. Let the cowards speak of us as they will; we will have executed our duties. No doubt, some fools will give weight to what the liars say. Lord Cao is no fool; he will surely know the full measure of our hearts and loyalty when he studies the field and our actions upon it."

Zhang Liao grunted. "What the hell were we feuding about last week? It seems I've forgotten"

"We were feuding?"

They both shared a laugh, now as brothers.

The Battle of Xiaoyao Ford

Was the Battle of Xiaoyao Ford as disastrous for Sun Quan as Red Cliffs had been for Cao Cao? The answer became painfully clear. Despite being vastly outnumbered, Zhang Liao and Li Dian mercilessly annihilated the already emaciated Wu troops manning the immediate front.

By midday, the two generals surged southward in determined advance, pressuring the remnants of the Wu force. At some point, hesitant generals within Hefei sensed that clinging to the rear meant only embarrassment and loss of prestige. One by one, they abandoned the safety of the fortress, going forward to consolidate gains behind the lightning thrusts of Zhang Liao's vanguard.

Channeling his mentor Guan Yu, Zhang Liao once again declared his identity on the battlefield, accepting all challenges and screaming "I come for the head of Sun Quan." For the legions of Wu, anticipating quick and uncomplicated victory, a daunting and intimidating spectacle.

His battle worn comrades, still emboldened from the first day's engagement, penetrated deep into the now retreating ranks. Their rallying cry, a chorus of "Victory or Death!" echoed across the field. Initially, Wu's retreat had been orderly, but now, discipline and morale were torn from their spirits, and they scattered wildly in disarray, each person for himself, hoping only to survive till nightfall provided ample cover.

Taking personal responsibility for the disaster, Sun Quan ordered his finest thousand to remain with him, covering his own retreat. Seeing this, Zhang Liao relentlessly pursued Sun Quan, decapitating his many doubles wherever he found them, then decimating his generals. Several times over, he nearly had him in his grasp until unkind fate, or simple turn of fortune saved Sun Quan's mounted ass.

By dusk, the remnants of Wu's legions lay scattered across the field, resembling pieces of meat strewn haphazardly for the approaching vultures and carnivores. Speckled red fields reached as far as eyes could see.

Sun Quan would have surely met his doom if not for the valiant General Ling Tong, who assumed the supreme role of "Defender of the Retreat." Ling Tong's delaying tactics provided the barest sliver of time for the escaping leader to reach the already burning bridge at Xiaoyao Ford. There, he raced forward only to find its middle section burnt through. With no alternative, he leapt the daunting gap on the fortune blessed wings of an indisputably valiant steed. Just as Sun Quan jumped from his mount to safety on the other side, the depleted beast staggered to recover balance, stumbling backward to its doom. Sun stared in disbelief, wondering what message lay scribed in all that had transpired.

Amidst the chaos, Yama and his miscreants danced joyfully, orchestrating a symphony of pain punctuated by screams and pleas for help. Accented by something as rudimentary as pleas for water. Demons thrive on irony, reveling in the anguish of those they torment.

Yes, it takes moments like these to recall what's really important. Pain is learning.

As Wei's forces enjoyed the rout, they lined the banks, sending torch arrows to ignite Sun's fleeing navy. For them, a sweet turnabout!

Ensuring time for his lord's escape, Ling Tong stood fast and firm. He and his men bravely held what remained of the failing rear until every one of his own soldiers had crossed dark underworld rivers of their own. By nightfall, only he remained. Under cover of darkness, he descended the banks, still in full armor, and slid into the gently moving waters, abandoning his fate to the river dragon. Satisfied only that he would not be captured and desecrated.

Against all likelihood, he survived. Come morning, a crewman on Sun Quan's very boat pulled him in, barely conscious, from the water. Sun Quan rejoiced at the discovery. He would yet have Ling Tong at his side to ensure his kingdom's survival.

Though deep in the gloom of defeat, spirits lifted when news of the miracle spread.

Among the victors, the breadth of Guan's spirit stretched far in many directions. It shows how it can be when we encounter someone very special. We may end on different roads, never again to meet as comrades. But somehow, our spirits remain tightly bound, always touching, with one there to support and uphold the other. A phantom elder keeping his sibling from harm or dishonor.

Zhang Liao understood this well, particularly after the episode at Xiaoyao Ford. So did Cao Cao, who was quick to study the parallels. As before, upon hearing news of the unfolding battle, Lord Cao sped with reinforcements to salvage whatever he might of the anticipated disaster.

Arriving but a day after the decisive battle, he found Zhang Liao and Li Dian before the gates, extending a formal ceremonial welcome. Contritely, they both dropped to the ground and tendered their apologies for failing to capture Sun Quan.

At first speechless, Cao than asked the two generals to accompany him as he personally studied the battlefield and reconstructed the events of the past days.

He knew the situation to be hopeless, yet these two men had delivered a decisive victory that he and all his own troops in the north and the west had been unable to achieve.

Though his steely facade didn't readily reveal his heart, the other generals all saw he was overcome with admiration. Undoubtedly grateful fate had blessed him with two men the likes of Zhang Liao and Li Dian. When questioned directly, the others had no explanations to account for their own timidness, except to charge Zhang Liao with recklessness. That only drew Cao's angry glare.

Li Dian, never one to ride the crest of another's righteous accomplishment, made clear, "It may be true, I contributed in some small way to the effort. But all will attest, it was Zhang Liao who struck fear into their hearts and broke their battle spirits. He cruised the field, never retreating, never flinching, proclaiming the open gate of Hefei just on the other side of his lance, and inviting all challenges. After dispatching what Li Dian recounted to be hundreds of enemy combatants, no more came forth to engage him. Then Zhang Liao demanded the coward Sun Quan to stand before his troops and fight him for the day, if only to spare the battlefield of any further carnage."

Lord Cao turned to Zhang, "Did you do as he described?"

Zhang answered, "Truthfully sir, it's hard for me to remember. This I know. I remained immersed in the moment, free from concerns of failure and consequence, undisturbed by thoughts of reward, and undistracted by lust for victory or fear of defeat. I knew well my duty to Lord Cao, as did brother Li Dian. That thought directed our spirits like missiles to the hearts of the enemy. All other concerns vanished. The aggressors from Wu became ambivalent against the certitude of our purpose. We remained free and in the moment, their minds drifted, then ran elsewhere, and before long, their bodies followed. For us, the field had become like the surface of a smooth sea, we could move freely, unimpeded. They found themselves caught within a ferocious storm, unable to find safe harbor anywhere."

"Only one other man could have managed what you did here, and we both know who that is. Our brother Guan has taught you well."

He reached his arms around both generals and said, "Truthfully, you two should have been my sons."

As had Guan Gong, both Zhang Liao and Li Dian achieved much deserved recognition and rich rewards.

We hear they never again feuded, but no one can say for sure. For not long afterward, Li Dian passed at age thirty-six. We have no details of how and why. History records he was loved and respected by all who came to know him. That included the hero Zhang Liao.

While Zhang Liao's legend had been carved with Xiaoyao Ford, his valor, loyalty, and righteous behavior glowed brightly on many more occasions afterward, before his flame finally burned to its final end.

Whispers say that whenever Lord Cao passed through the province, he insisted on stopping at Hefei. There, he would spend long hours studying the surrounding fields and reconstructing in his poet's vision, the events of those several days. He only wished he had been there with them.

Given the complex threads of their relationship to Guan Yu, confronting his end five years later forever marked both men. Not long after burying the reconstituted Guan with full hero's honors (gracefully ignoring what damage Guan had wrought to Wei when leading the armies of Shu), Cao, too, entered the present moment. Perhaps in that reflection, he saw the foolishness of all ambition, finally coming to terms with its destructive proclivities. He wanted so much more for his people, and to the very end, preserved the Emperor Xian, albeit as a puppet. Despite fears broadcast by others, he never fully usurped power for himself.

The sheer audacity of Sun Quan—desecrating the warrior saint. Dispatching the rotting head as tribute to Cao Cao! Can such be tolerated?

How could this be the same man we learned about earlier? Perhaps it had been calculated? Might Sun Quan have known of the lingering poison Guan's rotting head would sow onto Cao and Zhang? If so, the anticipated fruits may have seemed significant and tempting at first. Had it worked as intended, Cao Cao and Zhang Liao would have been out of the picture. Crushed under weight of sorrow.

Dharma teaches terrible deeds demand their own accounting. In ways often undetectable, cruel designs sometimes run amok, their unseen currents and back flows influencing the very doers in ways unsought.

Eventually Sun Quan consolidated his kingdom. Cao's successor, Cao Pi[35] saw fit to finally depose the Emperor

---

[35] Cao Pi - successor to Cao Cao. Though conflicts continued with Shu and Wu, Cao Pi worked to consolidate kingdom Wei still reeling from the disaster at Red Cliffs. He took care not to further dissipate Wei's stature in military adventures with unlikely prospects. Among his accomplishments was adoption of Chen Qun's proposed nine level civil service system. This created a system which at least in promise, opened access to power and influence to those with proven talent and high moral character.

Xian. At least he spared his life, dispatching him to comfort and insignificance. He then proclaimed himself Emperor of Cao Wei and backdated the same title to honor his father.

We can only speculate as to whether Lord Cao would have approved.

Sun Quan would be no man's vassal, and in a few short years declared himself Emperor of Wu. He had changed from the noble ruler who had earlier befriended Zhuge Liang.

Curiously, the usually brilliant Sun Quan, at first singular among leaders, seemed figuratively to have lost his own head. As Wu consolidated into empire, what had formerly been easy for him become very complicated. No longer could he read men's hearts. Shrouds of darkness and suspicion obscured his view. The young King who had surrounded himself with brilliant leaders and staff had aged. Now grown fat with power and targeted by opportunists, sycophants, and liars. Political factions, too many to count, emerged to pursue their own purposes. Purges ensued. Hoping to rekindle the past, he instituted what he termed "cleansings." A tepid word for mass executions of perceived threats. Among them his two sons, once groomed to be his successors.

How quickly times and heroes do change. Another reason Guan's example and influence remain steady through the ages.

Of the three, Sun Quan far outlived Cao Cao and Liu Bei.

But he wasn't happy. We wonder if toward the end, he saw his own life's true final reflection in his own empty mirror.

Guan's curse?

Perhaps, but I prefer not to think of Lord Guan as a maliciously vengeful man.

Karma perhaps!

The Grand Design

First the passing of Lord Guan. Then, the assassination of Zhang Fei.

Zhang went mad after Guan's desecration. Acting in desperation, his own men assassinated him rather than continue as targets for his lethal rages. With both gone, Chancellor Zhuge Liang knew Shu's trajectory had turned irrevocably toward descent. The dream of restoring Han would never be achieved. Not by Liu Bei or the Shu; not by anyone.

Remorse?

Not so much for the goal unrendered. Rather, the costs imposed—a terrible toll on all. Those who, but for the ambitions and intransigence of others would have happily gone about their uneventful lives. No degree of imposed ambition could have shown them more than they already knew. Leading lives intertwined with nature's cycles, integrating with and reaping the bounties of the land, raising more children than one had a mind to manage. Running about with goats and oxen, horses, dogs, cats and what else. Looking wistfully at contented sunsets. A community not of brothers in arms, but of family and friends for whom one cared, knowing so long as balance and restraint ruled, parents would pass before their children, who would pass before theirs. All as it should be.

Is it not a wonder how the ordinary and uneventful are so hard to procure?

Some would have you think it boring and mundane, but is it not a stark contrast to the pursuits of those who choose to exploit and deem their grand ambitions as most important?

Remorse?

Only for what had been lost.

Clarity, sharpened by hindsight, rendered Han's extinction inconsequential. Even those yearning to salvage remnants had wearied of the thought—a grim weight bearing down on all. In the long view, prior days of empire looked now to be no more than a fleeting dream. Just another quirk or twist of history, whose running stream of images passed from one's view like frayed themes on a tattered tapestry. Captivating in the moment, then gone. Dropped off the edge. The great empire would live on only as a lingering memory.

But how does one re-constitute what has unraveled beneath? The very fabric of civilization.

No two living men could agree on a method, though all remained fixed and certain as to the need, and the why. Life simply could not continue on this course.

Study the Tao!

Zhuge Liang once trusted that in time, Liu Bei and the others would come to appreciate the dreadful consequences of their aspirations. Right there before them. The pleading eyes of decimated and afflicted populations. He hoped if he remained patient and counseled restraint, all of them would eventually return to reason; and together seek the benefits of compromise and cooperation, for the betterment of all.

Here, he had miscalculated.

Those were his own words. He had believed leaders the likes of Liu Bei, Cao Cao, and Sun Quan would eventually come to terms with the obvious. Were they not paragons?

The finest mankind had to offer? Were not their own self-interests, and the well-being of the populace aligned? Why so hard to see? Peasants, possessing their own wisdom, have long told how leaders would do well spending time in the muck with pig farmers. From the bottom, they could see how their bad trickles down to the very silt. Perhaps, stewing a while in their own brew might provide them with a different perspective.

Yes, there he miscalculated. He believed the greatest minds would in time align action to righteousness, binding it inexorably with the well-being of the people and the vitality of the great land. The disconnect occurred just at the margin of their own conceit.

He trusted they would act rationally. They didn't. Agonizing over their shortcomings, he woke from sleep, calling into the night, "If not them, then who?" Who could weave the guiding thread and restore the way?

In another realm, Yama basked in his favored incense of smoldering bone, blissful over Zhuge Liang's dilemma. If the grandest wizard of all was helpless, who or what remained to get in his way?

Zhuge saw only one option remaining. It would seal his end. He would have to bear the burden himself. He knew of no alternatives. And with that, he turned his burning gaze to Yama, accusing, "It is you!"

Though laughing at this timid threat, the demon grew wary.

The dream of restoring Han lay in ruins, a stark contrast to the lofty ideals it held and the heavy sacrifices made by its people and their war-torn lands. The exact moment of this transformation is shrouded in uncertainty, but it's clear that the focus of the master shifted from Han to what would later be dubbed the Grand Design.

It's essential to note he never referred to it as the Grand Design; the title was bestowed by future generations. In fact, he never named it at all. He understood that once it existed in the open, malevolent forces would inevitably rise to oppose and undermine his carefully laid strategies. It had always been that way.

His objective was to dismantle the relentless urge for conquest, imposition, and destruction. But Yama, the harbinger of chaos, stood in opposition. Anything that Yama and his supporters perceived as a threat or resistance swiftly vanished from existence, made to disappear. This was hardly Yama's fault; he was, after all, the embodiment of destruction, the antithesis of order, distorting all that nourished life, leading it away from order and into chaos.

Civilization and life demanded order but teetered atop an unending wave of turmoil, uncertainty, and dissolution.

The Grand Design would provide a basis for maintaining control over Yama, or at least guiding his intentions and thwarting his plans.

He said nothing of it to anyone. Except perhaps a hint, or a reminder to do something, a friendly request or nudge, a hidden temple, a mural here or a bridge there. When pressed, he would answer only, "I will trust in what others have long dismissed. The integrity and determination of the people, when and if empowered."

The change could only come from where it was not expected. Once he placed the triggers and embedded the appropriate spotless souls deep within the mass of overlooked humanity, the Way would leverage its own return to balance. He would abide in the Tao, the proof being his absence when it happened.

The wizard finally understood. In the grand scheme, figures like Liu Bei, Cao Cao, and Sun Quan meant little more than insects strolling aimlessly on the fabric of Dharma.

Though he would never acknowledge it, Yama knew the same applied to him and his demon hordes. All, in the end, insignificant. Still, he had a role to fulfill, and whoever doubted his significance would first have to reckon with how well he did his job.

What Was He up To?

Always suspicious and ever cautious, Yama knew something was afoot. With no idea what it might be, he sensed a ripple in the fabric of existence. A quiet wave pushing quietly along the edges of his awareness. What could that wizard be up to? No trace, no clue, not even a word spoken. Until then, Yama had enjoyed the floundering efforts of the diminishing Zhuge Liang, but he knew better than to underestimate him. *Keep him in my sights and firmly under my thumb. The shorter the leash, the better—a mistake with this one could prove dire.*

Night guards, stationed near the wizard's quarters, often thought they heard Zhuge Liang arguing with some unseen entity. "It sounds like a devil is in there with him!" Concerned officers ordered checks for intruders, only to find Zhuge Liang seated in Lotus, surrounded by an impenetrable silence. No one else was there. Was he going mad? Were they too going mad?

Leaving, they would again hear blood curdling screams accompanied by the gnashing of teeth, striking terror into their hearts. Taking to the field without the likes of Guan Yu and Zhang Fei was already daunting, but otherworldly voices promising endless pain, loss and suffering stretched already thinned nerves to their limits.

They had no way of knowing. Zhuge Liang had shifted his sights to more sinister prey. His game board departed from the field before them and became the construct of reality. The battle for Dharma and the question of what deserved to remain; mirroring the once epic battle in the sub-continent.

For these many years, even he had failed to see whose hands pulled strings behind the scenes. Looking out for Han, protecting Liu Bei, defending against Cao and off balancing Sun Quan had distracted his awareness away from Yama and his slithering hordes. Sinister entities cloistered in unnoticed shadows.

Now, he saw everything clearly, and Yama, the beast, felt a growing concern.

How clever the demon had been. For raw material, he mined from the best humanity had to offer; the most righteous, the most valiant, the most creative, the most aware, even the most virtuous.

Then he turned them.

Mere playthings, they became his pawns. Blinded by spells of ambition, duty, greed, power, influence, wealth, status, and occasional tastes of success, they propelled his wheel of chaos forward, as if by their own design, crushing all order and normalcy beneath it.

Zhuge Liang carefully vetted these doings and sliced through the many layers. Perhaps it was the guiding hand of Ke Li Xi Na, perhaps the inner workings of Zhuge Liang's own organic alchemy. Answers streamed to him in dreams, secure from intrusive eyes.

To end this reign of chaos would require a new geometry, a new tilt on reality, a place where even Yama and the gods could find no traction.

Its heroes would be few and incorruptible. Untainted by ambition. Disdainful and distrusting of power and influence. Always challenging authority; fearless, and intractable. In preparing them, he ensured their insignificance was such that even Yama's ceaselessly roving eyes could not detect them. Then with his time remaining, he would set the stage. Dharma willing, its heroes would stand ready when the moment arose.

While his time drew short, he perfected the intricacies of his plan. He meticulously implemented its network of principals, pieces, resources, and triggers. All would actualize even should he not be there to initiate. He said little of it to anyone, mindful of the gods' broad reaching influence and their propensity to corrupt and subvert. To some extent, his apprentice Sying Hao and his trusted Colonel Sun were privy to his doings and intentions. But the underlying scope of his endless deployments, assignations and fabrications left even them befogged.

Most troublesome, there arose the matter of the Fifth Northern Campaign.

Overseeing the Battle of Wuzhang Plains[36], he took on all responsibilities, attending to every detail. No others of his

---

[36] 234 CE - Fifth and final of Zhuge Liang's Northern Campaigns. As always, his tactical brilliance proved to advantage as they engaged a superior Wei force. In the midst of this campaign Zhuge Liang died. Without revealing his passing, his troops discretely disengaged and began their retreat. Opposing general Sima Yi thought to seize advantage and mounted an aggressive pursuit, still uncertain what had become of his nemesis. Staunch counter by Shu's able generals caused Sima Yi to suspect Zhuge had lured him into a trap. He disengaged his own forces rather than risk humiliating defeat. Afterwards, some joked how a dead Zhuge scared off a living Sima. Sima Yi took it in stride, countering he could predict the strategies of the living, but not of the dead. With Zhuge gone, Wei no longer

caliber remained. The likes of Guan Yu, Zhang Fei, and the Tiger Generals were already gone, as was Liu Bei's steady and fearless hand at the helm of state. The heir Liu Shan inspired no confidence. He leaned toward gratuitous pleasure and self-distraction, valuing eunuchs above all as his mentors and advisers. We mentioned earlier, Liu Bei entrusted Zhuge Liang with the authority to depose the son should he prove inadequate. Zhuge Liang would never carry out such an order. He, more than anyone, knew that blood connected Liu's lineage directly to the Han. Fail to respect this, and all credibility deserted their cause and efforts.

Some speculated Zhuge Liang saw his end approaching. Others discounted the whispered concerns by affirming him to be an immortal.

The endless insecurity of fear fearing for fear itself. We are afraid because we are afraid.

Except for Colonel Sun, among those remaining, no one knew Zhuge Liang's full past. He would say nothing of it, except, "That's Brother Zhuge's business." The accepted narrative portrayed Zhuge Liang as emerging from obscurity. Like Sying Hao, he was reportedly an orphan, raised by an uncle in Jing. He showed immense potential early on, attending to and mastering the arts of agriculture, irrigation, and livestock while but a youth. He grew accustomed to dirt beneath his nails; yet still found time to immerse himself in the classics and the arts whenever opportunities arose. Even as a martial artist, he had few peers. To this day, it remains a great mystery that no one ever took credit for mentoring the development of this

---

felt threatened by Shu and turned its energy within. Sima Yi's own grandson would found the Jin Dynasty, bringing the warring kingdoms period to an end.

prodigy. Honing his breathtaking skills and broad spanning talents to their proven sheen would have ensured recognition and honor to any worthy master.

Then again, how can anyone take credit for teaching something they couldn't possibly have had or known in the first place?

Self-actualized? Hindsight would argue this to be likely, even probable. Suffice it to say, before he came there were none ever like him.

It wouldn't be inaccurate to think of Zhuge Liang as someone who had always existed. There, in the misty surrounds of our time, a subtle presence on the horizon, a flicker among our shadows, a light darting across the sky, or a lone figure walking a snowy field in the high, empty expanse. Could that be him over there, in a portico playing soft melodies to the ascending moon?

An older brother to each of us, born before, and willing to share lessons learned. Look there, even in our dreams, he whispers we can fly if we wish. Doubting, we hesitate, when invisible wings suddenly sprout to lift us from the weight and gravity of ignorance and doubt. Not knowing why, we know when to incline left or right, or to turn, or ascend and then to soar. We're not alone, but we don't know who's there. Or do we?

He knew too much for one lifetime, albeit complete with extraordinary challenges, laced with uncanny successes offsetting otherwise imminent cataclysm. Therein lies the proof. Whatever art, skill, trick, or device it might take to linger beyond one's allotted time, I trust he, above all others, had worked it out.

As to whether it gave him joy, you must be the judge. Sadly, after abandoning his onetime sanctuary to serve Liu Bei, he fell slave and prey to onslaughts that would have been insurmountable trials for others. They took their inevitable toll.

Liu Bei and his martial brothers marveled at how Zhuge Liang rose to every need, seemingly born again and revitalized proportionate to the degree of difficulty of whatever challenge befell him. This illusion held to the very end.

Even the young protege, Sying Hao, would sometimes confide he had seldom seen Zhuge Liang take rest, or sleep. As others recuperated and the battlefield paused, Zhuge would summon his young apprentice and together they would study and reflect on the internal arts, the changes, the properties of plants and compounds, the traps of time, and Dharma. Just like Ke Li Xi Na and Ah Ju Na but with a bit less drama and more deliberation.

It can be too easy to talk this conundrum into circles.

So, shall we leave it at this? He came to us first as an emerging immortal; but left us as a man. He had seen enough, done enough. This current manifestation, associated with Liu and his dreams of rekindled empire, had depleted the sage. As he prepared for Wuzhang Plains, he definitely foresaw his end. Others have confirmed he consulted the heavens closely as the fated day neared. In the background, unbeknownst to even Yama and his spies, he put the finishing touches on his Grand Design, trusting his instincts regarding the timing, and the placement of young apprentice Sying Hao as precautionary insurance that all would not come to naught for lack of vision and commitment. All in due time to be propelled by action.

Zhuge Liang Passes

Zhuge Liang knew what lay in store for Colonel Sun and regretted it. On this, he had to accept dictates of fate, and trust Sun would persevere.

Sying Hao told of how Zhuge Liang prepared for his end. Knowing it neared, he managed to conjure an elaborate ruse hoping to stall its approach one final time. He reckoned if only he might steal a few more years, he could still coax the land away from perpetual turmoil and restore some semblance of rational order.

It came midway through the battle of Wuzhang Plains. Everyone noticed the marked deterioration in the wizard, who now looked like any other member of the walking dead, which is what they had all become. Victimized by years of unremitting conflict, drained of life energy and will.

On hearing his spies' reports on Zhuge Liang's appearance, and the constant calls for his oversight over every aspect of the Shu campaign, Wei's commander Sima Yi turned to his staff and declared, "Not even Zhuge Liang can survive this. Our troubles will soon resolve." His staff attributed the comment to wishful thinking.

Referencing the sage, his tone evoked respect, tinged with remorse. He spoke of Zhuge Liang as he would of a mountain, a heavenly orb, or even a departing friend; one day there, the next day to be gone. An enigma and worthy nemesis he would undoubtedly miss.

Staving off the ever anticipating and unremittingly leering Yama, Zhuge Liang issued explicit instructions to his staff. On that fateful evening, no disturbance should interrupt his solitude. "Even should Sima Yi himself challenge us at our threshold, do not disturb me. Think of me as not being there!" His guards assured they understood the directive. He placed his trust in them. The success of his ruse depended on it.

Zhuge Liang's final scrutiny of the stars unveiled a solitary chance to outsmart Yama. To seize this opportunity required he access the deepest realms of meditation, transcending appearances, the grinding wheels of time and destiny, beyond chi itself, into the emptiness. Only there might he draw the vital energy needed to extend his remaining life thread by a crucial five years. In his unwavering resolve, those five years held the power to thwart Wei in the north, impede Wu in the south, and pave the way for the nation's self-regeneration, free from the internecine machinations of ambitious fools.

Could these be the meanderings of a mind teetering on the edge? Perhaps, but Zhuge Liang clung to an unshakable faith. Faith in the common folk and their innate wisdom. As always, he placed the utmost trust in those whose lives were marked by toil and purpose, individuals who understood the true worth of community and compassion.

This trust resonated with memories from places like Jing, the snowy expanses, and numerous other locales where he had lingered. It echoed the sentiments of Bao Ling in Ling Village and the understanding shared by Zhi Mei with her father and brother. Sying Hao, too, had experienced this profound connection with Colonel Sun.

How easily others were tricked and cajoled into forgetting, or into casting them off as weaknesses, mundane and pointless. Not these five.

But as to Zhuge Liang drawing resources from emptiness? How so? A place where galaxies spin on fingertips? The realms of wizards and immortals? Are there better explanations?

Just as he warned, the night had barely unfurled its dark canvas when Sima Yi, ever the strategist, directed his forces to probe for weaknesses along the battlements. Initially, the contacts unfolded haphazardly, like scattered pieces on a chessboard. Soon, however, reports of major engagements echoed from all quarters. Fearing disaster, the senior staff panicked. All inquired frantically "Where is Zhuge Liang?" By the stroke of midnight, ranking officers amassed outside Zhuge Liang's compound, trying to circumvent his personal guard, doing whatever it took to gain his attention. An unprecedented act even in graver situations. The guards, bewildered by this sudden turn, found the disturbance immensely peculiar.

Meanwhile, Colonel Sun and Sying Hao stood steadfast at the front lines, ensuring no one deserted their posts, trusting Zhuge Liang's guard to maintain order in the rear. They understood the gravity of the situation, yearning for a swift dawn that would reveal their restored friend when they returned to camp. The adage about letting others do what only you can do yourself lingered in the air.

Fear reached a fever pitch. From a distance, Sima Yi couldn't ignore the commotion emanating from the heart of the Shu encampment. He, with satisfaction, deemed it the intended consequence of his faux advance, warmly congratulating his returning troops for a job well done.

"Now we've got them where we want them, seeing attacks where none exist," he whispered confidently to his aides.

As midnight ebbed into darkest night, stars unexpectedly brightened the surround, as luminous as if the moon had been full. Mystified troops on both sides stared in awe at the flickering celestial display. It seemed to portend something profound. But what?

The spectacle prompted wild speculation among the troops. Had heaven opened its gates and thrown its welcome for one of its own? Long gone, but now returning?

The leaders of Shu, even more uncertain over what to do, fell to their knees, fervently imploring Zhuge Liang to emerge and dispel their fears. Colonel Sun and Sying Hao, their duties at the front line concluded, hastened back to the minister's retreat.

Upon arrival, their relief was eclipsed by sheer horror. Zhuge Liang stood outside his chamber, momentarily resembling the revered dragon sage of old before inexplicably transforming into a specter disintegrating before their very eyes.

A junior line officer had somehow breached the minister's guard, and stolen entry into the compound. Superiors credited and praised the young man for waking the minister from a deathlike trance which all believed would have been his end but for the young hero's determination.

In an instant, Sying Hao, overcome with fury, mounted an arrow intent on ridding creation of one more selfish idiot. Just at the point of release, Colonel Sun checked his hand saying simply, "My son, he who knows nothing should not be so harshly judged."

It took every reserve within for Sying Hao to quell his rage and spare the life of the ambitious intruder. Colonel

Sun pointed his chin to Zhuge Liang, "It falls to us to smooth his way."

Sying Hao turned, his eyes glazed and fixed on the unfolding tragedy. Paralyzed, he yearned to rush to his teacher's side, yet an invisible force bound him to the earth— a morass of horror and renewed uncertainty. In these dire circumstances, only someone like Colonel Sun could act decisively. He bounded to the side of Minister Zhuge who cast one final spell over his attentive audience in a last show of brilliance. By now, they all knew. It was over.

Minister Zhuge carefully laid out plans for the remainder of the engagement and lines of retreat should anything go amiss. He knew that on learning of his passing, Sima Yi would attack mercilessly, ensuring his troops reduced Shu to ashes. They couldn't allow this. They must trick him, making sure to reveal nothing of his demise. No funeral, no mourning, no trace. As his final act Zhuge Liang provided the strategy for escape and Shu's survival, then trusted they would all have the sense to go their own ways once given the opportunity.

That's what he told them! To his credit, an honorable man to the end.

Observing Sying Hao's pain within the somber assembly, Zhuge Liang smiled as if surprised, beckoning him forward and to his side. He gently scolded Colonel Sun for leaving his young shadow behind in his haste to serve. "Colonel Sun, you should know by now never to abandon one friend to the needs of another."

The two posted alongside the beloved minister, very carefully taking his arms and holding him upright as he bid final farewell to the legions of Shu. He wished only to endow them with his love and respect, affirming his unshakable confidence in their ability to follow his instructions. He concluded, asking only for a few fleeting moments to rest, turned briefly away, then faced them once more, "Never forget, you have striven for righteousness. History will show you served with loyalty against daunting odds and sought the highest moral purpose available to you in these confused and troubled times. Let others wander aimlessly in chaos and marvel over that which set you far above them all."

He spoke no more.

The starry carpet rolled into darkness just as the sage departed. In his absence the world leaned again toward uncertainty.

Yama reveled in the shadows.

Monkeys Are off the Menu

No one felt the loss more deeply than Sun Wu Kong. With each passing day, he found himself adrift, severed from purpose, and gradually detached from all connections. This eventually culminated in his baffling disappearance. A great mystery begging for a solution.

While alive, Liu Bei took special care to recognize and honor Colonel Sun's selfless contribution to the Shu Kingdom and its efforts to restore Han. His loyalty, indomitable spirit, and unparalleled skills were celebrated by all who knew him. A mysterious figure, Colonel Sun was initially brought into the fold by Zhuge Liang, and the origins of this half-man, half-simian enigma remained shrouded in mystery. His unusual appearance, accented beneath beetle-browed yellow-green eyes by a penetrating glare, occasionally made his colleagues uneasy. Yet, he was dearly loved and revered by those who fought alongside him. Of one thing his fellows had no doubt. It had been their exposed backs he protected, and their hides he felt compelled to rescue when others had written them off. Legends grew around the exploits of Guan Yu, Zhang Fei, and even Zhuge Liang. Deservedly so. But each would have conceded his share of honors to Colonel Sun, who most often preferred to steal quietly into the background, or into the silent company of his squire Sying Hao.

As the cycle of seasons brought winter's advance to Crystal Springs, Bao Ling spent more time in the temple.

Sometimes in the company of Shi-Hui Ke; more frequently alongside Zhi Mei. Together, they delved into the murals and the myriad portrayals, seeking the stories woven beneath the surface. Their quest unveiled a hidden intelligence, a mind and spirit that seemed to permeate not only the murals but every facet of the temple—the bridge, the disappearing river, the intricate maze of roads, and who knew what else? Bao Ling told Zhi Mei what lay before them could only point back to Zhuge Liang, all links in a vast chain, connected in the mind of one man. Might this be the key to his fabled Grand Design? Bao Ling had first heard Shi-Hui Ke talk of it, but even he had only a fragmentary perspective. What might it mean? The Grand Design remained elusive. When pressed for more, Hui could add nothing, responding only with a shrug of his shoulders, and a look of being lost. For that reason, they all remained captivated by the murals and mysterious allure, marveling over the images of Colonel Sun, Sying Hao and the many others. The long shadows cast by their deeds, somehow coalesced into new forms shaping the very moment where they stood—an unfathomable design known only to one. Just like long before, when Zhuge Liang predicted the wind would shift at Red Cliffs.

Without their even suspecting, Yama peered constantly over their shoulders, his clawed hand stroking chin whiskers as he surveyed all with great interest. Suspicions aroused, he too had no clue where the trail led.

One particular morning, Bao Ling and Zhi Mei stumbled upon a vignette showing Lord Guan and Colonel Sun, seemingly out-of-character, in what appeared to be a deadly standoff. This caught them off guard, prompting a search for clues that could unravel what led to this confrontation. They found a hint in characters scratched beneath, apparently added sometime after the mural came into existence, saying only, "Monkeys are off the Menu!"

Was it some kind of a joke?

Abbot Hui, at least, knew the story behind this particular episode. He explained how the incident had unfolded and carefully framed how the portrayal came to be.

Though he hadn't witnessed it, Zhuge Liang had been so delighted by Sying Hao's report, he couldn't resist memorializing it in one of the murals. He wanted no doubts in anyone's minds as to the true stature of these two titans, along with their eccentricities. "Sying Hao subsequently etched the words you see beneath, using the tip of an arrow. Everyone but Chancellor Zhuge thought he had desecrated the work. On reading the inscription, Zhuge burst into laughter, thanking Sying Hao and assuring, 'I knew something was missing from this, but I couldn't quite put my finger on it.'"

Elsewhere[37], we highlighted Colonel Sun's grand awakening during his commission to research and collect sacred sutras from the subcontinent. He emerged from this expedition awake and aware, standing foremost among all who undertook the arduous journey.

But what does it mean to be awake and aware? Integrated? Enlightened? While the terminology might be esoteric, Taoists and Buddhists have long understood, even if they refrain from making a grand spectacle of it. As they see it, we bump along in the course of life, often in a state of profound slumber. Deep asleep, if you will. I mean stone cold knocked out, incognizant, unaware, detached, dreaming, comatose, croaked, numbed, deadened, doped,

---

[37] Detailed in our prior work *The Wizard's Testament*.

dormant, dull, unconscious, mindless, senseless, unalert, zonked, and under the spell.

What's the cost?

Whole civilizations acknowledge the pragmatic reality that our ability to think and act can be wrested from our control by those who believe they can manage us better than we can manage ourselves. They rely on the usual tricks and devices. Whoever controls the weight of thought, controls the will and resources of the moment. Control the political landscape!

Empires, governments, merchants, armies, priests and scholars know full well the art of manipulation. Let them entrance you, and they will snatch your liberty right from under your weakening grip. Foremost among their tools— droning appeals to fear, greed, loyalty and heaven. Wherever you stand in the arc of time, you will not have to look far to see someone pulling these strings as they beckon and plead for your trust, your support, your sacrifice, and ultimately even your life and the lives of those around you.

History has shown two things certain. First, someone will try to hook you with this nonsense; second, when they do, you will really, really, really suffer. Lest you miss the point, when something repeats three times, pay attention.

Society tends to pedestalize the wealthy, powerful, and successful. We like to think of them as familiars, and often speak of them as we would of chums or neighbors. Inclined by our biases, we rivet ourselves to their every move while awaiting their pronouncements. Conned into anticipating fulfillment of wants, needs and potentials, but missing the boat as it floats away.

Amidst all this, where is the real "you"?

There are no excuses, Laozi set the record straight for all of time. Study his "Classic of the Way," then, beware. If you chase after their lures, not only do you validate them; but bite into one and you get hooked! That's the dilemma. Once on the hook, it's awfully hard to get off.

On returning from the subcontinent, Colonel Sun became complete. He strapped his root to center, and afterword emanated from the inside out, while maintaining balance, perspective, and restraint. Exterior concerns like fear, greed, demands for loyalty, and the professed will of heaven no longer concerned him. What did those who professed anything know that he didn't already. He stood where he stood, aware and awake. No more; no less. Plays for influence now reduced fundamentally to greed and indulgence. For him, distractions and nothing more. Smudges on his emptied mirror. He knew that which made him who he was was bigger and more important than all of it.

He remained a favorite topic among the others. They talked about him unceasingly. His strangeness, his outer worldliness, his hidden (or buried) past, his seemingly ageless countenance.

In fact, no one knew his age. Stare as you would, you couldn't tell anything from his incongruous countenance. Most would conclude, he appeared very mature, almost old, but not quite; and powerfully menacing if the situation required it.

Zhuge appreciated how nothing said it better than "Monkeys are off the menu."

As related to Abbot Hui by Sying Hao, the mural memorialized an incident where Colonel Sun and General Guan had come to disagreement over some monkeys the hungry soldiers had captured in the wild and were about to eat. Food had grown scarce, and troops had to look everywhere for nourishment.

Sun politely asked them to release the animals, explaining that they were allies and deserving of respect. One of them joked, "Allies? Do they carry weapons? Or are they spies on our behalf?" The others laughed at the suggestion, but of course the lads didn't understand any of this. The voice of their hunger spoke much louder. Some murmured discreet protests, accusing Sun of prioritizing his true family over his brothers in arms. When Guan arrived and overheard Sun's objection, he demanded they butcher the captured animals immediately, asserting that men were already going hungry, and monkeys were no different than deer or goats.

This of course deeply offended Colonel Sun, who, on another day might very well have looked like an appetizing morsel, tempting a near starving troop.

To everyone's surprise, the two suddenly faced off, motionless, flashing glassy eyed stares that seemed to freeze time itself. As did the troops, the captured monkeys studied the two with great interest, anticipating the immense explosion certain to follow.

Guan conjured his renowned battle mask, contorting his face and features to their most fearsome and grotesque limits. Cheeks glowed red, the superfluous beard echoed his fiery eminence, framing the huge, gritted teeth which ground menacingly beneath his rhinoceros breathing. A visage he usually reserved only for the heat of battle. More than one witness has confirmed it to be so fearsome as to steal life from enemies before they even thought to strike.

Colonel Sun emptied himself of worldly affiliation, and in an instant assumed the berserker cast of countenance from which he had gained combat renown as the "Monkey Prince." The half-man, half-ape lumbered impatiently, staring toward Guan, daring the next move. Just like in the mural.

The famished troops forgot their hunger, now shaking in terror at two man-monsters about to engage, akin to asteroids colliding. Fearing for their lives, they scattered in all directions, thinking only of finding adequate cover.

Even the monkeys chased after them, their evident terror driving them imprudently to their captors for some hope of protection.

The titans darted about, cycling their vocabulary of death stares, each throwing one mask after the other, upping the ante until even the horses broke from their moors.

Camp guards ran to Liu Bei, in the midst of conferencing with Zhuge Liang. Clearly, he did not expect, nor appreciate the interruption.

"What do you mean they're about to kill each other?" he roared, but not before Zhuge Liang politely signaled for his attention.

"What, counselor? How do you propose we break these two demons apart?"

Zhuge Liang simply smiled, "Sire, my suggestion would be we let the children play without uncalled for interference."

Liu Bei stared gravely at his trusted minister, then almost uncontrollably a spring of humor, tinged with irony pushed to the surface, ending with a slow and slight upward curl on the sides of his stress hardened mouth.

"Of course, counselor, we have more important matters requiring our attention."

Liu Bei dismissed the guards, who stalled in disbelief, until he turned to them, questioning, "Anything else?"

"No sir," and then they were gone, but not before encountering Sying Hao on their exit.

Hearing their concern, Sying Hao raced to where General Guan and Colonel Sun stood in face off, weapons raised, each glaring in his warrior mask, now probing one another, calculating possible openings to launch assault.

He was about to dash between them; no one else had the gumption to linger, help or interfere. His only thought being to push them apart; but frankly, expecting they would crush him when they collided.

Just as he positioned carefully to lunge between them, they both relaxed and turned to the young adjutant.

Guan spoke first, "What do you think Sying Hao, who won?"

Responding in disbelief, Sying Hao said, "Who won what?"

Colonel Sun answered, "Why the stare down; didn't you see us?"

"Of course I saw you. The whole camp's running for cover. Worried as to what untold scourge the two of you were about to unleash."

"Scourge, unleash?" they questioned, almost as one.

Concern tinted Guan's still fearsome brow, "Heavens, I hope we haven't stirred up any unnecessary trouble." To this, Sun added, "We were only practicing our Dragon stares for the battlefield," to which Guan corrected, "Actually, I was doing the Dragon stare; Brother Sun was doing rage of the Monkey King" to which Sun corrected in turn, "To be clear for Brother Guan's understanding, I was in fact channeling Monkey King, in his own manifestation of Dragon unleashed."

Guan responded, "Of course Brother Sun, I appreciated exactly what you were doing; but as you know, I do not have your gift for articulation."

Sying Hao stared incredulously.

"You two, you're impossible." He kicked dirt at both of them, muttered some expletives then turned about and stomped away.

Guan hollered as he left, "We were only trying to distract them from their hunger! You know … entertainment!"

"What's with him?" Sun asked Guan.

"Nothing that a little action wouldn't cure," answered Guan.

Looking around, Guan assessed, confirming everyone had indeed run off, even the intended meals had escaped, "Look Sun, the monkeys are gone."

"You're not thinking of rounding them up for the boys, are you?"

"Of course not. They've earned their freedom. Besides, I never eat them. It'd be like eating one of my friends," Guan explained, hoping not to offend, given the state of surrounding appearances.

"I know exactly what you mean," affirmed Sun.

Guan relaxed.

Finished with whatever it was they had been hoping to accomplish, the two turned together to walk off. Colonel Sun commented first, "Heavens Brother Guan, you really had me shaking there for a moment. I'd have all but given up my head just to get out from under the scorching heat of your glare."

"There you go again Brother Sun, a gift with words. For me, I all but peed myself back there. Trying to move but frozen still in terror by your Monkey Dragon focus dissolving my center."

"You're too polite Brother Guan, perhaps best we call it a draw?"

"How else can we call it? Now, how about we round up some food for the lads."

Colonel Sun agreed, "What do you suggest?"

General Guan stopped momentarily, "I would think venison, anything but horse again."

To which Colonel Sun added, "Or monkeys."

"It goes without saying," answered Guan.

And from that day, monkeys roamed unimpeded in the camps of Shu, where they forever found safe harbor, and on more than one occasion reciprocated with needed intelligence on enemy movements.

All declared monkeys to be off the menu.

Righteous Doubts

Understandably, the unanticipated loss of General Guan[38] struck a sharp blow to Colonel Sun.

Sying Hao often mused to Bao Ling. "It would be hard to find two men so completely different, while at the same time so much alike. Both were loners, existing onto themselves, of stuff much different than others. Each could spend days in utter solitude; simply listening. Re-experiencing the world as if becoming infants born anew. Always rediscovering and exploring. Looking to understand the underlying essence. Ever appreciating the innate beauty, while always on the lookout for another first moment. And finally, reconnecting to the reserve within. Boldly returning to the universe of ceaseless strife where they plied their unenviable roles. Those silent moments anchored their spirits, assuring their determination to go on.

"Guan Yu had the bearing and cast of a god, and people deferred to him as if he were. Colonel Sun had no such bearing. We suppose he could have, had it been his choosing. He had mastered the transformations after all. Rather, like a wild animal preferring solitude, he opted to vanish into his surroundings. Yet, if someone pushed hard enough, his frightening shape might emerge as though from

---

[38] Guan Yu is said to have passed in 220 CE, approximately fourteen years before Zhuge Liang.

air, and suddenly the man-beast with the lightning eyes revealed itself in full regalia before one's very nose.

Both lived righteously, and gave their all to every moment. Their efforts and determination bettered what followed. Their impeccable attitudes set prodigious standards for all to aspire. They rose from the bottom, from nowhere, and never forgot their roots. Without reservation or hesitation, they served whatever parcel of reality demanded the influence of their efforts and will."

Sying Hao recounted the dialogues and mannerisms of both and how taken he had been with their candor, not to mention their eccentricities. He marveled at the seemingly bottomless reach of their integrity. Neither would lie nor deceive. They didn't even know how to. Perhaps this, more than all else, explained their wrath and indignation when others tried to pull the fast one on them.

Hoping to mine all he might from these two masters, Sying Hao frequently cornered and queried each about his exploits in the field. He puzzled over whether their loyalty to Liu Bei's unwavering commitment to restore Han had been their inspiration. Or perhaps something else, deeper, hidden and within. If so, he wanted to know about it. Sying Hao of course, like all diligent young men, was forever pushing and probing. Skeptical and always searching for the essential reason things were as they were. He was not one to buy readily into superficial explanations and rationales. Particularly those first rendered and then broadcast universally from motivators on high. A dangerous proclivity even in those days.

Without apparent planning or collusion, they responded to his questions virtually identically. As though some time in the past they had worked out the underlying choreography, responses at their ready when and if questioned or challenged.

Typically, first a long silence, then a pensive studied gaze into the distance, then a hand to the chin, stroking downward as if milking thought. Either might answer with …

"Sying Hao, you have me at a disadvantage. Surely, I support the goals and objectives of Liu Bei. The Han brought a golden age to the land. We were productive, happy, creative, generally at peace and complete. The chaos today wasn't even a concern back then. The military fulfilled a domestic purpose, nothing more, and remained close in rein. The people were happy. Creativity blossomed everywhere. Wholesome thought found new roots and myriad paths, particularly with the spread of Taoism, Buddhism, propagation of the classics, and don't forget the sage Confucius, but also his contemporaries and their prescriptions for moral rectitude. Technology, art, medicine, metallurgy, coinage, communication, poetry. All flourished! Compare that to what followed, and you'll understand why there came to be a Peach Tree Oath, and why Liu Bei remains the sole vital lifeline away from chaos, away from despotism, away from self-serving ambition, and toward the ideal of our peoples' potential once again fulfilled."

Sying Hao at first thought, *Oh, of course, they are lockstep with Lord Liu. What was I thinking? I'll apologize for my impertinence.* He marveled at the depth of their convictions and the unity in their perspectives. It wasn't just about political allegiance; they shared a sacred duty rooted in profound understanding of history, culture, and the enduring principles that shaped their world.

But then they spoke from their hearts, acknowledging the cruel reality. Sying Hao listened intently as each unraveled his innermost thoughts.

"But to be honest little brother, I have seen decades of destruction, and at this moment, no endpoint emerges on time's horizon. Had I known I would become the emissary of chaos, albeit unwittingly; I would have walked into the western desert and turned my back on this nonsense. Now, I discern no ending to it, even with a careful gaze and close study. Without that, an honest man cannot state a true purpose remains, or in fact, ever existed.

"So, my motivation in the field has nothing to do with Han, or with Liu Bei. Certainly, I love, respect, and honor Liu Bei. He is a paragon among men. You won't find better, or more righteous. But we cannot resuscitate Han. Han has served its purpose and can be no more. It lies all about us, deader than the grit beneath our feet.

"As for us, we have become ghosts of our purpose now lost, and for all appearances, dead. It seems we remain only to haunt the surface.

"To be clear Sying Hao, I fight for those beside me, and behind me, and against those who come to do us harm. Would they contain themselves; I would be content to let them be. But they can't, and they drive their hordes into our domains, decimating and pillaging our people; stealing the lives of our youth while abandoning parents, the infirm, womenfolk, and the elderly to fend helplessly for their own survival. For those villains, life's purpose reduces only to the proposition of 'Serve us completely or die!' It's arrogance, Sying Hao, and the simple question is whether to tolerate such arrogance. Look about you. Where else in nature do you find this nonsense? It is our own doing. Mankind's. We stew in our own juices!

"No, Sying Hao, I can control only one thing. Whether the young lad beside me survives this day, and the next, and again the next. Perhaps with a token sprinkling of luck and shared insight, I preserve the possibility someday he might return home whole and spark the birth of a new direction. Perhaps it might be you, perhaps another like you.

"Apart from that, there is no purpose, no motivation. At the moment, assholes propel the winds which drive our sails!"

Sying Hao heard it time and again from Guan, and from Colonel Sun. Pretty much the same, seemingly polished and scripted but completely imbued with honesty and for that measure, extemporaneous. They had independently drawn the same conclusions.

Initially, what his two heroes said had put him off. How could they waiver in their commitment to Liu Bei's dream of restoring Han? Then, after seeing what was, and thinking carefully over their words and the experiences they shared, Sying Hao concluded likewise. If there were another peach garden, the three,—Sying Hao and his warrior mentors— might well have sworn a new oath, forged in the crucible of their shared understanding.

Part 5 - Tightly Bound

Hope as Common Ground

Doubts or not, Guan and Sun had given their word. Until the very end, their commitment remained unwavering. Despite surface disparities, those who knew them and witnessed their long procession of heroic feats deemed them brothers in common deed. On any given day, either could turn the battlefield singlehandedly. More than once, each confessed debt to the other for deeds rendered in rescue. Pulling victory from beneath chaos' cresting wave and the threat of imminent loss.

We already know what happened to Guan. An unprecedented lapse of focus, a misplaced trust extended to a boot licking enemy officer catering to obscure ambitions—among the greatest of tragedies. Can more be said?

Sun took Guan's death and subsequent humiliation viscerally, as though Yang had lifted unexpectedly from his own Taiji, leaving him floating aimlessly in shadowy Yin. A vital connecting cord now severed. Loose and adrift, he hungered for that special radiance which assured he was never alone and vulnerable. "Farewell my friend Guan Gong, a beacon among mortals, a true and kindred spirit. A brother!"

For Sun, tragedies like this were inherent to his choice to remain. Yin and Yang, never one without the other. But Guan's desecration raised troubling questions, and heightened doubts within. Learning the gruesome details, he wondered how one man could see fit to do this to another.

Didn't they know? Couldn't they see? It led to no good end. Not for them, not for anyone. Mighty as Sun was, he had no way of insulating himself. He chose to be here and to share in our experiences. Over time, he grew to care, tasting the sweet and knowing the bitter. Again, he would have to find a way to carry through.

He had trod this long plank many times. First, the descent into void, where nothing mattered; then, the sinking into silence and loneliness. Cursed by his eternal nature and by a need for companionship, which he now knew to be integral to his very being. He'd have to fight his way back. Pull himself from despondency. Somehow return to the surface, for what he knew would be more of the same. Guan had been among his greatest losses.

Long ago, Sun had crafted an algorithm of cold, hard detachment to preserve his sanity; without which, he knew he could not bear on. What made it so hard this time was it had been so good while it lasted. Sying Hao, having himself experienced these sentiments, compounded many times since pairing with Sun in service of Shu, understood completely. He knew … the colder, harder, and more distant Sun's detachment, the deeper the cut of his pain.

It was some time after the great stare down. Sying Hao happened to be sharing rice and greens with Lord Guan. He took the moment to recount with hilarity how fearsome Guan and Sun had been that day. Pushing their game to the limit; perhaps beyond the bounds of good sense; and how the entire surrounding encampment ran for cover, trailed by a herd of panicked monkeys.

As Lord Guan bellowed radiantly, Sying Hao smiled admiringly, then turned more serious. "Everyone feared one of you might kill the other, or, heaven forbid, you might kill each other. Where would that have left us? What would have become of me?"

Guan responded, "Who knows, Sying Hao? People will think what they think. One thing for sure, whatever their fear, it clouded what they should have already known. Colonel Sun and I are closer than brothers. Together, as duty demanded, we have done the impossible time and again. Alone and without the other, either of us might have failed miserably. We frolic, but never lose sight of the fundamental fact so many lives depend on us and our continued well-being. Why, we consider it a sacred responsibility to look after each other! And we do!

"Oh, and by the way, don't think we didn't recognize your courage, if not your slack wittedness, when you thought to stand us down. There you were, dreading all the while you might not survive. Yes, we knew what you were thinking! That made it all the more commendable. You did what no one else had the fortitude to do. You acted instantly, and with purpose. Valiant, if I may say. To this day, Colonel Sun still boasts of what you showed, saying it proved you were taking after him. But you and I both know it was my influence which inspired you. Let's just keep it our secret."

Sying Hao yet again rolled his eyes deep into his crown, signaling to the war god the last comment had already begun to lose traction, begging for a change of topic.

Affectionately slapping him on the shoulder (almost separating it from his arm), Guan continued, "Of course, your ultimate loyalty is with Colonel Sun, as well it should be. It's obvious to all of us that you and he have become like father and son, and that warms our hearts. You'll find no jealousy here. Lord Zhuge and I are content to be your uncles, and you can count on us to assist in guiding your proper upbringing."

Sying Hao grunted in humble acceptance, deep affection evident as he looked warmly across to his friend, the hint of an appreciative smile lighting his face.

As squire to Colonel Sun and apprentice to Zhuge Liang, Sying Hao had also gained opportunity to do what no other man but for one had done. He worked regularly with Lord Guan, learning the several arts over which Guan had acquired supreme command. Many had wished for the opportunity, but indeed, General Guan was a force of nature. All too capable of killing the unsuspecting or the ill prepared with what for him would be little more than a bump or a poke. History records only two to have survived training one-on-one with the daunting Guan: Zhang Liao, whose acquaintance you have already made, and Sying Hao, whom you will learn more of as our accounts unfold.

"If you'll kindly indulge me," Guan added. "Your concerns that we might hurt one another may have been a bit overblown.

"I admit Colonel Sun could take my life, should he manage to deliver the fateful blow. I can't promise it would be an easy task; but the likes of Sun, and even Zhang Fei, when all is at stake and nothing held back, who knows?

"Still, for me or anyone else, to deliver the same blow on Sun Wu Kung; a different feat entirely."

Sying Hao didn't understand, "Sir, please explain."

"Surely. Sying Hao, you and I birthed into this world … same as all men and all women, same as the birds, and the roaming animals. Like them, we have our talents and our vulnerabilities, foremost of which is our inclination toward mortality. When cut, we bleed; when broken, we die.

"Brother Sun never speaks of it, but in addition to his peculiar heritage, he is equally special in other ways."

"Go on," urged Sying Hao.

"Well, as you know, Brother Sun rarely talks about anything. When he does, it's never about himself. So, most of what I know comes from Zhuge Liang, who of course knows everything. I also have my own reflections on what I have gleaned from Brother Sun during our times together, particularly when sharing the lonely field of combat.

"You see my nephew, Colonel Sun simply showed up in camp one day, and petitioned for audience with Zhuge Liang. It later became clear they had some considerable history together. That explained why it was Minister Zhuge who presented Sun to Lord Liu Bei, along with his hearty recommendation, a rarity indeed. You know full well Zhuge's reticence in these things, always preferring to let others arrive at their own judgments. He explained about having made Sun's acquaintance when their paths crossed in earlier times, then crossing again during his period in the high mountains. He personally vouched Sun, among all knights, to be exemplar. For a brief spell Zhang Fei and I took offense to this. A stranger, spoken of as a peer to us.

"Lord Liu, as were others at court, was taken aback by Sun's ungainly appearance. It wouldn't be unjust to call it freakish. He arrived in rags. To all appearances, a wandering monk; a beggar even. Freshly emerged from some time in the wilds. Wandering who knows where? Doing who knows what? He even had a begging bowl. That tells you something. His hulking demeanor, his one-word answers to everything. Replies issued more in the form of rumbling grunts. And those frightening eyes; well, maybe not frightening to me, but everyone else cowered. I found their sparkle, and their threat enchanting. The court ladies still whisper about them today.

"Seeing Liu's hesitation, Zhuge Liang stressed, 'Lord Liu, please take my word for this. We will benefit from the likes of Colonel Sun and what he can deliver to our immediate needs.'

"As you know Sying Hao, it was a very dark period for us. Liu Bei had to evaluate this development carefully. He stepped down from his throne, and in a gesture seldom extended to others, put his arm around Sun and guided him to the courtyard where they spoke in seclusion.

"On their return, Liu proclaimed Sun to be an independent agent, serving at leisure. Recognizing his prior experience and honoring the strong endorsement of Zhuge Liang, Lord Liu pronounced Sun would bear the field commission of Colonel with all accompanying privileges. He would also be a member of the command staff as advisor, acting under Zhuge Liang's personal guarantee of integrity. And that was that!

"Understandably, I and the ever-skeptical Zhang Fei thought to bend the ear of our elder brother Liu. If only to find what had prompted the final decision. This fell ultimately to me, who pressed Brother Liu on what they discussed in the courtyard.

"Liu recalled how they hadn't discussed a great deal. 'The fellow truly had little to say.' Liu asked what precipitated his coming to serve our cause. Sun responded, 'I don't know precisely what your cause is. I heard my old friend Zhuge Liang wandered into this neighborhood and figured I'd drop in on him for once. Perhaps return one of the many surprises he had previously sprung on me. As to causes, they're all the same to me. Someone has some ideas, thinks they're better than the ideas of others, then tries to ram them down everyone's throats. Always a very messy business.'

"Liu Bei appreciated the stranger's candor and said so. At first, Sun didn't know how to take it. He knew from oft repeated experience. When he spoke candidly, it wasn't long afterward when someone came looking for his head. At least in this regard, Liu Bei seemed different; if only for the moment. For Sun, no matter. He anticipated all possibilities, always ready to act.

"Liu then solicited my thoughts on something peculiar, 'But what do you make of this, Brother Guan? I shared with him the substance of our Peach Garden Oath. Our commitment to restore Han. And to serve the weak, the troubled and the threatened. No ambitions but to blanket the land, west to east, with peace, prosperity, and contentment.'

"I answered, 'Yes, our Oath, enforced by our sworn fraternity. How did he respond to that?'

"Well, he looked me hard in the eyes. I must say brother Guan. I fear no man. But this is no ordinary man. I studied those two yellow tinted pools set deep beneath his brow, and for a moment felt I had fallen into a timeless torrent. Same as I felt when first caught on the frozen mountain. I sensed a great well of experience riding the dragon wings of a broad spanning history. I found no discernible end point. Yet, no happiness, no contentment. Only uncertainty. But also hope, it was the hope I saw within him which caught my attention. I knew then we would find our common ground."

"Did he have anything further to say about our Oath? About anything else?"

"Yes, he said the Oath was commendable. He had heard others much like it in the past. Then he laughed and said to me, 'Look about you. See where it's led.'

"Then he told how he had once fought alongside the Western Han, begging his leave to move on only when they finally achieved some degree of stability."

"The Western Han? Why that was four hundred years ago!"

"Liu Bei hesitated, then added, 'Yes, I thought he was joking also, and said as much to him. He replied he never joked with truth. I begged to learn of his exploits. It quickly became clear from the plethora of details and litany of recounted events that whether true or not, Sun had intimate knowledge of those campaigns and the tactics which prevailed. I proceeded to test him with details of battle routes already known to myself, but not to others. He knew of opportunities and pitfalls which even I had failed to discern, but which on close study of his account, revealed only the flaws in my own thinking, paling against the soundness of his assessment. Seriously Brother Guan, he reminded me of you!'

"I pondered, then answered, 'Well, that certainly argues he deserves a look at, especially if accompanied with the endorsement of Zhuge Liang.'"

"Yes, I thought so too. No need to belabor his secrets. We all have them. Places within, where outsiders, for whatever reason, may never go. Counselor Zhuge Liang has never erred in his assessment of others. Still, it wasn't clear what Sun intended, or wished of us. Rather than prolong the session and impose further on his good will, I told him I remained yet uncertain as to whether our inclinations or goals were compatible. I assured we would not detain him if he chose to move on, and as courtesy to a welcomed guest would see he had supplies and provisions should he decide to seek destiny elsewhere. I closed with a suggestion he remain with us a bit. A test, if you will, of whether our feeble efforts aligned with what he aspired to for himself."

"Yes, an exceptionally good proposition. What did he say?"

"He said that would be acceptable."

A Chip off the Primordial Block

Guan looked at Sying Hao, "So nephew, we had a riddle in our midst. I quickly grew to respect the man, particularly once I witnessed what he brought to the battlefield as fate soon placed our survival into his very hands. Suffice it to say, he could be relied upon.

"Still, the riddle of his past itched and burned. I lost sleep over it; and you already know how battle-weary bones crave sleep. The more I tried to ignore it or let it rest, the more troublesome it became. Eventually I knew of only one person who could set these irksome thoughts to peace. Zhuge Liang.

"In the end, I took it right to the man. I asked if he trusted me, he responded 'With my life.'

"'Then would you please grace me with more insight into Colonel Sun?' He answered, 'What would you like to learn?'

"That smart-ass. He knew I'd have no idea where to start. Honestly Sying Hao, it would have been easier for me to read answers in tea leaves or to ponder the Book of Changes. Still determined, I told Zhuge Liang I'd still be standing there tomorrow, if he could not help me that day.

"Zhuge laughed politely. I'd be first to vouch the Sage always keeps a good humor about himself, though he harbors closely in reserve. He told me, 'Guan, we are faithful friends and brothers in a destiny bound like no others. That is also the case for me and Colonel Sun. So, I will tell you this …'"

A tint of weighted gravity arced and pulled at the war lord's grim visage when he continued, "First thing he tells me is Sun Wu Kong was something other than a man. Of course, that gave no cleaner footing than before, and I emphatically said so. Of one thing you can be certain. Colonel Sun was indeed other than a man. He was ten, a hundred men; and more! That's what I shouted in response. 'Please tell me something I didn't already know!' I demanded. Zhuge, with a hint of impatience, raised his hand, basically signaling me to pipe down and let him continue. Well assuredly I did. Nephew, you know how it sometimes is with me.

"He explained how Sun had come from an earlier time, an ancient time," Guan recounted, looking at Sying Hao. "Zhuge continued, relating how Sun had appeared and departed at many points and intervals in the history and changes of our people, and even of many others who came before us.

"Of course, I argued that could not possibly be. Sun was not an immortal. Why as brothers in arms, even I'd seen him cut and bleeding. More than once mind you. That of course made the wizard laugh even harder, then apologizing for his impertinence.

"Zhuge Liang resumed, recalling for my benefit how at times he and I had come upon great footprints, mammoth tusks, and even the occasional, but inexplicable icy carcass of some incomprehensible beast. Bound forever in some remote and forgotten frozen grave. From within its crystal chamber, it looked up at our inquisitive eyes, as we stared down in disbelief.

"At least I did, from the warm blooded above. Zhuge told of how there were many things of which we had little awareness; but were present, nonetheless. Then he looked seriously to me and stressed, 'We should always be on guard against those forces which, though not discernible to our first inspection, were there regardless, and quite able to deflower our lives and destinies. Just as they had done to others before us.'

"He said that for a reason. He wanted me … us to know something. That's why I'm taking care you hear from my own lips, exactly what he said to me.

"He continued, telling how, much like the mystery beasts, Sun came from an age preceding our own. The minister confessed he wasn't entirely sure of anything since he preferred not to trouble Sun with meddlesome questions. In fact, he was very respectful of their relationship. And that necessitated restraint and the civility of some distance, if only to credit the weight of Sun's history. However he did explain that just when humankind began to manifest in this present form, there were others; similar, but not the same. Just as with us, there were kings, wizards, warriors, and the plenitude of others who simply went about their business and enjoyed life. At least to the extent circumstances permitted.

"Zhuge never said this directly, though I knew it always to be on the tip of his tongue. Folks as we know them are prone to propagating great mischief and nonsense. And with that, there is seemingly no end of associated grief. It was not the same with those others. He told how in the beginning, they roamed untamed and free, seemingly in alignment with their essential natures, and forever in the moment. They lived happily, arguably lacking for only one thing. Society as we know it. Hardly a problem by my reckoning; others might disagree. Zhuge felt their needs and characters reflected their world, not ours. He said we were obliged to respect that. So be it.

"Zhuge explained how that resolved in time when one of them emerged as a supremely gifted leader, and in less than a generation a prosperous kingdom grew from nothing. Wouldn't you know, it replicated itself repeatedly, first here, then there, until a formidable empire emerged out of their combined efforts. Serendipity. Almost unintended; but there, nonetheless. These creatures, for want of a better word, were in many ways superior to what we find in ourselves. They were more intelligent, and had no inherent inclination toward greed, power, selfishness, dishonesty, self-promotion, or imposing themselves onto others. Their king had very little to do, except what every king should learn to do. He kept out of everyone's way, tending only to the Tao, or whatever it was called before Laozi was born, and trusted his subjects to oversee their own affairs.

"He was our Sun Wu Kong of course, and as Zhuge Liang explained, Sun was very special, even among those creatures with whom he shared in part a common heritage. He differed from them, just as from us, and that brings us to the strangest anomaly of them all.

"You know well the metaphysics of Wu Chi, and how from the void and the ascent of consciousness emerge the Taiji, the Yin and the Yang. Then, once they begin their dance, the two become the four, then the eight, the sixteen, the thirty-two and sixty-four. Until arriving to where all which we think of as real explodes into existence right before our eyes, as real as our noses.

"Zhuge Liang suggested I take a moment to think of Wu Chi; and what marrow lies within. Rather than the emptiness we know it to be, and from which all originates;

what if instead, it were a shoe, a banana, or some other tangible object? I laughed, saying I preferred to think of it as smoked duck; figuring my visualization of 'nothing' could at least promise a tasty morsel. The minister, not knowing how to take my jest, testily responded we should try to stay with his conceptualization, adding I could do without the added nourishment. Fine with me. I protested of course. You and I both know that as soon as you think of Wu Chi as something else, why it's not Wu Chi anymore, it's something else.

"Zhuge chastised, 'Relax Brother Guan, walk with me a bit further on this.' Then, amazingly, he suggested a stone! Maybe even one we could hold in our hand if you believe it. This insignificant shard of nothingness simply existed unto itself, when suddenly it exploded, and from its minuscule core came the many worlds and manifestations; multiplying as we know them to have done, and as so convincingly articulated in the Tao de Ching.

"I followed every step of his metaphor, without issue. Until Zhuge proposed something to me that I struggled with then and do so even to this day. He said the stone had a complete awareness of its own. What we perceived as material manifestation in what surrounds us, call it our universe if you wish, was nothing less than an extension of this consciousness. Sying Hao, you're well aware. That guy Zhuge Liang can tie anything into conjectural knots. Here's what he said next, take it as you wish. This stone, which we now know as Wu Chi, became our manifest world. But there's a catch. After the explosion, a piece of the stone remained, a counterpoint akin to the 'eye' in Yang or the wee freckle in Yin. Here on one side, is everything we know. There, its counterweight. A little speck, barely visible; but in the realm of reality, there for a reason. Ballast? Almost as if its not being there violated the fundamental dictate of change and Dharma; where once here, everything constitutes with the seed of its complementary aspect. If that were not the case, all would become a dream, evaporate to nothing, then dissolve into emptiness, ending again as a rock."

"And what might the significance of that lingering sliver be?" asked Sying Hao.

"I don't know; but I do know this."

"What?"

"If you can believe Zhuge Liang, that speck became Sun Wu Kong. A timeless spirit coursing the stream of history. A reflection of the great void onto itself. Bearing witness and participating in all which the great consciousness manifested in its enduring cosmic dance."

A stunned Sying Hao answered, "You're saying he's immortal!"

Guan slapped his knee for emphasis, adding, "and that's exactly what I said to Zhuge Liang!"

"Then what?"

"Why he said nothing, he never denied it, never disputed. Just stood in front of me like a statue. When the ice finally melted, he looked to me, 'Anything else General Guan?'"

Zhuge Tells of the Monkey King

Guan continues recounting for Sying Hao all he learned from the wizard regarding the mystery of Colonel Sun.

"Staring directly into his face, I nearly screamed to Zhuge, 'Anything else? For the first time in my life, I'm knocked out of my saddle, and you're looking at me like we've wasted enough time on the matter. *No way*, thought I, *let's joust!'*

"'Why yes minister, just a few incidentals if you'll humor me. Is he truly immortal? Is he a god? Can he be killed? Where are the others like him? Was he not someone's king? Where are his subjects? What powers does he possess? What does he gain by serving us? Does he sleep? Why is he here?

"Finally, he started talking sense:

'Of course Brother Guan, those are things you should know. However, what I say as to the points of your questions will be little more than poorly informed notions. You'll have to weigh what you hear today and take from it what you will.

Sun Wu Kong stands unique among all life forms. He birthed directly from Wu Chi into common awareness. He is not a god. Gods are part of what followed in the spiraling evolution of the many. He may be an immortal, but only in the sense he has not yet succumbed. He can be speared, spiked, shot by arrow, or felled by the poisonous bite of an insect or viper. In that regard, he's no different than you or I. It

speaks remarkably to his vast array of skills, senses
and inclinations that he has survived thus far. But you
have seen him in action. Openings cannot be easily
had. As to the others like him I can only relate what
I've managed to put together. Bits and pieces gleaned
from Brother Sun those few times we spoke of it.
Even among his own, he was unique, though in
appearance and demeanor he looked to be one of
them. Being a direct manifestation of Wu Chi, and
respecting its timeless dimension, he too evolved and
perfected those things within himself which made
him most special. There is, of course, his amazing
strength. Then his mastery of the transformations,
seemingly able to disappear into any background,
then erupt from nothing right before unsuspecting
eyes. Yet again, his remarkable connection to the
elements, and to the animals, they seem to unite with
him. Not at all like today's towering aristocrats,
thinking all subject to their inflated sense of domain.
He stands with innocent creatures as one, perhaps
having been one himself. And they respond to his call
when issued, as though all of nature were his lute. In
fact, a good deal of what I learned on these very
things came under Sun's tutelage.'
"Stunned for once, I questioned 'Truly?'"

'Yes, it is so, and hopefully I taught him a thing or
two to reciprocate his courtesy. But this takes us back
to the great change, and how it is he is here; but the
others like him are not.

As it was, his people flourished, and their empire
grew seemingly without bound. Sun knew and spoke
to me of the gods and the heavenly emperor and his
hordes. How they too staked claims on the myriad

manifestations of Wu Chi, which they felt had become their exclusive lot, subject to their whims. They demanded subservience and loyalty, under the guise of friendship and mutual support. Then they required Sun agree to what would have been hostage domicile in their domain, presumably to keep a closer eye and tighter rein on him.

Frankly, he spooked them. Until Sun entered their sights, they supposed only they had been here forever. Now, before their faces, a creature whose span of awareness went far beyond anything they had ever experienced or imagined. It's true you know. When you think of yourself as the center of the universe, you tend to feel pretty important, and can easily fall into the trap of imagining you were there at the beginning. Even if you weren't. Moreover, when the gods sent their legions to test their will against his, the immortals and their stooges always came out on the short end. Why … to their dismay … he even seemed to be playing with them, stealing their thunder and blanketing it in buffoonery!'

"'Good man,' I said, 'Why hurt your opponent if you can deliver a life enhancing lesson instead? A little humor never hurt anyone. I commend him on this but would expect nothing less of him!'

"I tell you Sying Hao, on that point, the gods will take issue. Tweak their noses and see how nasty they become. They soon had their fill of him. Particularly when he began to opine how the heavens would be much happier and content if someone like him were emperor and had the good sense to forgo meddling. Was he joking? Threatening? Mark these words … it's true what some say. The gods are much like us in their whims, fancies, ambitions, fears and lusts for power. I would venture one could plausibly argue they come of us, rather than we of them. How else can anyone explain it? They clearly bore no relationship to Sun or his kind. Their abysmal conduct made it seem as though the original thread had gone awry.

"As Zhuge further explained to me:

'They couldn't kill him, and they couldn't manage him. Uncomfortable with him around they did what any cluster of self-serving entities would do. They returned him to his domain where he presided over his own kind as if nothing had ever happened. *Ignore the whole lot of them. Out of sight, out of mind?*

'Predictably, that didn't end it. Sun's empire continued to flourish and grow. For those in the heavens, concerns mounted. They couldn't let it go. Perhaps foolishly, perhaps not; they dreaded Sun's kind would someday set sights on heaven itself. They presumed Sun and his subjects were of like yearnings to the gods, which of course they weren't, but it didn't matter. Fear and self-interest create their own realities. Those with tainted hearts think the hearts of others to be even more tainted. It has little to do with what really is. The ill intent you see in others more often reflects the worst in you. Gods, more than any other beings, crave survival and will resort to any deception necessary to preserve it.'

Guan explained to Sying Hao, "According to the wizard, Sun didn't see it at first. You might say it was so insidious as to pass beyond notice. Like Sun, the gods had gifts and talents of their own. Among them, the ability to manifest havoc. Not like Yama the destroyer, though he was certainly one of them. But Yama was always obvious and open about his doings—an honest demon.

"Think of them like someone sabotaging a large boat. To escape all suspicion, gods respond to prayers and supplications for blessings by seeming to protect, allowing the vessel to sidestep all overt threats. But beneath the surface, a little nudge here, a slight tug there. Soon enough, the ill-fated craft bumps upon unseen shoals, made helpless and doomed. Prayers be damned. Tragically, this particular vessel turned out to be their world. Everyone's world. The flagship. A living piece of the rock itself, upon which all were meant to sail effortlessly through the void.

"Then making matters even worse, the gods dispatched their sinister minions to the surface. The changes barely perceptible, if you weren't specifically looking for them, you'd at first see nothing. Unnoticed flickers of the rudder, a shake here, a vibration there. Before anyone had an inkling, the great ship came undone. First the rains, then the floods, followed by endless eruptions, toxic winds and darkness. Jungle expanses turned to beds of dust. All capped by interminable sun and the withering disappearance of edibles and food sources. Species diminished, as did entire echelons of beings. Many whose kind had shared eons with Sun Wu Kung. Unchanging and eternal, his ageless eye witnessed the eventual diminishment of his own kind and their slow but certain mutation into something entirely different. Emerging as cloned images of the very gods whose trickery and deceit sought to derail Wu Chi's yielding of itself into paradise freely given. The empire dissolved, the kingdoms crumbled, those who remained looked first to their own survival. Society meant little when food, comfort and safety could no longer be had. Even the land soured, its sweet aroma gone. All fruits turned bitter.

"Zhuge explained to me how what emerged became humankind as we know them. When the scale finally tipped away from Sun's people to those who followed, Sun, the once Emperor, became an outcast. Humankind bore the look, stamp and proclivities of the gods and seemed imbued with their fear, anxiety, and mistrust of this strange being who simply wished to be above and apart from it all. The gods tugged further at their vapory threads and doggedly unfolded their plan to its intended end. A process of meticulously fine tuning the changes, and locking them in. They had but one major unanticipated disappointment.

"Sun Wu Kong remained, unchanged and aware of all, a constant reminder of what they sought to forget. They had counted on his demise. With no other choice, they brought their full game to him. Whatever they put in his path, he withstood. When they poisoned the air, he disappeared beneath the earth. When they sent plagues, he mastered the herbs and plants. When they sent ferocious beasts, he spoke to them and won their loyalty. It would seem Wu Chi, the mindless void, had the last laugh. Leaving no doubt, the fullness of folly and its arrogant outreach held little sway against Sun Wu Kong, the embodiment of nothingness. You think you have him, but you don't.

"Sying Hao, I've often said what doesn't kill you, leaves you stronger. It's a fact lad. Nowhere truer than in the case of Sun Wu Kong.

"Sun eventually put it together and understood. A poison seed. Bastard children of the gods would supplant his kind. They spread like a contagion until the new displaced the old. The scale finally tilted full, giving way to the uncertain future and the finalization of their intended change. When that moment arrived, seemingly only Sun remained of the originals. He was there when the last of his own kind passed, an incredibly old woman. Her final words to Sun were, 'Live in peace, Lord Sun; let your example be your seal.' A final directive for him from all who came before.

"And from there, he walked the earth. Alone and searching, perhaps hoping to find another. Who really knows?

"Though initially an outcast, repulsive to the ever-multiplying god reflections, some eventually warmed to the bestial wanderer. Inspired and taken by his accounts of bygone days, a time free of fear, overreach, and loss, which by then were becoming the lot of their own earthly existence. At first, Sun avoided them, repulsed by the 'vile' traits inherent in their god sourced alchemy. In time, however, even he took note of their suffering. Grudgingly, he admired how the weakest and most downtrodden still looked hopefully to the next day, always anticipating an end to suffering and a change for the better. Sun thought they deserved credit for managing even that, given their pitiful existences. He let go of his reticence and ventured through their communities, acting overtly to protect the weak; then saw fit to share the healing arts, and what he knew of cultivation and agriculture. In turn, they were touched by his compassion, and even his playfulness, though clearly, he tendered few words and favored solitude. Preferring to manifest by living example whatever it was he had to say. To them, this seemed very real and true.

"Many generations passed after the great upheaval. Stories grew among the people telling of a great and munificent creature who by then had touched all corners of the land and even regions beyond. New kingdoms grew and tired ones receded, empires came and went, and always, reports of the fabled monkey-like immortal weaved through the tapestry of human history. The creature seemingly showed himself where and when his presence mattered, then disappeared just as suddenly, once his contribution had finished.

"But his shadow lingered, particularly in the form of stories which bounded from the memories of those he had served. As is the case even today, the stories and lore far outnumber what history has trimmed and provided to any formal record. Suffice it to say, by the time of Han, the legendary exploits of 'The Monkey King' were already part of the culture, with plays and operas regularly found in every village and marketplace.

"Of course, no one mistook the fearsome Sun with the now universally propagated, and admired Monkey King. Zhuge Liang affirmed how we alone stand fortunate knowing in fact, they are indeed one and the same, which of course will remain our little secret. Brother Sun has enough to occupy his mind. Those who embraced the legend would be rapt in wonder, realizing the reality of Sun's adventures had been far more noteworthy; and at more considerable sacrifice."

Merely Centered in the Moment

Concluding his account of Sun's story, Guan continued, "As Sun's reputation among humans grew, the gods became further incensed. Witnessing their own progeny enamored by the one they feared and despised complicated matters. Sun may not have understood why the gods were what they were or did what they did. Nor could he fathom why they did what they did when they did it. He wanted to avenge what happened to his kind, if only to balance the ledger and prevent a repeat. Unfortunately, gods were gods. Immortality shielded their daftness from even the most determined inquisitors. They threw countless trials at Sun, each of which he met. From what Zhuge told me, I understood those trials brought him new awarenesses; and opened channels into the otherwise unfathomable energies enveloping our reality. Inadvertently, the gods had made him stronger.

"Zhuge tried explaining all of this to me. I'm not even sure I understood, but for your benefit, Sying Hao, I'll repeat what I remember of his words …

'Sun's thoughts always flowed like water. But now they seemed to escape the bounds of time quickening into a raging torrent. At a glance, he could take full measure and account of any situation. No matter how complex or faceted; he found the essence.

You may already sense this Lord Guan, but others don't. The gods do not see the future—no more than the mules. I concede they have a clear view to the here and now. But their untoward idiosyncrasies forever dull them to the moment. Hence, they know only what they choose to see. Always the circle, never the sphere. Sun Wu Kong possessed an eternity of experience. His never wavering from direct involvement or commitment had disciplined his lightening eyes to see all possible endpoints of all contemplated actions. This, combined with the thundering engine of his unfettered mind, gave him purviews of time and outcomes no other human, wizard or god could lay claim to.

That proved to be their vulnerability. Ever scheming and plotting, gods deluded only themselves, never him. Knowing this, Sun conceived a meticulous trap. He surgically inserted his unique gifts in service of each one's plotting against the other, recommending actions and predicting outcomes with uncanny accuracy. In less than a millennium, the gods became so entangled in selfish machinations, the balance of creation flourished without their interference. Down below, a golden age unfolded for humans, and they advanced admirably, all thanks to Sun's intricate game. From the shadows, he surveyed their growth, not without appreciation; sometimes even thinking the poor misfits had a chance.

The Celestial King, however, saw through his charade and was not fooled by the skillfully executed sleight of hand. He summoned, actually asked quite contritely, if Sun might favor him with a visit. Perhaps re-establish connections, let bygones be bygones. "You're one of us Sun Wu Kong. Better for you to be here than continue wasting your time among them."

You see Lord Guan; gods prefer to distance themselves from lesser beings. From their point of view, this meant mortals. Before, it meant Sun's kind; but now included the humans and their rapidly multiplying progeny, whose unanticipated evolution had begun to draw renewed concern. Though humans were created in the gods' own image and stamped with their traits; the gods had no more attachment to them than to Sun's kind. A problem they thought already solved had again raised its prickly head. The growing sophistication of humans threatened them. Having witnessed it before, they understood the power and impetus of evolution. Watching it unfold and accelerate brought them great fear and trepidation. Where might it lead or end? Why couldn't they do it? Never evolving, frozen always in their godly habitus. One thing for sure ... they certainly weren't interested in the prospect of new gods crowding their universe, their domain.

Sun had become the supreme eternal constant, and this concerned them immensely. He was always there, inscrutably going about whatever it was he did, continuously grinding at their all too sensitive nerves.

As to the meeting with the Celestial King, Sun agreed enthusiastically.'

"A bad choice," Sying Hao muttered.

... asking when the heavenly King would next come to the surface.'

Guan blurted admiringly, "Ahhh, now that's my buddy Sun. Setting the forum to suit his needs. He knows, or suspects something."

'Sun made an important discovery observing what transpired over the ages. Initially unnoticed, so subtle as to be invisible—a chink in their armor. Who would have suspected?

The celestials rarely came to the surface, and even more rarely did they have direct contact with the surface entities. Sun always figured they didn't want to get their hands bloodied or soiled. In their stead they used spies, agents, allies, servants, saboteurs, spells, curses, plagues, famines, drought, flood and pestilence. During the devolution of his kind, Sun had witnessed it all; but never had he seen one of the gods directly stirring the change. If he had, he would have acted. Considering what he was up against, he confronted a puzzling dilemma. Why would these seemingly all-powerful beings deliver such nonsense? *Why destroy everything if I am what you wish gone? Why haven't they come directly for me?* At first, the answer eluded. Why had they not? What characteristic of the surface world concerned them? Granted, Sun Wu Kong could fight them to a stalemate. But he couldn't kill them, and without that possibility, their avoidance of the surface made no sense.

Though the reason lay clouded and tucked carefully away from less inquisitive minds, in the end it did not escape the probing eyes of Sun Wu Kong. The answer lay revealed in his contemplation of an entire history of contacts or absence of contacts with the celestials. They feared him! And this fear could only root in a single fundamental reality, which he now understood completely.

When a god, otherwise immortal, came to the surface, he or she became vulnerable—same as Sun Wu Kong. They could bleed! They could die! Who would have thought? Over the mortals, they were still gods, in the sense their powers remained daunting against the common and ordinary. But, unlike Sun Wu Kong, the god who trespassed upon earth did not have an eternity of evolved survival skills trailing in his or her wake to assure safety and continuance when exposed. In contrast to Sun Wu Kong, gods had become inbred, lazy, and two dimensional. Actual fighting? They left such to others more capable. By default, they steered clear and away.

But for what they had done, and become, he might almost have pitied them. For sure they had their heaven, and they had all those powers we associate with their kind. But they also had cabin fever on a divine scale. They knew each other inside and out and no longer seemed to like what they saw. Only the mortals, and that infernal Sun, seemed to be having any fun. That really pissed them off!

For the Celestial King, the situation became untenable. Heaven had become engulfed in endless bickering and mayhem; and the monkey-man had snubbed him. He demanded Sun Wu Kong accede. Sun demurred. Then Sun said something that planted fear and anxiety enduringly into the hearts of all the celestials. They knew of his awareness into outcomes but had no understanding of its scope, or its limitations. Sun counted on this when he told them, 'I have calculated when life will conclude for each one of you, and can promise your futures stand on not so nearly certain a footing as you once supposed. A time will come when you seek this insight, and nowhere else will you find it when you need it. To leave me be is your only hope.

Was he bluffing? Celestials wanted no part of death. Simply beneath them, undignified. So of course, Sun captured their attention. Yama, though one of them, didn't help the matter of their concerns confirming they would all be welcomed warmly into his underworld pit.

Among humans, stories of the Monkey King continued to abound, and legends grew regarding his Dragon Bow, which could hurl arrows from one horizon to the next. Then there was his golden ringed staff, which floated like a feather in his hands, but landed like a mountain on the head of anyone who chose to oppose or threaten him. You see Lord Guan; Sun had mastered nature's alchemy. Just as he connected to the creatures, he connected to the elements and the myriad changes which manifest. He learned their secrets, and his endless experiments and improvisations ultimately yielded results far surpassing the ordinary. The Dragon Bow arose singular, a weapon with no peers, seemingly possessing a consciousness of its own, responding only to an untarnished heart.'

"Yes, the Dragon Bow. Appropriately named. Truthfully, in the heat of battle, I'd prefer to have Sun and his bow over a celestial dragon, and that's a fact."

'As would I, Lord Guan.'

"And what of the Golden Ringed Staff?"

'Well, the legends are exaggerations. It cannot grow or shrink, and it does not rest as a pin hidden away in his abundant hair. It certainly is unique, though, and possibly the equal of the Dragon Bow.'

"No, the bow is peerless. I speak from direct experience."

'Perhaps, but the staff serves only Sun; no other man or god has been able to wield it with the apparent ease and overwhelming effect of Sun Wu Kong.'

Lord Guan reminisced "I remember. One day we worked staff together, trading ideas and tactics. I asked if I might try his weapon. He hesitated at first, then responded, 'Of course' handing it to me. He handed it to me with one hand. I accepted with one. When he let go his grip on the other end, it felt as though a bridge were collapsing. Trying to recover, I turned side to front and caught the front half with my free hand, expecting to stabilize it. I felt like a turtle trying to bear the weight of creation and could scarcely move. Even as I struggled with the thing, I could see my feet starting to sink into the earth. These were things beyond my comprehension. I looked helplessly to Colonel Sun, whose eyes left no doubt he recognized my predicament. He stepped forward, asked, 'May I?' I responded, 'Please!' and he lifted it with one hand from my now quaking arms.

"I told him his Golden Ringed Staff might even surpass my Green Dragon Blade. He told me the staff carried the weight of his sorrow, then he made sure to show me an inscription circling the middle of the weapon. It read, 'Golden Ringed Staff, bane of the immortals.'

"On my telling this to Zhuge, the wizard reflected, 'It said that did it? Well, it looks like old Sun has more than one trick up his sleeve should the immortals ever again cross him.'

"Stunned by his words, I asked the wizard, 'You're not saying the staff has power over the immortals?'"

'Whether it does or doesn't, only Sun knows for certain. The immortals will be wary, and that, in itself, will give him a wide berth. I suppose that would be enough for him.'

"But how is it I could barely lift the staff from the ground? More baffling, how is it that when Colonel Sun said it would be light in my hands, it became light in my hands. Why, he even let me practice with it on occasion. A fine weapon it truly is; though I still prefer my Green Dragon Blade, if only because of our long acquaintance."

'He let you take it from him, did he?'

"Of course, we share like natures; chipped from the same stone if you will. If he can't trust me, who is there for him? I mean no offense; your relationship with him goes without saying."

'Understood Brother Guan and spoken well. The answer is simple. Recognizing your righteous and loyal essence, the staff befriended you.'

"Are such things possible?"

'Lord Guan, you now know what I know. As to what might be possible, you and Sun define that for all of us, with everything you do, and represent.'

"Who else knows of these things?"

'You and I; and Colonel Sun; and the immortals.'

"What about the boy (meaning Sying Hao)?"

'When the time is right Lord Guan, you have my permission to tell him. You may decide the moment.'

The war god then turned his eyes to Sying Hao. "There you have it. I can only add this. After leaving Zhuge Liang, I sought out Colonel Sun. As usual, I found him alone on the high ground, surveying the field below. I walked right to him, and before he could say a thing, I dropped to one knee and bowed my head in deference. 'Colonel Sun, of all who live, only you are my hero.' I then stood, looked him hard in the eye, turned about, and left him to his solitude.

"From that day, he knew that I knew."

Sying Hao studied Guan closely, "Did you ever learn anything more about Sun?"

Shaking his head, Guan replied, "I didn't need to know more, I filled in the details from my own life experiences, and respected Brother Sun's privacy and solitude, knowing there were sound reasons for this. Perhaps, but for you, young nephew, he might have returned to stone. Still, we do have yet another wrinkle in this account."

"What could that be?"

"Well, once Zhuge Liang satisfied my curiosity regarding Sun, I still had that itch. The Minister looked at me standing and staring at his front but not speaking. Finally, he asked, 'What else Lord Guan?'

"For once, I hesitated. I could see he sensed what I wished to ask. His body relaxed back, and his head arced, much as the tiger does when encountering a threat. Finally, I got it out. 'Brother Zhuge, are you an immortal?'

"Had he simply answered yes, everything would have made sense."

"Well, what did he say?"

"He responded that he was not. As soon as he answered, all began to unravel. How could anyone know and do what Zhuge Liang did and not be an immortal. There could be no other explanation. Even to this day, no one knows anything definitive regarding his past, except that King Liu brought him back from some frozen expanse, where he is rumored to have been communicating with the gods and other entities of which he never speaks. Why I've even heard stories of how he encountered beings not unlike our own Sun, roaming the desolate and frozen wastelands. Making their home where no man could follow and expect to survive. The story goes it was by earning their trust he eventually encountered Sun Wu Kong and they became fast friends, and more importantly, allies.

"So, you can see nephew, my question to Zhuge Liang followed naturally in the footsteps of what he had shared regarding Sun."

"Yes, quite true, I can see you wondered about the extent of their history and their shared experiences. But more importantly, if both were immortals, their view of time, likelihoods, and consequences might help those of lesser purviews gain needed confidence in the expected outcomes of their present endeavors. Matters always clouded in the uncertain fog pervading the present."

"Exactly! Nephew, you are good! Another Zhuge Liang in the making! It's as if you picked the fruit right from my thoughts.

"So when I asked him if he too were an immortal; he answered, 'No Lord Guan, I'm merely centered in the moment.'

"Stunned by his words, I paused to reflect as they rooted in my consciousness. At first nothing, then doors began opening everywhere. And no sooner did they open than the frames dissolved along with their associated architectures and dimensions, taking with them the past and the future, stealing the relevance from time itself.

"I looked to Zhuge Liang and presented the only thought which remained, in the form of yet another question.

"Immortal? Centered in the moment? Brother Zhuge help me! Is there a difference?

"To which he answered, 'Not really, just a matter of how one becomes subject to the illusion and whims of time.' I pondered his words for quite a while, then replied.

"Time, I never think of it. Not like others. I suppose I'm centered in the moment too."

'Yes Lord Guan, I suppose that also.'

"Now nephew Sying Hao, I'm not sure I can explain why, but having Zhuge Liang say that of me felt like all of creation had turned and validated my meager existence to that point."

"I turned back to Zhuge, asking 'Immortality isn't that big a deal then, is it?'"

'No Guan,' he said, 'It's like a cage.'

"Then shouldn't we pity our Sun?"

'No.'

"Why not?"

'Because he's centered in the moment also.'

"Ahhh, then we are brothers!"

'Yes, all three of us.'

One Becomes Two

Sun Wu Kong believed in hope. "Hope commands creation to go forward. No telling what will happen without it." With Zhuge's death, Sying Hao knew things had changed. The months following were painful for the young officer to behold. Looking more like a worn and tired old man, Sun frequently turned dejectedly to his protege, muttering "Zhuge Liang is gone," as if reminding himself the universe which had been one way when the wizard lived, had become something entirely different. When going together about their duties, Sun often stopped. Then, as though asking only himself, whispered, "Where will we find hope now?"

Sying Hao did not possess Sun's time spanning gaze. Nor was he privy to Sun's hard earned awarenesses into the ways of the world, humankind, wizards, mystics and celestials. Sun's eternal gaze took full measure and study of all which preceded, culminating in the present. All lay there within him — an empty mirror reflecting an eternity of direct encounters. Above all other sentient beings, he recognized the significance of Zhuge Liang's role — a solitary fulcrum; the point of pivot for the restoration of natural order. With him gone, where could one like Sun look to replenish hope. For so long, relying on his own devices, Sun had failed enough to know it was beyond his solitary efforts. Alone, he was simply lacking. Through time's long stretch, the pattern had devolved into a troubling constant. The celestials scrutinized, studied, and countered his every move, proving ever again they had nothing better to do. They worked ceaselessly to frustrate his protracted efforts to restore what had initially been the Way[39]. While he strove for earthly peace, they delivered conflict and bedlam. But why?

These humans troubled them. Constantly growing, developing, and evolving. Where would it lead? Fearing an uncertain future, the Celestials were determined to stifle any potential threat of competition. Their concerns brewed a potent mix of suspicion, jealousy and fear. Hate perhaps? From within this tumultuous mix, their cruel vindictiveness took shape.

Can't say they were greedy though. That's more of a human trait. They didn't need greed. They figured they already owned everything. Their method? Constant accumulation. Simplicity itself. Amassing little bits here and there over broad spans of time. On the surface world, while others less celestial struggled to survive on little more than crumbs, they'd be set. But up there, things were different. Housed in their celestial domain, gods found the accumulation of wealth, gems, precious metals and artifacts didn't have nearly the same import and effect as it once had for those on the surface.

Down here, we take wealth and its manifestations very seriously. The more one has of it, the more respect one accrues. Even becoming targets of reverence, and other things of course. In the celestial paradise, all of it reduced to becoming simply more "stuff." They possessed immeasurable amounts of it and frequently tripped on the junk. Because it no longer served to differentiate and stratify

---

[39] An oblique reference to what later became immortalized by Laozi in his "Tao de Ching."

celestial status, at least in terms of amassed holdings, in the end, it served no purpose at all, except to distract, clutter and get in the way.

Or to perhaps impress mortals when on those rare occasions, they gained access to the heavens. An understatement perhaps; mortals were more than impressed by it, and very tempted. Make off with some of those captivating trinkets. That's all it would take. With some of that stuff in hand, on returning to the surface a man's destiny would instantly swing positive.

A procurement not so easily accomplished. The celestials, though bored out of their minds with managing their vast collections, couldn't bear to part with any of it. And since they seemed to see and know everything, except perhaps the inscrutable mind of Colonel Sun; making off with a bit of their "stuff" remained nigh impossible.

So, there they were, surrounded by it. Piled so high they could barely penetrate as they moved about. Unable to escape this rut, they spent much of eternity re-inventorying things which brought them no joy, and no utility.

Despite the risks, rumors circulated that on occasion, celestials had ventured onto the surface. With a few handfuls from their treasure troves, they could pose as earthly royals or aristocrats, astounded at what all became available to sate their needs and fantasies. Those clever humans seemed to have no limits as to what they could conjure. Yes, even celestials had fantasies and needs. As surface beings took aim on their bounty, the celestials marveled at and reveled in the unbridled greed and ambition of humans, genuinely appreciating the extremes undertaken to provide them unbounded pleasure in exchange for what the immortals perceived as mere tokens.

A marvelous place, this earth, when one knew how to properly beguile it.

But for the celestials, boundless pleasure and dissipation, like all things else-wise inscribed in broad expanses of time, proved in the end to become tiresome.

Among themselves they wondered, "Why doesn't Sun Wu Kong share our affliction with endless repetition? How does he manage to keep his mind fresh and alive?" You see, Sun Wu Kong walked the earth. They did not. They feared and avoided risks; he welcomed them. In that, they differed. For Sun, the surface world and its limitless gifts, guaranteed one's own prospects to evolve and actualize. How could one fail to do so within this circus of inexhaustible experiences? Many as fresh and new as just ripened fruit, some joyful, some tragic, but always there for the picking. That, after all, was the promise of Ke Li Xi Na; immerse yourself in the experience with a true heart and an impeccable spirit, and you will unite into the unbounded moment, becoming one with your true and limitless nature. The celestials clung to their immortality, leaving them limited and essentially pickled in their own juices. Sun, on the other hand, clung to life in the very act of living it.

Though never openly admitting it, the celestials were indeed bored beyond measure. Infinitely so, if such were possible. How might we think of it? Endless repetition: the same neighbors, the same disputes, the same uninterrupted bliss, the same repeated trysts. Infinite boredom; reducing to infinite purposelessness. All-powerful entities, but moribund, dead and useless in the ether. It's no wonder they took out their frustrations on surface dwellers—first Sun's kind, now these humans. Neither meant piddle to them, beyond their transient value as entertainment and fleeting diversions from the immortals' own plight. In this convoluted sense, their focus on Sun and the mortals served a very considerable purpose. Without them, the celestials would have nothing to do but stare at their hoards and each other for all of time.

Heaven forbid.

That's why they had become toxic. Their very touch soured the planet; and promised ruin, suffering, pestilence, and heartbreak. Even when at first, it appeared in the form of a blessing.

"Better them, than us," or so they reasoned.

Sun had often wondered, coming upon no others, whether he and they were the only ones untouched by time. Perhaps that underscored his profound change after visiting the subcontinent and encountering the Buddhist scriptures—a more recent embodiment of a timeless understanding. He found within them yet another ageless voice, coming from one who had reconciled and reduced the cycle of suffering into the nothingness he demonstrated it to ultimately become. So much for the gods and their gangrenous meddling. Now, there were paths of deliverance. For Sun, a grand awakening.

But as to checking or countering their malevolence, Sun's efforts were simply not enough. On more than one occasion, he had almost given up, contemplating ending it all; something he knew to be within his capacity. He once arrived precisely at that point when luckily, fate delivered an equal, someone who would ultimately tempt him back from the precarious edge.

Zhuge Liang!

It didn't take long after their first meeting for Sun to appreciate how chance and serendipity had deemed to grant the possibility of an ally. A human nonetheless, but one possessed with a far-reaching eye; much like Sun, able to tap into and skim the wisdom of the ages. Once better acquainted, Sun begrudgingly came to appreciate that perhaps in this regard, Zhuge Liang had the advantage. His span of understanding reached to assimilate everything and imbue it with his own sense of purpose. Of such construct and complexity that it looked to match the flow of life itself.

Like Sun, Zhuge Liang did not easily fall prey to distraction. As to ambition, he sought only to be awake, aware, and free. No easy task. So many things within the surround of our existence aim to keep us entranced, distracted, befuddled and bamboozled; and with that, enslaved to the whims of others, or even worse, to our own imposed limitations.

If you don't believe it, ask the celestials; those who like to think they pull and guide our strings. They or their servants are at it all the time.

Can you keep a secret? They're no different than us! They even do it to themselves!

But Zhuge Liang, here was a piece of work. Until fatefully walking down that slope with Liu Bei, there seemed to be no limit to his consciousness. One so gifted with insight into the moment, it seemed at times he knew everything, and could tilt creation on its very axis if he were so inclined. Believe you me, the celestials took notice. Of all beings, only Zhuge Liang could draw their wrathful attention from Sun.

"Who is this guy?" they whispered among themselves.

Sun and Zhuge Liang

We know Sun had witnessed and partaken of earthly paradise only to lose it to the treacherous meddling of the immortals. He then traversed subsequent eons of chaos, laboring ceaselessly to restore order to the troubled world, with no discernible effect. "Fall eight times, rise nine" became his mantra. His resilience baffled the immortals. Their victims usually stayed down once put down. Sun demonstrated fervor beyond the measure of the gods, pushing back and even making progress, prompting them to escalate their efforts. Incessant, infernal, and mindless meddling eventually returned all to chaos, accompanied by renewed harvests of ashes and rotting corpses.

Before Zhuge Liang, there were occasional companions for Sun, but only a few. Understandably, Sun kept to himself by choice and necessity. A simple equation, he outlasted all those he loved, while his pain from their passing lingered seemingly without end. Still, from time to time, a mortal, perhaps a man, sometimes a woman, might somehow push through his wall of induced isolation. Typically, at first, he would resist, considering it another indulgence best avoided. But then, something would draw his attention or catch his fancy. It might be something new he saw in them. A special talent or quality of character perhaps, or maybe a kinship in suffering. Could it be he sometimes just felt overwhelmingly alone? We all do at times. Would it be unfair to say that when isolation weighed too heavily, he reached out in hope to others, seeking completion and the solace of companionship?

Admittedly, the endings never went well, nor did they come without their price. Sun had a great and immortal heart, rooted in loss and sorrow as much as in the lively moment. Because of this, and fully aware of both life and departure, he knew the inherent preciousness of all beings and things. An appreciation of truth far beyond the grasp of the gods. When finally relaxing his guard, he did so with a commitment of love and compassion which ran as deep as the wells of time. Though he couldn't keep these relationships for the distance, and always swore he would not again become invested in a mortal, he loved his companions dearly. Though the pain of loss often tried his capacity to endure and to contain, it did not steal from him the joy of the experience risked and gained. Yet another quality distinguishing him from the celestials.

When each of those granted companions had come to the end of their allotted time, Sun would imagine it as yet another pearl. A new addition to his endless strand of memories. There, deep within, hidden in its entirety and completeness, subject only to his recall.

He never forgot … anything.

So, when some mortal somehow pushed through his reserve, and shared with him the common trail, he reveled in the moment. Together traversing the unabated twists, trials and tests; while deep within he knew the day would come, soon enough, for them to part. Only he could go on.

He had no method for handling this. The greater the love and the more profound the relationship, the harder the parting. Each loss reduced him to helplessness. It would not be an exaggeration to say Sun wandered aimlessly after such passings, sometimes for years. Murmuring the once companion's name over and over with every step taken; sounding like a mantra or perhaps a prayer; its owner seemingly satisfied and prepared for all purposes to continue with only that for the balance of his journey.

You've heard "Time heals all wounds."

"Yes," Sun would say, "It is true; but the healing is difficult and seems to take forever."

So, by choice Sun walked alone, except perhaps for the accidental mortal who managed to penetrate his shell and befriend him. Beloved for a moment, then turned to dust in what, to Sun, would have been little more than the seeming blink of an eye.

Perhaps that best explains his reference to the "moment" as his timeless companion.

But everything changed with Zhuge Liang. Sun did not keep time carefully, but he knew there had been many blinks of his eternal eye. Zhuge Liang was there as it closed, and still there when the eye opened once again. To Sun's immense joy and surprise, his friend had not reduced to a pile of dust.

This at first confounded Lord Sun. First time around, he thought he had lost focus or somehow miscalculated. But then, a second time, and after that, a third. There were no mistakes. With no other possible explanation, Sun began to suspect a second being had been hewn from the timeless rock of his own origin.

He would have been wrong thinking this of course. Zhuge Liang was as mortal as you or I.

Over time, Sun learned much from Zhuge Liang, just as he taught much to him. Each complemented the other, and perhaps even kept the other from madness. As certainly the tainted creation and its incessant chaos, which beleaguered them both, would doubtless have best dealt with them and their incessant meddling.

Instead, they united. Combining their gifts and diligence, they pushed back against the onerous tide. Indeed, they pushed hard, sharing many wondrous adventures. More than once, they descended to the eastern coastlands, the cradle of empires. They would spend a generation or two, always hoping for a return to harmony, and the potential for peace so integral to life's promise.

In their travels, they met and studied with great mystics and philosophers who really seemed to get it, and whose teachings for a time wielded broad influence. Even leaders of state had to recognize such gifted teachers. Naturally, honoring them and placing them on pedestals proved inevitably to be self-serving. It brought their teachings, and their influence in-house, and removed them from the general populace. What went out to the people were only the finely filtered crumbs of now shattered awareness.

It was for that very reason, Sun urged the young guard Yinxi to stall the sage Laozi at the western gate. "You must beg the master to record his teachings. If only to leave a trail of rice droppings for those who might choose to follow."

There was the Han Dynasty of course, and for a while, things looked up. Both partook in various roles, some hidden, some visible, some influential, some not; hoping in some way to keep it viable, and to hold the ever-present demons and patrons of chaos at bay. Sun informed Zhuge of a distant time when those demons and perpetrators of chaos were not there. But the memory had grown thin and distant and painfully hard to recall in all its detail.

Now, it seemed they too had rooted themselves into the eternal moment. As part of the fabric, their combined efforts belayed the end. But they could not stop the inevitable.

Humanity seemed hellbent on milking chaos for personal gain; or if on the wrong end, survival. You'll find few choices but for one or the other. If not for the powerful reaping immense profit and reward from this mix, chaos would be little more than a harmless whiff of foul air.

Together in Time

Eventually Sun figured his friend Zhuge had somehow unlocked the secrets of immortality. For Sun of course, they were not secrets. Immortality was his state of being. It required no study or chicanery. No different than the hair on his arms. Simply a fact of his nature. But for his companion, a different story.

You can see how this has no easy explanation. Let's start by observing and studying what's around us. Note how the manifestations of life come and go. Babies birth, and they do so by bubbling forth into the plane of existence. Fruits, flowers, birds, fish, even the clouds and stars, as well as the rocks and the sand. They bubble forth, manifest, recede, and finally disappear. Like the tides—at first rolling in, then out. Or grapes flourishing robustly, then eventually withering on the vine.

Picture in your mind a silk cloth draped over your arm. Lift your arm, keeping the hand within. Upward to where it's enveloped by the cloth. Form your hand into a relaxed fist. Tighten the silk around it, and the surface above will appear as a new form—perhaps a ball or a rock. Or, by spreading or moving your fingers, it might resemble a tiny, wriggling fetus. Playful imaginations might infer the silky lump had an independent identity, an existence of its own. Perhaps a puppet become real. But it's still really you, as its creator, and your hand. An extension of your underlying self. A manifestation of your consciousness. If you ponder and observe carefully, you'll sense how all which presents to awareness comes into our "outside the cloth world" in much the same way. What does that say of emptiness, and the mystery of fullness implicit within?

Alternatively, picture reality as a cord of indivisible protoplasm with countless strands, running from head to tail spanning all of time. Along these strands are knots and twists, billowing like waves. Imagine if these knots could think; they might forget their essential interconnectedness, seeing only each other and losing sight of the underlying consciousness—the creator. Why you can do it yourself. Take a rope and tie a half knot. Tighten it. Seems real to the feel, doesn't it? Now loosen it and stick your finger in the loop. Run it to the end of the line and it's gone. Only the rope remains, and the consequences of what occurred. Some like to think of those consequences as Karma, but that's a different topic. Besides, it stretches our metaphor beyond the reach of our reason.

For the moment, let us stand with Sun Wu Kong, confronted with Zhuge Liang who has lived far beyond his time, but is decidedly not the rope, nor the protoplasm, nor the hand beneath the silken cover. Nor is he deceased. He is a mortal, but he has somehow learned to defy the great and common singularity of death.

For nearly a hundred years, Sun sat with his friend in the frigid wastelands, spending long evening hours by the fire. That is, when not meandering in joint contemplation and scrutiny of the evening stars, the planets, and the mysterious phenomena which forever unfolded, dancing in counterweight to the affairs of men and immortals. To the surprise of both, Zhuge Liang made a profound discovery. After undertaking careful study of Sun Wu Kong, particularly in regard to heavenly biases and portents, he concluded Sun seemed to exist outside their influences. Appearing almost to be a universe unto himself. He had never elsewhere seen the likes of this; and once told Sun that even the gods fell subject to the persuasions of the heavenly bodies.

It seemed that each of the friends posed a riddle for the other; making each the more grateful for that lucky day when the two walked toward each other from opposite horizons. Practically stumbling on one another in the middle of a frigid field of ancient ice at the remote western rim of creation.

During those exchanges, Sun picked away at Zhuge Liang's insights into the core elements of existence. Together, they tried to assemble the myriad pieces into some explanation which made sense to both.

Pushing for understanding, Sun questioned extensively about the properties of the elements. Not the five classical elements Wood, Fire, Earth, Metal and Water. Those he knew intimately, as he did their underlying metaphysics, and the cycles of generation, opposition, and insult[40]. Broad as the metaphysics of the five elements might be, he knew from his long experience there existed paths of knowledge and insight well outside their scopes of account. This was where he gained most from the exchanges.

At first, he theorized somehow Zhuge had unlocked the secrets of mercury, or of gold or perhaps jade. For eons, the greatest earthly minds looked to these elements for the secrets of immortality. During his travels, Sun made acquaintance with some of them. He encountered many

---

[40] Insult is one of the natural cycles defined in the metaphysics of the five elements. Water for example can extinguish fire, but fire can boil water.

fools. So blinded by selfish and conceited quests, they were deaf to his protests. Foremost of which was, "Why would anyone want to live forever; if they had a choice?" He had even known several emperors who gleefully consumed their silvery cocktails of mercury, satisfied they would become earthly equals to the celestials. Sun recalled how they even welcomed the shedding and peeling of their skins as signs affirming the changes within.

Dead, all. Very prematurely. Their empires forfeit in the end to those who most encouraged the mindless pursuits.

But Zhuge, here was a clever chap. Apart from the five elements, he had mapped out nearly a hundred others. Many of which had their own unique properties and traits, as well as relationships with, and sometimes against other elements, either alone, or in complex combinations. While the metaphysics of the five essential elements remained in tack and continued to provide great insight into the nature of energies, these new elements and their propensities left no doubt how the wheel of Dharma, and life itself was vastly more sophisticated than anything previously imagined.

The ever-attentive Sun struggled mightily as his friend patiently explained. Then, he meticulously mapped out the new channels of relationships. What originally had been little more than the five points of a star, and the lines and arcs relating them, had now transformed into a seemingly endless tapestry. One which appeared to blanket all of creation. Now you have the reason for our earlier metaphor of the silken cloth. They also talked endlessly about the herbs and the concoctions. Both were masters of the healing arts and Sun seemed to know everything about every plant and creature, though he could never reduce himself to harming any creature to extract something like a horn, or a liver or even a testicle to humor some ancient fool looking to enhance his sexual prowess. There existed many such fools to be sure. Sun found workarounds for every formula, relying exclusively on vegetable matter, or his keen eye for minerals, and the traces they left on rocks or in streams. From such places, he would glean harvest.

Until meeting Sun, given the paucity of alternatives, Zhuge Liang had in fact used the heads of snakes, wings of bats, or even tusks of jungle giants. But now, appreciating Sun's example, he bound himself to respect and spare all innocent life.

Sun still drilled Zhuge on whether he too was an immortal. He wasn't. Sun queried how many life cycles he had lived. He had lost count, essentially saying he stopped recording it at the twenty ninth. "Keeping track no longer fulfills any purpose and steals time from other pursuits." By coincidence, twenty-nine was his physical age when he first succeeded in slowing time's grinding wheel. Sun noted how he appeared to have aged beyond that, to which Zhuge Liang explained he had not stopped the running of time, he had only managed to slow it. Still, he felt it remained possible he might someday have even that constraint worked out.

"Then you'll be ageless, like me."

To which Zhuge Liang responded, "I'm not yet sure I would want that for myself."

This greatly saddened Sun who by then had grown to love this most exceptional companion. He could only counter, "Yes, Brother Zhuge. This I understand. I had been thinking selfishly. Of all who seek, you are the best qualified to understand the folly of the pursuit. Should you ever choose a time to leave, I beg you tell me first, so that I might prepare. Always know the sorrow of your loss will run without end."

"… and you must promise likewise, my friend."

To this, they agreed.

This truly touched the wizard. Few could match his span of awareness as did Sun. He considered him an equal in these things. Recognizing his own qualms about immortality, he had once asked Sun if he had ever thought of leaving this existence. Sun had already shared with Zhuge Liang that though he was ageless, he was not an immortal. He could be killed; and in theory, he felt he could become ill. No matter, both knew full well his prowess in avoiding both. But as to Zhuge's question, Sun answered, "There have been times where I contemplated ending my long path. In fact, I can truthfully say there have been stretches where every waking moment centered on the very thought, waiting only for my will to firm a decision to act. Something would always arise to distract me. Curiosity perhaps, or some new trace of purpose. Perhaps a calling where only I could have influence. Tying me once again to this plane. I must say, our time together has certainly been worth the wait."

Silence, pondering the sentiment, then to ease the weight of the moment, Zhuge assured his friend he was not leaving anytime soon. Their adventures spanned another twenty-nine lifetimes before Liu Bei happened upon a now middle-aged Zhuge Liang in his mountain hermitage, and first met (though he never remembered the encounter) Sun Wu Kong at the door, seeming to be a servant.

As to the wizard's secret for longevity, "Mind over matter."

He saw the true nature of our reality. Through deep meditation, supplemented by the potency of herbal mixes, bolstered by minerals combined under the influences of the five elements; and keeping all their inherent cycles in perfect harmony with the heavens, he learned to hold the dogs of Yama at bay.

Yama fumed!

When the day came for Zhuge Liang to return to the lowlands with Liu Bei, a great wail descended from what had been their mountain sanctuary. Sun, and those reminding of his own kind who still made this their home called farewell to their friend in the only way they knew. Though mixed with the wind and the cacophony of all embracing nature, their wails found only the ears of Zhuge Liang as he trekked ever downward with Liu Bei to the valleys far below.

Others heard nothing but what they chose to hear. Howling in the wind.

Zhuge Liang walked toward his future and eventual end with a heavy heart, and no small regret.

Demons, Death, Celestials, and Men

The departure of Zhuge Liang left Sun in a void. Of all all he befriended through time, only Zhuge Liang matched him in stature. Now, the wizard dwelled in the recesses of Sun's memories. An emerald jade standard, foremost over all lingering phantoms from his lonesome trail of righteousness.

Sun once dreamed that together they might accomplish what neither could alone: restore freedom, deliver independence to the people, and shape a world to flourish free from obstruction. Aspirations that intertwined their thoughts, aiming to ascend to new heights and turn the collective will away from implementing death, coercion, and tyranny.

Sun's compassion manifested as an unyielding compulsion, a mystery even for him. If asked, he wouldn't find it easy to explain why he bonded to the humans. He could just as well have moved on, hidden away, or simply watched passively as their existence slid to its end. He was after all experienced in this sort of thing.

But something always gnawed at him to push the other way. Sun Wu Kong concluded long before, he had no real choice in these matters. It seemed his very nature embodied resistance, opposition to imposition. When he saw the helpless, the weak, the abused, the abandoned, or the infirm, he acted—like water following its path to the sea. One way or the other, heading unerringly to that end. True, it brought him toils, snares and sorrows. But he had a place for them, and somehow managed despite them all. What he didn't have was a lack of compassion. All his instincts and reactions started there. It would do well to remember. Sun came from the stone, and not from the myriad manifestations. Is it possible compassion emerged with him? Both as one; the two propelled into existence from the void?

So, he accepted it. A quirk over which he had no control, but wouldn't deny. And in this instance, it meant he would go the distance with these humans. If he found a way, he would free them from disorder.

Somehow, they must return to Dharma's harmony and nurturing influence. He had seen the possibilities once—the innate potential and benefits which he had so long ago witnessed and knew had been real. *Might they still be?* If only the interlopers, some earthly, some not, could just get the hell out of the way or be made to stop.

It serves well to remember that whatever the motive, whether for better or worse, nothing complicates like meddling! Easily said, not so easily appreciated. Something rooted within us, yes, you and me, and even the gods, makes it nearly impossible to resist. To forgo meddling is life's great test. Fail it at your peril.

For him, it proved to be a lonely path. Often, he lost patience, frustrated at the very thought of always having to do it himself. Better than anyone, he knew meddling when he saw it. Once, when castigating the Celestial Emperor on the very issue, the self-proclaimed supreme entity laughed directly into Sun's face, accusing, "Ah my friend, you don't like it? We do a little this and a little that, and it upsets you? Walk in our slippers for a moment, then look at who's talking. Why, you are the very embodiment of meddling! If it is as bad as you say it is, then you, more than anyone, bear responsibility for the current state of affairs. Remember, it was your infernal meddling over the course of endless time which got us here in the first place."

The argument could be justly made. He knew it, but he would counter in his defense, it didn't ring with truth. Once meddling starts, it's like a demon unleashed. You're forced to meddle again to undo the earlier meddling, which has already taken a devious turn. It always does. It's one of the natural laws! Then you do it again and again and after enough iterations, meddling is all that's left. Laozi knew the answer. Leave things the hell alone, trust in emptiness and in life itself. Only stir the mud a bit, nothing more. Then with innocent eyes, learn to appreciate what marvels arise! Accept! Be alive! Enjoy!

Sun rebutted by reminding the Emperor who had first meddled with whom. Older than the immortals and possessing a greater span of awareness and recollection than all of them, he chastised the Emperor, giving him no quarter over who did what and when, leaving no doubt who bore final responsibility for the consequences. Once, he even declared to their trepidation, "Just because your kind doesn't plan to die, doesn't mean you're beyond the reach of karma." Implying even they would be held to task for their doings. Their wrongs rendered, and what he assured would be karma's payback for their meddling.

The Celestial Emperor laughed at this suggestion; though within, he fretted over it for nearly an age. The Emperor had seen Yama at work, commendable in his diligence unpacking the karmic debts of wrongdoers. Until hearing Sun's words, he and the gods felt themselves immune and above such prospect. But then again, Sun Wu Kung had seen more than they. Did he know something they didn't?

Transitioning to broader reflections, we've all struggled with these same issues. Where are the good guys? Who are the real culprits? Are there devils? Why do they exist? Do they threaten us? Can we contain them? What motivates them? Why are we taught they focus on us, as though we were trophies or prey for which they scheme and battle endlessly? What do they gain if they win? The right to stare at our mounted heads for the balance of eternity? A hand hold on our depleted spirits? Our money and gold? Our children? Our possessions? What? What could they possibly find so enticing or tempting in this mix, when viewed from the perspective of eternity and how insignificantly we bob about in its gyrating stream? It boggles the mind how we remain targets of their enduring focus.

What's the concern? Compared to them, we're insignificant? I confess, my understanding of these things is meager. Surely you can make better sense of it. No? Well then, that's the two of us.

Consider for a moment the celestials. Call them gods if you will, they'll like you the better for it. But I ask you, what makes a god a god? Are they benevolent? Do they nurture us? Provide for us? Answer our prayers and petitions? Help us keep even keel with the struggles of existence? Where did they come from? Were they always there? Did they make us? Did someone or something make them? Why are they there? All we seem to know of them is what we know of ourselves, our foibles and our idiosyncrasies. We love those celestials. Like loving one's own image in the mirror. It seems they don't, us, though we strive to convince ourselves otherwise. But is any of it love? Or perhaps greed? Cloaked in the form of wanting or needing a favor from someone better positioned than us, sweetened with devotion. They don't admit to needing or wanting anything from us. Perhaps that best explains where their love resides?

Gods and devils, are they all so different? How so? Where is goodness in this mix? Where is righteousness? Where does the good come from? What about evil? Where does one find compassion? Where does that come from? Them? Us? It? Nothing???

Well, in those troubled times, no one on the surface had even a clue about any of this. Mostly, they were all too busy trying to fill their stomachs and to stay healthy, warm, dry, and alive for the coming day. No different than dogs. Even today, shedding light on these things isn't any easier. Can you?

Sun Wu Kong, a different story. There from the beginning, he saw what followed. He knew what had been and what had caused it to change. Just as he knew from where those ill humors first sprang. The celestials had great power and awareness, but in the net, they were petty, selfish, self-centered, uncompromising, cold, suspicious, mean spirited, and downright callous. Above all, it was their fear that made them straight-out dangerous. A single, solitary fear their spark of life would by fluke or fortune slip out and away from their clutching grasps, leaving them with nothing. The thought of emptiness, or not ever again being there and alive, moved them invariably to terror.

When you've been around for a long time, such a predicament can be endlessly unsettling. Oh sure, they might still function, just like any of us would. Fiery missiles could be dropping on our heads; disasters befalling; but before long, we'd come up with ways to adjust and accommodate. It's in the nature of living things to find some degree of normalcy, even when swimming in shit. They had ample time on their hands, so they did too.

With time's gentle urge, whatever attitude sticks around long enough tends to become the norm, even when it shouldn't be, or when it's not natural for it to be. Therein lies the prospect of great tragedy. Tagged directly onto the engine driving our very struggle to survive. We forget what once was and know only what now is. This afflicts even the gods. If you were to ask them why they didn't simply turn back and retrace their steps, possibly correcting their follies, they would answer, "Turn back to what? Follies? Where?" Though, by human measure, they were all-knowing, the celestials simply didn't remember so well.

In that, we exceed them, we are ever homesick for what could be or might have been; but modeling them, we too get stuck in our fears of the moment. For both, once chaos has become norm, and fear its promise, sound judgment and recall are trapped in a place where they no longer see outward or are ridiculed as what got us there in the first place. It may be only Ke Li Xi Na who remembers and sees what truly is. We have already spoken of that, and we know what he is capable of.

The fear of death and the possibility of an unwanted end weighed heavily on the celestials, far more than it would ever for us. From their eternal perspective, such loss spanned beyond any measure. What we forfeit in death barely counted as a trace against their unending line of experience. By their underlying nature, they weighed life's intrinsic worth by what one had left to lose. Humans, in their eyes, remained on thin ground—decidedly insignificant. Yet, something about us stuck in their craw. Though insignificant, and not worthy of mention in the same breath as the celestials, humans had made strides like no other creatures before. Except perhaps for Sun's kind, now only a distant memory. For all purposes forgotten, except by

Sun and Zhuge Liang who do not forget. But humans, those inconsequential bags of flesh, had the supremely annoying habit of being remarkably resilient. In theory, if their race survived and prospered over time, one could well conjecture and speculate on the outcome. Their potential, should it continue the demonstrated trajectory, might be limitless. Humans, these inconsequential beings, posed the main threat on the celestial horizon. A threat is a threat; it cannot go ignored or unaddressed. That's how peculiar the thinking of gods becomes when ruled by fear. Jealousy? The question begs asking. Regardless, why complicate things? Since we were already deemed expendable, they determined we had to go.

Have they ever imagined what it would have been like without these inconsequential humans? Certainly, and that too brought them no peace. Not before destroying Sun's empire had anything so bolstered their sense of self-worth. Their meddling and mingling with humans provided a sense of mission and purpose, a perception of fundamental merit. The celestials tried to rationalize why this was so. "There's a big difference sharing time with humans, as compared to flatworms or chickens, though all are equally insignificant." They recognized amusement when it befell them and learned to enjoy if not crave it. For their victims, an unintended benefit. The toll of chaos slowed, even lingered haltingly. The gods were beguiled, faux sense of purpose stalled their fears.

Indeed, the gods possessed an extraordinary ability to forget, they scarcely remembered the particulars of Sun's people. Though omniscient, they elevated forgetting to a divine art. The apes troubled them. The simians, seemingly without limits, emerged from nowhere, transforming the surface into an endless garden with life forms of every imaginable type and shape, flourishing without any apparent order. No one even seemed to be minding store, no hierarchy, no system of laws, all looking to be doing whatever they pleased, with only the occasional nudge, or correction of course, executed delicately and with much precision by the incomparable Sun Wu Kong. His touch was so light and gifted that no one knew or suspected its influence. Yes, the simians too were a threat and they too had to go; though the rare and occasional thought of them evoked a deep sense of loss, if not regret among the gods. That species had been endlessly amusing!

Enough of the gods; by now, you're likely grasping their peculiar ways.

Regarding angels, Sun knew of none, though among those he aided many referred to him as such, but usually only after he had moved on. He would hear none of it directly. As to whether such entities existed, he could not say with confidence. He simply wasn't sure what an angel was supposed to be. For him, one should first actualize compassion and restraint. See where that led before reaching for angels or "rescuers" in other shapes and forms. "If they're there, let them do their jobs; if they're not, transform yourself. Take ownership. Start with compassion, or restraint. Pick one or the other, or both. Either way is better than whining and pining. Combined, they're unrivaled."

As to devils, and demons, he knew them to be all too real, and to be just as base and sinister as anyone else might have been if evil were their sole motivation. They had after all spent an eternity cultivating their requisite skills. If it's not out of place to say so, they were frightfully good at their jobs. Devils were no different than anyone else in the ever-changing creation. They evolved and acclimated as their environment dictated they should. The same for the celestials; and the same for Sun Wu Kong. But seemingly, only Sun Wu Kong had grown from those influences. As the tests became more formidable, so too had he. The others held tightly to the foibles of their underlying natures. They remained as they essentially were, devious and uncompromising.

Once, for Sying Hao's benefit, Colonel Sun began talking of the types of devils, and their hierarchies, purportedly so the young squire might better recognize them if and when they crossed his path.

"What's there to recognize, isn't a demon a demon?"

"That's true Sying Hao. In their native forms, you'll easily recognize the legions and familiars of Yama. Generally though, they are very clever. While they don't have my skill with the transformations, they do have the gift of merging into shadows and even events, at times assuming the shape of words or strategies, flying like poisoned breath on gossamer wings of deceit into the ears of the unwary. They might be hiding within a spark of light, or in your lingering shadow. Many times, they are there at your side, or beneath your feet, openly looking for ways to trick your will and push you through the door to chaos. You spin about to find them, and everything turns instantly still. They take on the appearance of stone or wood, immobile, non-threatening. Don't look too soon away. Instead, remember everything. Map it out and commit all to memory. Only then, when you look again, will you find it has changed, and how. They move cautiously at times. Only the quick and wary can catch them.

"Mostly though, for someone with your skills and awarenesses, they can be found out and dealt with. As with the celestials, while on the earth and away from the protection of their domain, they are vulnerable. They steer clear of me, long ago concluding I was an unresolvable threat, and as such, a misuse of their precious time. Why, more opportune targets could be found virtually everywhere! I figure they're afraid of me. Possibly they even consider me a demon. It's like that you know. Everything is relative. No one looks at their reflection in the lake and sees they are monsters. I don't, you don't, and the demons don't. Demons don't even know they're demons, they only see themselves as driven to succeed at wreaking havoc, knowing chaos to be the grist of hell. They exist that way. They'll tell you it's all like this for a damned good reason, though they can't tell you what the reason is."

"Then I needn't be overly concerned?"

"Not about Yama's legions. They are what they are, and they do what they do. Just like vultures. You will know them when you see them. In time, I trust they will come to fear you as they do me.

"But there is yet another creature, perhaps the most sinister and dangerous of them all. That demon is not of Yama, nor has it a relegated place in nature, which of course makes it even the more demonic.

"You've seen the great red mushroom. Common folk call it the lobster, because of its bright red color. But what you are seeing is a parasitic growth which has overtaken another type of mushroom, and stripped away its true essence and nature, turning it into something it never would have been otherwise, but for the parasite.

"You mean there's a devil parasite?"

"No, no devil parasite. A devil human. An entity, once as human as yourself or any other, turned away from its own nature and mutated into something completely different. An entity dedicated to chaos, and evil."

"But how can that be? Zhuge Liang teaches our essential spirits root within us and can't be tampered with, compromised or despoiled."

"What the wizard means is that others cannot do to us what we are not prepared to first do to ourselves.

"These devil humans represent the embodiment of evil, the very beast itself. Even Yama cringes when in their unnatural presence."

"You've seen this?"

"Sying Hao, you know I do not speak of what I have not seen.

"These are the demons whose ears tune closely to the whispers of the gods, turning their every trick, hint or ploy into immediate reality, raining incessant chaos until its uncontrollable torrent floods the empire north to south and lays all to waste and ruin.

"Yama and his legions merely pick up what is left."

"How can a human be so possessed? Is this not truly the work of a parasite?"

"Parasite is just a word. Think of it how you will. Demons among us are what they are, and can be dealt with. But humans who have crossed over? They wield unseen influences beyond our purview or reach. You would think rising as leaders would enhance their humanity, guiding them toward higher purpose. Like I said, when they gaze at their reflections, they're blind to what they've become. The parasite within their soured spirits has already worked its changes. Finding root and nourishment in their greed and ambition; annihilating all traces of underlying humanity. With auras red as the War Star, lit with singular intent: conquest, acquisition, and possession; heedless of consequences."

"Then they should be easy to root out?"

"What's that you say?"

"They should be easy to root out. Glowing as red as the War Star. Who could miss that?" No sooner had Sying Hao said it when his mind raced to Guan Gung, and the thought of him being a devil cut quick to his conscience and stopped his words cold.

Old Sun saw the dilemma and before the next question came, answered, "Be straight on this. Brother Guan was not a devil. Just a man, a fine man, the standard by which I measure them all!

"No Sying Hao, these demons are not so easy to see or to pluck out. Many good intentioned people would and do follow them right off the great precipice of calamity, so convincing are they. They take great care in cultivating the images they project to us, in essence controlling precisely whatever it is we know of them, their natures, and their doings. They are supremely skilled at turning and manipulating the truth, just as they can make facts read like lies, and conjure deceit into righteous purpose. Their machinations readily turn the hearts of men who already know better, but fall under their enchantment, sliding toward ill purpose with no easy return."

Relieved Guan had been spared, Sying Hao continued, "Then how will I know them? How can anyone know them?"

"Know them, and all men, by their hearts. A poisoned heart will speak poison, think poison and do poison; a true heart will not. Having a true heart is not easy. Having one will get you scorned, branded and impoverished. Only one thing is certain, it leads to no green pasture. Let that be your standard. You will travel a hard road and trudge a lonesome valley, but you will not fail. Should someone look to have you sow chaos, stare hard into their essential nature. Start with their heart. Show them for what they are."

"And what if I determine them to be demons?"

Sun only looked at him, raising his eyebrows slightly.

From the Void
(Much From Nothing)

Sying Hao had long ruminated on these primal
mysteries. Especially following his rigorous sessions with
Zhuge Liang, which left his head spinning. Once, after
finishing with Zhuge, he returned to camp hoping for Sun's
input, expecting to find more clarity.

He wanted to know why there existed demons and evil
entities; and why the celestials were not loving and
supporting gods as they had the potential to be. How had
things become this way? Did gods not have the power to tip
the balance toward good?

Sun only laughed, then added he had been pondering
those very same questions from when he first encountered
them and assumed his current form.

"And ...?"

"And what?"

"What explanation do you have?"

"You know Sying Hao, the gods and the demons have
been asking the very same about me; wondering how it was
possible for someone like me to even exist. For them, I am an
interminable nuisance. An infernal impediment! As you
know from lore, there are stories of the famed Monkey King,
and tales of him proclaiming himself 'Great Sage, Equal of
Heaven.' Well, I don't know about that, or how the stories
came to take that form. Folk tales are what they are. Some,
the workings of imagination; some inspired by events, or

legends. They fulfill a needed purpose and tap deeply into roots which cannot otherwise be seen or discerned. Roots nurtured by an eternal stream delivering to humankind its singular character. I can truly say, over time the others have tried on many occasions to do me in, yet have not succeeded. Heaven and hell have sent their finest, and they have failed. At great cost to them I dare add. Those whom they sent and lost can never be replaced. It's not like they're birthing new immortals up there.

"So, when direct assault failed, they chose the back door, opting to bypass me and avoid further catastrophic losses. Instead, they targeted my kind, and all that I held dear. Unable to defeat me, they figured to deplete me, severing the purpose for which I lived and fought. Purpose! It defines who we are. Defeat me by rendering me useless and insignificant. That became their endgame. Stripped from my people and Shambhala[41], I found myself alone, seemingly purposeless; stewing in the juices of complete isolation; certainly not the 'Great Sage, Equal of Heaven.'

"Did they keep me for their amusement? Gaming my misadventures, living vicariously frustrating my exploits, foiling any hint of strategic design or ploy on my part. To fend off madness, I learned to be useful in the moment, moving where righteousness took me. Until now, it has sufficed, though it's never easy.

"Maybe you already suspect this because of who I am and where I come from. I can traverse heavens, worlds, and realms of consciousness. None are beyond me. I have in fact tested those waters. Heaven's company doesn't suit me, and elsewhere … let's just say, I've been to many elsewheres, but

---

[41] The now mythical realm which had once been reality for his kind.

I've chosen this as my home. I like it here! My history lies here, and here, all games will play to their conclusion, whatever that might turn out to be. On this point, Zhuge Liang and I share common mind. Besides, humans have captured my fancy. In my recollections, nothing compares to them. A species plagued with trouble, often feeding on themselves, and ever targeted for extinction by the celestials. Yet resilient, always pushing through. If nobility were the true measure, they would be the immortals, and the celestials would share rotted carcasses with Yama. The immortals may be eternal, but my span of memory begins long before theirs. Believe me, this greatly offends and frightens them. But then, everything seems to frighten them, prompting gods to scheme and demons to torment the living at their constant urging."

"I still don't get it … it seems they act from panic and malice; but I don't see what causes or justifies their terror."

"Why, you and I, Sying Hao; we are the causes. As are Zhuge Liang; and humankind itself. Humans—even with their limitations, and their propensities for making terrible choices, and their greed, and their ambition and ruthlessness; somehow yet manage to survive. It mystifies how they become more resilient with each passing debacle or cataclysm. You would think the ordeals would long ago have finished them. Always, they emerge, worn and tattered, but not long sullied. Always ready for more. I bow in appreciation and admiration for the humans. They have spanned a longer mark of time than even my people, though their trials have been equally severe and arduous.

"You see Sying Hao; it is within humankind's dogged resilience wherein they reckon the portent. They have no choice but to become intimate with the possibility of their own end. Humans, those infernal creatures! Per the gods, barely one step removed from slugs. Undaunted by eons of trials, pestilence, death and suffering; they somehow push onward. Lifted and bettered by what others sent to mark their end. Celestials don't possess such fortitude. But for having eternity already handed to them on a jade palette, they would long ago have become extinct. You and I, our kind, have long been acquainted with death. For us, just another unavoidable twist of nature. An inevitable curve in our road. A pivot toward new unknowns. Doubtless, terrifying for some. But from where we stand, can anything be done about it? No! We accept it for what it is.

"They don't have the benefit of that exposure. Unlike us, they haven't witnessed it among themselves. But for the loss of those they sent to slay me, it'd be another's problem, and not their own. Now they have something to worry about. Yes, they took something from me. I, in turn, took something from them. I showed them they could be had. We both lost peace of mind. For them, death is an imponderable oblivion. How can the eternal be here one day, then gone the next? Is such even possible? Is their fear reasonable? Can they indeed die?

"I have my suspicions. By doing what they have done, they have become what they are. They have chosen chaos, and ultimately, that may seed their end. What has caused the humans to become resilient has clearly diminished the gods. Yama knows that. Even now, he postures ever cautiously to preserve all plays. He chooses not to warn them, secretly delighting in the prospect they too will someday be in his grasp. The gods have consistently cast their lot by becoming the proponents of chaos. In time, I expect that will prove to be their undoing. Dharma has no place for chaos, nor for those who choose to seed it, even if they are sometimes the patron saints of its victims."

"What of the demons and devils?"

"Why Sying Hao, they are as natural as the fruit on the trees. Creation birthed them as agents for change, and they have not failed in their responsibility. It is the gods and us who have failed, allowing compassion, care and soul to slowly drain from life's experience. The demons did not do that; that is beyond their power. They only act upon it, like a dog sniffing fresh meat. The weight of responsibility is on us.

"Only when we re-kindle 'the Way' will the demons take their rest. They'll simply run out of things to do, and we will learn to just ignore them."

Sying Hao laughed at the thought, then said after thinking it over, "Won't they become even more dangerous with more time on their hands?"

"Possibly, but I have great faith in compassion, and where it can take us, and lead even them. Besides, I figure they'll have entertainment enough, with the celestials in their grasp."

Sun was already well familiar with the holy men and mystics of the age. He sometimes related how he encountered them during his endless meanderings, sharing what he found or learned. Most, he assured, could be ignored. "Just like everyone else," he said. Afraid, hungry, somewhat ambitious, and possessing a game or method that produced food and shelter and sometimes even wealth from cleverly engaged words and tricks.

Colonel Sun for one could not be tricked or deceived. He had witnessed every scheme and con, just as he had studied the arts of the charlatans and magicians. Perfecting, for his own interest and fascination, the many ruses, misdirections, ploys, designs and illusions which were their stock in trade. It brought him immense pleasure toying with the "holy" ones, letting them try to lift his staff or watching their amazement as he seemed to disappear into thin air—leaving them bewildered, while everyone else laughed uncontrollably. Still able to see him standing motionless; comically holding back a yawn for added effect.

He would be quick to add, "That's not to say all were without merit. Some certainly possessed deep insight into this reality of ours. The best among them peered through this mist we think of as life, anchoring their consciousness in the great void. Admittedly, one thing surprised him. Though themselves mortal, they somehow gauged the cycles and passages of ages and even civilizations as mere wrinkles in the blanket of time. That's indeed how it was. These things he knew intimately. But to see others discern them, trusting some seed of awareness within the very self. Possessing the same clarity as if they had in fact lived the experience. For him, it proved the worth of their understanding and insight. It also spoke to the value and content of their method. For that reason, he lingered with them when he could, sometimes even assuming the role of disciple.

But they already knew of him. They seemed to know everything; only the other seekers were deceived. The elders considered him a peer and spoke to him of ages, and enormous bridges of time, where entire worlds, universes, even creations came and then went. Even the immortals and the creator, himself then herself, would exist, then not exist, then birth, then perish, then birth again in endlessly repeating cycles. Hearing this made Sun uncomfortable. He trusted what they said but could not reconcile it with what he knew. When he first became aware, he was formless and alone. There were no others. The void felt to him like a great sea without limit, capable of holding all the infinities of all the celestials and all the ages of creation, as he remembered their very passing like clouds rolling over the earth. The void didn't frighten him. He recalled it to the mystics, and together they puzzled over how he had come to exist as a piece of emptiness, mysteriously manifesting independently and apart from the root of creation as they thought they had come to know and understand it. He thought no less of them when they freely admitted they could not fully account for him in their awarenesses. He had hoped they would shed light. He told them he had been neither dead nor alive, nor did he expect to be dead when he was no longer alive in this creation. He described it as very restful, as though being in a deep sleep, yet still aware … of everything. In the form of its emptiness, and a singularity which included him, but everything else too. He expressed an expectation of someday returning to that state but didn't know if and how that might come to pass, or when, or even if he had to do anything to make it happen. Not knowing for certain, he asked them, "Do you suppose earthly death is the doorway?" They assured him that what others feared as death was not the death they feared. Regretfully, there was no explaining that to others. You either knew or you didn't. If you didn't, you became fearful. For them, true death was the inability to manifest compassion. "It's why we're here. Look to compassion for your doorway."

Politely, they confessed how Sun Wu Kong confounded them in other ways. They could attune to the energies as well as the chakras, and they understood the threads of time in the form of manifest ages. But encountering Sun Wu Kong demanded they look hard again at their own cosmology. They felt him to be of this age, this Yuga (the Yuga of Kali) but wondered if he had been the same in other ages. Sun likened their struggle to that of Ah Ju Na with Ke Li Xi Na.

They responded that even Brahma has his days and nights from which all we know comes and goes, and that at some point even Brahma goes, then returns. So, they reasoned it might very well be the same for Sun Wu Kong. They could only speculate of course. For all they knew, he might have been the very incarnation of Brahma.

He told them he had never met this Brahma, and assured he came from emptiness, in the manifest form of what seemed to be a massive black rock, the large part of which broke away and exploded into the limitless manifestations of existence, endless permutations of matter, energy, and then life as we know it. The residual part, though merely a speck compared to the former, simply grew aware. Starting from within this newfound consciousness, the speck marveled at the manifestations bubbling forth, and transforming everything, all around. With awareness, the speck became substantial, and once substantial, assumed the form of Sun Wu Kong, but only after looking for a shape and visage perfectly matched in beauty and elegance to the birthing reality. From the pulseless material heart of the larger portion emerged the gods. They intuitively felt themselves to be the very center of it all. Suddenly they were awake, and, not fully understanding awareness, felt they had always been awake, always there, all powerful, all knowing, sensing limitless opportunities to do anything, anyhow, anywhere, with no discernible limitations. Sun saw them, and knew that unlike him, they were not truly of the stone. They grew from the manifestations. He had seen with his own eyes, there could be no doubt. Though time did not yet formally exist, he had been there long before, and knew the state of reality before they emerged. It was the first of only two times he had ever been frightened. They frightened him. Like all untamed creatures, he knew predators when he saw them. It was for that reason, he determined to watch them closely, just as surely as he had grown insatiably curious and compelled to immerse into the myriad manifestations of existence which seemingly demanded his unique and undivided attention; a demand he could no longer muster the will to resist.

The Great Ruse

Now, left with only threads of memories during this spell of new mourning, Sun reminisced how the wizard listened in rapt attention while he recounted days long gone. Brother Zhuge particularly relished tales of the once proud and prosperous empire and the particulars of his people. He marveled at how they flourished and harmonized. Conflict, sickness, poverty and deceit were so rare as to be unknown. A once paradise, now lost.

He shared with Zhuge one particularly fond memory from that time. When one simply stilled and listened, the community could be heard resonating with creation's "Om." The very sound and wheel which propelled all life forward. To which the wizard affirmed in wonder, "Until the day it is again silenced, and all returns to one."

Sun begrudgingly acknowledged. Until hearing his friend's words, he had never considered the possibility. Now he felt it to be true and wondered what it meant.

He remembered a particular day, recalling the joy on the wizard's face. Sun seized the moment to build and color an enticing narrative when suddenly he stopped mid-course. Only then realizing the wizard had never in fact experienced any of it and was learning of it all second hand. Zhuge knew of these things only from what Sun shared. There were no other records or histories. Sun understood then the true breadth of Zhuge's commitment to know and learn. From that point, he decided to hold nothing back. It was one thing to have experienced earthly paradise and lost it, quite another never to have known it, but to believe it might exist yet again. Sun spoke from direct experience. Zhuge Liang had only his hope. That was his gift in return to Sun.

Together, the two were formidable; apart, simply not enough. Together they pondered and debated the great questions. Why would anyone tolerate the current state of affairs? What made humans so wrongheaded in their choices? Why would anyone tolerate this degree of suffering? Always, mankind found a way to veer from the promise of life itself, seemingly preferring its antithesis, and accepting its dreaded consequences as though no other practical alternatives existed.

Who could explain it? Who could manipulate what was into something which made sense?

Celestials were no different. They had their own hierarchy of imperatives, none of which promised any turn for the better. They remained ever alert and ever on guard, captive always to their rampant insecurities and associated suspicions. Somehow, others, though in all respects insignificant (their assessment), threatened their contemplated continuance into eternity. It demanded a reckoning. "Disappear them," was their favored expression. Sun shuddered when he said it.

So, Sun and the wizard became allies treading a common path. Leaving nothing to chance, they swore blood oaths to one another, giving requisite weight to their own individual realities. Each promised to tell the other in advance when and if his time to leave drew near. Colonel Sun knew the hardness of the road, and the toll of the grind, but had been at it much longer. He seemed most times to be the least affected of the two; but it was only that his hide had grown thick. To survive, Zhuge Liang had on occasion found it necessary to abandon the affairs of men. The toll on him required such. It was during one such period when he took retreat into the forbidden mountains. There he would have remained alone for who knows how long. He stumbled upon Sun, and then the mountain dwellers. The two became quick friends, eventually inseparable and together shared lifetimes of adventures. The forbidden mountains remained his lifeline. Leaving for several generations, then returning. A refuge and sanctuary, as needed. There he felt safe and impervious in his hidden lair, until his fateful show of compassion to the stricken Liu Bei. We've already spoken of that. Zhuge Liang saved him from freezing, then escorted him safely down the mountain; stepping hard and full into the trap that was Liu Bei's world. A trap from which the wizard knew he could never escape. Stuck like all the others, until his own end in a world torn by ambition, greed, insecurity and conflict.

Colonel Sun had seen with his own eyes the toll exacted upon his friend. The two never spoke of it until the final days approached. Even then, the debilitated Zhuge seemed assured he might still somehow trick and belay death. The price for serving Liu Bei proved far steeper than even he had imagined.

For the two friends, time became of the essence.

Then, not long before the ill-starred day neared, Zhuge Liang came alone and unannounced to where Colonel Sun kept his post. Vigilant at the front line. Sun quickly turned about when he heard approaching steps crackling through the surface ice on the frozen tundra.

"How does it look Brother Sun?"

"I've seen better. The line will hold, for now. But the weather is hard, and the men hunger. As you can see. All along our line, the enemy watches. They are fresh, and well supplied. True, we have been more severely tested and I can assure this is not the day that will be our end. Yes, we can still hold our own, but we will not ever break their will or spirits, and in the end, will not take Wei for the Han."

The wizard only smiled, nodding his agreement and understanding.

He looked very old to Colonel Sun. He had grayed, and his skin had dried. In the frigid wind, Sun noted how Zhuge's usually resonant voice, now clogged by phlegm, had reduced to a rumbling near growl. He limped on approach. Sun saw how the once stout and robust wizard leaned on his staff for support as he came slowly to Sun's side.

Looking to his friend, Sun asked, "It seems you never did find time to complete your explorations into the final containment of Yama's waiting hand? How will you ever outlast me, if you keep losing your focus?"

Laughing at the thought, the wizard answered, "No Brother Sun, as you know, other issues intervened and demanded my full and constant vigilance. Truthfully, from where I stand today, it is only you who will remain unique among all beings, a precious gift and reminder of what underlies all existence. A grand mystery!

"As to me, it is no worrisome loss my friend. Eternity will not miss me, nor I, it. Your brother Zhuge is simply an impostor. One who has been found out and is now called to task."

Still thinking of both as one, Sun asked, "How much time do we have?"

"If my machinations are able to run their true course, five more years."

"You have doubts?"

"Unlike you Brother Sun, I am subject to the whims and influences of the heavens. They speak to me of uncertainties beyond my means to reconcile."

"So, we wait and see?"

"No my friend. Suffice it to say, the portent is not favorable. If I have learned anything, it is not to trust fate to bend to my will, or to my needs. It will simply laugh in my face if I beg again for its patience."

"So, you come today to tell me that our time is short, as you once promised you would?"

"Yes, Brother Sun, too short indeed."

The two friends did the only thing they could do. They sat silently and stared to the horizon, seemingly barren but for the occasional frozen corpse or partially butchered horse's carcass abandoned on the frigid plain. Almost majestic in its reduction of reality into near monotones, all so simply summarized for their joint scrutiny.

They spent the long day recalling their many lifetimes of adventures and explorations, even at times trying to one up each other, arguing that but for one saving the other's sorry ass, he would certainly have met his untimely end, enchantments be damned. To which the riposte would be, "… and whose sorry ass would die of loneliness and abandonment, if I were the one first gone?"

Recalling their long alliance, its many successes, and its sometimes failures, and saddened by the prospect of parting, Sun turned to his friend and asked, "How do you think we've fared, Brother Zhuge?"

"I cannot say. Those who swore to restore Han have found only an unrevivable corpse. And the others? These hard years have changed them all, and not for the better. Given these times, and the uncertainties confronting whoever remains, why, even submitting to rule under Cao

Cao looks to have been a better prospect than where we stand at this moment."

Colonel Sun could only gaze silently to the distant horizon, surface glistening white. Lingering sunbeams glittering along its frozen skin. He had no counter for the conclusion. All he could offer was, "We did our best, no one can ask for more than that. As to mysteries, there's no greater mystery than change, except perhaps, how to find change for the better. Above all others, you and I know what we've been up against. To our credit, we never wavered."

"True, yet I have a troubling question. Given what you now know Brother Sun, why did you come to join us? You of all should have seen through the great charade."

"I came because you called me!"

"Yes, but why? Did you not sense where it would all lead and end?"

"Have we reached the end? How can one ever be sure of that? I came because you called me, and because ... because, I had become bored in your absence. Yes, that's right, bored. Sure, I had a sense where it would all lead; but that damned optimistic spirit of yours, always driven by hope. And your cursed propensity for always pulling off the impossible. If you ask me, it's like a contagion. Can anyone resist it? It drew me like a magnet. For a moment, just a fleeting moment, I thought we might succeed, disregarding the impossible odds. Numberless opponents, incessant conflict, populations reduced to all but dead; let alone the constant mingling and interference of demons, and celestials. Now, look at the mess we're in!"

"So my friend, you blame me?"

"Never. It was just me being practical. If there's blame, I accept it. I came because I came. If I hadn't chosen to come, how in hell would you have kept your promise to tell me your end drew near? Where do you think it would have left me? There on top of the world, hearing nothing, knowing nothing, then looking for you and finding only that you were already gone? You know how I feel about these things, I don't deal well with surprises; and besides, a promise is a promise!"

"Yes, perhaps I am the fortunate one, I never once fretted it would be you who would have to tell me."

"Besides, dammit … I … I missed you!"

Zhuge Liang looked warmly toward him, "Yes, it was good you came, I could not have gone much further on alone."

"Oh, so now this sour ending is on me?"

They both smiled at the jest.

"Brother Sun, you know I am not one to give up so easily."

"You mean there's still hope?"

"For me, I'm afraid not. But for an end to this plague of chaos, possibly."

"How so? You've already conceded we can't revive the Han."

"It's not about the Han my Brother. The Han were already dead before even they knew it, before we came to know it. The problem was us. We lacked imagination and failed to see where the true battle line lay. Guan Yu agonized over this very question, as did Liu Bei. Perhaps even Zhang Fei, but as you know, he never spoke to anyone about anything. They all had good heads on their shoulders, no disrespect to Guan, of course. If they knew what we know now, they might have helped us overcome our own ignorance and blindness."

"A riddle, how does anybody know now, what they don't know yet?"

"That very question, Brother Sun, may be the key."

"The key? To what?"

"Well, is it not true the celestials know everything there is to know?"

"Can't deny that. They're probably listening to us as we speak."

"Yes, but they don't know what is in our minds; and they don't know what they don't know yet. If we are ever to find an end to chaos, we need to be where they don't know yet."

"Brother, I'm lost, can you explain that please?"

"Yes, but if I do, then they will know what they don't know yet, and we will languish further in our predicament."

Sun's face seemed to fold forward upon itself, creases of concern and deep reflection covering every aspect, his mighty right hand and its gnarled fingers stroking downward from his brow until coming to rest at his chin.

He stared at Zhuge. Though gravely ill, and at death's door, his stricken friend kept his wits honed to their keenest edge. There was more to his words than met any mortal eyes, or immortal eyes for that matter.

Looking intently at the wizard, Sun remarked, "I gather there's nothing specific you can tell me?"

"There's nothing specific that can be said."

"So, you're saying all of our efforts, our plans, our strategies, our sacrifices have been pointless."

"If you agree we are no better off than when we started, then yes, they have been pointless."

Colonel Sun studied his friend's face closely. The statuesque cut of his every feature said nothing. He knew that with Zhuge Liang, this was intentional, an enigma to be considered part of the message.

As his gaze veered into the flames, he felt he had just learned of a new plan, a strategy which even the gods would not be able to decipher. Over the recent years, others had commented or expressed concern about Zhuge Liang's erratic behavior. Stories abounded of him sending resources to construct battlements and citadels where there were no contemplated actions. Companies of artists were painting murals in remote temples where they would never be viewed. Sun took no issue with those reports. He trusted Zhuge Liang above all others and never questioned his actions, his motives, or his foibles.

Now, everything returned in a flood of images to his consciousness. His gaze remained fixed on the fire before them, hand still resting on his chin. He knew, in fact, a plan had been set. He couldn't see it, and the wizard couldn't tell him. Even a hint, or token detail, and the meddling gods would know. Then, from their quarter, more hell would rain down. Sun saw things more clearly now. As illness debilitated the sage, the erratic behavior and misguided inclinations seemed proof of his rapid decline. But all unfolded under the constraints and manipulations of careful, though unspoken, purpose. Others, even the gods, suspected he had lost his mind. What seemed to be proof of his decay were, in fact, decoys and elaborate mechanisms carefully placed and set, each to fulfill its purpose when the designated moment arrived.

He couldn't be privy to the specifics; no one could. The plan had to remain in the wizard's head, beyond the spying eyes of the gods. Yet, even the cautious Zhuge Liang would not keep his friend in the dark, or depart this existence leaving his friend devoid of hope.

Hence, this meeting. So quintessentially Zhuge.

In turn, Sun needed his friend to know the message crossed and that he understood, albeit only partially. For a moment, he bobbed within, hoping for a response on point but still beneath the purview of the gods. Something which would keep them off.

He turned to Zhuge Liang, "Forgive me Brother, but what you've just said gives me nothing, and leaves me with nothing."

The wizard searched for traces and turns in his friend's expression, finding only the stoic face of an ageless being. He knows, thought the wizard, and the ever-so-slight crease of a smile teased the ends of his mouth.

"Well, if that's truly the case, Brother Sun, perhaps it is best we end it with that."

"I'm sorry."

"Me too."

Chaos and Compassion

Celestials were in high spirits that day. Their two most formidable rivals all but conceding defeat. One of them sure to be dead within days, the other just as certain to rot hopelessly away. Until, ultimately, his will abandoned the body, turning it back to stone. With no imminent threats to their immortality, they only needed to persist in thwarting humankind to ensure their own continued existence.

Further playing the deception, Sun continued, "Well, if all we said is true, where then should we have drawn the battle line?"

The wizard hesitated, not sure whether to answer, "The solution to this riddle, my friend, may point to the ultimate answer. It's become my belief our true battle wages where compassion confronts chaos."

"You know Brother Zhuge; we've spoken of this many times before. Compassion, chaos; chaos, compassion. Like Yin and Yang, tails and heads on opposite ends of the same fish. But a line of battle? What is there to battle? What influence do we truly yield over them, beyond our internal discovery, and acting upon them within ourselves."

"Excellent, Brother Sun, undoubtedly the face-off wages right here ... within us. Compassion is what separates us from the rocks and the worms. We can demonstrate; and may not always understand. Just act and radiate it outward. It doesn't even have to make sense. The quest to surface one's spiritual potential. The puzzle of finding and freeing it." He touched his palm over his heart, "Like Yin and Yang. They are always together. From the ripples of their gyrations spin those many fragments of reality which drive all destinies forward or downward. In the end, there is only the one, compassion … or its absence. We know from experience where that leads.

"For a time, the influences stood in balance, as their natural state should be. We coalesced into the Han, an empire which brought many blessings to the land before it too fell to the designs of those more inclined toward chaos."

Sun acknowledged, "I remember as if it were this morning. A respite spanning generations, then too quickly, everything spinning wildly out of control. Don't know if we can blame it on the gods though. Eunuchs, would-be dowagers, sycophants, usurpers—leaders catering to selfish interests and bent philosophies. The very plagues infesting all human empires."

"Yes, the time-tried formula for chaos. A wicked alchemist couldn't have scribed better. And once tricked from its lair, so very hard to get back in."

"I see nothing new Brother Zhuge, we've spoken of this often in our long journey. Some men just seem inclined to it. Some can't see it until too late. An evil entity boring about in the muck of their greed and their ambition. But the battle line is not us trying to contain chaos. Even you and I can't do that. It's us trying to get humankind to understand and effect compassion. Or do you think we failed there too?"

"No. No mistakes there. I have come to believe compassion is the proof we are never alone. Never abandoned. Not even you Brother Sun, in your endless trek through time! We can puzzle endlessly over how we got here, and from whence we came, or to where we will go. Only one thing is certain. Between the dawn of each day, and the final setting of its sun, there will be endless opportunities to exercise compassion. And in so doing, bond with those about us in igniting our common essence to its full radiance. Look no further to conclude we are not alone or forgotten.

"It was you Brother Sun. The stories of your people ... your account of the changes which took place right under your nose helped me to see the line clearly. Who would have thought the gods to be so heartless? Or to be so devoid of compassion?"

"I, for one, did not. It never crossed my mind as a possibility, until too late."

"Well Brother Sun, look what they've done once again. Right under our very noses!"

Quite some time passed. Colonel Sun, with his perfect recall, ran silently through the stream of events which drove mankind's fate through its many twisted gates and turnabouts these several years. Always seeming to push them further down the road to perdition and away from the dream of restoring Han. Finally, from the seemingly undecipherable mix of events and personalities, the hint of a common causal thread emerged.

"The bastards," he murmured, "They seeded the world with chaos. Yama and his legions chased after and thrived upon it. Then using their trickery, they harnessed the frigid hearts of deceived men, ensuring its spread over all aspects of life. Twisting once paradise into just another shit show."

Zhuge Liang only looked at him.

"It took an age, but they poisoned my people from existence. The earth shriveled from abundance to a death field. But at the least, we had life of a kind. We never turned on one another. But why have this? Why this chaos, and the interminable conflict, want and suffering?"

"Well my friend, my thought is the gods learned from the first experience."

"Learned?"

"Yes, chaos is a more effective poison. It does its work quickly, and lingers long in the aftermath, ensuring its victims cannot undo their end, nor regain what they've lost."

Mulling over what he had just heard, and concerned for his frail friend, Sun left momentarily to gather more fuel for the fire. He moved about it quickly. One could hear the stream of profanities, invectives and insults hurled at the gods as he raced expertly through his task. Finally, he told Zhuge Liang to bear up against the now-howling wind. He quickly anchored a leaning cover over the fire, where they might both sit and warm.

The contours on his face left no doubt of his pain when he finally spoke again to Zhuge, "Then there is no hope?" He made sure to say this loud enough for all the gods to hear. This was his gaming them of course, for he already knew of Zhuge's message of hope, hidden in their earlier exchange. The charade they proffered now was solely for the benefit of the intrusive eternals.

A seemingly dejected Zhuge Liang gave no response.

They sat together as friends and stared at the fire, while the day drew to its close. The wailing wind continued blowing its protest, driving the animal skin cover to flutter chaotically, as though taunting them. Sun set about to boiling water. His well practiced hands tore through his sack and its collection of herbs and teas, finally settling on the right combination to bring quick warmth to his friend, and to draw contentment from the inside out.

Handing the cup to the wizard, he re-iterated, "Then there is no hope?" thinking perhaps his friend had not heard at first.

The lack of response concerned Sun, and he stared at the wizard. Zhuge's head was lowered over the beverage, as though fighting off exhaustion and the need for sleep. Then, slowly, the wizard raised his head. When his lazy eyes opened, they again sparkled with the hint of new life. Sun studied him closely. Only when Zhuge had fully raised his head could Sun recognize the undeniably mischievous grin, punctuating what they had shared earlier. There was his answer!

"No Brother Sun, none at all. The sorry joke falls on us."

The gods thought the wizard was delirious, if not already gone. The ruse had been well set and played.

Zhuge Liang let his tired head lower once again. There it remained until the fire dimmed. After some time, Sun whispered to him, begging leave but promising to return shortly with more dried dung for the flames.

He returned to find the wizard standing upright, facing into the evening gale as though in defiance, barely able to keep balance. Hearing Sun's soft tread across the freshly fallen snow, now ice, he turned to his friend.

Sun spoke first, "They do hear everything, don't they?"

Zhuge nodded, affirming to his friend that fundamental truth of the celestials.

"Brother Sun, thank you for the warmth, and for your good company all these years. It was great fun spending an age with you. Oh, and thanks for the kick in the butt" (looking toward his emptied cup as he said it).

Colonel Sun stood and advanced slowly to his friend. He set down the newly gathered fuel along with his armament and put both hands on the frail wizard's shoulders. He had known him first as a young man, and after a millennium, as a worn, tired, and depleted old man. But always the incomparable wizard, the one who towered above all others.

His fiery eyes lit deep into the well of Zhuge Liang's heart. They shared their long final embrace, ending only when light's last threads danced their slow retreat into darkness. Sun first, then Zhuge, each whispered into the left ear of the other, "I will always have you in my heart."

They say a parcel of your own spirit leaves with the parting of a faithful friend.

Now, Zhuge Liang was forever gone. Sun remained. Alone, and for only the second time in his life, afraid. He feared what he did not know, and what he knew he must do. What the wizard told him made it clear. Colonel Sun would have to abandon his role and decompensate; prove to the gods he too had lost purpose, surrendered hope, and given up. He could explain to no one, lest the advantage be lost. He held only a sliver of hope that Zhuge's great ruse would somehow come alive and inform itself and others as to its purpose, then actualize its own foothold into reality. Decompensating would not be hard to fake. In many respects, he was already there. The breath of his own life had already begun to lift from the troubled embers within. The winds had shifted and now everything stood at risk. Without his wizard friend by his side, all seemed lost for Sun. Without that final conversation, and the single splinter of hope, he would readily have joined the wizard. There he stood. Fragile, and depleted. With all motivation seemingly gone, he could barely muster the will to move.

For Sying Hao, the obvious toll on his proxy father was a call for deep concern. Colonel Sun seemed aged and worn. During lulls in the interminable campaigns, he would choose to sit alone, motionless in some hideaway. Usually in his fetal semi crouch, looking almost froglike as he rested, often balanced on some rock overlooking another adjoining field of death. Close by would be his bow and his light armor, near at hand in the event of surprise and attack.

By now, Sying Hao had become well acquainted with Sun's mastery of the transformations and learned to never be surprised by what he found and saw. Or did not see.

Still, what passed pushed him beyond surprise. Sun's melancholy had driven him to sanity's precipitous edge. As though fallen into an abyss, he had not been seen nor heard from for days. Concern spread wildly among the troops, none of whom wished to take field without a hero of Colonel Sun's stature anchoring their efforts and spirits.

Normally, Sying Hao knew Sun's mind, and where to seek him when he craved solitude. This time he came up short; a first. It seemed the aged warrior had simply vanished. Sying Hao trusted his friend wouldn't leave without a word or explanation. They too had made their promises. At some level he felt Sun remained in their midst, somewhere in the shadows perhaps, or bent into the form of a boulder, barely beyond the plane of sight, but nonetheless there. Such was his skill at the transformations. Though by experience and training, Sying Hao had learned to look deeply, and to see what others could not. He found not a trace.

So, Sying Hao listened … nothing. He searched … nothing. He tried to feel using his instincts … nothing. Mind you, the bonds and ties between these two went far beyond the ordinary. Why, not once had they ever become separated in the maelstrom of battle, some deep attraction between always pointing the whereabouts of one to the other; and each always finding and covering the other's back.

But now, nothing at all.

It felt as though Sun had never existed.

"Impossible!" thought Sying Hao.

He struggled to keep up appearances, and issued assurances, but felt lost and adrift.

Within, he wondered. Had his father companion simply chosen to let go? No longer able to bear the weight and responsibility imposed by an epically troubled existence.

Part 6 - A Summons

Liu Shan Summons Sying Hao

Concern spread among the general staff, then sped quickly to higher levels, eventually winding its way to Emperor Liu Shan. On first news of this troubling development, he summoned Sying Hao to Chengdu to settle firsthand the question in everyone's minds. Had Colonel Sun betrayed them?

Sying Hao, as Sun's aide, and himself bearing the battlefield commission of Colonel, had been to the capitol in the past. He had participated in and contributed to the war councils and planning sessions of Liu Bei. More so than those of the son, Liu Shan. Early on, the senior Liu took quick notice of the young man. Barely an adolescent who at first seemed to be little more than an appendage or shadow to the mighty Colonel Sun. The King often wondered what thread connected the two. No matter, it wasn't long before Liu Bei heard accounts of the young man's exploits on the battlefield, then witnessed and ultimately tested his wisdom under direct fire in the war councils.

The young Sying Hao, barely out of his childhood, had grown tall among the men.

In the asides, Liu would take the arm of Minister Zhuge Liang and nod toward Sying Hao. "We were fortunate in finding this otherwise insignificant seed," he remarked. "If he survives, there may be no limit to his potential." To Liu's consternation, Zhuge tersely replied, "Yes, Brother Liu. Think for a moment: how many other insignificant seeds we have all trod upon in our follies?" Liu held the wizard's stare only long enough to respond, "Brother Minister, you have always kept me well aware of the price of folly, and I am in your debt. Here, we find a seed and an opportunity to make a difference. That was my only thought."

No matter. Sying Hao had already drawn the wizard's ever inquisitive eye. Zhuge Liang first studied him from afar, then more closely; seeming often to bump into Sun and his protege as they went about their normal affairs. On the battlefield, it took only a few short months for battle-scarred veterans to accept Sying Hao as full equal in their fraternity. They only smiled, admiring when he purported to be nothing other than Sun's squire.

Think about that. An apprentice among titans, yet able to fend for himself and to hold his own. Zhuge Liang finally went to Liu to get his blessing and permission to mentor the youth. He had barely begun his request when Liu begged to interrupt, suggesting "Brother Minister, I have taken your words to heart. Indeed, how many seeds have we trod upon in our follies. Well, some things we can't control; some we can. We know of young Sying Hao's potential. What a tragedy if this potential veered from its natural course through oversight on our part. No telling what mischief might ensue. Can I trouble you to take the young man under your guidance and tutelage? I trust through you his mind will find clarity and righteousness."

Zhuge Liang laughed at King Liu's suggestion, saying only, "Got me." You see, King Liu was no slouch either. He knew Zhuge Liang's intent even before he entered the royal chamber and saw no reason to waste their time waddling through Zhuge's polished and undoubtedly convincing rationale justifying the undertaking.

Zhuge continued, "I will do right by the lad, and by Shu."

Liu Bei acknowledged, "Of course you will; but let's not forget. The boy is bound in heart and spirit to Colonel Sun. My generals tell me, they have become as father and son. We must respect that. To ensure the young man reaches full potential I will also request Colonel Sun be mindful of our motives and beg his assent to your guidance for the boy."

"Not necessary Lord Liu," the minister replied, "Sun has already consented."

Sun, though not originally intending it, had begun to have his own thoughts of Sying Hao perhaps becoming a third, alongside himself and Zhuge Liang. Only the wizard could open that door; but he would not do it without good reason; nor would Sun impose to ask. It had to come from Zhuge.

Liu Bei continued, "Then it is decided. Oh, and I'm inclined to also involve Lord Guan in this endeavor; particularly the martial training."

"You don't think it will put the boy at risk?"

Liu answered, "It certainly will. But there is no technician so gifted as Guan Yu, and from this point we will spare nothing to fill this young man's cup for the future, whatever that brings."

Zhuge Liang mused, "Lord Guan teaching Sying Hao. Well, I suppose what doesn't kill the young man, will make him stronger."

"And along with righteousness and wisdom, strength of character is our most pressing need. Guan will ensure that."

In time, Sying Hao grew well acquainted with Liu Bei. The more he saw and knew of him, the higher rose his regard. Young Sying Hao could easily understand how Lord Liu had won the hearts of untamed men like Zhang Fei and

Guan Yu, as well as the respect and loyalty of Colonel Sun and Zhuge Liang. There were no others quite like him. He had an even hand, and an ability to draw truth and honor from deep within the bowels of chaos.

But on this day, Sying Hao faced Liu Shan. As different from his father as night from day. Why, just to get to his chambers, Colonel Sying Hao had to pass through a gauntlet of eunuchs, sycophants, and courtesans, explaining himself each step of the way. Then being pumped for information, targeted for exploitation, and blatantly propositioned with sexual adventures of every imagining, as tokens to be exchanged for favors. All looking for a niche, an ally, or a new angle on a fresh play to new advantage.

Liu Shan was only a boy, 16 years old, when he assumed the throne with the passing of his father. Now he had ruled for eleven years. Only the efforts of Zhuge Liang had prevented Shu from descending to utter extinction. The court toadies had already bent the ear of Liu Shan to the possibility Colonel Sun had sold out. They even questioned the loyalty of Colonel Sying Hao, raising the suspicion he had now undertaken the role of a spy, planning to eventually reunite with his mentor beast-father; now likely enfeoffed in Wei. Yes, ugly thoughts indeed! They even held the passing of Zhuge Liang in suspicion—just another part of the grand deceit. The former minister was in fact capable of anything, was he not? Who's to say he hadn't already floated on some cloud to the halls of Wei. What better explanation for the string of recent strategic failures?

Some will speak anything to gain status or notice.

This congregation of sentiments greeted Sying Hao as he entered and stood before Liu Shan.

Soooo different from his father.

That's what Sying Hao thought as he dropped to his knees and paid due respect.

He never found this comfortable. A person dropping to their knees before another. In the field, a man was a man, and a person's worth was a person's ability to produce under duress. Liu Bei understood this, as did every veteran in the field. So too did every person running a farm, household, or business. Demeaning practices like this came from the sycophants, and the status brokers. Great power meant further apart. Separate oneself from the common. Keep them aware of their status, or lack of it. Why if anyone felt otherwise, they were free to go mingle with the many. The only way one group forced another to grovel was to keep them close to the ground, and to "convince" them of their place relative to those in charge.

It was in these majestic halls where one supposedly found the cream of Shu—the finest minds, the noblest of the many. Sun often cautioned Sying Hao, it's never only the cream which floats to the top. Decades of what seemed perennial conflict and dispute yielded this—the grandeur, ceremony, and the clinging blooms and detritus of countless blooded fields—spread wide before him.

The grandeur and ceremony existed to instill awe, and pride; but just as importantly, fear. Nothing worked better to keep another humble than instilling a nervous sense of insignificance and impermanence.

But then again, Sying Hao knew exactly who he was, whom he trusted, and to whom he owed loyalty. Everything else paled inapposite.

He smiled at the possibility that he, the grandeur, and all the symbols of power spread imposingly before him would someday turn to dust. Who knows, perhaps Sun Wu Kong might yet be defecating on this very spot as he meandered through time.

With what he had already learned from Zhuge Liang, Sying Hao might entertain the same prospect for himself.

To the evident glee of the courtiers and political schemers in attendance, the Emperor grilled him regarding Colonel Sun. A grand charade. Sying Hao of course, knew nothing of Sun's status or whereabouts, but also knew whatever he said before this court wouldn't suffice. Even those who believed his every word, could not safely acknowledge.

He explained as best he could. He spoke of the slaughter of Lord Guan and the assassination of Zhang Fei, followed by the passing of Liu Bei. Then the five interminable northern campaigns with no clear outcome, culminating with the untimely passing of Zhuge Liang. The combined weight of these tragic losses left the once formidable but now diminished Colonel Sun emotionally crippled. The noble warrior had aged and deteriorated, often issuing random and incoherent thoughts leading to pointless or disjointed conclusions.

He added how he had made it his responsibility to keep close eye on Sun, if only to protect him from harm until this ill humor had run its course, which he assured it would. All the same, as his adopted son, Sying Hao was bound to uphold his filial duty and allow Sun's request for privacy and solitude. He confided his concern Sun may simply have wandered off and lost his way. Or had perhaps been captured, or even killed by enemy infiltrators or wild beasts. He reminded all of what had befallen Guan Yu, adding no one lasts forever.

None of which possibilities he believed for an instant.

As Sying Hao faced the court and explained Colonel Sun's condition, the young emperor's counselors laughed derisively. They had already painted the beast to be a traitor, and that is where they weighted their fates.

Sun was Sun, depleted, worn, and emptied, for a fact. But diminished; and without his senses—never. He would do what he chose to do. The realization that Colonel Sun would act according to his own will left Sying Hao with a profound sense of emptiness, even as the thought flashed in his mind. Momentarily recalling in him a sense of the great aloneness he once felt. Until so long ago when an unexpected friend emerged and brought him slowly back to purpose. Now he would have to do likewise. That would take precedence over all other considerations.

We've already heard elsewhere that Liu Shan was a nincompoop. From the highest general staff down to lowliest regimental elements, all felt the young King overly taken with hedonistic pursuits, propelled by an intellect far wanting of average. At least to them, it seemed that way.

How could this be the son of Liu Bei? Was this the same child, now become man whose legendary rescue at Changban by the peerless tiger general Zhao Yun stood etched permanently into record and legend?

In retrospect, one might muse whether history benefited from the feat. We mean no disrespect to Zhao Yun with this postulation. History's confirmation of Zhao Yun's peerless character, and absolute commitment to morality, stand far above and impervious to any devaluation from our opinions and retrospections.

Zhao Yun had in fact outlasted Liu Bei, Guan Gung, Zhang Fei and even Cao Cao. He passed five years before Minister Zhuge Liang, and only after rendering six years loyal service to the young Liu Shan. He did the impossible, sealing the East from invasion while the northern campaigns rolled endlessly on. It was none other than Zhao Yun who once urged Liu Bei to keep his focus on Wei; and not to become distracted by Wu. The costs of ignoring this wise counsel proved decisively dear.

As he continued spinning his story, Sying Hao studied the emperor's gaze and expression intently, hoping to read reaction and character. He wondered if those victim's eyes were truly those of the one here enslaved by all which his noble father abhorred. He explored every nuance, every crease, looking hard for character within this flawed rose. Would the young monarch assent to the exhortations of his counselors. "Execute Sying Hao today, now and on the spot. A ruler can never bend when confronted with the likelihood of treason and conspiracy. Sying Hao's brazen attempts to cloak the irregularities speak for themselves and leave no doubt as to his guilt and complicity."

Sying Hao knew from confidences of others. There had been much of that in recent days. What better way than suspicion, fear, and distrust to eliminate your competition. In that, they mirrored the celestials.

We can only speculate what whirled about in the young king's head. He looked hard at Sying Hao, nodded in what appeared to be understanding, then turned to his counselors, on occasion bobbing like an imbecile and smiling ingratiatingly, as though saying, "See, no problems here, all makes sense to me."

Sying Hao saw how disappointment etched their brows. Some moments passed. The young ruler timed the pause carefully, and only when the murmurs subsided did the emperor turn to Sying Hao. He tasked him to find Colonel Sun, instructing also they both return to court for a full accounting of his disappearance; carefully noting the imperial expectation (for the benefit of listening ears) that all would make perfect sense once Colonel Sun explained himself. He would do so in person, allowing all who wished to question him a proper opportunity to do so.

This turn came unexpectedly to Sying Hao. Even as he entered the inner sanctum, he took careful note of the guards and assassins placed strategically. Only waiting for the signal, from either the Emperor, or whoever pulled the back strings, to resolve whatever questions and uncertainties attached to this upstart Colonel Sying. Sying Hao was no easy prey. But to invite Colonel Sun into the court, and to entertain his removal. Mad! Or was it a ploy?

As would have been the case with Guan Yu, few would willingly lift a hand against Sun. Not so much from fear, or respect for his abilities, though certainly those were factors, but because anyone who served in the field before becoming bound to the court knew of his accomplishments, witnessed his loyalty, and trusted his heart.

This puppet emperor left no doubt. He still had plays in counter to the schemes, ploys and plots spinning all about. Like a spider, he moved ever so adroitly from web to web, never tripping, never falling, playing each trap off the other as somehow, without true power, and without the presence of command, he managed to still rule Shu. Despite the hundreds in constant attendance, he remained completely alone, and often mused how much like the recently deceased Emperor Xian he had become. Late at night, staring at the heavens, he mourned his failure to better steward his father's legacy.

He knew the end drew near and wished only to cause no further harm or damage. A plague on all the others. Along with that, and for reasons he could not give or understand, he grew certain of one thing above all. Sying Hao must live!

A Recollection Emerges

For a fleeting moment, time froze as Sying Hao allowed his thoughts to wander from the imperial chamber, soaring through memories of better times.

Sun had once shared a story, emphasizing its authenticity and marking the day he recognized the preeminence of Guan Yu.

It happened before the siege at Red Cliffs when the forces of Cao Cao stood on the brink of military supremacy, a superpower if you will, or perhaps just another domino. Lord Cao first looked south to Wu. If successful there, he intended to promptly close westward on Shu. He would implement an epic pincers deception from north and south, then thrust westward through the mountain passes into Shu. This echoed the three points move in the internal arts and left no doubt as to Cao Cao's great skills as a strategist. Consummately able to infuse the global, with the subtle nuances of the subjective within.

Zhuge Liang, recognizing the looming danger, argued for an immediate alliance between Shu and Wu. Failure to unite meant both kingdoms would succumb to Cao Cao's dominance. Those who survived would become vassals, losing whatever autonomy and character they aspired to achieve for their own people. Sun, imparting his wisdom to Sying Hao, emphasized the importance of autonomy and character. "Autonomy and character! One cannot overstate their importance. Never forget this: Mankind's birthright is to become free; and all are meant to actualize their essence. Take that away, and there will be no will or reason to live."

Sun then spoke to the plight of Sun Quan, who ruled the fledgling Wu empire at the time, surrounded by ministers not so different from those of Liu Shan in whose "august" presence Sying Hao now stood. They wanted nothing that would augur against their continued and assured comfort, influence and prosperity. They counseled Sun Quan to align with Cao Cao, "Swear fealty, and with Cao's assistance, partner against the others. Ask only for Jing Province in return. Surely Cao would find the proposition attractive."

In those days, Sun Quan still possessed his legendary acumen, as well as his sense of heritage and independence. The state of Wu had its own culture. Even the spoken language differed markedly from that of the north. The span of time had spared them the turmoil and conflict which came to characterize the north. Until recent events, Wu might very well have continued its independent course. Unfortunately, it had become wealthy, prosperous, and full of promise. You may already know this to be the time-true perfumed scent of temptation. Beckoning to those already established as powerful and acquisitive. Wei wanted all which Wu had, and would take it before Wu became a viable rival.

Sun Quan also knew and venerated his clan's history and influence. In no small way, they had been instrumental in preserving the broad, rich and fertile southeastern sector. From a throng of warlord and bandit states, his ancestors had forged this bountiful expanse into Wu. Once a land of varied lineages and cultures—now melded into one. Current inhabitants freely credited this remarkable family, enshrining their name into state heritage, often calling their kingdom "Sun Wu" to distinguish it from the historical

"Wu" and recollections of the once troubled and fragmented past.

But where Lord Cao and the court sycophants of Wu gravely miscalculated was on a simple matter of protocol. Words like "fealty," "vassal," and "liege" left a sour taste in Lord Sun's mouth. So much the case, he fought to hold back the blind compulsion to spit whenever he heard them. Never in his life did he think to demand "fealty" of another. He knew, perhaps more than others, "fealty" was earned, and rooted in silent agreement, never in open subjugation. He recognized the thinly disguised threat inherent in the suggestion he accede and swear loyalty to Cao Cao.

"What has Lord Cao done to justify our sworn fealty, besides frightening some of our more timid ministers?" he would ask.

Still, he knew the bones must be cast for all to see. Their shadow's incline would show what they determined auspicious.

He agreed to Zhuge Liang's suggestion that he and Liu Bei should meet. What harm could come of it? This meeting would provide Lord Liu with the opportunity to present his case and engage in a dialogue with Wu's general staff. Together, they would assess the prospects, likelihoods, risks, and possibilities before making final decisions. Through this exchange, everyone present could thoroughly evaluate the man.

Sun Quan's ministers were initially stunned by the development. They swayed toward assent when they successfully persuaded the pre-condition Sun Quan only agree to meet with Liu Bei if he came alone, accompanied solely by Zhuge Liang and one personal attendant. This left no doubt the threat of his renowned war band would not be tolerated on Wu's sovereign soil. A smart precaution, as no one wished to offend Lord Cao.

Liu Bei, of course, saw it to be a trap, which it may well have been. While he respected the reputation and propriety of Sun Quan, as a practical person, he knew many in the general staff and ministry opposed an alliance. Recognizing the inherent risks to lives and fortunes, many were hesitant to embark on the righteous trail, a path fraught with uncertainty and peril. The prospect left them cold. From his own experience, Liu knew the natural tolls of righteousness; and why so few chose the path. Cao Cao, a master strategist, exploited these reservations in others skillfully, enticing conspirators with promises delivered through back doors.

Did it work for him? Was he successful?

It is enough to say only this. History had borne out his promises made to have been promises kept. Even his enemies reluctantly concurred, "The bastard keeps his word."

Many had prospered by turning to his cause. In a world of constant uncertainty, a strong endorsement indeed.

Amidst this political landscape, Liu Bei delved into Wu's history, supplementing what he learned with the reports of spies, traders and merchants. He confirmed it to be in fact the haven of resources which had long attracted Cao's covetous eye. Despite the allure, Liu Bei harbored no ambitions for Wu. He felt that Han, once restored, would be its own beacon, drawing others to its righteous purpose. That would suffice.

Some of course are forever bound to their dreams. Can we fault Liu Bei for being among them?

In a different creation, he might have been proven correct.

Yet, even the noblest dreams have their shadows. Liu Bei's righteousness bore a blemish—a festering wart resembling Jing Province on his righteous cheek. Unspoken during his interactions with Sun Quan or anyone else in Wu, Liu Bei harbored a desire for Jing, viewing it as integral to stabilizing Shu and restoring Han. He knew an opportunity would present. Like a bolt of lightning, he would act. Practicalities, not reckless ambition, guided his intentions. But who's to say; validation rests in the aftermath and the consequences. Liu Bei would ultimately sink his teeth deep into this alluring fruit. So deeply in fact, he would never be able to pull them out.

So entangled was the web that, if Liu agreed to the meeting terms as stipulated, he did not expect to return. Sharing this sentiment with Zhuge Liang, he added, "Minister, if you can unravel this conundrum, I will attend your meeting, and together we will persuade Sun Quan that, at least in this instance, our destinies align."

Having already pondered the matter, Zhuge Liang swiftly responded, "Lord Liu, they said you may bring one attendant. Sun Quan has already agreed to my insistence the attendant may come armed, to serve as your personal guard, as you deem fit."

Then he smiled toward Liu, like the cat who had just caught the mouse.

Lord Liu considered the response for some time. When it hit him, the contours of his mouth lifted in smiling appreciation of Zhuge's acumen, "Guan Yu, of course! He will be my attendant!"

"Precisely."

The two sat in a silent, knowing exchange, resembling leopards contemplating what might follow. Both were acutely aware that even alone, Lord Guan could freeze an army dead in its tracks.

The much-anticipated day arrived. The conspirators, numbering in the hundreds, perhaps thousands, waited, some yet to declare their allegiance, preferring first to see where the will of heaven leaned. The warriors of Wu had heard tales of the dreaded man-god of war, his legendary escapades resonated everywhere in awed whispers. Higher-ups dismissed the stories as fabrications and hype, particularly as they regarded the taking of Yan Liang's command (meaning his head of course; but you know all about that and its authenticity).

They may have mocked and downplayed Guan Yu's rumored accomplishments, but the atmosphere shifted as soon as they laid eyes upon him. He entered the royal compound mounted on Red Hare, his full regalia accentuating his rank and accomplishments. Liu Bei and Zhuge Liang seemed mere shadows in his presence. The conspirators stared, mouths agape. This was far more hazardous than they anticipated. While Lord Cao posed a distant threat, out of sight and out of mind, Guan Yu's immediate presence instilled a profound fear. A panicked minister echoed the sentiment to all he met, "Even our own generals say he is the equivalent of 10,000 seasoned troops on the battlefield."

If this continued, the conspirators would lose their nerve. It was enough to churn the stomachs of even the staunchest would-be abettors.

While they all fretted and plotted, Liu Bei and Sun Quan met and counseled for several days. Motivated in part by the urgings of his general staff, Sun Quan called a break to the rigorous colloquium to commemorate their new acquaintance and the possibility of alliance. He proposed a feast, where all the impacted generals and ministers might make Liu's better acquaintance and perhaps vent their concerns in a more relaxed setting.

So there be no misunderstanding, I will tell you Sun Quan's intentions were honorable (for the most part). He meant no harm to Liu Bei, and in fact had started to admire the elder statesman's practical insights, as well as his clear focus on the righteous path—great rarities in those days. Zhuge Liang was of course a commodity of immense value and attraction. Sun Quan had already tried to turn his loyalty several times, without success. As to Guan Yu, no less than having a volcano in their midst. Seemingly dormant; quiet and unassuming. But beneath the surface, one sensed rivers of flame itching to explode into manic incandescence. There where all could see, ever positioned never more than one Green Dragon's Blade distance from Liu Bei. Lord Sun could only wonder what planets had conjuncted to bind these three so tightly together, when in every respect, they appeared to have so little in common. He didn't fail to note how they rarely even spoke to one another, but each seemed to know the other's mind and thoughts at all times.

Frankly, it made him jealous.

Others among his staff had a different focus. Getting a grip on their awe and trepidation, plotters devised more elaborate schemes for the elimination of Liu Bei. They hoped to execute when they found Guan and Liu to be most compromised, with their guard relaxed. Sun Quan's call for a feast could hardly be believed. They couldn't have planned for a more serendipitous turn of events. The feast presented a singular opportunity. To act decisively, that is. Kill Liu Bei and Guan Yu; then present Zhuge Liang the options of eternal imprisonment or opportunity to serve Wu, with the promise of great reward and advancement. Who could resist that? They had it all mapped out. With Liu and Guan gone; Shu would be vulnerable. Forget about alliance with Wei. It would be a simple task to move on Shu. And then to permanently re-secure their coveted Jing Province, which long history and spilled blood had already deemed to be Wu's. Once done, kingdom Wu would surpass Wei, and Cao's threat to Wu would become Sun Quan's threat to Wei.

Why, if things fell into proper place, they would have an unprecedented empire on their hands.

Friends, observe the intricate web of deceit woven by influential individuals, like those surrounding Sun Quan, who conceal their greed and ambition beneath banners of loyalty. They proudly sport crests of distinguished clans alongside imperial banners, forever waving national colors, while repeating how honored, proud, humbled, and unworthy they are at every opportunity. Yet, they scheme ceaselessly—riding the sacrifice of the masses on one end and eroding the imperial house on the other. They orchestrate chaos to force change, then connive to leverage it for their own gain.

Should such individuals ever invite you to dinner or attempt to hitch you to their purpose, be wary! Oh, and never let them dictate your thoughts or draw your conclusions!

As for their ill-considered ambitions—how far do they reach? How high is the moon? Remember, once let loose, these ideas grow and take on lives of their own. Nothing is inconceivable once unleashed. You needn't look far to witness how quickly these escapades run away with those who entertain them.

One would think it unimaginable to entertain thoughts of assassinating their own Sun Quan along with Liu Bei and

Guan. And perhaps even Zhuge Liang. Why not? They're there, aren't they? Why else would the gods have made it so?

Wouldn't it leave a clean slate for the future? Some wondered why they hadn't already considered it; perhaps anticipating rewards or credit for their audacity. But, oh, the doubts. No one seemed to have spleen enough to take out Sun Quan. Believe me, they checked under every slimy rock. No matter what size the promised reward, not one would commit to the deed. As though enchanted, young Sun Quan had already become an icon to his people. The populace would not take his demise lightly. Worse, the conspirators could not come up with a salable spin to cloak their treachery. How could they justify the supposed removal? So, the schemers tabled the thought (for the time being).

Always complications—given their unending internecine rivalries, the thought of taking out Sun Quan naturally floated other concerns among them. Who would protect them from each other? Running these thoughts to likely outcomes led to a single conclusion: alliance and fealty to Cao Cao; there could be no other way forward.

Why, where would that leave them? How did that differ from where they already were?

Time to rethink matters. So, Sun Quan lives, and if he does, he's stronger with Zhuge Liang than without. Reason dictates Zhuge Liang lives too. Presumably, Zhuge Liang, once master-less, would welcome a distinguished new role guiding the future of Wu. He's no fool. He'll see the sense it makes. But, of course, that meant Liu Bei had to go.

I say this friend. Should you choose to follow a righteous and loyal path, others will unyieldingly work to bend your will. Arguing you're no fool, all the while contemplating the two inevitable possibilities: your end or your enslavement to their needs.

Anyone Who Comes Forward, Dies!

It was to be the typical Chinese feast, a grand assembly of course after course, featuring exotic cuisines from all reaches of the land. The air was thick with the aroma of rich dishes, and the atmosphere buzzed with toasts to friendship and bright aspirations for everyone's futures.

Excepting Lord Cao of course.

Through intermediaries, the conspirators discreetly instructed servants to keep the guests' cups full. Their plan was meticulous - by late evening, the senses of even the vigilant Guan would be blunted, whether from drink or from standing frozen and attentive for so long. The combination would surely dull the vigilance of any sentry against planned chicanery.

How is it a head of state has so little insight into the hearts of trusted associates? Not to mention servants. Might Sun Quan's youth explain it?

No wonder so many envied Liu Bei. Through his actions and deeds, he had earned unwavering loyalty from those surrounding him, a tangible force which showed. No one could dispute it. Loyalty flowed to him like water running to the sea.

It was to happen at midnight. The general staff were to rise to their feet en masse and propose a toast, acknowledging Wu and Shu's joint and shared interests against a common and imminent threat. Many in fact already felt this way. It would be little more than leading the horse to a poisoned well. Outside, a legion of assassins disguised as stationed troops would be chanting for alliance against Wei. Their orchestrated chorus would draw the attention of those inside.

The designated interior security officer would step to the rear and order the hall doorways opened, allowing the outside clamor of support to be better witnessed and appreciated.

Who could suspect anything from this? Leaders live for accolades; do they not?

For timing and calibration, the counselors designated a spokesperson: a singular and trusted figure. He would stand and call for "Alliance!" A second time: "Alliance!" And finally a third: "Alliance against the fiends of Wei. All who support this stand, come forward and show your loyalty!"

On each call, the assassins would hasten their entry, covering all exits, pushing forward to the strategic front. The attack would come on the word "loyalty." A fickle twist. But then, isn't that their way? Always cloak the dagger beneath the promise of hope and solidarity. No one will ever see it, or if they do, they won't believe their own eyes.

The more experienced Liu Bei recognized the ominous signs of an ambush ready to spring. Past tragedies, the loss of cherished friends, and even a beloved wife had honed his instincts for deception. As the generals converged, Liu turned to Sun Quan, acknowledging the display with a nod. Behind his smile, he pondered Sun's role in the unfolding events.

Lord Sun, seemingly surprised, rose to acknowledge the apparent unity among his generals. Showing humility, Liu remained seated, offering a respectful acknowledgment to Sun Quan with the ageless left hand over a closed right fist.

As his eyes swept to the right, facing toward Sun Quan, Liu mapped and calculated the three steps it would take to close distance on Lord Sun, pick a blade from the table, and slit his throat in retribution for the anticipated treachery.

Zhuge Liang subtly nodded in acceptance but warned against hasty action with a slight turn of head and flicker of eyes.

Trusting his minister's unerring instincts, Liu Bei relaxed, rooting back into his chair.

Catching the signal, Lord Guan staked position behind Liu. Serenely still, one hand supporting the Green Dragon Blade and staff; the other anchored over his yidian, centered in front of his gilded mail belt. The belt, a fearsome weapon in its own right; more than once, its abrasive sides had downed charging steeds.

Guan too sensed treachery. But then he always did; that was his gift. He hoped for the best in others but expected the worst. Liu often said how nine times in ten, Guan proved correct.

We already know what happened the one time he failed; no need to belabor it. On this particular day, his compass pointed true.

Triggered by the generals' signal to toast, his warrior spirit immediately ascended from within its molten pool. Their unanticipated call for alliance contradicted what he already knew of their prior wrangling. The discongruity drew Guan's close study of every face in the room. His red-tinted visage flared into its war-god frown of doom. Framed beneath its fiery mane; the beard of which he was quite proud. Spewing sinister streams of stringed lava downward to his breastplate.

Standing tall beside him, the Green Dragon remained the sole manifest weapon in the room, a symbol of both power and potential destruction. The generals of course had their hidden arms. The usual blades, dirks and darts. Some laced with exotic poisons. But nothing to match the Green Dragon. They also noted Guan's famed belt; and could only wonder what else lay further concealed on his person.

In fact, Guan needed nothing else.

Lord Guan, ever pragmatic, discreetly leaned and whispered to Lord Liu, "If I move now; we can finish off all the generals; and still have time for a final toast and dessert."

It was Zhuge Liang's side darting glance which cautioned him to hold back. After his gesture of respect to Sun Quan, Lord Liu turned to Guan smiling, looking more like a betranced lotus eater than the renowned warrior prince he had become. But Guan read its meaning, "Patience, but make ready!" Guan Yu knew these smiles well.

First, he prepared by cleansing his mind of all distractions, reducing it in mere moments to an inexhaustible chamber of emptiness, a grand mirror able to register all.

Others in the surround sensed only fumes, and a towering figure to their front unleashing a nightmarish protoplasm. Were their eyes deceiving them? A phantom and resinous atmosphere gummed all movement in the assembly. The evil doers, with their stalled intents, now simmered in their own juices.

Lord Guan hadn't moved a finger, but air had drained from the room, consumed by some invisible flame. Judging by reactions, the heat inside had grown oppressive, for some who dropped groundward, unbearable. Liu Bei, Zhuge Liang, and Guan Yu remained stunningly unfazed, the only ones not perspiring profusely or gasping like fish out of water.

A puzzled Sun Quan briefly suspected the three had somehow poisoned everyone; then immediately dismissed the notion. *Simply impossible. Completely out of character for Liu Bei, a man as reputed for righteousness as Lord Cao was for promises kept.*

What was going on?

Some things are a bit hard to explain. Those versed in the internal arts would know better than most. Regardless, I have some experience and can say that chi, while cloaked in many alluring mysteries, possesses certain characteristics, and abides subject to propensities which have served to perpetuate its reality and transmission over the ages. To the initiate, it will seem mysterious, even frightening—a maze riddled with distractions and dead ends. To the more dedicated and experienced, it simply exists, its full nature known to only a studied few. Though many may doubt, once witnessed and felt, there is no choice but to reconsider. All in the room were doing just that!

Those like Lord Guan, who had made its full acquaintance, knew of its power[42]. For him, it came without end or limit. Ancients have taught, "The more you engage it, the more of it you have to engage; the better you are at using it, the better you become."

Magic? Maybe, but masters laugh at the suggestion, countering the only magic is its utter simplicity. "It's right under your nose. There! Right before your eyes. Quick, look

---

[42] We use "power" for want of a better word. Where chi diverges from power is in the realm of integration, and the avoidance of dominion; relegating it, for many, to no more than idle distraction.

again!" I can attest to having heard the same from my own teachers.

For someone like Lord Guan; who seemed somehow able to morph at will from ordinary man into the crimson-tinged god of war; chi clung to his steady rein much as did the famed steed Red Hare.

Which brings up the other affectations of chi, which I'm happy to relate to you as I was taught; so long as we agree it's our little secret.

It all goes back to Wu Chi—the primal emptiness, and the underlying elixir. Which of course is not an elixir at all, since there's nothing there. Forgive me, we have only words and thoughts to describe a place where words and thoughts are not.

Think of it as reality distilled to its essential element. All impurities removed, all non-essentials and distractions excised. Nothing there at all, at least nothing our weighted mass of opinions and perceptions can set upon. Let's just agree you can think of it as you will, or title it how you wish. Whatever it is, it is this which underlies and propels the wheel of Tai Chi, actualizing all manifestations into consciousness. A great and shining sea, reflections filling its surface.

Go deep into that sea. That is where you will find your chi.

One cannot deny the connection between chi and consciousness. It's a part of our human inheritance, yet often elusive, much like water is to a fish. Imagine you're that fish, exploring the vastness of your underwater world. Now, quickly, tell me where the water is. You look around, scan all directions, move freely about, almost like a bird in flight having no limitations. You glance upward, then check the bottom, look far and near, then finally report you have found sky, sand, rock, other fish, crabs, urchins, coral, seaweed; but no water. Whatever this "water" is supposed to be, there's not a trace of it. You, the fish, doubt it even exists.

Chi is like that. To understand Lord Guan; and his magnificent talent; one must come to grips with the similarity of chi to water, if only to sense Guan's immense potential to channel emptiness into eruption.

Imagine again, you are the fish, now caught in a net. Stolen from the depths, puzzled, frightened, and displaced. Anxiety tearing from within. *"Where am I? What happened to my universe?"* You begin to gasp. Something has severed the unseen link which previously nurtured your being and brought life. You flutter helplessly about. There ... through the net and far below, you see it clearly for the first time. Water! So Beautiful! Everywhere! Its secret, once and forever unlocked.

When connected with our chi, we achieve our full potential, as demonstrated by Lord Guan. He embodies the essence of what was "water" for the fish, the universal chi.

Here's something the celestials know, which you don't. Chaos steals us away from our chi. We become just like fish in nets.

It is nature's way for water to follow the most efficient path, it can't do otherwise. Still, as its course is run, barriers and obstacles arise, which at first, appear insurmountable. No matter. There exists within an efficiency seldom outdone, though not always apparent. Think about it. Blocked by a dam; it goes around, or perhaps sinks into the soil seeking new routes, or maybe evaporates and lifts heavenward. Impossible to grip, almost slippery, by next week, some will already have flown to other parts of the globe. You already know how water carves mountains and shapes canyons. But again, it may just sit there, patiently biding its time. Knowing time to be an ally, and the dam, or the wall, or the rock will eventually fail beneath its patient and otherwise unnoticed touch.

For Lord Guan, possessing an earnest heart and an impeccable spirit and whose essence flowed as water, any choice made, and any path taken neared him to his goal. As with water, issues of success or failure, correctness or incorrectness become meaningless. If the heart is true and the spirit impeccable, the course will be appropriate. Just like water! Call it faith if you will; others certainly do. All else loses meaning. All else is distraction.

As to distraction, the generals and their ministerial colleagues in the grand hall now stewed in it. Each stared at the other, shaken by what they saw. Water dripped from their bodies to the ground, their silken garments darkened, soiled with sweat (or worse). Then, an even more ominous portent. Temperature in the room rose dramatically. The air no longer nurtured when inhaled. Had they become fish out of water?

Why, they were panting; like dogs sweltering under the oppressive tropical sun of their southern provinces. All but for the three guests who remained unaffected. *What sorcery might this be?*

Lord Guan knew. He had mastered the Taoist practices and was now turning the wheel of Kan over Li within his abdomen, water simmering over fire. Frankly, he poured it on. Deep within his emptiness, chi raced about like a mad hound, chasing closely behind the hare, propelled by Guan's own will in the form of his intent manifest as thought. He stood there motionless before them all while his thoughts raced about like a madcap hare to every corner of the hall. A fiery dragon acting the ravenous hound bounded in rabid pursuit.

Though eyes of others might be deceived into seeing nothing but effects, Guan knew the room had become incandescent with his energy.

Chants continued unabated from the legion outside. The traitor officer designated to open the doors now froze to his post along the perimeter, eyes locked to those of the smoldering Lord Guan. Only when Guan issued a barely perceptible nod did the officer's soaked and weighted limbs loosen to allow his already delinquent race to the rear of the hall where, after opening the floodgates for the assassins, he hoped to run outside and exit the seething furnace within.

The carefully chosen assassins numbered in the hundreds. Best not to leave anything to chance, so their principals calculated. As the doors swung wide and their orchestrated chants supporting alliance poured forth, the counselor spokesperson recognized the signal for his own presumed step into history, and the promise of new influence along with hoped for riches.

The horde inched forward, having already prepared their weapons for the intended dash of slashes and finishing thrusts, targeting the honored guest and his bodyguard aide.

By now, Sun Quan sensed something had gone deeply awry. Too many things had unfolded too rapidly. The carefully planned script for his evening with Liu Bei had clearly gotten trampled beneath these uncertain developments.

He questioned within, *"What before me is real; what is ruse?"* Certainly, many supported the call for alliance. But Sun already knew there were many yet opposed. This robust outburst of solidarity came not only unexpectedly but seemed incongruous.

Then it hit him. Something was adrift. Could it be rebellion? He studied the group closely and noted the passing of signals amid furtive glances. Flashing and rolling like waves among the attendees. Then he saw the massive portals to the grand hall opening wide. But at whose signal? Only he had the authority to issue the order; and he had not!

He looked with concern to Liu Bei and Zhuge Liang; both of whom acknowledged him with faux airs of resignation.

Lord Sun made to the ready, placing himself to the front of his guests, as a last barrier to any arrows or projectiles.

Liu smiled at Zhuge Liang. Sun Quan's true heart had become clear! Their patience played well.

Simultaneously a loud voice rose from the center of the gathering, "Alliance"! A hush rolled through the crowd.

Guan had already spread his burning focus to every corner of the room. Now its tentacles reached even outside, racing through the portals into the corridors beyond. The officer who earlier thought to have made his escape now felt a new wave of rolling heat washing through, draining whatever remaining energy he had, driving him to the nearest wall if only to find something solid to support his hobbled body. He pushed so hard against the wall with his back, one might have thought he was trying to hold it up.

Another call from the spokesperson, "Alliance!"

Guan knew well the rule of threes. Treachery danced to triplets, and clearly the evening's mischief somehow related to this call for alliance.

Liu Bei and Zhuge Liang both turned toward him. Then, without words, they jointly opened the space between for Guan to step forward into battle posture. But not before Lord Liu, first begging excuse for the arguable discourtesy, nudged Sun Quan toward the already anticipating Zhuge Liang.

The Green Dragon blade exploded into a circular arc; snapping to ready as Guan readied his war scream and the challenge of "Anyone who comes forward dies!"

Sun Speaks Well of Guan

At that crucial moment, the spokesperson's voice echoed for the third time, "Alliance against the fiends of Wei, all who support this, come stand at front and show your loyalty!"

For the conspirators, this cued their moment of destiny. The assassins pushed forward into the portals. To their dismay, with each step their collective strength waned. An evil spell had befallen them; ill winds countered their purpose. Their horrified faces registered the countenance of the now enraged Guan. They realized a demon threatened their advance, waiting only for their crossing the threshold to extinguish any wayward ambitions.

On that night, Guan never did have to issue his war cry.

In retrospect, he mused and even expressed regret; but justified that doing so might have seemed impolite. Perhaps even to the point of embarrassment before his host Sun Quan, whose sincere heart had by then been revealed.

No one in the grand hall or in the corridors had any further inclination to do anything but remain motionless, frozen before Guan's threatening visage. Hoping only for the evening to quickly close before they involuntarily dropped to the ground, life draining from their now functionless torsos.

Their thoughts reduced to getting the hell out of there! Forget aspirations. Seek a swift steed, or better yet, a boat disappearing beneath the cover of darkness.

Except for Sun Quan, who immersed himself into the moment, calculating carefully before making his next move. Time seemed to stop, as all eyes followed those of Liu Bei and Zhuge Liang and turned to Sun Quan.

When he spoke, not a sound came from the group before him, "Am I to understand the leaders and ministers of Wu have concluded we are to ally with Shu?" To be clear, many tried to speak out, or to object, or to voice their protest; but for the moment, all that emitted from their throats were barely audible hisses. Air passing over frozen lips with no prospect of taking the shape of words.

Such things happen even to the best of plans, or plots and conspiracies. For that very reason, one must choose one's targets and enemies with great care, reservation and restraint.

As Lord Sun surveyed the gathering, a gracious smile masked the heaviness in his heart. His thoughts involuntarily gravitated towards Zhou Yu, the trusted military commander he regarded as an elder brother. Zhou Yu, tasked with securing the province against spies and intruders during these delicate deliberations, had foreseen treachery within their own ranks, a foresight Sun Quan had cavalierly dismissed. He had urged Zhou to have more faith in their compatriots, more trust in their commitment to Wu's future. Once again, Zhou Yu had proven right—treachery held no inclination toward loyalty or restraint.

This night forced Sun to confront a harsh reality. Even among those he trusted most, temptations had grown, threatening the deep roots of enduring loyalties. The irresistible pull of allure had worked its magic, twisting one's needs into fears, inclinations, and ambitions, endangering the well-being of the nation. Zhou Yu, Sun knew, would have stood beside Lord Guan, despising treachery as much as the war demon of Shu. *I wonder where he is right now?*

The spokesperson for the group, the man who had led the chant for "Alliance" was none other than An Mou.

Lord Sun knew An Mou well. He had served his father Sun Jian with distinction, particularly as a once young field officer tested in battle. He later served his brother Sun Ce, both as a commander and counselor, until Sun Ce's untimely demise. An Mou continued in what all thought to be faithful service under Sun Quan. He had grown into a mature statesman, a valued influence and sounding board among the ministers.

Unlike Shu and Wei, kingdom Wu held a stable base throughout the southeast and a sense of common identity and united purpose. These constituted its greatest assets. And the key to success for others, like Cao Cao, who understood the importance of subjugating Wu in his dreams of forging an empire. But what did An Mou's faltering portend? Sun Quan, viewing him almost as an uncle, wondered what actions he must take to set a clear example for all to see and remember.

Lord Sun already knew what would be in the heart of his trusted commander Zhou Yu. *Death for treachery!*

He looked back up to the group, still smiling warmly, and nodding to his guests, "I am not thrown by your silence. In my heart, and from your past comments and deliberations, I know there remains strong opposition to an alliance with Shu. Friends and brothers, we have come too far together to diverge on token principle and forgo mutual deliberation in making choices regarding our shared destinies. I value your freely given thoughts, concerns and recommendations and plead for them now. Before our final decision, this moment will be your opportunity to stand forth and speak your heart freely, should you choose."

He stepped aside, then lowered his left hand to a spot at the proscenium, reserved for whoever wished to stand frontmost and speak. One might think of it as a very hot spot, immediately proximate to Liu Bei and mere whiskers away from the still wary Guan Yu.

The hall remained motionless, and quiet, but for the undertone of breath pushing through clenched teeth in the sounds of sssssssiiithhhhh.

Fish, out of water, suspended in a net carefully cast!

Lord Sun followed the steady gaze of Guan Yu as he scoured the room in one final clearing scan before stepping back to his ready position aside Liu Bei.

Lord Sun allowed a generous span of time. Still, no one stepped forward. If anything, most would have preferred to run for the exits. Anything to increase the distance between themselves and Guan Yu.

Eventually, Lord Sun closed the curtain on the opportunity for free opposing voice. "Brothers, friends … I judge from want of opposition we stand as one. I ask now you call your choice; alliance with Shu, or accommodation with Wei."

As Guan stepped further rearward, the oppressive weight seemed to lift from the group. Even the air felt restored. A light breeze flushed through the assembly. In the halls behind, one could hear scuffles. Though not ordered to, and perhaps even against orders; Zhou Yu had positioned himself and his select cadre in the immediate surrounds to the Grand Hall. In effect, assuming full personal responsibility for the safety of those gathered within.

When he heard the earlier pandemonium and the boisterous calls for alliance emitting from the corridors within, he knew the portent immediately. Acting on his own authority, he entered with his vanguard and found the corridors packed with armed men, weapons drawn and clamoring inexplicably for alliance.

Seeing through the masquerade, Zhou Yu determined to confront the assassins on the spot when he sensed a significant shift in the underlying ether. He attributed this change to Zhuge Liang, whose reputation for sorcery had already drawn his attention. As the assassins struggled with what appeared to be standing asphyxiation, Commander Zhou's vanguard flooded the rear, apparently immune to the noxious spell; and neutralized what threat there was just as he heard Minister An Mou call "Alliance against the fiends of Wei, all who support this stand to front and show your loyalty!"

Quickly, Zhou Yu ordered his personal guard to the front, sealing the Grand Hall entries from any further hostile penetration. He could only trust Lord Guan would do likewise and seal the interior.

This is how it is friends, the essence of greatness. Respect, trust, faith, and mutual support.

Zhou Yu once again felt the shift in the ether. He observed the impaired bodies of the assassins slowly recovering from their incapacitation as the spells receded.

Ever wary, Zhou Yu moved cautiously forward to the threshold of the Grand Hall. There, he met the welcoming gaze of Sun Quan as he called, "Brothers, friends, we stand as one; call your choice: alliance with Shu, or accommodation with Wei."

From his rearward post, Zhou Yu cried out like a heralding trumpet, "Patriots of Wu will stand with Shu, against Wei and the usurper Cao Cao!"

It echoed as the sole voice in the room, shaking the rafters. Even Lord Guan had been startled, then quickly recovered, staring hard, but with respect and approval directly into the eyes of Zhou Yu. In that moment, Guan witnessed the spirit of a great warrior and a deep root of righteousness. Until that instant, Zhou Yu had made no decision, preferring to reserve judgment. What he found this evening showed the risks of any further vacillations or, in the alternative, accommodation. His unexpected outburst swayed those still on the fence back to the arc of loyalty and restored full personal commitment in those who had withheld judgment pending their final assessment of prospects and risks. The gathering erupted in symphony with Zhou Yu.

It seemed Lord Sun had redeemed the day, but for the straddlers and the just moments ago about-to-turn-coats still present in the mix.

Now, a question of great delicacy for Lord Sun. He needed the full support and loyalty of every person in his domain. The decision to ally with Shu would determine their very future, and whether the state of Wu would survive with character intact; or be sacked in retribution for opposition. He had no margins for error. Any deviation from the agreed course, or second guessing, doubt, or hesitation would threaten the kingdom as much as outright treachery.

On this evening, there had been just that. An undermining of his authority by those who prioritized their interests ahead of Wu's, and ahead of righteous conduct. Two unforgivable sins, as Sun saw it.

Was his only choice to consecrate this new alliance in a sea of blood?

Liu Bei observed and recognized the unfolding events, understanding the stakes. He knew that whatever the future held for Sun Quan and the state of Wu depended on first steps anchored in sound principle, and proper example.

He turned looking toward Lord Sun, just as Sun sensed to turn toward Liu. Though unintentional, the symbolism of the gesture proved vivid to those in the hall. Liu Bei knew to hold his silence. Opinions could be cheap and intrusive, when not invited. His had not; though Guan Yu noticed Zhuge Liang's slight tug at Lord Liu's sleeve, encouraging he move closer to the somber Sun.

In the passage of a breath, they paired side to side. Sun faced toward Liu and remarked, "I fear I have a bit of a dilemma."

Liu answered, "Yes, I can see that."

"Any thoughts?"

"Yes, three thoughts. First, seek the counsel of Zhou Yu, consider it carefully, then act upon it; second, you must forgive those who vacillated before this evening, trusting they will grow spleens when duty demands; lastly, set a clear example of what is at stake, and the consequences for treachery. The specifics are for you to decide. Do these three things tonight, and your position will stand secured."

Lord Sun hesitated, then darted his eyes to the pensive Zhuge Liang, who had listened intently, and through his silence sent a clear signal of agreement.

Sun Quan beckoned Zhou Yu to come forward, then cordially invited him onto the dais, asking "What happened in the entries."

"A regiment of assassins Lord Sun."

"Ah general, I see you have saved my ass once again."

"They are currently in our custody Sir."

"What do you recommend as to their disposition?"

"There is no option, death for treachery. No telling where their intentions would have taken us had they been able to act out their plans."

At that, Lord Sun turned toward Lord Guan and raised his cup, "A toast General, from me to you, in recognition of what to others might not be believed—but for us who witnessed, will be our sworn testament in commemoration of your extraordinary skills, etched forever in our memories."

Zhou Yu walked straight before Guan Yu, then placed both hands on Guan's shoulders in fraternity, "But for you, and perhaps my small finishing touch, tonight would have spun our worlds into chaos. I remain in your debt."

Though Guan did what he did because he did it, and not for reward or accolades; on hearing Zhou Yu's words, he raised his head and adopted the stare of eternity, affirming his acceptance of General Zhou as a peer. Then turned to stare deeply through Zhou Yu's eyes, to his center, responding only, "Thank you for your kind, and timely assistance. You sir were the hinge, on which all ultimately turned. I commend your coming as you did."

Though he said nothing of it, Guan carefully mulled Zhou Yu's comment regarding worlds spinning into chaos.

Sun Quan summoned An Mou to the front, then signaled Zhou Yu to his side.

"As to the assassins; should the execution be public?"

"No sir, that is the way of Cao Cao. With your grace, I will provide fair hearing and review of their planned game this very evening; and effect the executions before sunrise. Come morning, their corpses will be floating with the current, eastward toward Cao and his troops. In that sense, they will perhaps restore some portion of their usefulness to Wu, signaling our message for Cao Cao, and those of Wu who still struggle with indecision. Wu knows how to deal with threats and deceit. We need no announcements or formal proclamations; our actions will speak clearly as to who we are. As to the traitors, by their fate and their absence will others know how thin our compassion becomes when tested by treason."

"Agreed General, and I will add but one small detail, a finishing touch on your little tapestry."

At that, he signaled An Mou forward; took both the elder's hands in respect and gratefully acknowledged with a gracious smile, "Thank you Uncle; I don't quite understand how, but it seems your calls for Alliance were just the right-timed catalyst to turn the will of all present to come down from their fences of indecision."

For once, An Mou went speechless. He looked hopefully to Sun Quan, whose hard but compassionate eyes were glistening with tears. An Mou knew then, he stood naked and exposed.

"General, once you have finished final disposition of the assassins, I ask you also provide Minister An Mou and his entire family a vessel adequate to their needs, along with their valuables and possessions. Assure them safe passage beyond the borders of Wu.

"… for they will no longer find welcome or home among us."

Zhou Yu took the older man by the arm and led him to the rear of the hall, politely but firmly. All now understood the extent of Sun's wrath, but also the breadth of his restraint, and if you will, compassion.

He invited Liu Bei to his side then turned toward the gathering and asked, "Who will stand with Lord Liu and me against the insolence and arrogance of the usurper Cao Cao?"

To a person, they affirmed; and … they meant it!

"Then it stands decided. Let us celebrate the birth of our brotherhood."

The events of that evening diverted Wu from its otherwise certain path to ruin, solidifying Colonel Sun's profound respect for Lord Guan.

You might wonder, Sying Hao had but one question.

"How can you be so certain all this truly unfolded as you describe?"

"Why, I was there, of course!"

"How is that possible when only one attendant was permitted?"

"I hid in the hallway."

"Surrounded by assassins?"

"Sort of."

"Were you with them?"

"Yes, it's best to let me explain. Zhuge Liang informed me of the necessity for an alliance with Wu and his plan for Liu Bei. Aware of the great risks and agonizing over his calculations and portents, he sensed immense uncertainty. The stars wouldn't speak to him on this matter. He needed eyes within, and well in advance, I entered Wu. After a few challenge matches, I drew the attention of the conspirators. To them, I represented an unknown, making no claims of loyalty to anyone beyond my feigned desire for reward and recognition. It was that which hooked them. Remaining in their midst until I saw Zhou Yu had matters fully in hand, I then simply disappeared."

Knowing Sun's gift with transformations, Sying Hao smiled and continued, "Oh, so Lord Guan already knew you were there?"

"No, I never told him. Only Lord Liu and Brother Zhuge knew, and the wizard made me swear never to speak of it to anyone as long as Brother Guan lived."

"Why is that? Shouldn't you have included him?"

"Yes indeed, we were worried about his feelings, that's all. Sadly, that was our only mistake; we now know he was a much bigger man than our concerns over his feelings."

Sying Hao nodded silently in assent, tears welled in his eyes once again, even as he stood there in the present moment, daydreaming before the Emperor, in the midst of a hostile imperial court. Awaiting his own fate.

Ripples in the Chi

The days grew shorter as early winter's frigid fingers etched white upon the ridges. The atmosphere lightened to festive when the final autumn moon showered its fairy luminance over the highlands. For several sleepless days, festivities, games, song, and dance became the norm. Such times reaffirmed one's connection to friends and the natural rhythms of seasons and planets. Together, they coursed their anticipated cycles, lingering momentarily—barely time enough for appreciation before they were gone and life again pushed forward. The elders knew what the young did not, often saying little and preferring to teach by silent example: "Seize the moment!" Life's twists and turns could and would intervene, pushing thoughts of survival, vigilance, and preparation before those of fellowship, frolics, and diversions.

As summer's dryness and the unbroken run of radiant days receded to realms of fond memories, winter's teeth already nipped the air. Early morning white caps graced the surrounding peaks, each day dropping their baselines lower. Soon, the seasons would fully turn and only white would remain, settling its weight and silence upon all beneath. Stillness would ascend to its wintry throne, punctuated regularly by avalanches and shifts of the surface mass, which never let anyone forget their footing or to always mind carefully what threatened from above, and what lay beneath. Though most life-forms elsewhere took refuge, the mountain folk found no rest. In these conditions, the margins for survival were thin; small errors came with dire consequences. Liu Bei could attest to this. Those living here knew, "The Shu Mountains have no tolerance for arrogance or carelessness. Enter them humbly, and respect them always. Be prepared for the unexpected."

When winter finally arrived in force, it would return like a long-anticipated but irascible old uncle. One who would soon enough outstay his welcome; appearing first in the guise of a needed change, then unleashing relentless frigid gales from the north and west.

Bao Ling's thoughts went to Southern Mountain, where he knew the first snow would have already fallen. The way back would now be considerably more difficult. Three lunar cycles had passed, and he had no instructions for his return. From that, he knew developments in the Southlands had delayed Sying Hao, or possibly worse. There had been no recent news from the South. Even the traders who bartered with the monks and the villagers could offer nothing about goings-on. They told how in the lowlands, things simply weren't moving; people weren't traveling, deeming it best to keep close to what they held most dear and could depend upon. Uncertainty loomed beyond every horizon.

What the traders could say was "Those in the towns would have you believe nothing was happening anywhere. Ask them a question and they stare at you as though you were some kind of stupid for not already seeing what looked you straight in the face. It seems they're all afraid to talk. But glance about and you'll find changes wherever you look, as well as puzzling curiosities. It's hard to miss the concern written on everyone's faces. Town elders now reported regularly to military commanders. About what? Who knows? Even they had fallen from trust. Others came guised as provincial magistrates, followed soon after by superfluous hordes of tax collectors. Collecting tax for whom? Where is the edict? Show us the emperor, or the imperial court, or even the government for that matter. Opposition, you ask? Protests? Few had the gall to object once they learned the potential consequences. Initial resistance had quieted to near nil. Outspoken critics became subdued or disappeared mysteriously. Constables, with no credible investigation, only reported they had moved off to be with relatives elsewhere. Their free pass to doing nothing. Townspeople bought none of it and knew to do what they had to do. Parents everywhere spirited daughters and young sons away under cover of darkness to the homes of relatives in remote villages. Older sons remained with their fathers. During the day, streets clogged with idle men, many armed, while commerce slowed cautiously to a shadow of its former self."

No one was gaming this situation for anyone but themselves. The common folk, beyond being exploitable, were of no concern. Taxes lined the pockets and funded the ambitions of warlords, along with their kin and toadies. Undisciplined and loosely garrisoned thugs milled along the walkways. Protecting against thieves, vandals and malcontents; for a fee, of course. Then thieving and vandalizing under cover of darkness, ensuring the market for protection would still be strong come morning. When not doing one or the other, they listened carefully. Hoping to mete out a needed thumping or better yet, silent justice to anyone their finely tuned ears determined to be a potential threat. Best to be safe, rather than sorry. If they played their options carefully, even small beginnings promised to yield bounties in the form of bribes or ransoms. One brash elder cried out for all who would hear, 'This villainy would never have been tolerated under the reign of Liu Bei; or even Cao Cao for that matter.' A death wish quickly granted by disciples of the new order.

Rumors of major infiltrations from the far north became fact. Incoming caravans confirmed garrisons and camps in the western plains. For what purpose? Feelings mixed on the matter. Supplying military camps always promised high returns, though never without jeopardy. Long stretches of barren expanse posed risks. Particularly when transporting commodities, or holding gold from payments received. Traders and merchants able to produce and deliver received favorable status from those they served, even extending to protection. For the invaders, it made sense. Even scoundrels had a practical side. Why not hire or pay for what they could not do or get, if the only alternative were not to have? Remote outposts could only survive to the extent they had reliable supply channels. Lines from the eastern provinces had stretched to non-existence. Locals who could be relied upon were highly valued and compensated, mostly from the exorbitant taxes imposed on their brethren. The elegance and simplicity of it all. Apply force and intimidation with a bit of cleverness. The engine seems to run on its own. In such matters, one must keep in mind the practicalities and the justifications, never the impositions.

Again, compassion; it's what distinguishes us from stone and from cold hearted aberrations. Surely you can see how easily things become muddled in all of this. Never entirely comfortable with the unprecedented uncertainties of this nascent commerce, or the bastards they were dealing with; many traders funded their own security. Thank heavens for the limitless availability of hired hands, those willing to risk their lives for the promise of a next meal and a cut of the action. Might it be that in time some of these traders would grow to be warlords themselves. Doubtless, if they pushed, stomped, tread and sliced carefully enough, they might even rise to the top. Celebrated in the end perhaps as statesmen or sages. Just like the honorable others who preceded. Or so they imagined. Even the offspring of the abused-to-near-extinction peasants would look first to these examples as behavior to emulate. It's a perverse but wondrous thing. A system which all at first agree to be aberrant somehow hooks them all.

Does any question remain as to why Laozi left?

By this time, the Shu empire and its court was long gone, as was its governance, regulation, and protection. Warlords vied for what remained of the imperial presence in Chengdu, in effect a complicated network of "bosses, uncles, godfathers and nephews." Even those on the inside couldn't get it figured out. Heaven help everyone if they ever did! More troops with their more sophisticated armaments were continually trickling in from the circuitous northern passage, the arduous trek taken only because of the impregnable Shu roads, and the newly re-surging resistance of the Shu people; once decimated, now seemingly reborn, and no longer easily managed.

But under who's leadership? Where were the guiding hands?

Rumors of similar events in the far south trickled northward but lacked confirmation or detail. What happened in the far south mattered little to them; beyond the curiosity of who was doing what to whom and what might that portend for their own future. Best to focus on the matters before them.

Past days of massive troop movements were gone. Forces the size of entire populations that had characterized the rivalries of Shu, Wei and Wu had become unsustainable.

New groups vied for power in the Northeast. Liu Shan[43] had already surrendered to Sima Zhao, marking the final assimilation of Shu into Wei. Sima Yan, the even more ambitious son of Sima Zhao[44], in turn forced Emperor Cao Huan[45] to abdicate, bringing the tale of once mighty Wei to its tired and whimpering close. From that carcass, emerged the Jin Dynasty. Within a generation, Wu also fell to Jin, and just when one thought to expect sweeping change, all hell again sprang loose.

That history, and the myriad subsequent manifestations and re-emergences were behind the observed troop movements, both in the north and the south, as well as the chaos erupting everywhere in the east from the fertile plains, to the midlands, to the very foothills of the western ranges. No one seemed spared. In virtually every region, the land again lay fallow, grown coarse, untended, and depleted; the populations torn, weakened and impoverished. Only the remote west and one time Shu held any semblance of order, thanks to what remained of Liu Bei's efforts to emulate the civil structure and hierarchy of the once Han. Perhaps in that sense, he succeeded. For others, elsewhere, the rekindled chaos promised fine pickings. As yet undeterred, the wild dogs of ambition scurried about, scouring for bones and fresh remnants. Anything to fuel yet another rise from the ashes. Snake charmers?

Though seemingly isolated from these unfolding events, news traveled quickly through the passes of Shu. Zhuge Liang had seen to it. In designing his network of temples[46],

---

[43] Son of Liu Bei. Last emperor of Shu.

[44] (211-265 CE). Second son of Sima Yi. Military general, statesman, and eventual regent of the state of Cao Wei.

[45] Grandson of Cao Cao. Last emperor of Wei.

he just as meticulously crafted an effective logistical network and a system of assured and rapid communication; both by mounted riders; and by carefully bred and birth-calibrated messenger pigeons. The Shu people had spent well over a hundred years perfecting these tools, and at this point, it augured their common identity, their unity, and their prospects for survival.

What they gleaned from this intricate network was that events were unfolding rapidly, threatening to spin once again from any semblance of order or control. Competing princes and warlords raked the eastern plains. Finding no firm hold, they turned to look south, but also west for resources and ways to replenish and grow their depleted war machines. Only one thing promised certain: a new reign of terror would soon envelop all.

Abbot Hui determined for himself, the time for secrets among friends had passed. As the celebrations unfolded for the close of autumn, he spent more time with Bao Ling, taking every opportunity to share and glean insights. Hui confirmed there had been no recent contact from Sying Hao, quickly adding he trusted his friend's ability to survive. Bao Ling sensed uncertainty in the assurance, leaving no doubt as to Hui's underlying concerns.

Though time between the two had been short, Hui felt he had taken the full measure of the outlaw archer from the midlands. He came to think of him as a brother and knew he could be trusted with anything. True, Bao Ling yet inclined mostly to solitude. Too often, his blighted past seemed quick to weigh heavily upon him. For one with such highly polished skills, he certainly resisted having to use them. He

---

[46] As with Clear Springs, the network of temples functioned in essence as fortresses.

should have been a farmer. Perhaps it was the thought of death itself; or maybe the lingering ghosts; which had combined to stretch his patient humanity to its very limit. What might push him beyond this enforced restraint? Who or what might he become then?

If even half the stories proved true, Bao Ling, though still a young man, had to fight many times over for his survival. While possessing a compassionate and gentle spirit, he is reckoned to have killed ruthlessly, and without reservation. At least that's what others have told. From his network of roving ears, Hui had learned of the incident in the mountains where a battle-hardened troop of seven reportedly disappeared into thin air. A girl was rumored to have been in their company, presumably a hostage, but no one knew for sure. The mystery would have remained just that but for an unexpected anomaly. He had been making inquiries into restoring the stolen valuables delivered to his custody by Bao Ling. From the many he spoke to, he learned of an incident in Mei Village.

He already knew of the loss of Zhi Mei's father and brother. But hearing further details and accounts from those who came upon the scene afterwards, he accumulated enough pieces to lift the puzzle into full view. He found the two incidents somehow intertwined. It was the number of attackers and the report of a captive girl which threaded his logic. Not to mention the four mules, even now harbored in the village. Zhi Mei figured significant in both incidents; Bao Ling, only in the second. He had done what normal men would have deemed impossible. Slaughtered a squad of seasoned combat veterans, then disposed of them so completely, searchers found no remains. Abbot Hui marveled at the wonder of it.

As if anyone genuinely cared about the missing troop or their unkind fate! Bao Ling would care of course, or at least Abbot Hui theorized as much. Like any man who valued compassion, Bao Ling would see himself in those dead men. With his special sensitivity, he would come to know who they were, where they came from, and who remained in their wake, heartbroken and desolate. No human being wanted that for anyone. No human being deserved those fates. Bao Ling had only this as perverse reward for his valor.

And yet, he sustained nary a scratch. Truly remarkable. It didn't surprise Abbot Hui though. He had seen the man in action. As to the heavy burdens and consequences among those who have chosen unwaveringly to act, he could offer no consolation beyond his understanding and his compassion. Righteousness! A rare commodity—its high price met only through personal sacrifice.

Having great sensitivity of his own, and having played through the same emotions and pushed through the same toils; Hui always questioned, replayed, and second-guessed everything he had ever chosen to do or to stand for. Invariably he ended with only doubts and more questions. But never an inclination to change or to succumb. In his mind's eye, he could see Bao Ling stumbling upon the group of soldiers. Sensing something amiss, he elected to encounter them rather than to tempt their interest by coursing around their camp. Abbot Hui hated to admit the truth of it, but in uncertain times, trying to avoid unwanted trouble was the best way to back into its midst. Regardless, Bao Ling took the frontal approach. Hui knew of no better way to foil an ambush. It must have been quick and ruthless. Survival would have tolerated nothing less. As to the untainted innocence of Zhi Mei? Who could say or even speculate what she had been through? Or even what Bao Ling knew, suspected, or saw? Neither he nor she ever said anything of it. These things would certainly induce scars of their own, on even the strongest of men or women. Hui had been there. Now he lived in monastic retreat. A transformed, but not a lesser man. You could take Hui out of the mountain passes, but you couldn't take the mountain passes out of Hui. For him, the mountains lived. When defiled or put at risk, he would act without hesitation. And just as did Bao Ling, he too communicated with and made constant offerings to the ghosts of those he had killed. A gesture yielding not nearly as much solace and comfort as one might hope.

Zhi Mei embodied compassion, and in that, she had become strong, even radiant. Abbot Hui had no worries for her. Except perhaps what would become of her should she lose Bao Ling. Hui marveled at her work in the village, using song, poetry, and the ebb and flow of life itself. Reminding all of who we truly were and where the best lay within each of us. He could see how Bao Ling positioned himself carefully, always on her periphery. As though hanging on to her every word and movement, utterly lost and adrift, should he turn away for even an instant.

Abbot Hui laughed to himself, recalling how once the young herdsman, Kuan-Yin Ting, had referred to her as a goddess. "Just look at her, the embodiment of caring, giving, and compassion." When Hui laughingly asked how Kuan-Yin had uncovered her secret, he quickly answered, "Because she lives by powerful example and asks nothing in return."

On hearing that, Hui thought the words fit equally well to Bao Ling.

As to their true natures, what they have done, and what they would likely do again, Hui had no misgivings. For him, only one question remained. Was not his pursuit of enlightenment the ultimate self-deception? Given what he too has done; and what he would do again if the needs of his people required it?

He could only shake his head in resignation, noting with sadness the question would not find its answer in his lifetime. Laughing to himself, he whispered, "Maybe in another thousand incarnations. Perhaps then I will at least stand a chance. But only after we have eliminated all threats, or turned to dust for trying."

Because he understood precisely how it was, Hui had long concluded it remained within the realm of possibility Bao Ling would one day simply walk off toward the western horizon. Not unlike Master Laozi, or even Sying Hao for that matter. Choosing to leave all behind and disappear into his unfathomable aloneness. In that, Bao Ling was no Laozi. A true sage was never alone. Bao Ling most certainly was.

So … one morning, Abbot Hui decided to make a gift to Bao Ling. It would be freely given, though he hoped his friend might reciprocate with something in return, if only to affirm their bond. Though an Abbot, Hui's values still rooted in mountain tradition, which dictated generosity reciprocated to be the truest measure of respect. Hui knew that with respect came the possibility of loyalty, and brotherhood. From this point forward, they would need that from each other.

Bao Ling Remembers a Prank

"Bao Ling, wake up!"

Bao Ling's eyes snapped open to find Abbot Hui standing before him, this time sans robe. Attired in mountain garb, fleece vest over short coat with pants bound tightly into soft leather boots. He looked more like a seasoned hunter than a monk. There, leaning aside the doorway, Bao Ling noticed several of the scrupulously shaped light ash frames, cross laced with sinew. He had seen these devices before. The mountain folk fastened them to their feet when undertaking prolonged treks in the snow. He was familiar with the concept, as they were a sometimes tool of necessity on Southern Mountain.

Taking it all in, he wondered why his instincts hadn't alerted him before Hui entered the room.

"Trouble?"

"No. Every thing's fine. Just thought we might take the opportunity to have some time together. Run off quietly on our own. Perhaps look ahead a bit ... and plan."

Bao Ling rose quickly, and readied in moments, bow slung, quiver at the side, all blades positioned on his person.

"Where to?"

"To the high country; we'll be gone several days. We'll have to pack our food, conditions may be harsh. We'll likely be in the snow; I don't expect finding much to eat out there."

"Do we need to alert anybody?" Though he framed his question broadly, he was thinking only of Zhi Mei. Having spent so much time together, he had no doubt she'd have concerns over his absence.

"Zhi Mei will be informed when she checks on the elderly villagers this morning."

Bao Ling flushed. Was he so obvious in his thoughts of Zhi Mei that others were now taking notice? It was a conundrum for which he had no answer. He lived with constant threats and danger, and new she'd be at risk if they kept together. But he had found great joy in her nearness. *What would I do without her?*

They packed carefully, though still opting to travel light, knowing the weather could turn murderous even in early winter. Sharpened poles, used like extra feet for leverage on ice, and generous lengths of hemp rope were essential for emergencies. Lashes and binders, proven valuable in unexpected situations, were packed alongside kits of medicinal herbs, a habit ingrained into the character of outlanders by harsh experience. Nothing wasted, no tolerance for excess. Only essentials came along, each serving multiple purposes. Even the snow feet could double as shovels should the need arise to dig in quickly.

Trekking straight east, they ascended the entire day. Just after midday, they crossed above the snow line and bound the ash and sinew-laced paddles to their goat skin boots. Fleece inside warmed their feet, even with the accumulating moisture. Freshly fallen snow from earlier covered all. Light and dry, velvety soft and powdery. They glided swiftly across the windswept, undulating surface, the white crystal vapors dancing in the light, matching the tempo of breezes tracing the surface contours. The sun sparkled off the galloping forms, all suspended atop the harsh glare constantly emanating from the surface below. Before long, it would have blinded them, if not for the devices Abbot Hui pulled from his pack, handing one to Bao Ling.

It was a plank of white oak, carefully shaped and polished so it fit comfortably onto the brow, laying over the eyes like a thin mask. On its sides were strips of seasoned and tanned sinew, which slipped over and behind the head, binding the apparatus securely. The top line extended upward just enough to cut the sun's rays from angling into the eyes from above. Bao Ling saw two narrow slits carefully cut and positioned so that the eyes could look forward. He already knew these would solve the issue of glare. He had seen them before with Sying Hao, who had once tried to explain their use and their effect. Sying Hao had shaped his own from antler and, as was the case with his hand-fashioned bows, they were wonders to behold.

When first introduced, Bao Ling saw no purpose in the contraption and would not don it, arguing with Sying Hao no true archer would cut his field of vision so drastically. Until that point, Bao Ling had been a lifelong mid-lander and knew nothing of snow blindness. So, with only a small degree of trepidation, Sying Hao reckoned it fell on him to drive the point home for Bao Ling's benefit. He said nothing further, deciding to let him get a full dose of snow-reflected sunlight. He knew the lesson of harsh experience would best loosen his friend's misplaced intransigence. So, together, they trekked across whitened fields under a constantly glaring sun until the young protege felt like his eyes were boiling out from their sockets.

There was no resistance to the device after that. Straightaway, Bao Ling puzzled at how well it worked. He found even with the narrow slits, through which he at first could barely see anything; once practiced and familiar, he could see quite well. This of course led to streams of questions for Sying Hao.

"Why do they work? How do they work?"

"The field of white overwhelms our vision with light and brightness. Picture a drinking glass filled to overflow. Except with light, unlike the cup, the eye continues to drink in the excess and becomes so blighted it loses its ability to function. It would be as if the cup broke apart from the influx of water. For some, the loss of vision remains."

"You mean you let me go through that, knowing it could have blinded me?"

"You needed to learn; I was tired of arguing with you. My patience had filled to overflowing. For a while there, the prospect of a blinded companion seemed better than having to deal with more quibbling; besides, now you're fine. Right?"

Bao Ling understood where that came from. He too knew what it took to survive. Always excise the non-essential. What works works, what doesn't, doesn't. Attitude can be lethal if wrongly engaged. More often than one would like, it gets in the way. Resistance has its place, but often runs counter to essential purpose. Excise it; avoid it; purge it, or risk losing your center. Be without your center in troubled times and you'll drift aimlessly. That remained the core of their relationship. Heart. Centered, forged and shaped by shared purpose. Sying Hao knew, as did Bao Ling, sometimes one simply had to take chances, though with great reservation and care. To drive the lesson home and beyond all argument, looking to avoid time further wasted, Sying Hao had done just that.

"But I can see better with them on than without them? Why is that?"

"Well, that's because on a sunlit snowfield, all you need to see is what's immediately to your front, and the horizon ahead. You've already seen what's behind. Everything else becomes an impediment. All that glare from every direction works against your purpose. The bone mask gives you only the horizon ahead and cuts away the unnecessary. You learn to assimilate and distinguish from what's left; much the same as what you do on entering a darkened room. For a few moments, you adjust, move your eyes, tilt your head, listen intently. Then you begin to see more, registering the shapes and shadows, as well as whatever light passes through. You can shift that horizon by adjusting the angle and elevation of your head, and your mind consolidates the information, re-creating within, all that is already outside. Just like when you've had to fight in darkness. You learn to compensate and adapt. In short order, you find yourself completely at ease."

And that proved true. Before long, Bao Ling could see just as well with the contraptions as he could not without.

Abbot Hui didn't know this, but Bao Ling had also learned to use a silken head wrap for this same purpose. Sying Hao had shown how something simple as a silk wrap over the eyes could reduce the harmful effects of glare. Learning that, he made it a habit to always have some silk fabric on hand, and in fact, had been reaching for it just when Hui offered the mask. He chose the mask of course, knowing to trust the mountain people, who would long ago have found the best solution to the problem.

After donning the device, he asked his friend, "Are we going anywhere in particular?"

"Yes, tomorrow, we'll cross those ridges to the east and descend to the snow line below. You'll have a chance to see the real Shu, the never ending mountainous maze which has baffled invaders since the beginning of time. There, I'm hoping to share some things with you. Perhaps you'll do likewise for me. An exchange of skills and sharing of talents if you will."

Bao Ling knew not to press. After some steps, he asked, "And tonight?"

"Tonight, we'll sleep and rest in the snow. Darkness will soon be on us. Best we prepare our shelter before the night chills and the freeze comes."

When the midday sun shines brightly, melt develops on the high icy surfaces. The frozen snow underneath becomes wet and saturated. Soon enough becoming an annoying and strength-sapping mush making upward trekking difficult. The combination of steep vertical angles and constant backsliding tests even the strongest.

Then later, if not suddenly, certainly faster than one might expect; as the day cools, it all freezes to solid once again. Then, with every step, the risk of slipping and cascading to one's doom.

By now, Bao Ling had become well acquainted with the cycle of late day freezes. On the slopes, the snow and ice would soften to pliable with the daylight, particularly on a day such as this, where the sun shone brightly. When afternoon shadows began to creep down, a chill in the air would come first, then the downslope winds. Before long, deepening bites of cold drove through to the very bone. By dusk, slopes took on an icy sheen, and steps thereafter loomed uneven, slick and treacherous.

Of necessity, the snow paddles came off on hard ice, where they served no purpose. If anything, on ice, they complicated the already escalating risks.

Lashed atop their packs were iron flats, each with sharpened spikes beneath. Seasoned hide straps threaded through the plates and, when worn, cross-tied to the feet and ankles. On ice, the spikes punched through the slick top surface, not deeply, but enough to generally hold one's feet firmly in place. However, they weren't foolproof. Bao Ling had learned this the hard way. Once, on Southern Mountain, one of the plates failed on his downslope foot. The ankle harness snapped just as he leaned his weight forward onto the foot. His ankle buckled, nearly broke, and he flew disoriented until dropping hard onto the glossy ice. It took all he had to find his long knife and drive it into the surface. Initially, nothing. But after much effort, with bleeding hands spiking frantically downward at the ice, he slowed his descent to an eventual stop. A few moments more would have been too late. When he finally turned about, he saw a gaping crevasse just below. Given his history, he had learned to keep fear in rein. But that meant fear of the known risks. It remained in check even then, at least until curiosity drove him to the edge of the crevasse. There he could fully see what he narrowly avoided. A harrowing emptiness descending to nowhere far below.

Though his mind remained still, his body shuddered involuntarily. He decided then and there he wanted no part of these creature devouring holes. It was one thing to die; another to drop into a mountain's bowels and disappear without a trace, sealed forever within an icy tomb, never again to resurface. The very thought grated the core of his mid-land sensitivities as he limped back up the slope.

On the caps of their walking poles, Shu metal smiths fashioned curved grapples of one to three fingers—much like claws of a hawk, thick, sturdy and protruding outward. Some bore images, perhaps aberrant spiked jester crowns, or horns of goblins, widened and sharpened for their intended purpose. The hill people called them eagle talons. Bao Ling

had never seen their likes. On first encounter, he regarded
them as weapons or implements to loosen earth or ice. In
those days, tools often served multiple uses. It was not
unusual for common implements and tools to double as
weapons benefiting those who knew. But it was the pole
with its eagle claw that most captured Bao Ling's interest
and curiosity. Early on he begged Hui's explanation of what
it was for.

Hui explained that when falling on slick ice, one could
secure the pole with both hands, then drive one or two of the
spikes downward into the sheet. He said it was a sure brake
if executed properly; carefully adding that in an attack, it
made an equally fine weapon. Spiked on the bottom end,
with the eagle claw doubling as a grappling snare on the
other, and perfectly weighted. Heavy enough to knock an
enemy down with one strike, but balanced for vertical
comfort. Clearly these mountain folks left nothing to chance.
To seal Bao Ling's understanding, Hui had the monks teach
him its use on the snow fields above the temple. Bao Ling
didn't look forward to sliding uncontrolled down
treacherous slopes. He came from the midlands, after all. But
he knew he would need the skill. So that was that. Even
Abbot Hui made a point of joining in the exercises. The robe-
clad monks frolicked like a bunch of otters dashing about on
the snowpack, so intimate were they with their slopes.
Chasing, running, bumping, racing, all thoroughly enjoying
the play.

Hui had only the right arm, and Bao Ling hadn't
expected him to be adept with the snow staff. Yet,
witnessing Hui mentor his acolytes on its use as a weapon,
Bao Ling learned never to underestimate his friend. The
Abbot had reconfigured traditional staff movements to
accommodate his missing left arm. Bao Ling noted how the

monk's right arm had developed and muscled to offset what the left had lost. What remained on the left, in the form of a stumped upper arm, now served as the ballast, pivot and anchor for the back end of the shaft. The right arm became the rudder and guide for defensive flows and lethal counters at the front. Hui's adaptation turned perceived limitations into unanticipated strengths.

Hui had reconfigured the traditional nine opposing hand staff sequences, along with the nine common hand sequences and the twenty death strikes into a system of his own design. What others thought constituted limitations, had become unanticipated strengths. When Hui assumed the role of monkey, all became evident. Simply standing there, immediately in front of an attacker or attackers, relying on barely perceptible shifts in angle and movement. Tilting his still rooted staff little more than a hair's width, this way or that. Or sometimes lifting it lightly from the ground, in subtle contacts and responses, immediately neutralizing whatever came at him.

Bao Ling had already witnessed, and been duly impressed by Hui's "thought arrow." This was something entirely new and different. As swarms of monks moved on him, Hui brought to mind the Monkey King in the enchanting effortlessness to his flow. Almost implying that still having the left arm would have impeded what he now so nimbly accomplished.

Cloaked in the core of his movements was something else Bao Ling discerned but did not completely understand. The attackers seemed off-balance. Confused from the geometry spun by Hui and uncertain of their footing as they moved on him. Hui had become like a spider weaving a complex web which his prey could neither detect, nor ever comprehend. In the midst of even this, Bao Ling's sure eye caught shifts in the attackers' movements for which he could make no account or explanation. Something nudged or tugged at them, delicately altering their timing and rendering their attacks futile. By what cause, he could not say. As they weighted to step forward in attack, they tilted ever so slightly, one here, one there, one way or the other, barely appreciable. So delicate even they failed to catch it, and with that their timing and their attacks came to naught.

Bao Ling had the underlying mechanics of similar principles drummed into him by his own teachers. He perfected them over the course of his trials and hard gained experiences. When someone came forward in attack, for just an instant, their weight passed entirely over the leading or planted foot. In that instant, all balanced precariously, and the spread of their root reduced to only a fraction of its normal breadth. In that state, it took little more than a nudge, or bump, or push to either off balance, or neutralize the attack entirely. He remembered how his grandfather said of Iron Hand Gao that he "Rarely had to use his iron hand. With his precisely honed timing, he could neutralize, disable, even kill an attacker with nothing more than a bump." Or, in the case of Abbot Hui, a carefully placed thought arrow. That was the only possible explanation. *He must be breaking their balance with his will!*

Hui's legend as a great archer spoke of dedication over a span of years evolving into realms not at first imaginable. It would seem Hui's proven triumph over adversity fueled a level of discipline and determination more than matching anything Bao Ling had ever before encountered.

As the day grew late, Hui pointed to where the slope they ascended capped in a thin ridge. "Best we follow the ridge line. The ascent will be smoother and less tiring."

For the mountain folk, ridges were the preferred arterials, offering a straight path unimpeded by obstacles and crevasses, avoiding energy-depleting steep angles. Ridges provided clear views in all directions, a strategic advantage in troubled times, allowing a quick escape at the first sign of approaching danger. The teeth-rattling plunge down the icy slopes demanded experience, training, and courage, skills the mountain folk had mastered to the point where it was as comfortable as walking.

They sat on their oilskins, then slid downward, using the pointed or hooked ends of their poles as rudders and brakes in precisely controlled descents. Their command over the process proved remarkable to an admiring Bao Ling. They, in turn, had great fun drumming the skills into the head of their archer friend, who, to their chagrin, mastered them all too readily. The need to have a little fun at his expense was somewhat appeased when they insisted he join in one of their competitions. A test of nerves, plunging downward head first and then upside down, racing as though hell-bent on meeting death at the bottom, only to spin about at the very last moment and brake to a stop amidst howls of laughter.

But then, a mishap. For some reason, unable to gain traction on the icy surface, two of the monks sailed helplessly over the edge of what appeared to be a bottomless crevasse. Unfazed, the others quickly set anchors in the snowpack, burying their staffs with lines lashed securely about the middles. To this anchor, they looped several ropes together and tossed the improvised rescue cable over the side. Peering cautiously from over the edge, Bao Ling saw nothing. He heard a roaring torrent of ice melt racing far below. Appalled at the loss, Bao Ling declared the exercise pointless, expecting they'd find no one alive down there.

He might have been fearless on the surface, but the deep unknown now confronting him presented challenges for which he had no familiarity or ready solutions.

Politely acknowledging his voiced opinion, the Shu offered no response except to continue in silence what they intended to do. Respecting their example, Bao Ling held his tongue. *Who am I to argue what we won't find? These are friends! Stuck below, hurt and freezing, I'd sure want someone to come looking for me.*

Joining the common mind and purpose of his friends, he watched as one of the monks removed his robe and donned hunter's topskin and slacks with stiff boots and iron claws attached to his feet. The monk then secured himself to the main line using a hemp loop which he ingeniously circled over and through itself several times until it pulled tight anchoring to the main line. To that loop he attached another, the larger residual crisscrossing his upper torso where it supported his full weight. Bao Ling, spellbound, absorbed every nuance as the monk carefully dropped backward over the edge and descended confidently into the fissure. Others showed Bao Ling how this worked. One could loosen and tighten the looped segment attached to the main line. This allowed for descent with great control, and even provided support should one tire. Once the monk reached bottom, he signaled. Another immediately prepared to follow; that is, until Bao Ling insisted he be next. *No better way to overcome one's uncertainty and fears than to push through them* is what he thought.

And that's what he did.

The surface monks initially resisted his request. They tried to persuade him away from it, emphasizing the considerable risk. Should the rescue or the equipment fail, he'd be stuck with the others until exposure did them in.

They had no rope for a second shot. There could be no margin for carelessness or error. Or ego.

All part of their game of course. Mountain folk loved their pranks. They knew Bao Ling would insist on getting involved. It was his nature after all; their resistance nothing but a charade; their threats of dangers, real, but exaggerated; they were as adept in the crevasses as they were on the surface. "He doesn't have a clue" is what they gleefully whispered amongst themselves as he gingerly stepped over the edge for what he expected to be his likely end.

The descent proved rigorous for Bao Ling, a revelation in its solitude. With neither bottom nor top in sight, sunlight somehow filtered through the walls, casting a blue aura that illuminated the underworld. He stopped to breathlessly take in what he had never before seen or imagined. So quiet and still. Except for the stream below, a raging testament that dragons did indeed exist in the form of seething torrents ever shaping and molding the world above, all from the inside out. Finally, he passed over the last outcrop, the rope now nearing its end, and through a chute. Just below, he saw the two who had fallen, sitting alongside the third, enjoying rice and dried fish on a rocky bank. Smiling and waving, they passed around a flask as Bao Ling descended nearby.

They waited patiently until he touched down. "Bao Ling, come have some tea with us," called one of the monks, "We'll have to hurry though, the light above is getting thin. We don't want to make our way up in darkness."

Bao Ling knew they had tricked him, but could do nothing other than smile lightly, and nod his acceptance to their offer of tea. As he neared, he saw a third rope, which he surmised the first two monks had employed to make their safe descent before being loosed from above and dropped below.

He said nothing to them on the return, preferring to focus on and copy their climbing technique, noting how carefully they studied the fissure walls looking for optimal foot placements.

In turn, as they ascended, they took great care to ensure Bao Ling knew how to work the friction loop. Lift and climb, root your feet into the wall, slide the loop upward, lock it, then repeat the process. Once he found his rhythm, Bao Ling surprised even himself with how quickly he made it to the top. All the monks were smiling broadly, saying nothing, and doing their best to look otherwise engaged.

It was Abbot Hui who broke the ice, "It seemed like such a clever prank, I couldn't in good heart deny them."

Only when Bao Ling nodded his head, affirming with his usual subtle smile, "Yes indeed, a fine prank ..." looking about as he raised his voice, adding "... perhaps someday I'll find a way to reciprocate."

Only on hearing his words did they relax, knowing there would be no hard feelings.

In short order, the adroit Bao Ling became the equal of any of them. One day he heard them joking amongst themselves. On snow-draped hills sounds traveled far. One who listened well could make out conversations, even whispers, from others in the distance. They spoke discreetly of how the Dragon of the Midlands, when unmasked, was indeed a snow monkey. A term they often used in referring to themselves. Bao Ling deemed it a high compliment, electing to best acknowledge by acting as though he hadn't heard it at all.

But he did take it close to heart.

Epilogue

And so they cast their common lots as friends fated
No different than the many before them

In due course, some would emerge as heroes and legends
Others would fall or fail
No different than the many before

In their far-off time and distant place
They had only hope, and each other
One might go a long way
With little more than that—and some luck
No different than the many before them
Nor from us

Picture if you will. We bob our way through eternity
Innocents amidst streams of turbulent uncertainty
Seeking futures somewhere to be had
But never quite within reach or grasp

But then again
Let's not forget the unseen guiding hand
Of a long since departed wizard

Or his friend—the immortal one
Who roams yet amongst us, and knows for all
What must follow

Characters and Incidentals

Abbot Shi-Hui Ke - see Shi-Hui Ke, below.

Ah Ju Na - see Arjuna, below. The great archer and companion to Krishna, whose spiritual dilemma confronting imminent cataclysm provides setting for the core teachings and lessons of the Bhagavad Gita.

An Mou - A conspirator in the failed attempt to seize control of Wu and ally with Wei. A trusted counselor to Sun Quan, and longtime minister, officer and servant of Wu. While Wei declares to assimilate Wu and leaves no alternative but to submit or be defeated, Sun Quan and his staff rigorously debate whether they should resist. Should they elect to resist, their only hope of success would be an uneasy alliance with Liu Bei—a troubling and uncertain proposition which has left Wu divided. An Mou favors accommodation with Wei, and agrees, as Grand Hall spokesperson, to trigger a dramatic coup when all assemble to make a final decision.

Arjuna - Third of the five Pandava brothers and key protagonist in the Hindu epic Mahabharata. He possesses Gandiva, the divine bow, and among archers is supreme. He is the famed student of Drona and constant companion to Lord Krishna who, in mortal form, serves as Arjuna's charioteer.

Bao Ling - "The Dragon of the Midlands." Protagonist around whom many of our stories revolve. Raised in a remote agrarian community, he opted to resist oppression, taking up arms to defend the weak and helpless. Branded as a rebel outlaw and constantly on the run, he came upon a mysterious stranger, Sying Hao, who offered sanctuary on Southern Mountain. The bargain soon proved to extend far beyond the promised protection. Sying Hao became his mentor, and teacher, honing his talents and abilities to their highest realization. In some ways Bao Ling is everyman … just trying to make sense of the unknowable and the uncertain, while preserving his connections to the simple life of his forbears, and to the land and people he loves.

Cao Cao - (155 - 15 March 220 CE). King of, and then posthumously declared Emperor of Wei. Ambitious and talented general who sought to harness the will of heaven and establish a new empire in place of the failed Han. A talented leader, warrior, strategist, and scholar, as well as a renowned poet. Universally regarded as ruthless, cruel and merciless in securing his objectives, but grudgingly acknowledged for love of family and remarkable loyalty to friends and allies. History tells how he succeeded to a considerable degree. His portion of empire is now remembered as the "Cao Wei." This should not be confused with lesser successors, also named Wei. All mere shadows of the original. What he forged, though formidable in its prime, lasted less than half a century. Hardly a blip in the roll of dynasties. His doings unfolded long before the events of our stories, but lingered as factors, nonetheless. What remained after his demise were many conflicting ambitions, driving lesser personalities to propel the great land deeper into chaos. Pervasive suffering beset the masses. Generations came and went with no promise of any ending. The warring kingdoms alluded to in our accounts were mere shadows of the original "Cao Wei." No more than specters of what once was. Except in the degree of violence and torment which they wrought. Vying for control of everything, they scrounged every which way to replenish resources depleted by unprecedented waves of war machines foolishly unleashed. Therein lies the significance and relevance of once ignored places like Ling village and the Shu mountain passes. Perhaps they might be of consequence going forward.

Cao Pi - Son and successor to Cao Cao. Forced the Emperor Xian to abdicate, sealing the demise of Han. Also a renowned poet.

Cao Zhi - Lost the succession of Cao Cao to his more politically astute brother Cao Pi. Managed to have his life spared by meeting two impossible poetry challenges issued by his brother. He spent the balance of his life barred from court and courtly influence. But for his poetry, he would likely have disappeared from history.

Colonel Sun (Sun Wu Kong) - Honored officer and counselor in the service of Liu Bei. Close comrade to Zhuge Liang and colleague to Guan Yu. Mentor and fatherly influence on Sying Hao. Possibly an immortal, possibly a descendant of a distinct species. Forever shrouded in mystery. In no small part due to his guarded and reticent demeanor, barely offsetting his foreboding and ever solemn presence. His life and deeds linger as monuments preserved in legend and enshrined as myth. Directly, or indirectly, his influence and spirit can be felt throughout our tales and seem to ripple through the ages. We speak of him at considerable length over the course of many accounts and recollections.

Deshi Ku - "The ancient one." One of the mountain people. Esteemed tribal elder and regarded as chieftain. A healer and facilitator revered for his knowledge, and his life connection to heroes of the past.

Dragon Bow - The incomparable bow of Sun Wu Kong. Recognized by those who knew of it to represent perfection of the bowyer's craft. While simple in appearance, close inspection showed it to be complex in every detail, designed so its very core resonated with and drew strength from the character of its holder. One unworthy could scarcely draw the string, let alone shoot with it. Supreme in its authority, it came to be known as the "Hundred Li Bow." In the hands of one with righteous character, and the requisite skill, there seemed no end to its tactical reach.

Erge Lafah - Ekalavya. A character from The Mahabharata. Rejected by master Drona, Ekalavya returns home, but being resolute and with singular purpose to master archery he enters the wilderness and fabricates a mud and straw image of Drona before which he undertakes a disciplined program of self-study. He achieves exceptional prowess … rivaling, perhaps surpassing Drona's best pupil, Arjuna. On seeing this, Drona demands payment in full for his lessons, asking for, and receiving the thumb of Erge Lafah's release hand.

Five Northern Campaigns - (228-234 CE). The final attempt by Shu, under the guiding hand of Zhuge Liang, to defeat Wei. In the end, it proves unsuccessful.

Golden Ringed Staff - Second weapon associated with Sun Wu Kong. Despite legends, it did not grow or shrink, nor did it rest as a pin hidden away in his abundant hair. It did appear to have mystical origins, serving only Sun Wu Kong. In the hands of others, it proved unwieldy, its unimaginable weight making it nearly impossible to lift or move. Even Lord Guan said, "… as I struggled with the thing, I could see my feet starting to sink into the earth." Inscribed on it were the words, "Golden Ringed Staff, bane of the immortals."

Guanyin - Bodhisattva of compassion, somehow connected in pedigree to Zhi Mei.

Guan Yu - (160-220 CE). Also referred to as Guan Gong (Lord Guan), or simply Guan. Sworn brother to Liu Bei and Zhang Fei (bound three as one by their Peach Garden Oath). Virtually peerless among human warriors. Revered as a staunch patron of righteousness. Protector of the oppressed, guardian of the weak and vulnerable. Particularly the Shu tribes, in whom he took an unshakable personal interest. In the lineage of our accounts, he becomes companion and peer to Sun Wu Kong (Colonel Sun). He is the only human ever considered by Sun Wu Kong to be his martial equal. In his prime, with no more than his Green Dragon Blade in hand, Guan Yu could alone, stand down an entire enemy army.

He Ling - Paternal Grandfather to Bao Ling. Of considerable influence in shaping his character and developing his unique talents. Though we say little of him in this account, in time he will be shown connected to a history of mysterious influences which only become apparent to Bao Ling as his own journey into uncertainty and challenge continues.

Huang Gai - A commander in the army of Wu, and strong right hand to Field Marshall Zhou Yu. Huang Gai had a long and prestigious history as a military strategist and leader of men, and as such, commanded the Wu marines during the siege at Red Cliffs. Along with Zhou Yu, he forged the ultimate and risk filled strategy which turned fortunes about at Red Cliffs. But all depended on the ultimate test of his loyalty. Would he meet the challenge?

Iron Hand Gao - Friend of He Ling, Bao Ling's grandfather. Martial and life tutor to the child Bao Ling. He is mentioned only in a passing reference. A master of iron-hand and the internal disciplines and revered as benefactor and protector of his village and surrounds. After encountering a man like Iron Hand Gao, one is unlikely to fear any other, or anything else for that matter.

Jin Dynasty - (265-420 CE). War of the Eight Princes. The period leading up to and enveloping our stories.

Kong Kong - A young and gifted mountain archer who threw the brazen challenge to Bao Ling which resulted in an archery contest. The village elders feared the talented young warrior's unbridled need for reward and acclaim might lead to his ruin. The turns of the contest defied all the young challenger's anticipations. In the end, though not victorious, he seemed changed, and to have found his proper place within the community. Among themselves, the elders became hopeful of a beneficial outcome.

Krishna - Lord Krishna; eighth incarnation of the Hindu deity Vishnu and in his own right, the Supreme deity. Embodiment of compassion, tenderness, and love. Lifetime companion and charioteer to Arjuna. Their story depicts the bond of trust and devotion which ultimately links man to the divine.

Kuan-Yin Ting - Orphaned mountain herder who first encounters Bao Ling while minding livestock for Shu-Ting tribe. In short order, he becomes friend and disciple to Bao Ling. On accepting the archery challenge from Kong Kong, Bao Ling opens the game to all who would test their skills. To that end, he specifically brings Kuan-Yin Ting into the match, albeit against the herder's reticence. Though nearly opposite in personal nature to the brash Kong Kong, as events in the challenge unfolded, the two soon enough recognize the ascending skills and character, each in the other.

Lady Sun (Sun Ren) - Younger sister to Sun Quan. A legendary beauty who from the first, captured the heart of

Cao Cao. He does eventually come to regret this. Though immensely talented, it is her audacity and fearlessness which make her a factor in events which follow. She eventually became wife to Liu Bei. The move had been meant to keep peace between Liu and her brother. While Liu was on campaign, she snuck away and returned to her home in Wu, but not without attempting unsuccessfully to kidnap Liu Shan, the royal son. An attempt fortunately foiled by Zhao Yun and Zhang Fei. Little more of her is known beyond that.

Laozi - (604 - 532 BCE). One of history's great sages. Said to have authored the "Tao de Ching."

Li Fung - "Master Li" of the Mountain People. Village elder. Martial master. He figures prominently in the personal development of Shi-Hui Ke, both as child, and as man. In our book *Seed of Dragons*, we give full account of the man and the considerable influence he has over his people. Now he is older. His onetime protege, Shi-Hui Ke, stands nearly his equal in the high esteem of the mountain tribes.

Ling Tong - The Hero of Wu's forces during the disastrous retreat at Xiaoyao Ford. But for his valor and sacrifice, Sun Quan would not have survived the day. Fighting virtually alone until the end, he felt certain his time had come. To avoid desecration, he dove into the torrent. Defying all likelihoods, his body rose from the waters the following day, still breathing and vital.

Liu Biao (142-208 CE). Fierce warlord, who ruled Jing Province as the once Han Dynasty fell into warring factions. Adopted a posture of neutrality which at first spared his Jing subjects from the chaos and turmoil surrounding disintegration of the empire. This even as Cao Cao's Wei forces pressured constantly from the north, and family Sun's Wu forces pushed relentlessly from the south. Like Liu Bei, he was a distant relation to the once emperor. As a distant relative, he extended sanctuary to Liu Bei when he and his fledgling forces faced annihilation from the pursuing Cao Cao. Liu Bei proved to be an able ally and general, making Jing Province under Liu Biao virtually unassailable.

It was Liu Biao's talented general Huang Zu who devised the plan to kill Sun Jian, the fierce warrior King of Wu. That loss ultimately bred the blood vendetta which fell to his son Sun Ce and finally to Sun Quan; forever linking their family honor to the once father's desire to capture Jing.

But for Liu Biao's untimely death from illness, Jing would have remained secure. As it were, upon his demise, a conniving spouse manipulated the second son (her own child) into leadership, circumventing the designated heir. The second son proved weak, the situation worsened when avenging Wu forces killed the great general Huang Zu. Defenses within the province disintegrated beneath the withering onslaughts from Wei in the north, and Wu in the South.

Liu Bei - (unknown 161 – 10 June 223 CE). The incomparable man of righteousness. A common man, though distant relation to the Han emperor. A sandal maker who rose to prominence as a formidable military commander—driven by his unsparing dedication to restoration of the Han Dynasty. After a lengthy retreat to save what remained of his forces, he founded the Shu Han empire in the remote west, and prospered beyond all expectations—his achievements the stuff of dreams and legends. Until his demise, he remained a key principal during the period of the Three Kingdoms. He felt the Shu tribes to be a most noble and honorable people, believing that so long as they remained viable, there would be no direct path for Cao Cao and Wei to attack from the east. To that end, he ensured the Shu remained independent, and always, a respected ally. He nurtured, encouraged, and taught them how to fend for themselves.

Liu Shan - (207-271 CE); son of Liu Bei; ascended throne at age sixteen on the death of his father; initially under the charge of Chancellor Zhuge Liang. Ruled for 40 years, longest of all in the Three Kingdom era. Today, his name connotes one who lacks sense or ambition and could not achieve anything even with significant assistance. Surrendered to Wei in 263 CE. Few specifics are known of his court as Zhuge Liang banned official historians, leaving no formal record.

Longzhong Plan - Zhuge Liang's grand plan for the restoration of the Han. Liu Bei would first solidify his position and stature by acquiring Jing and then Yi, setting a springboard to the West and then South, where he could vastly expand his base and influence by assimilating new peoples and territories. It called for the early alliance with Sun Quan to counter Cao Cao, thus setting the stage for planned eventual conquest of the north through the North China Plain, while also recognizing the need to have a final reckoning with Sun Quan as last phase of the Han restoration.

Peach Garden Oath - Three desperate young men meet in fate and find themselves of common heart. They agree to bind their destinies to hopes for a just and prosperous land. Liu Bei, Guan Yu and Zhang Fei swear to become brothers in united purpose. Avenge the Han, restore the nation, bring peace, exercise compassion to the helpless and needy. Liu Bei as eldest, becomes leader. Guan Yu his second. Though not born on the same day, by their oath they commit themselves unto death, memorialized in their expressed hope to die on the same day, in the same month and year. They call upon the immortals to seal their pact, and to strike dead whosoever fails its purpose or betrays their sworn fraternity. 14th century playwright Luo Guanzhong preserves the actual oath in Chapter One of *Romance of the Three Kingdoms*.

Red Hare - Many during that era regarded Red Hare to be the greatest warrior's horse to ever grace the battlefield. Chroniclers record the steed could cover five hundred li in a day, and that it never even broke stride ascending mountains, or crossing deserts. In battle, it moved forever forward, fearless, and completely attuned to its master. Its coat glistened red, not a single hair of any other shade. In battle, the sweaty sheen on the coat took on a light of its own, casting a red glow on the faces of all who closed to do it harm. Among horses, it stood as Guan Yu did among men. At first, wild and intractable and of no use to Cao Cao, in an unexpected turn Cao gifted the animal to Guan Yu. A match of destinies; each completing the other. From first meeting, they remained inseparable.

Shi-Hui Ke - One of the Shu Mountain people. Abbot of Crystal Springs temple, a mysterious preserve and one of several fortresses meticulously conceived by Zhuge Liang to secure the Shu Roads from invasion. Created, in accordance with Liu Bei's directive, to protect and preserve the culture and heritage of the mountain people. Although a monk and man of peace, Shi-Hui Ke remains an ardent patriot, and has found purpose in his role as defender of his people and their ways. In his youth, he had attained renown as a singularly gifted martial artist, particularly in archery, before losing his left arm midway from the shoulder resulting from unlucky encounter with a sadistic band of Wei mercenaries. In some ways, the unfortunate loss proved a blessing ... in time, the once consummate archer, now monk, found within his higher states of awareness, the secret of the "thought arrow." Bao Ling had opportunity to witness Abbot Hui's remarkable skill, projecting nothing but concentrated thought to strike and deter a stalking tiger. We present the full account in *The Wizard's Testament*. He also appears to have gained privy to the alchemy of longevity, or so concludes Bao Ling; but that's a different story.

Shu Han - Most remote of the three warring kingdoms … the Western Empire established by Liu Bei and his followers. Originally on the run, hoping only to survive, they took refuge in the remote western wilderness and wastelands. There, under inspired leadership, they won the loyalty of the inhabitants. In less than a generation the region consolidated into an empire recalling the once great Han.

Sima Yi - (179-251 CE) Talented general, politician and administrator of Wei, charged with defending Wei against Zhuge Liang's Northern Expeditions. He proved to be a valuable right-hand presence to Cao Cao, as well as an ally and staunch defender of his son and successor Cao Pi, who in turn entrusted his own successor Cao Rui to the general's charge. Despite many years of credible service to the Cao line, Sima Yi eventually turned on the great grandson Cao Shuang, ultimately executing him and his clans, and himself taking charge of Wei. He did, however, win the support of the populace by governing with an honest hand, and encouraging beneficial change. His own grandson, Sima Yan, founded the Jin dynasty. Considering subsequent developments, some have questioned the true nature of Sima Yi's loyalty and designs, starting from his very first emergence in Wei.

Sima Zhao - (211-265 CE). Second son of Sima Yi. Military general, statesman, and eventual regent of the state of Cao Wei. He worked to weaken the hold of the imperial Cao line on what remained of Wei and may have been complicit in the death of Cao Mao (grandson of Cao Pi). As general, he moved to finish what remained of Shu, eventually forcing the surrender of Liu Shan. Even while he appeared to have the trust of those he purportedly served, insinuations left no doubt, "Everyone on the street knows what's in Sima Zhao's mind." His ambitions could not be fully cloaked.

Sun Ce - (175-200 CE); Eldest son of Sun Jian and older brother to Sun Quan; a naturally talented leader, brilliant tactician and gifted martial artist. Assumed oversight of his father's warlord domain while still in his teens, and quickly established himself as a leader around whose charisma and penchant for success, others of notable talent could willingly serve. He won loyalties with his demeanor, his fairness, and his inclination to encourage others to rise to wherever their gifts and skills might carry them. Before his untimely assassination, he had carved a significant warlord state in southeastern China, which ultimately became the state of Wu. He had one son ... still a child at the time of his passing. Rather than complicating the fate of his infant son, he passed control of the state to his capable younger brother Sun Quan, in whom his trust proved well placed.

Sun Jian - Warlord and progenitor of what would become the powerful state of Wu. Father to Sun Ce and Sun Quan.

Sun Quan - (182-252 CE); ruled as King of Wu 222-229 CE, ruled as Emperor Da of Wu 229-252 CE; combined total of 30 years; initially a great leader, warrior and patriot, intent on the survival of his nation against the overwhelmingly powerful forces of Wei under the leadership of Cao Cao. Enters the controversial alliance with Liu Bei which proves decisive in the momentous Battle of Red Cliffs. Their on again; off again alliances over the course of years darkens their relationship and leaves little to show for their once parallel life paths. In later years, his youthful greatness becomes lost and swirled in the constant distractions of power, insecurity, confusion and ultimately mistrust.

Sun Tzu - (544 - 490 BCE) Renowned military strategist and philosopher whose landmark work The Art of War stands foremost among the finest portrayals of strategy ever conceived. Even today, its lessons impact military and transactional philosophies throughout the East and the West.

Sun Wu Kong - See "Colonel Sun."

Sying Hao - Mentor to Bao Ling. A onetime war orphan who became apprentice and adopted son to Sun Wu Kong. Friend of the Southlanders and archer supreme. Scholar of the classics and bow craftsman of singular caliber. Guided by Sun, he mastered the transformations, learned to project consciousness, and to move about undetected. Thought by many to be a ghost. Sometimes called "Fenghua Yan" (weathered rock), or "The Man from Southern Mountain."

The Five Tiger Generals - The five generals who served Liu Bei with uncompromising loyalty throughout his reign. Many times, their valor and exemplary leadership proved decisive against what others deemed insurmountable odds. By Lord Liu's designation they were:

Guan Yu - General of the Front;
Zhang Fei - General of the Right;
Huang Zhong - General of the Rear;
Ma Chao - General of the Left; and
Zhao Yun - General of the Center.

History honors them as "The Five Tiger Generals."

Wei - Foremost among the three warring kingdoms. Ruled in its prime by the brilliant and formidable Cao Cao.

Positioned in the northeast, extending from the western highlands to the eastern sea.

Wu - One of the three warring kingdoms. A vast empire situated predominantly in the southeast, ascending for a time to its full potential under the leadership of Sun Quan.

Yama - "King Yama." A devil of sorts, or perhaps what we might think of as the incarnation of death. Presides over hell and is accountable for the death and transmigration of human souls. Keeps true the final ledger and ensures his fearsome legions bring the newly departed to their end judgment. Relishes chaos and induces strife. Genuinely enjoys his job, particularly the part where he gets to torment those deserving. Once, when confronted by the Creator for his evil doings, he defended himself most eloquently, arguing to the Creator, "Hey ... isn't this my job? Did you make me for any other purpose? Can you think of anyone who can do it better than me? Forgive me sire, but I fail to see where we have a problem." Convinced by his logic and impressed with his integrity, the Creator ordered his release declaring him free to go about his business unimpeded.

Zhang Fei - (unknown - died 221 CE). Sworn brother to Guan Yu and Liu Bei. Also, a singular warrior, one whom Guan Yu deemed his peer and often boasted of. Known for his uncontrollable temper, it proved to be his ultimate undoing, in the end assassinated by his own men. But not until fulfilling a life of epic feats and undeniable heroism.

Zhao Yun - One of the illustrious five generals serving Liu Bei throughout his lifetime, and beyond. Zhao Yun passed in 229 CE. His day of birth is unknown, but most believe him 60 years old at the time of his death. He dedicated his entire life and lived above all things to serve the cause of Liu Bei and the Shu Han. In our prior work,

Token Tales and Fragments, we allude to the possibility his direct blood line includes Bao Ling.

Many remembrances of his deeds echo within *Romance of the Three Kingdoms*. Typically, they recall his supreme martial skill, unbounded courage, penetrating intellect, as well as the loyalty and admiration of those who served with and under him. To the present, his high principles and righteous character remain common knowledge throughout the land, modeling standards revered by all.

Even today, in Henan Province he may sometimes appear as entrance deity, along with his comrade Ma Chao, together protecting Taoist temples from the influence of evil spirits.

Zhi Mei - A farm girl discovered hiding after Wei marauders killed her father and brother. Kidnapped and abused until stumbled upon and rescued by Bao Ling. Alone and vulnerable, she accepts Bao Ling's offer to partner as traveling companions to Crystal Springs. She comes from a family of skilled poets, and though a common farm girl, possesses consummate skill in rhyme and song. In time, her words become the voice of the resistance, and her accounts and stories record the noble deeds of its heroes, particularly the Dragon of the Midlands.

Zhou Yu - (175-210 CE); Died age 35 of uncertain illness while preparing for conquest of Baqiu. Though only a young man, as a general under Sun Ce, he established his reputation as strategist, and one able to deliver consistent victory. He possessed an imposing figure, and prodigious talents. Handsome, kind, and especially skilled in music, he won even the loyalties of those who first rejected him. They attributed their turnaround to the eventual awareness of his immense talents, much like the discovery of a very fine wine. At first too complicated and delicate to appreciate, but ultimately dazzling in its final complexity. After Sun Ce's untimely death, Zhou Yu accepted the younger Sun Quan to be rightful sovereign, acting first among those paying dutiful respect, and soon becoming strong right arm to the new ruler. Zhou Yu received prominent credit among those responsible for the great victory at Red Cliffs, and the subsequent victory at Jiangdong, among many others. His premature death proved to be a great loss to Wu, as his singular talents went unmatched by any other.

Zhuge Liang (181 - 234 CE) - Sometimes referred to as "Kongming" the Sleeping Dragon, attesting to the splendor of his essential nature once unleashed. A wizard, scholar, musician and hero whose influence and guiding hand threads either directly or indirectly throughout our accounts, and perhaps beyond them. Despite his many deeds of record, historical abstracts say little of his past, or his background. No one can account for how he gained his remarkable talents. For that reason, he remains an enigma. In our recitations, the dates of his life are indeterminate. He has achieved longevity; though, not having fully mastered its alchemy; he is not a true immortal. As a Merlin-like sage who has perfected awareness, he stands singular. Among humans and other creatures, his name is spoken of in the same breath and with the same reverence as only the likes of Jiang Ziya and Sun Wu Kong.

Acknowledgments

A work like this challenges one with numerous tasks, hurdles and twists. Endless revisions and fine-tuning are just the beginning. Then there's the layout, necessary for both print and E-book formats. Life's usual demands don't quiet during the creative journey. Crises, illnesses, and daily distractions vie for attention. So too, the deluge of texts, memes, and emails.

I often struggle with distractions and losing focus. That's where friends come in. Renee Knarreborg, a longtime friend and artistic collaborator once again graced our effort with her artwork, creating the cover drawing and interior map. Renee devises these wonders while navigating regional power and utility issues and running audits. I told her the "Gift of Red Hare" was intended to be a metaphor for something larger, relating to our isolation in life, and what it means to find good-fellowship with another, whatever form it may take. I believe she nailed it!

And then there's the editing. This particular endeavor necessitated no end of review and revision. Someone once asked how many re-writes I do. In this instance I stopped counting at fifty. I owe my survival (again) to Bryan Smith. Long ago, Bryan, a retired professor of mathematics and computer science, generously offered his expertise to edit and provide valuable feedback on my ongoing works. He's tackled whatever I've sent with a relentless yet fair-minded passion, always aiming for excellence, clarity, and relevance.

This book is undoubtedly better because of him. Bryan, I thank you again for your kindness and commitment to excellence, all freely rendered while you were undergoing life challenges of your own.

Lastly, I am deeply grateful to the many mentors[47] and teachers who have guided me over the years, sharing their wisdom and skills. Most have passed on, and I now stand in their shoes rather than on their shoulders. To those still among us, please accept my advance apologies. Whatever I got wrong is not your fault or doing.

---

[47] If you're curious, here's a link: https://ironcrane.com/IC_Flowchart.jpeg

About the Author

Billy Ironcrane was raised in inner city Philadelphia during the 1950's and 1960's. He partook in the revolutionary currents of change, protest, activism, and idealism which characterized the era. While a teen, he spent summers on the Jersey coast hawking newspapers, tossing burgers and exploring places like Atlantic City where he encountered flea circuses, Gene Krupa hanging between sets at the Steel Pier, petrified mermaids and the fabulously wealthy promenading the boardwalk at night flashing mink stoles, diamonds, tuxes and studded canes. Atlantic City dubbed itself, "The World's Playground." All the stuff of dreams as he returned to Mrs. J's boarding house where he slept for ten bucks a week, sharing occasional space with his grandfather and other Polish immigrants working the summer trade. Not to mention the landlady's ever-present legion of cats.

He departed the inner city still in his teens, and pushed blindly into the unknown never to return. There he found his many stories and mapped his own insights into the nature of existence. To remain static and have done nothing would have been terminal, as in fact it proved to be for many of his mates.

In the decades following, he pursued new awarenesses. He swam exotic currents, wandered through remote tropical forests, and became a soldier. He ambled through southwestern deserts at night, slept through thunderstorms alongside petrified forests, and trekked the Rockies. He mastered the martial arts, jogged with blacktail deer in the hills surrounding Monterey, explored Zen, and motorcycled the California coast. He scaled Pfeiffer Rock, freelanced, traversed the Cascades, and slept beneath ancient redwoods in remote Los Padres. Along the way, he raised a family and bridged the corporate jungle. Then, he hung a shingle and lived on wits and ingenuity until the muse of the 60's again tapped his shoulder, ordering, "Time to shift gears, Billy."

So there you have it.

Other Works by Billy Ironcrane

Returning to Center
(A Collection of Stories, Vignettes and Thoughts)
2018

Seed of Dragons
(Surviving an Empire Undone)
2019

Token Tales and Fragments
(Recalling a Time of Heroes and Sages)
2020

The Wizard's Testament
(An Unexpected Challenge)
2021

Di Xin Emperor of Shang
(A Tale of Two Kings)
2025

www.ingramcontent.com/pod-product-compliance
Lightning Source LLC
Chambersburg PA
CBHW070828260626
47170CB00007B/2298